Worse than Dead

Stephen Puleston

D1534004

ABOUT THE AUTHOR

Stephen Puleston was born and educated in Anglesey, North Wales. He graduated in theology before training as a lawyer. Worse than Dead is his second novel in the Inspector Drake series

www.stephenpuleston.co.uk
Facebook:stephenpulestoncrimewriter

OTHER NOVELS

Inspector Drake Mysteries

Prequel Novella– Ebook only
Devil's Kitchen
Novels
Brass in Pocket
Worse than Dead
Against the Tide

Inspector Marco Novels

Prequel Novella– Ebook only
Dead Smart
Novels
Speechless
Another Good Killing

ISBN-13:978-1523423606
ISBN-10: 1523423609

:

In memory of my mother
Gwenno Puleston

Prologue

The air was filled with the damp smell of sweat and unwashed clothes. A carton from the galley, which once had carried fish and chips, had been stuffed into a metal bin and cans of cider were piled into one corner. He lay on the narrow bunk, his head vibrating from the music blasting through the earphones. He cursed when he noticed the roll-your-own cigarette had gone out, but his annoyance grew when his lighter failed to spark. He got up and fumbled for some matches in a bag. Through the porthole he could see trucks moving on the quay next to the ferry's berth.

He slumped back onto the bunk, reached down for a can of cider on the floor and took a deep slug. He knew he needed to clean. But why should he bother? Nobody ever came into the cabin. And he could give it a quick wipe when his watch ended.

He drew a hand over his stubble. It had been three days since he had last drawn a razor over his chin. That morning the deck officer had given him a sullen glare when he walked over the car deck and he guessed that a reprimand would follow. But he never saw passengers. Never saw the drivers of the lorries. He barely mixed with the crew, come to that.

The first time he had killed a man had been the hardest. The excitement had built up in his chest until he thought he might collapse but after he'd squeezed the trigger and the smell of cordite had evaporated exhilaration pulsed through his body. The second time had been easier. He'd never thought about the victims afterwards: there had always been another job. Now he was older and when they came looking for his help he could never ignore them.

They had arrived at his home late one evening the week before. He had left the rear gate off the latch and he was waiting in the kitchen when they pushed the door open. He had motioned to the chairs by the table, but they had stood.

'Not going to be long,' one of them had said.

He had nodded.

'We've got a problem.'

It had sounded like they were stuck on a crossword puzzle.

They had been right – they were not long. The instructions had been clear and then they had left.

A text purred on his mobile – his only contact with the real world. After reading the message he punched in his reply and pressed send, before throwing the phone to the bottom of the bed.

They were worried. They needn't be. He'd told them that.

He would see to it. It would be clean.

He reached down for the can by the side of his bunk, shook it around, before realising it was empty. He cracked another open. He had time enough.

He turned up the volume on his iPod and let the music crash around his ears.

Once he had finished drinking, he stood up and belched loudly. He looked at himself in the mirror, drew his hand over his face and rubbed his head. There was a small basin that he filled with hot water before dowsing his face – a shower could wait until tomorrow.

He glanced at his watch. Almost time.

Chapter 1

Ian Drake bowed his head and stifled a yawn. Then he tried to focus again on the inspector from Southern Division, a tall, thin man who wore a cheap suit and a battered white shirt with a tie that had an enormous brown stain running down its length. He had given up the prospect that his fellow officer could make data protection sound interesting. Caren Waits, sitting by his side, was alternating between keen, intense stares at the speaker and scribbling notes.

Since the police forces of Wales had been unified into one service, Drake often found himself sent on courses to Cardiff or Swansea but today it had been the turn of officers from Southern Division to make the journey up north. And over lunch Drake had become increasingly annoyed as he'd listened to jokes about *sheepshaggers* from voices trying to mimic the North Wales accent.

Drake drank some water – maybe he was dehydrated and that was the reason for his lapse in concentration. He could ill afford to waste a day on this course. He had the appraisal of a junior officer to undertake, a pile of reports to read and a missing person's file to review. Irritation was building in his mind.

A fragment of pastry from the lunchtime sausage roll had dislodged itself from his teeth and was rolling around in his mouth. His father liked sausage rolls; he remembered that from his childhood – perhaps that's why he had scooped one onto his plate with the sandwiches and crisps at lunchtime.

'Data protection is central to our policing policy,' the inspector droned on.

Drake swallowed the pastry and could feel another yawn starting. He pulled the edge of the newspaper out from underneath the course materials and cast an eye over one of the difficult squares in the morning's sudoku.

'There are organised gangs in Nigeria, Eastern Europe and China – all targeting our economy.'

Caren was still scribbling.

Drake watched another slide of the presentation, which was full of text and bullet points. The inspector had a sing-song voice that made it difficult to concentrate and his attempts at humour had been met by stifled grunts. Drake looked again at the sudoku but any pleasure at solving part of a difficult square was interrupted when he heard the noise of a door crashing open behind him. A uniformed officer strode down towards the front and handed the inspector a slip of paper.

'I'm sorry for the interruption,' the inspector said, before scanning the room. 'Urgent request for DI Drake to call headquarters.'

Drake got up and gave the inspector a look of feigned regret. Caren began sorting her papers, stuffing them into a black folder. Drake inched his way along the row of seats, mouthing the occasional apology to the others present.

The uniformed officer stood at the end of the row. He had a wide stance and broad shoulders, the sort of officer assigned to a late shift in Rhyl on a summer's night when temperatures ran high and tempers frayed.

'What's up?' Drake asked.

'Superintendent Price wants to talk to you, sir.'

He led Drake and Caren out of the conference room and down a corridor to reception. He pointed into a small ante room and Drake picked up the telephone lying on the table.

'Drake.'

'I tried your mobile,' Superintendent Wyndham Price's voice sounded edgy.

'I … ah. Must be in my coat.'

'Inspector. There's an emergency.'

'Sir?' Drake could feel his body relaxing at the prospect of leaving for good the presentation and its statistics about data protection crime. It wasn't the same as proper criminals. There were victims of course – every crime had a victim – but these gangs seemed to operate in the ether, in cyber space.

'I wouldn't have called you out of the seminar, but you're the nearest senior officer.'

Drake gave Caren, standing by his side, a knowing look.

The super continued. 'On the one day when we've got all of the DIs committed, a body turns up.'

'Sir?'

'DI Rogers is in court, before that idiot of a judge in Mold, and Geoff Burnell is on a train to London for a conference in Scotland Yard,' Price continued. 'You'll have to take the case.'

Drake's mind started to concentrate. If there was a body, then the scene needed to be preserved and evidence secured. The crime scene investigators would have to be in place.

'What are the details?'

'There's a ferry arriving at Holyhead in an hour – full of lorries. They found a body. Better get over there.'

Drake barely concealed the smile on his face as he left the room and then made for the exit, without a second thought to the intricacies of data protection. Outside in the car park, he strode over to the Alfa Romeo GT and pointed the remote. The car bleeped and the lights flashed. Overhead, thick storm clouds scudded across the sky, and over the mountains to the east he saw dark columns of rain.

Within minutes, they'd turned onto the dual carriageway and Drake fired the car westwards over Anglesey towards the darkening sky. Soon it was raining heavily and water pounded against the windscreen. He feathered the brake and the cruise disconnected. The car slowed and he peered out as the wiper blades swept back and forth.

After half an hour, they crossed the embankment to Holy Island, and the cooling tower of the closed aluminium smelter loomed out of the shadows. Drake followed the signs down to the port area. Two men were standing at the entrance, their heads lowered against the rain, wearing high-visibility jackets, their hands stuck deep into pockets. Drake pulled up beside them and flashed his warrant card. One of the men spoke into a radio. Soon a small van, with flashing lights and the livery of the ferry company painted over the side, parked alongside Drake, its driver gesticulating for Drake to follow him.

The driving rain made the dilapidated buildings of the town to his left look depressing, and the long wall running along the boundary of the port seemed to separate it from the activity in the harbour. The flowing lines of the steel tubes of the footbridge that linked the port with the town towered above Drake.

Eventually, they reached a wide concourse lined with articulated lorries. The flashing lights of the van came on again as it approached a small office building. At the far end of the concourse a ferry was unloading; another was reversing slowly into a berth.

Drake parked alongside a police van and they left the car. He dragged on the Barbour that had been lying on the back seat, pulled the collar close up to his cheeks and ran over to the building, as the rain soaked his face. Inside telephones were ringing and there were shouts from an office for somebody to answer the calls. Two uniformed officers stood to one side and nodded acknowledgments at Drake and Caren; moments later the door opened, Detective Constables Gareth Winder, and Dave Howick entered, rain dripping off their jackets.

'Got here as soon as we could,' Winder said.

'We've only just arrived,' Drake replied.

Drake had barely finished his instructions for the team when a man with a wide chest and a swarthy beard

9

emerged from the rear of the building. The telephones continued to ring. Drake held out a hand. 'Detective Inspector Drake,' he said, before nodding towards Caren. 'Sergeant Waits.'

'Huw Thomas.'

Drake started to take off the Barbour.

'There's no time for that now. She's almost alongside,' Thomas said.

'What ...?'

'Need to get you down near the ramp and on first.'

They were outside again and Drake was certain the rain had intensified. It seemed to blot out the town and, squinting into the distance, he saw the shape of the ferry company's offices towering over the harbour.

'Into the van,' Thomas said. He barely squeezed into the driver's seat, struggling with the belt, the jacket rustling against the chair. Drake sat alongside him, Caren, Winder and Howick in the rear. The van wouldn't start the first time; Thomas cursed then fiddled with the ignition until the engine fired into life. A couple of minutes later they reached the ramp and watched as the ferry finished her manoeuvre. A siren sounded, more lights flashed, and the ramp descended from the stern of the vessel. The group left the van and walked over to the edge of the ramp.

Three members of the crew stood on the car deck as Drake strode down into the vessel. Despite the rain he could see their dark, intense stares.

A man with a wide jaw and a shaved head stepped forward.

'Captain Seymour,' he said, thrusting out his hand towards Drake.

'DI Drake. Where's the body?'

'Follow me,' Seymour said, turning towards the lorries parked on the deck.

'How many passengers are there?' Drake asked.

'Not many. We were light this morning. All of the

passengers are in the lounges on the top deck. What do we do with them?'

Drake turned to Caren. 'Sergeant Waits will take care of that.'

Seymour raised his hand and waved at another man in a high-visibility jacket.

'Howard. Take Sergeant Waits up top.'

Drake watched as Caren followed the crew member to an open doorway, Howick and Winder close behind her. Turning, Drake heard the gears crunching on the Scientific Support Vehicle, as it thudded onto the ramp and began a slow descent into the bowels of the vessel. There was a deep grinding noise behind Drake and he looked towards the bow doors.

'It's standard operating procedure to open the bow doors when we're alongside. We have to clear the vessel of any fumes,' Seymour said. 'Follow me.'

The captain led Drake past the lorries and trucks parked closely together and stepped over cables lashed around tyres. Drake was expecting the heavy smell of diesel oil and petrol fumes, but was surprised by how clean the deck seemed.

Seymour stopped below the cabin of a large lorry. 'He's over there,' he said, nodding his head.

'What's the dead man's name?'

'Frank Rosen. He was the chief engineer.'

'Who found the body?'

'One of the ABs – able seaman.'

Drake nodded. He walked over and knelt down. Rosen's head lay tucked against his chest, drooping slightly to one side. Drake guessed he was early forties. There was a large red stain on the one-piece suit, and the handle of a knife protruding from his chest had dark blotches along its length. Then Drake heard the familiar sound of Mike Foulds's voice, turned his head, and saw the crime scene manager looking down at him.

11

'Mike,' Drake said.

'Has anyone interfered with the scene since the body was found?' Foulds sounded edgy.

'Can't tell. Captain Seymour?' Drake said, directing Foulds's question at the captain.

'I gave instructions for no one to go anywhere near the body. Exactly as I was instructed by your superintendent.' Seymour folded his arms together tightly and gave Drake a defiant stare.

'Do what you can,' Drake said, returning his gaze to Foulds, already realising that there were problems ahead. 'If there's contamination of the scene, then there's nothing we can do about it.'

Foulds nodded and moved away, looking around, assessing the task in hand. Drake had been on cases with him before: Foulds always made sure there was no doubt who was in charge of the crime scene. Drake could hear the bustle of the crime scene investigators behind the tyres of the trucks.

'This could take hours,' Foulds said.

'Keep me informed,' Drake replied, as he turned his back on the crime scene manager and motioned for Seymour to leave the scene. As they moved back towards the open section of the car deck, it struck Drake that this would be the first case in which he knew where the killer was right from the start. They had all the suspects in one place. It was only a matter of establishing the motive and opportunity. He could keep everyone on board until he had a confession.

Seymour was saying something that interrupted Drake's thinking.

'Inspector Drake. The port manager is on his way.'

'What?'

'The shipping and port manager.'

Another tall man strode down the ramp.

'Who's in charge?' The accent was estuary English and a decibel too loud.

Drake held out his hand. 'Detective Inspector Drake.'

The man looked at Drake's hand for a moment and then shook it. 'How long will you be?'

'As long as it takes.'

'That's no good.'

Drake stared at the man before replying. 'Sorry?'

'I've got a schedule to keep. Look at all these lorries. Perishable goods mostly. Massive claim against us if we can't offload the ship.'

His tone suggested that arguing wasn't an option.

Drake straightened a little. 'What's your name?'

'Mortlake.'

Drake raised his voice above the humming of the engine noise. 'Mr Mortlake. This is a crime scene. I've got a team of crime scene investigators beginning their work. There's a murderer on this boat.'

'It's a ship,' Mortlake said, through gritted teeth.

'What?' Drake said.

The mobile rang in Drake's pocket; he reached in, feeling the damp seams. His feet felt damp too, and he worried that the bottom of his trousers would be sodden by the time they finished. He wasn't dressed for this – he reconsidered the advantages of the seminar, now somewhat regretting being on the deck of a ship, having to debate who was in charge. His suit was one of his best – a German designer brand that his wife had bought as a birthday present and oil and grease would ruin it.

'Can you come up here, sir?' It was Caren's voice.

Drake turned to the two uniformed officers standing on the ramp. 'Nobody goes off this ship, without my authority. Understood?'

They nodded and Drake gave Mortlake a hard stare.

The stairwell to the top deck was wide and clean. Caren stood by a large wooden door underneath a sign that said 'Irish Bar'.

'There are a couple of smart-arse passengers in there.' She tipped her head towards the doors.

'Really?'

'Demanding they have to leave.'

Drake was in no mood for any further dissent and pushed the door open, clenching his jaw. One hundred pairs of eyes turned towards him and he stood in front of the bar, clearing his throat before raising his voice.

'I'm Detective Inspector Drake. There's been a murder on this vessel and until we've completed our investigation nobody is leaving.'

He was about to continue when the door burst open and Winder crashed in. 'Something you need to see, sir. Now.'

Chapter 2

Clothes were lying in piles on the floor, the bed linen torn, pillows ripped to shreds.

Winder stood by the door as Drake stepped into the cabin. He walked to the bottom of the bed, noticing an Elton John *Greatest Hits* CD discarded into a corner. He snapped on a pair of latex gloves and picked through some polo shirts and boxer shorts. He fingered the front cover of a Louis L'Amour Western novel detached from the rest of the pages. Somebody wanted to find something very badly – desperate or angry or both.

Drake turned to Winder who was standing by the door. 'Better get Mike Foulds up here.'

Winder nodded and left.

Drake knelt by the bed and flicked over more of the clothes with a pencil he'd found in his jacket. There was nothing to identify the occupant of the cabin, no family photograph. Not even a newspaper. He stepped over to the small bathroom behind him and noticed the narrow shower door, wet from recent use. But there was no wash bag or shaving foam or shower gel. The bathroom had been stripped of personal belongings. They were probably under the clothes on the bed, waiting for the CSIs.

It was quiet in the cabin as Drake waited for Foulds. He walked carefully over to the window and peered out into the harbour, watching a small fishing boat churning its way into the fish quay, the crew huddled in the small wheelhouse for shelter. He looked back over the discarded possessions just as Foulds arrived by the door and groaned.

'Somebody's been busy,' Foulds said.

'How are you getting on?'

Foulds took a step into the room and reached for a pair of gloves, as one of the CSIs appeared in the cabin door.

'Slowly. The chance of getting anything useful is

zero,' Foulds said, turning to the investigator. 'Andy, get to work here,' he said before looking over at Drake. 'We need space on the car deck, Ian. Some of the lorries will have to disembark.'

Drake nodded. Time was what they did not have. The fact that he must be so close to the murderer was all he could think about. He could easily touch him, speak to him, and look him in the eye. Or maybe it was a woman. All he had to do was get all the passengers and crew into one area on the ship and demand a confession. But it only happened that way on the television for Poirot or Miss Marple.

'I'll come down with you.'

Stepping over the high threshold into the car deck, Drake noticed activity in a small office in one corner. Mortlake stood near the cab of a lorry and when he saw Drake, he mouthed something to a crew member who immediately picked up a radio unit.

Drake strode over to the crime scene. Foulds looked worried and he pointed under the lorries behind him. 'We need to move these wagons.'

Drake didn't want to let anyone off the ship. Everyone was a potential suspect. He dreaded to think how many foreign nationals might be on board: could he confiscate their passports? Keep them in the UK until he was satisfied they had nothing to do with the murder?

'It's important, Ian,' Foulds continued.

'Yes, of course. Get it done,' Drake replied, still thinking about the murderer sitting somewhere on board.

Caren appeared on the car deck. There was something different about Caren that morning, Drake realised. Her clothes were smart and her hair had been carefully and tightly pulled back behind her head. It had irked him before that she'd arrive at work looking untidy. On one occasion he'd been convinced that she had carried some manure on her shoes from her farm into his freshly cleaned Alfa. It had taken him a couple of hours to clean the car properly afterwards.

'I've left Gareth and Dave finalising all the passenger data,' Caren said. 'Some of the passengers are getting restless.'

Drake felt his mobile vibrate and fished it out of his pocket. 'Drake.'

He heard the voice of Wyndham Price. 'I've had the port manager on the phone.'

Drake glanced over at the office. Mortlake was standing in the doorway now, feet wide apart, a smirk on his face. Drake muffled a hand over one ear, hoping he'd hear everything Price was saying.

'He's complaining about the cargo on the ferry. I know this guy from a local business forum. He can make a lot of noise and his head is so far up his arse ... well. You know the sort.'

Drake glanced over at Mortlake again – arms folded now. 'I know the sort, sir.'

'Go through the motions and leave him to me. Make certain you get the names of everybody on that ship.'

'Of course, sir.'

Drake didn't need the superintendent to tell him how to do his job. He stood for a moment after switching off the mobile. Keeping everyone on the vessel was impractical. He would have to let the passengers and lorries disembark, but at least he would have the name, address and personal details of the killer. It would only then be a matter of time.

The noise from the engines powering into life was deafening and the car deck filled with exhaust fumes. Drake and Caren stood by the office as the first of the tractor units lurched forwards before pulling a container. It crawled over the deck towards the ramp and then upwards onto the harbour concourse. A second followed and soon the area near Foulds was emptying of lorries.

The smile on Mortlake's face grew wider.

Drake left Caren with the officers on the ramp and

walked back over to Foulds and the crime scene investigators working near the body. The car deck near the body was clear: a proper inner perimeter had been established. Foulds appeared more contented when Drake approached him.

'Anything?' Drake asked.

'Oil and grease and diesel. But sod all else.'

'Doctor been?'

'No. Been delayed.'

'When are you going to move the body?'

Before Foulds could answer, his mobile hummed into life and he read the text. 'Andy's finished.'

Drake said nothing but nodded at Caren and they left the car deck to head back up to Rosen's cabin.

Chapter 3

Captain Seymour stood outside the cabin when they arrived. There was pale wash to his skin and the apprehensive look of a man unaccustomed to not being in control. The CSI was packing his equipment away and Drake peered into the cabin, seeing a resemblance of order.

'What was Rosen like?' Drake said to Seymour.

Seymour hesitated. 'Kept himself to himself.'

'Did you know him well?'

'Not really.'

The CSI hauled a box of equipment into the corridor.

'Did you get on with him?'

'Yes. I suppose so.'

'Don't the senior officers all work together?'

'Of course.'

'Why was he on the car deck?'

'Don't know.'

'Is that his normal place of work?'

'No. Of course not.'

'Any ideas then?'

Seymour looked at Drake. 'Look, I have no idea why he was on the car deck. He should have been in the engine room.'

'Why wasn't he in the engine room?'

'How the hell would I know?'

Drake wanted to say – *Well, you're the captain*: instead he said, 'Was there a problem in the engine room?'

'I wasn't aware of anything.'

'Did he have any friends on the crew?'

Seymour seemed puzzled by the question. 'I ... don't know.'

A junior officer walking down the corridor towards them caught Seymour's attention. 'And what do you want, Berkley?'

'I might be able to help.'

Seymour let his mouth fall open.

Drake said to Berkley. 'How well did you know Rosen?'

'He helped me with my studies.'

'How often?'

'Depends.' The man shrugged a little. He was barely twenty, his face still covered in pimples.

They stepped into Rosen's cabin.

The CSI and Seymour stood outside. Inside, order had been restored. The contents had been tidied and bagged. The chair was against the wall and the bed and mattress reunited.

Drake turned to the CSI standing by the door. 'Any personal possessions?'

The investigator gave him a sullen look. 'Not much to talk about. CDs, wash bag. Usual stuff – toothbrush, shaver, etc., etc.'

'Have you found his iPhone?' Berkley asked.

Drake and Caren looked at the investigator.

'And what about his laptop?'

Drake almost fell headlong at the bottom of the last flight of stairs in his haste to reach the car deck. Eventually he heaved open the door and stepped into the deafening sound of engines, air choked with diesel fumes, crew members gesticulating wildly, directing drivers towards the exit. He hurried over to the uniformed officers standing at the bottom of the ramp, their heads turned away against the driving rain. He shouted instructions and they nodded confirmation, pulling the zips of their jackets tightly under their chins.

He walked over to the office with Caren and stood for a moment watching the flickering images from the various CCTV cameras, suppressing his anger that he had not been shown the monitors before. Both screens were divided into four segments, each image tagged with the date and time. He stared at the two screens as though they had some hypnotic quality and it struck him that there might be a record of Rosen's last seconds of life. He heard voices behind him.

'Where do these record?' Drake said directly to the white-suited crew member standing at the door.

'All over the car deck.'

'Anywhere else? And why the hell weren't we told about them before?'

Before the man could answer, Mortlake appeared in the office doorway. '

Why have you stopped the disembarkation?'

The port manager's eyes bulged; he'd loosened his tie. Drake raised his head and stared at him.

'I wasn't told about the CCTV images,' Drake said, pointing at the screen. 'The record from the cameras could be crucial. We are talking about a man's life.'

'I want to know about the disembarkation.'

'Where are they stored?'

'What?'

Drake squinted. 'The images from the cameras. I want copies of everything. I don't want anyone to have access to these computers without my authority.'

Mortlake gave Drake a tired look and nodded sharply. Outside on the car deck the noise was diminishing, making their conversation more audible.

'Inspector Drake, I want to know why you've stopped the disembarkation.'

Drake straightened his posture, drew his shoulders back and stared at Mortlake. 'This ferry is a crime scene.'

'And it's full of containers, mostly with perishable goods.'

'And whilst it's a crime scene, I can stop the disembarkation.'

'But …'

'Rosen's laptop is missing.'

'That could be anywhere …'

'And his mobile telephone. So we'll need to search every lorry and car leaving the ship.'

'You can't be serious.'

Drake clenched his jaw.

'I'll get Special Branch and the customs officers to assist.'

'This could take hours.'

'In the meantime, no one leaves.'

Chapter 4

By the time Drake pushed open the cafeteria door he was starting to think clearly, the anger with Mortlake abating. The smell of fried food made Drake feel both hungry and thirsty.

'Coffee, boss?' Caren said.

Drake mumbled agreement. He had to quench his thirst, but the coffee would be thin and tasteless. He walked over to the table where Winder and Howick were sitting. Winder was short with a round, flabby face and a shaved head that made him look older than he actually was, and he gave Drake a brief acknowledgment as he sat down. He wore a faded red denim shirt under a grey jacket. Drake had suggested in the past that Winder should wear a tie and he made a mental note to mention it again sometime.

'The passengers are getting really twitchy,' Winder said.

'Have they had something to eat and drink?' Drake said

'Yes, boss. But you need to talk to them,' Winder said, urgency in his voice.

'Have we got a full list?' Drake asked.

Dave Howick, sitting by Winder's side, opened the folder on the table and pushed over a list. Howick wore a navy suit, his white shirt looked unironed and his tie, a blue-and-red striped variety, was knotted untidily. A recent haircut had made his face look more gaunt than usual. His work and appearance – and his social skills – had all suffered since he had failed his sergeant's exams a few months previously.

'This was the list we got from the ferry company. But it's only the drivers. We had to add the names of the car and foot passengers. At least the company had the name of every lorry driver.'

Drake raised an eyebrow and looked over at Howick. 'Really? I thought they had to have lists of everybody travelling on a ferry like this.'

'The paperwork is all over the place, sir,' Howick said.

Drake considered for a moment how Mortlake would react if he challenged him about passenger records. 'And the list of crew members?'

Howick pushed over another list.

'And is this list complete?'

Howick nodded. 'At least they got that right.'

Drake studied it as Caren sat down by his side, sliding a mug of coffee over towards him. Winder took a doughnut from the plate piled high with multi-coloured cakes Caren had plonked on the table.

Drake was right about the coffee; it was almost transparent: decent coffee would have to wait. His hands felt dirty and he wouldn't be able to eat anything until he'd washed so he excused himself. Standing in front of the mirror by the washbasins in the gents toilets, he undid the cuffs of his shirt and filled the basin with hot water. He brushed away some mud on his trousers with a paper towel but he cursed when he noticed the oil stains. He poured liquid soap onto his hands and began washing, knowing he would feel better once he'd finished. The ritual cleared and cleansed his mind, as did sudoku: fill out all the squares, solve the riddle. He looked at himself in the mirror, wondering if being a policeman in his early forties meant that he had to have bags under his eyes and grey streaks through his hair.

There were a couple of doughnuts left when he arrived back at the table. He chose one with green-coloured icing that he ate between gulps of tepid coffee. 'Every lorry and every car will have to be searched thoroughly. There's a laptop missing. And an iPhone. All we have to do is find them.'

'This could take days, sir,' Caren said.

'How many lorries are there?' Drake turned to Howick.

'Forty-two.'

'Each search takes ten minutes. That's seven hours,' Caren said. Drake could see that she was about to launch into one of her customary speeches where she'd share her plans for how the investigation should be run but before she could say anything Winder cut in.

'And there are forty cars.'

'Can we realistically do a search in ten minutes?' Caren put down her empty cup and started tapping into her mobile. 'That's another five hours,' she said.

Drake's mobile hummed into life and he quickly read the message. 'Backup's arrived.'

'I don't think it's one of the passengers,' Caren said.

Drake pulled the door of the lounge closed, knowing he'd left behind a hundred disgruntled passengers. He'd tried to sound helpful but instead he'd come across as vague. As he strode towards the stairs, Caren kept in step.

'Maybe not,' Drake said. 'But we can't take that chance, can we?'

They made their way down to the car deck, Drake unsure if he'd just said the right thing to placate the travellers. He certainly didn't want any more dissent.

'Make sure Seymour gets them enough to eat and drink,' he said, as they reached the pneumatic entrance door to the car deck. Immediately he felt the rush of damp air on his face. He looked over towards the ramp and noticed the rain still sheeting down, driving water into the ship. He took a couple of paces and saw a team of officers swarming like ants over a lorry, the tarpaulin drawn open, exposing the boxes in the shipment. There were three men in the cab slowly dissecting the driver's possessions and another half a dozen squeezing past crates. The driver stood by Winder, a resigned, bored look on his face.

'How is the search going?' Drake said, as he stood by Winder's side, zipping the Barbour as high as he could.

He shook his head. 'We're doing quite well. This is the tenth lorry,' he added after consulting the list on the clipboard in his hand.

'Any luck?'

'Three is about the maximum number of officers that can work in any one cab.'

'What about searching the actual cargo?'

Winder blew out his cheeks. 'Some of them are very easy. It's the ones with the tarpaulin down each side that are the simplest. At least that way we can see all the cargo. A couple of the uniformed lads from the station in town scrounged torches from the customs department. Without them it would have been a nightmare.'

'Have the crew been getting in your way?'

'Something's going on. Mortlake has been talking frantically into his mobile.'

Drake crossed his arms and looked towards the office, but couldn't see Mortlake or any of the other crew members. As the senior investigating officer, Drake was in charge. This was his crime scene and he would organise the investigation as he wanted.

'So how long is it going to take us to finish all the lorries and the cars?'

'Hours, sir.'

'And if we had more manpower?'

'Might help.'

The team had finished on the lorry in front of Drake and Caren. The driver dropped the tarpaulin and fastened the tabs before jumping into the cab and starting the engine. Drake waved a hand in front of his face as fumes filled the air. Then the driver slowly pulled away towards the ramp and out into the rain.

Drake hadn't noticed Mortlake approaching until he was standing right by his side, his jaw jutting out, his hands thrust deep into the pockets of his fluorescent jacket.

'I need a word, Inspector.'

'What about?'

'Not here. In the office. Follow me.'

Drake nodded briefly to Caren, noticing the reassuring expression on her face.

Mortlake slammed the door closed behind Drake. He seemed to draw himself up, swirl his head back in a movement Drake had seen in men about to head-butt someone and then he drew his tongue over his lips. 'How long is this fiasco going to take?'

Normally, Drake would have made an attempt at being courteous but he had taken an instant dislike to Mortlake, a dislike that was clouding his judgement.

'This is a crime scene.'

'I bloody well know that.'

'And I'm the senior investigating officer.'

'And I know that too – you keep reminding me.'

'It's going to take as long as it takes.'

'I don't know what you think you're going to find. But it's totally over the top to insist on searching every single lorry and car like this.'

Mortlake had a finger pointed at Drake. 'This company employs a lot of people in this town. We've got some important connections. You can't just close the ferry service down.'

'As this is a crime scene, I can do what I want.'

'We'll see about that.'

Before Drake could say anything further, the door behind Mortlake opened and Superintendent Price walked in. Drake's initial surprise gave way to an uneasy feeling that he wasn't in control of events.

'Ian.' Price acknowledged Drake before turning to Mortlake. 'I want to discuss the investigation with Inspector

Drake.'

'Of course, of course.' Mortlake managed a brief, snide look at Drake as he left.

'He's been really obstructive, sir,' Drake said.

'Bring me up to date.'

'There's a laptop and an iPhone missing from Rosen's cabin.'

'And you're searching every vehicle?'

'Have to, sir.' Drake widened his stance. 'And they didn't even tell me about the CCTV camera until I came into this office. If we don't find this bloody laptop we'll have to search the entire vessel.'

Price nodded slowly, a look of resignation on his face, acknowledging that Drake was right. 'Let's get the passengers off as soon as we can.'

'There's a murderer amongst them or the crew.'

'Probably not the passengers.'

'We can't be certain. We have to check everybody.'

Price folded his arms.

'Mortlake was able to get the MD of the ferry company to call the Chief Constable in Cardiff. Banging on about the company's margins and how important it was for the ship to sail.'

'We've got a murder investigation,' Drake said, measuring every word.

'For Christ's sake Ian, don't you think the Chief Constable knows that? I've got two dozen off-duty officers coming in the next half an hour to assist. We need to get the passengers off first.'

Drake linked the fingers of his hands together and rested them on the top of his head. 'We know where the murderer is: he's on the ship. Once we let everybody go, they could be taking valuable evidence with them.'

'I know you're not happy, but there's nothing more we can do. Get all the passengers and crew photographed, logged, all their details taken. Maybe then we can get

Mortlake out of our hair.'

When they left the office a stream of policemen in high-visibility jackets walked down the ramp past Mortlake, nodding acknowledgments to Price and then to Drake. Price breezed past them, heading for the ramp where he stood talking with Mortlake for a couple of minutes before leaving.

Drake spent the next three hours crouching over officers who were rifling through passengers' suitcases, children's rucksacks, double-checking everything. He stared at every passenger and lorry driver, wanting to memorise their faces and clothes and belongings, convincing himself that, this way, he might not miss something important. As the last of the vehicles left the ferry, Caren walked up to Drake.

'Waste of time, sir.'

'We didn't have a choice.'

Drake noticed that the rain had stopped. It was the first time he'd looked outside for several hours.

'I suppose we need to check out the crew?' Caren asked.

Drake nodded as his stomach reminded him that a doughnut was not really adequate sustenance. 'I need something to eat.'

The table in the cafeteria was sticky as Drake ran his finger over the surface. He opted for a bottle of water and ate a single ham sandwich whose sell-by date had just past, feeling his appetite disappearing as he watched Caren vacuuming up a plateful of stale chips. He looked round the cafe area for a newspaper, hoping that he'd find a sudoku to solve. He only needed to solve a couple of squares. Enough to make him feel in control. Caren paused briefly and looked at him as he checked the tables without success.

Howick and Winder joined them at the table before finalising the day's work. The crew members had been logged and told to expect a visit for a formal interview. A little before midnight Drake found himself on the quayside staring at the ship, wondering which of the faces that he had stared at today, spoken to in the lounge, or seen photographed was actually that of a killer.

Chapter 5

Overnight the rain clouds had disappeared and the early spring sunshine streamed into the car as Caren drove through the tunnels along the A55, the main trunk road that stretched along the North Wales coast. Drake sat by her side, a folded newspaper on his lap face-up at the sudoku page. He turned a pencil slowly through his fingers.

As they approached the bridge over the Menai Strait Drake looked up, stopped fidgeting with the pencil and stared out of the window. It was the same every time he had to cross the bridge, memories flooding back, recriminations swirling and, more than anything, guilt as he thought about the deaths he might have prevented. A difficult case, a year previously, had hit him hard but the counselling the Wales Police Service had insisted he needed still nagged at the back of his mind. Soon they were onto the island and Drake focused on the task ahead: they had a widow to see, condolences to offer.

Another thirty minutes passed as Caren wound her way through the country lanes towards the cottage Janet Rosen had shared with her husband. Caren slowed as she neared the property: its windows were small, the outside walls shaped from large boulders. Small wooden windows had been neatly painted a brilliant white to match the exterior. Drake had often seen cottages like this, their uneven roofs covered with slurry to delay further decay, but Janet's cottage had a gleaming slate roof that looked clean and newly rain-washed.

Drake was surprised to see a marked police car parked by the low stone wall surrounding the cottage. Caren parked next to a log store, full to the brim with neatly chopped pieces of timber. A woman Drake assumed to be Janet Rosen stood by the back door next to a uniformed officer who was speaking into his mobile. When he saw

Drake he finished the call and walked over towards him.

'Constable Iwan Morris,' he said. 'Good morning, sir. There's been a break-in.'

'When?' Drake said.

'Last night. Mrs Rosen was staying with her brother. She got back first thing this morning. She called 999 once she discovered the break-in. She told me you'd called her last night to arrange to see her this morning.'

'CSIs?'

'Shouldn't be too long.'

Janet had her arms folded when Drake walked towards her and he could see her pale complexion and her eyes swollen and pink.

'Detective Inspector Drake and Sergeant Waits,' Drake said. 'My condolences, I am very sorry for your loss.'

'Has this break-in got anything to do with Frank's death?' Janet said.

'It's far too early to tell. Have you been into the house?'

She nodded.

'Is there anything obviously missing?'

'His computer and the television and the stereo. He had one of those fancy touch-screen computers in the study at the back of the house.'

'We want to have a preliminary discussion. Let's sit in the car,' Drake said.

Caren sat in the rear seat behind Drake, who'd swivelled around to face Janet in the passenger seat.

'Can you think of anyone who might want to kill your husband?' Drake said.

'The officer yesterday asked the same thing.'

'I'm sorry. I know it's painful.'

Janet looked older than Drake had expected: he reckoned she must be nearer fifty than her late husband had been. The lines around her eyes and grey bags didn't help. Turning away from Drake, she peered out of the window.

'Frank and I were having difficulties. Arguing, not seeing eye to eye.'

'What was the reason?'

'He was never here; he worked a week on, a week off and during the time he was off I never saw him. I thought he was having an affair with one of the girls on the ferry.'

'Did you confront him?'

'We argued a lot.'

'Did he have any financial problems?'

She gave a noncommittal shrug before replying. 'We had separate bank accounts.'

'Did he have any enemies?'

She gave Drake a sharp look. 'What on earth to you mean?'

Caren interjected before Drake could respond. 'Somebody had a motive to kill Frank and anything that you can tell us about his background, his family, work, will all help. We need to build a picture of your late husband. Something that will enable us to understand more about him.'

'I can't think,' Janet said.

'There must be something, surely,' Drake said.

'How were things at work?' Caren asked.

'He'd just been promoted to chief engineer. He was delighted. It was always something he wanted.'

'Did his promotion cause any ill feeling with the other engineers?' Caren continued.

Janet looked puzzled. 'And you think one of them could have killed him?'

'Janet, tell us if you know something about his colleagues.'

'Well, I know it was between him and the other second engineer. Frank could be very determined and he really wanted the job.'

'What was his name?' Drake asked.

'Robert James.'

'What about family?'

'We didn't have any children,' Janet said, an edge of disappointment to her voice.

A silence hung in the air for a moment.

'Frank was an only child and his parents died a few years ago. It was their inheritance that meant we could buy the cottage.' Janet looked towards the house.

'What about friends?' Caren asked.

'He spends a lot of his free time at the flying club.'

'Where?'

'The flying club at RAF Mona.'

'Did you meet his friends there?'

'Not really.'

'Did you have the names of his friends?'

'All the details will be in his study.'

A Scientific Support Vehicle pulled up and Drake saw the CSIs jump out and walk over to the young uniformed officer.

'Ellis-Pugh,' Janet said, loudly enough to break Drake's concentration.

He looked at her.

'Ellis-Pugh is one of the officers of the flying club. Thinks he's very important.'

'Did Frank fly a lot?' Caren said.

'All the time,' Janet replied wearily.

'Is it an expensive hobby?'

'Yes, I suppose it is.'

'How often did he fly?'

A shadow fell on Drake's window, followed by a brief tapping sound. He wound down the window. 'Do you want to see inside, sir?' Iwan Morris said.

'In a minute.'

Janet continued. 'Most weekends when he wasn't working. More often than that in the summer. Because he had a licence to fly at night, he was popular with some of the other members. What happens now?'

'A family liaison officer will be calling later,' Caren said, smiling at Janet.

Janet just nodded.

'The post mortem will take place this afternoon. If there's anything further, then we'll contact you.' Drake was already out of the car before Janet could reply.

He walked over to the door and stepped into the crime scene. Every drawer and cupboard in the kitchen had been opened and the contents strewn over worktops. He went through into the sitting room – cushions had been shredded and chairs upended. He heard the voices of the CSIs down a corridor and found them staring at the chaos in what must have been Rosen's study, the books and CDs now in piles on the floor. He threaded his way back through the cottage and stood looking over at the car. There was an old dilapidated workshop and pigsty at the far end of the driveway, covered in slate waste. Caren had wound down the window and was still talking to Janet. Drake leant over and rested a hand on the sill of the car door.

'Have you got anywhere to stay tonight?' he asked Janet.

'My brother and sister-in-law. That's where I was staying last night.'

'The house is a mess.'

'How long will they be?'

Drake straightened. 'Hard to say. All day at a guess.'

'Anything in the sheds?' Drake looked over at a door hanging off its hinges.

'Of course,' Janet said. 'I should have remembered. Frank had a box he kept hidden. It had his mother's jewellery and a watch his father bought in Germany after the war. He was afraid of losing them in a burglary.'

Janet got out of the car and strode towards the door. Drake and Caren followed. Their footsteps made a crunching sound, reminding Drake of his parents' smallholding and how reassuring the noise could be. He hadn't spoken to his father for a couple of days and with the course of treatment for his father's cancer coming to an end, Drake's mind felt heavy with possibilities.

Janet led the way around the rear of the building and through an open doorway to a small passage that eventually opened into a working area, full of old rusting tools, and a pile of timber shaving under a saw-horse.

'It's over here.' Janet squeezed through a small gap.

Beyond was a dark room with a large old fireplace in once corner. She knelt down and reached up into the breasting, struggling at first, but then she pulled her hand down and looked at the small metal container. Drake stepped over towards her as she opened the top.

There was an old Rolex watch, a gold chain and jewellery. But lying on top of some old, pristine one-pound notes was a data stick. Drake lifted it out carefully.

'I wonder what's on this?'

Ron Flanagan from the forensics department was waiting in reception when Drake and Caren arrived at headquarters. The excited look on his face matched the enthusiasm in his voice when Drake had warned him he had a data stick that he needed to access. Flanagan held the device tightly as he headed for his office.

Drake fished out his mobile and dialled the forensic team that was still conducting the search of the vessel, hoping he wouldn't have to spend another afternoon on the ship. Mike Foulds answered after one ring.

'Is there anything to report?' Drake said.

'Do you know how many places there might be to hide a laptop on a ship?'

'It's slow going then?'

'Glacial would be a better word. Can you spare a hundred officers?'

'Don't be daft.'

'We'll do what we can.'

Caren raised her eyebrows as though she expected Drake to tell her what Foulds had said, but his mind was distracted.

'What did Mike Foulds have to say?' Caren asked, standing by his door.

'Nothing. I didn't expect him to find anything; the laptop was probably taken off the ship in a car or one of the lorries.'

'But we searched everything.'

'We were under too much time pressure. It should never have been like that. We should have done a more thorough search of everything.'

'It was as comprehensive as we could have made it, in the circumstances.'

On the first floor Drake pushed open the door to the Incident Room where Winder and Howick were busy at their desks. A board had been assembled along one wall and a photograph of Frank Rosen had been pinned to the middle.

Drake looked over at Howick who was scratching a day's worth of stubble, his shirt cuffs flapping untidily. Gareth Winder had shaved his head the night before, Drake concluded from the light that was reflecting off the young officer's skull.

'What's next, boss?' Winder asked.

Drake dragged a hand over his wrist and looked at his watch. 'Caren and I are going to the post mortem this afternoon. Gareth, you get over to the port office. I want to find out everything about Rosen. There must be a personnel file – you know, appraisals and training. Everybody does training these days.'

Winder nodded.

Drake turned to Howick. A spasm of annoyance rippled through his mind as he watched Howick chewing gum. 'Dave, I need you to go through all the crew and get a PNC check done for them all.'

'Everyone?'

Caren broke in. 'Do you think it's someone from the crew?'

'Could be a passenger,' Winder suggested.

'Once you've done the crew, we'll look at the passengers.'

Howick made his first contribution. 'Might have been a crew member and a passenger together. One kills him and the other takes the laptop.' Howick scooped the gum out of his mouth and wrapped it in a shred of paper.

Drake didn't need reminding about the laptop and he narrowed his eyes at Howick. 'Forensics haven't finished the search of the ship yet. So they might still find the laptop.'

Drake left the Incident Room and slumped into the chair in his office. It was exactly as he had left it two nights previously. The bin was in its correct place and he reassured himself that the papers on the small bookcase were in the same precise order. The photograph of Megan and Helen stood by the side of the computer and he gave it a reassuring nudge. The telephone handset was clean but the computer screen seemed smudged, so he took a handkerchief and gave it a gentle wipe before switching it on. As he waited for the machine to flicker into life he checked the Post-it notes that had been left in two neat and orderly columns on his desk. Not all of the notes had the same colour and the insertion of red ones had been a recent innovation that Drake hoped would help him prioritise better. In his inbox, he trawled through the emails, checking them individually before deleting those of little value.

Then he started a sudoku from one of the books of puzzles in his desk and for the first time that morning felt properly in control.

'What's he like?'

Superintendent Wyndham Price stared at Simon

Lance, wondering how he'd answer. The secondment had been finalised more quickly than he'd expected and tomorrow he would be facing a new challenge in the West Midlands. But in the meantime, he had Superintendent Lance sitting in his office asking about Drake.

'You've not met him?' Price avoided answering directly.

Lance shook his head.

'He's a good officer. Difficult to get to know him and he can be prickly. He won a Chief Constable's commendation medal a couple of years ago.'

Lance raised his eyebrows.

'But a case last year hit him hard.'

'The murder of the two officers,' Lance said, nodding now. 'I remember the case, of course. Very high profile.'

Price sat back in his chair and threw a biro onto the desk. Lance had a certain reserved personality, as though he didn't want anyone to get to know him, rather like Drake, a little too buttoned up and formal.

'Drake is having counselling as well. Paid for by the WPS.'

Lance raised his eyebrows again and kept them high, a little longer this time. 'I didn't realise—'

'Don't worry. You won't be expected to discuss anything with Drake.'

Lance looked relieved.

There was a knock on the door and Drake came into the room.

'Ian,' Price began. 'This is Superintendent Lance from Southern Division. He's replacing me for three months while I'm on secondment to the West Midlands.'

Lance stood up and leant forward to shake Drake's outstretched hand. Both men gave each other a wary look. Drake's brief smile created a fold on both cheeks that framed his mouth. There was sense of balance to Drake's face –

eyebrows, nose and mouth perfectly proportioned. Normally his clear blue eyes had directness, but this morning Price could sense the hesitation. Price looked from one man to the other guessing that Lance at six feet tall was the same height as Drake. When Price motioned to a chair, Drake sat down.

'I thought you could bring us both up to speed with the latest on the Rosen case.'

'I've just come back from the post mortem. He was killed with a knife wound to the heart.'

'Any forensics?'

'Nothing yet. We'll have the results of the clothing quite quickly.'

'Anything from the search of the ship?'

'It will take some time.'

Drake's mobile hummed into life and he smiled as he read the message.

Lance butted in. 'What's missing, Inspector?'

'A laptop. At least it was.'

Chapter 6

The following morning Drake parked near Caren's battered estate car and glanced inside, noticing the shopping bags and piles of old clothes. He couldn't imagine how someone could live with such untidiness. To reassure himself he stepped back towards his car and looked inside: all neat and tidy. Reception was already busy and he skirted around a stationery delivery and wound his way through the building to the CSI department.

Mike Foulds sat by a long table, in front of him a mug that had *KEEP CALM BECOME A CSI* printed on it. Caren leant against another desk. She was drinking tea that she sloshed around her mouth noisily, a habit that annoyed Drake, but he never had the courage to suggest she change. She'd discarded the smart clothes from the day of the seminar and was back to looking like a farmer. Her unruly hair looked like it had seen an attempt at brushing, but there were still knots that she'd missed, and under her coat Drake could see her blouse needed ironing.

'Good morning, Ian,' Foulds said.

'Mike,' Drake said.

'Help yourself to some coffee,' he said, nodding towards the electric kettle on the bench behind Caren.

Drake spotted the cheap instant brand, turned up his nose and declined. Foulds clicked the mouse, and the screen on the laptop in front of him came to life. Drake and Caren stepped over towards him.

'Anything on it that's going to help us?' Drake said.

'There are no fingerprints. The memory is empty. Nothing – no files or films or music.'

'Someone must have deleted them.'

'Looks like it.'

'How long would it take?'

'Not long. Depends.'

Caren asked, 'Where did you find it?'

'It had been pushed into a store cupboard, full of cleaning materials. It was just lucky that we'd started the search nearby. Otherwise we'd still be there.'

Immediately Drake considered what Mortlake would be making of his ship still being out of action. He looked down at the laptop humming silently on the desk; he had to make sense of who might have moved it. 'Can you tell when the laptop was last booted up?'

Foulds took another sip of his tea and wiped a hand across his lips.

'Should be able to. Let me ...' He started clicking the mouse and staring intently as various screens came to life.

'Any sign of the iPhone?' Caren asked.

'You're joking.' Foulds was still staring at the screen. 'I've still got three CSIs trawling through the crew quarters.'

'Did you see Mortlake?'

Foulds lifted his head and fixed Drake with a narrow glare. 'Kept floating around. He's your number one fan ...'

Before Foulds could finish Flanagan came into the room, an excited look on his face like a child at Christmas.

'Something you need to see,' he said.

Ron Flanagan didn't do eye contact. He kept alternating his gaze between a point just above Drake's left ear and his right elbow and Drake could feel himself following the man's darting glances. Drake pondered whether a black shirt and a multi-coloured sleeveless sweater really was in keeping with the WPS dress code. He could imagine Flanagan listening to folk music in a small bar, drinking real ale from a straight glass.

Flanagan sat down by his computer. 'Mr Rosen must have planned this very carefully.'

'Get on with it, Ron, just give us the details.' Foulds folded his arms.

Drake stood immediately behind Flanagan in the room he shared with two other civilian technicians, with Caren and Foulds on either side of him.

'Mr Rosen had created a lot of folders protected by passwords. At the start I thought it was a bit of a challenge.'

'But?' Drake said, realising that Flanagan was one who enjoyed suspense.

'When I first started with the two main folders you can see on the screen now,' Flanagan said, not distracted by Drake for a second, 'I tried all the usual sorts of passwords – date of birth, first name, last name, name of wife, house name. Some people even have a file with their passwords in them. Eventually I was able to get into these two folders. Just so.' Drake peered at the screen as Flanagan clicked through the various images.

'And of course within each of those two folders there are more files, each passworded in turn. So I had to start again.'

'I can guess,' interrupted Drake. 'Eventually you got through.'

'Yes, sir.' Drake ignored the hurt expression in Flanagan's voice.

'Inside each folder there is a file with a number. In fact, everything about Frank Rosen is about numbers. He's probably a really compulsive character.'

Drake sensed Caren, Winder and Howick staring at the back of his neck. Although he'd been able to conquer the compulsions and rituals recently, and things had got better, even at home – his wife, Sian, had reassured him of that – still he sensed the nervous, embarrassed stares. Glancing around, however, he saw them staring only at the screen, oblivious of him, waiting for Flanagan to finish.

'Once I got through all the passwords I could open the fifteen individual files. And they've all got various lines of numbers and letters. It's obviously a code of some sort.'

Flanagan double-clicked the mouse until the screen was dominated by the numbers contained in one of the files.

06	10	8
G	N	G
LK	WX	D
1589	3985	15146
0630	0524	0218
351	1652	2568

Then he clicked through it to each in turn. Each list was different in its order, but similar in content.

'What do these mean?' Drake said.

Howick was the first to make a contribution. 'Maybe Rosen was in a betting syndicate.'

'We'll probably find something in his personal possessions,' Drake said. 'We'll need copies of everything that you've been able to open'.

'Already done,' Flanagan said, adding as an afterthought, 'sir.'

'So what do we know so far?' Drake played with his cufflinks, pulling at the light-blue, quality fabric of his shirt, as he stood by the board in the Incident Room. Occasionally the links glistened as they caught the artificial light.

He had a pained expression that Caren had seen earlier that morning when Foulds had mentioned Mortlake. She had seen the same troubled look when she spotted Drake in the canteen at lunchtime, obviously uncomfortable with the two road traffic officers who had sat down at his table.

Caren sensed that it was better not to interrupt him. Winder still hadn't returned from his trip to the ferry company's offices at Holyhead and she guessed he was extending his lunch hour. Howick sat by her side, a surly, uninterested look on his face. She had been tempted more than once to speak to him, but decided it was down to Drake.

'We'll need to dismantle Rosen's life,' Drake continued, folding his arms. 'There must be something about these codes: the numbers must link to something in his life.'

'Do you want us to look at Janet Rosen?' Caren asked.

'But you can't think she was responsible? It would have meant somebody else being on the ship,' Howick said, still slumped in his chair.

Drake ignored him. 'Caren, we look at Janet in detail. And Dave, we need to build a clear picture about Rosen. Get all his mobile phone records, we'll need to find his bank statements, go through everything. I'm going to see the flying club later.'

'Maybe he was blackmailing somebody? Perhaps he knew somebody's guilty secret,' Howick said.

'Whatever the reason for his death, somebody had a good motive. And that somebody is on one of the lists that we have. We know who the killer is, just remember that.'

Caren sensed Drake's mood lifting as he continued. 'There's a list of passengers and the crew members. All we have to do is find out who it was. Simple.'

Caren wasn't certain what sort of response Drake expected. She glanced quickly at Howick who had a Drake-like pained expression on his face, so she decided against saying anything.

Chapter 7

Drake played the entirety of Pink Floyd's *Dark Side of the Moon* on the journey from headquarters to RAF Mona. He only ever played it in full when he was driving and usually it gave him the opportunity to think clearly. The final bars of the last song faded as he parked next to a sign that said Anglesey Flying Club – Guests. Apart from a securely locked control tower, the only evidence of its use by the Royal Air Force was the gleaming new tarmac of the runway.

He locked the car and walked over towards a ramshackle building. Drake imagined the fighters that would have filled the airspace over the island when it was used as a major training base during the Second World War. Now all that remained was the old structure, badly in need of redecoration, new doors and windows. Behind it was a hangar where Drake guessed the planes of the flying club would be stored.

In the distance, towards the mainland, Drake saw the late afternoon sun catching the mountain peaks and, looking over towards Caernarfon, he thought about his father, knowing that he wouldn't be in the fields, mending fences or tending to sheep.

Screwed to the wall near a door was a simple weather-beaten sign – 'AFC – Entrance'. Drake entered the narrow hallway and shouted a hello; he half expected the secretary and chairman of the club to have been waiting outside for him in leather bomber jackets and long white scarves.

From somewhere in the building he heard voices that became louder when the door to the office was opened. A man stepped out into the corridor and called over at Drake who recognised the deep, laid-back tones of Wing Commander Ellis-Pugh's voice from his telephone conversation.

'How do you do?' Ellis-Pugh was dressed in a one-piece green suit and his well-groomed moustache seemed strangely out of place below a balding head and a narrow nose. Drake shook his hand and exchanged pleasantries; he guessed that Ellis-Pugh was in his early fifties, but he could have been older. The other man standing by a desk was nearer sixty.

'This is Tim Loosemore,' Ellis-Pugh said. 'The club secretary.'

'Good morning, Inspector,' Loosemore said.

Drake shook the secretary's offered hand and sat down.

'Absolutely dreadful business,' Ellis-Pugh began. 'Dreadful. Rosen was an awfully decent chap, you know, very popular. Can't understand why anyone would want to kill him.'

'I appreciate your help. I need a list of the members and then some information about the club,' Drake said.

'I've prepared a list of all the members, Inspector,' Loosemore said, passing an envelope to Drake. 'What other information do you need?'

'Coffee?' Ellis-Pugh said, more as an order than a question.

'Black, no sugar,' Drake replied. 'Who were Rosen's friends?'

Ellis-Pugh was fumbling with the electric kettle until eventually it started a gurgling sound.

'Can't really say much about his friends,' Loosemore said.

'What was he like as a pilot?'

'Frank Rosen was a natural pilot. Great intuition, good responses and patient with younger pilots. It was a hobby he could have turned into a profession had he chosen to do so. He had been a member of the club for many years, certainly over ten years,' Ellis-Pugh replied, pulling three old mugs from the bowels of the cupboard. He gave them a cursory glance, presumably to check for life and then thrust a spoon into the coffee jar and quickly tipped granules into the mugs.

'How long have you been secretary of the club?' Drake asked Loosemore.

'Just over two years. After I retired actually. I'd sold my company in Marlow and I had a holiday home here so I came up to live here permanently. Before that I had been a member and I knew him vaguely.'

Ellis-Pugh put the steaming coffee mugs on the table for both men. From a drawer he drew out a packet of digestive biscuits that he scattered over a plate.

'What was Rosen like?' asked Drake.

'Generally unflappable, bit quiet.'

'Did you notice anything different about him recently?'

'What do you mean?'

'Anything really'

'Can't think,' Ellis-Pugh said.

Tim Loosemore added, 'Frank Rosen was well liked and approachable. He was a regular flyer for our syndicate.'

'Syndicate?' asked Drake.

'Yes of course. I should explain. A syndicate is a group of individuals who pool their resources and buy a plane together.'

'Who were the others?'

Ellis-Pugh passed Drake another piece of paper. 'The names are on this list with contact details.'

'Where do the members fly? Do you go very far?'

Loosemore replied, 'All over really. England, South Wales, Scotland, Ireland, the Isle of Man. Most of the members are professionals or local businessmen. It's not a hobby without cost.'

Ellis-Pugh snorted. 'Damned expensive sometimes. And Rosen was as keen as mustard.'

'He had a night flying qualification,' Loosemore

added. 'Made him very popular for overnight trips.'

'Are you aware of anybody who might want to kill Frank Rosen?' The question sounded lame but it was the sort of enquiry Drake had to make.

'I think I can speak for both of us, Inspector Drake,' replied Ellis-Pugh. 'From my knowledge of Frank I can't imagine anyone who might want to harm him.'

Loosemore nodded solemnly.

Drake drank the coffee as he listened to Ellis-Pugh and Loosemore exchanging banter about their flying trips. By the time Drake had finished he had the impression that Rosen was no more than the hired help for a group of wealthy businessmen.

'Would you like a guided tour of our humble surroundings?' Ellis-Pugh asked.

The *surroundings* comprised a changing room with some old lockers, without locks; mess room with tables, some armchairs and a very peculiar smell; three further rooms were occupied by a collection of furniture that would not have been out of place in a Second World War movie. Finally there was a grandly titled Committee Room, its hallmark being a clean carpet, tidy and unmarked table tops and a board on the wall inscribed with the names of the club chairmen. In the last few years Ellis-Pugh's name featured regularly.

Outside, Ellis-Pugh took him towards the hangar used by the flying club. It was large and cavernous, the wind rattling the zinc sheets that kept the building together. Drake counted twenty aircraft, all neatly parked.

'Any security problems?' asked Drake.

'Not really, it's not like having a car,' observed Loosemore. 'Occasionally the Special Branch from the port pay us a visit. Meirion sorts out all the notifications.' He nodded towards his friend.

'We lock the hangar every day,' Meirion Ellis-Pugh said, raising his voice slightly, 'and none of the aircraft have any valuables left in them.'

Drake zipped his Barbour up to his chin as he made his way back to the car. In the distance he could make out the shape of the Carneddau mountain range rising beyond the flatness of Anglesey. Sitting in the car he rifled through his CD collection, choosing a Springsteen *Greatest Hits* album for the journey home.

An hour later he pulled into his drive and switched off the CD player. He picked up the newspaper lying on the passenger seat with its unfinished sudoku, which he knew he would have to complete later.

Sian wore a pair of denims that made the best of her slim figure, a powder-blue blouse, the one he'd bought her as an anniversary present, and as a gamble, and an expensive, dark plaited leather belt had been threaded through the loops of the jeans. She kissed him lightly, before he slumped onto a chair in the kitchen, having taken a bottle of Peroni from the fridge.

'Where are the girls?'

'They're at my mother's. I did tell you this morning, Ian.'

Drake nodded; he'd forgotten, of course. Sian sluiced water over broccoli spears before checking the stew bubbling on the hob.

'I've just spent two hours in the Anglesey Flying Club. Did I tell you that I went flying once with a friend of mine years ago?'

Sian nodded.

'Rich man's game, I suppose.' He slugged a mouthful of lager. 'Place was run by two real old-fashioned types. I'm sure I've seen Loosemore on the news, and the other one – Ellis-Pugh – was like something out of a comic.'

'Is that Tim Loosemore the bio-scientist?'

'Yes. He's the one who's been in the papers.'

'His daughter was a year ahead of me at medical school. She'd look down her nose at those of us who wanted to be GPs. More money than she could spend. Her own Audi and a flat that Daddy had bought for her.'

'Not bad.'

'She's a consultant in one of the London hospitals now. And I've come across Meirion Ellis-Pugh through one of those charities our practice manager wants the surgery to support. His daughter has a very rare illness.'

Drake didn't say anything; he was thinking about the codes that Rosen had created. If he could bring the numbers under control the answer would surely be there.

'And I don't suppose you've spoken to your mother,' Sian said.

'What?'

'Your mother. We discussed it this morning. She wanted to talk to you about your father's treatment.'

'No, today has been a blur.'

Before Sian could respond Drake's mobile buzzed. He didn't recognise the number.

'Inspector Drake,' Lance said. 'I've had the MD of the ferry company on to me. They're insisting on getting the ferry back in service.'

'But we need to interview the crew properly.'

'You've got tomorrow. After that the ferry restarts its schedule.

'But that could mean delays—'

'Do your best.'

Drake stabbed the mobile's *off* button and cursed Mortlake. Then he took another mouthful of the cold beer before going in search of the sudoku and a pencil.

Chapter 8

It was still early morning when Drake crossed the railway bridge at Holyhead as a train pulled out of the station. Grey clouds shrouded the terraces and port buildings, but the promised rain had kept away. He turned left at a set of traffic lights and then down towards the port. Drake had spent a few months based in the town as a young officer, dealing with the drug dealers and petty criminals. Not to mention being entertained by the older officers with their tales of the *terrorist movements* through the port years before. It always had the air of a place that people passed through: nobody stayed except the locals.

Long queues of lorries were parked, waiting for the next ferry; a few cars had already arrived and staff milled around the concourse. On the other side of the port Drake caught sight of the twin funnels of the ship.

Drake collected a security pass and then they snaked their way through the port, passing the buses waiting for foot passengers before reaching the terminal. It was a short walk down the ramp into the vessel where Drake could see Captain Seymour and Mortlake waiting for them.

He pushed out a hand. 'Good morning, Captain. Mr Mortlake.'

'Morning Inspector,' Seymour replied. Mortlake made a brief grin and a nod.

Upstairs in one of the lounges a table had been set out for Drake and Caren at different ends of the room. Mortlake stood, arms folded as Drake dumped a folder of papers on the nearest table. A clean antiseptic smell filled the air.

'We've almost finished getting the vessel ready,' Mortlake said. 'You've got until this afternoon to interview all the crew.'

'We'll see how long it takes,' Drake said, taking off his jacket and draping it over the back of a chair.

Seymour now. 'The ferry has to be clear by late this afternoon. We've got a sailing this evening and I've a hundred lorries booked.'

Drake knew from his conversation with Lance that he was under pressure to complete the interviews before the vessel restarted its service. But he wasn't going to give either Seymour or Mortlake the certainty that he'd finish in good time.

'We'd better get started then,' Drake said.

An hour later Drake had seen four crew members and Caren had managed only three. He calculated that taking fifteen minutes for each of the individuals on his list would take just under seven hours without having lunch or toilet breaks.

He took off his wrist watch and propped it into a position where he could read the face. It would have to be twelve minutes each from now on. Then he glanced down the list of standard questions Caren had drafted, wondering how many he could ignore.

'Anything of interest?' Caren called over to Drake when they'd finished seeing two of the crew at the same time.

'Nothing,' Drake said. 'Bloody waste of time.'

'Nobody liked him much.'

Drake nodded back, as a young girl with dark freckles came through the door and sat down opposite him.

By two o'clock Drake glanced over at Caren and saw her shaking hands with one of the crew as he stood to leave. Drake walked over to her, finishing the last dregs of a bottle of spring water. He could tell from the look in her eyes that her conversations had been a waste of time.

'Somebody must have seen Rosen,' Caren said.

'Maybe we just haven't seen the right people yet.'

'Who have you got next?'

Drake glanced at the name of a second engineer – it didn't sound Welsh.

'Foreign-sounding engineer.'

Drake noticed a face at the door and waved towards it. Second Engineer Stewart Van de Melk was a pallid, spotty youngster; Drake thought he looked far too young for the job. There was a nervous and agitated look in his eyes.

'What was your working relationship with Rosen like?' Drake said.

'Fine.'

'Did you find him easy to get on with?'

'OK.'

Drake realised it was going to be a struggle so he diverted from the standard script.

'Did Rosen help your career?'

'Well, yes, sort of.' He sounded defensive, before he explained about the qualifications he was aiming to complete. Rosen had helped him with his revision for an exam. Van de Melk drew a picture of Rosen as a straightforward colleague, helpful to subordinates.

'Where are you from?'

'Holyhead.' Van de Melk sounded surprised. 'My family's originally from Holland. The Dutch navy was stationed here in the war. My grandad stayed on.'

'Was Rosen good company?'

'What do you mean?'

'Did you socialise with him?'

'No.'

'Who did he socialise with?'

Van de Melk shrugged.

'There was something ...' Van de Melk paused. 'I heard an argument between Rosen and James about the promotion. I think James was annoyed that Rosen had been promoted before him. There was a lot of swearing and I heard James say he was going to kill Rosen.'

Drake moved uneasily in his chair. James was further down on his list. This could be nothing more than a jealous argument, but on the other hand.

By the time Drake reached James three witnesses had recalled an argument between James and Rosen, making Drake decide that he needed more time with the engineer. James tried to protest that he had to work when Drake told him he'd have to call at the police station the following day. Drake assured him, tongue in cheek, that Mortlake would be more than happy to release him.

Drake had five able seamen to interview and he guessed they would be long on brawn and short on brains.

'Call me Daz, mate.' Darren Green spoke with a strong Liverpool accent. He was thickset, in his mid-thirties. Drake noticed immediately a film of grease over the seaman's large hands and placed his own in his lap. Green sat back and narrowed his small, dark eyes until they were barely visible.

'How well did you know Rosen?' Drake asked.

'He was sound. Never gave me any grief.'

'Did you see him on the car deck on the morning of the murder?'

'Look, the engineers never come down onto the car deck, it's just the lads and the deck officers and a couple of the ABs.'

Drake pursued this line of questioning and grudgingly Daz agreed that Rosen could have come down onto the car deck whenever he wanted. The air smelt dirty after Green left.

When Seymour appeared at the door of the lounge, Drake knew that time was running short so he finalised the last interview. Drake was tired and hungry and he wanted a decent coffee. Caren stood up and stretched her back as Seymour strode into the room.

'I hope you've finished,' he said.

'All done,' Drake replied, tidying the papers on the table.

Within ten minutes, Drake and Caren were sitting in the car on the quayside listening to the roar of tractor units firing up, as the first of the lorries were taken down into the vessel.

'I'm starving,' Caren said. 'I know a decent place.'

They drove back to the main entrance where Caren directed Drake to a nearby side street just after a sign for all-day meals. The staff at the converted chapel seemed to know Caren as she ordered a full breakfast – adding an additional fried egg. Drake settled for a bacon sandwich.

'Makes you hungry,' she said.

'What?'

'Being on the water.'

Drake noticed the tin of a decent instant coffee brand and gave specific instructions about how much hot water should be added to the granules. They found tables to one end of the café and sat down to wait for their meals. When the plates arrived, Caren poured brown sauce all over the food and prodded the fried egg with her toast.

'Lots of the girls think he was having an affair,' she said through a mouthful of food.

Drake nodded.

'And there's a lot of conflict and rivalry between the staff,' Caren continued.

Drake tried the coffee, pleased that the result was decently palatable. He took a bite from the sandwich and found himself enjoying the only food he'd had all day. 'James and Rosen had a blazing row when Rosen was promoted before him.'

'I'd heard about that too.' A large dollop of sauce fell onto Caren's plate.

Once she had finished she pushed the plate towards the middle of the table and slurped noisily on her tea. Drake turned the mug around in his hands and finished the coffee. A message beeped into his mobile – can you talk? MC. Drake hadn't heard from MC since his release from jail and was intrigued as to why he'd made contact now. The small café was too full for a confidential conversation, so Drake stepped outside. A couple of older men stood by the front door dragging on cigarettes, so Drake walked down the steps and along the pavement. He pressed the number.

'MC. How are you?'

'Are you looking for Rosen's killer?'

'Yes. How did you know—?'

'I've got some information. We should meet.'

Chapter 9

It had been over two years since Drake had seen his cousin and a year since he had been sent down for robbery. As Drake pushed open the door of the café, he thought about his mother's comment that MC was just like his father: *un gwyllt* – a wild man, with a temper to match.

MC sat at the far corner of the café nursing a glass full of a clear liquid that he turned slowly, sending a lemon slice swirling around the edge. He nodded at Drake who ordered an Americano at the counter and sat down.

'Been a while,' MC said.

'Your mother's birthday party,' Drake said, recalling a buffet in a local hotel with lots of family present. He'd spent an embarrassed few hours sitting on the same table as MC, knowing that his cousin was facing prosecution and jail.

MC nodded. He wore a leather jacket and a white cotton shirt with yellow and green stripes. His hair had been trimmed neatly and two days of stubble couldn't hide the lean appearance.

'When did you get out?' Drake asked.

'Last week.'

'How's Auntie Gwen?'

'Mam's good.'

'Where are you living now?'

'I moved back into the house in Bangor.'

Drake sipped the coffee, it was more bitter than he liked but better than most local cafés' attempts at authentic coffee. 'Look, you know the score with handling informants. I should have another officer present and everything recorded.'

'Fuck that.'

'Regulations, MC. Let's make this a social meeting shall we?'

'Yeh, old times' sake.'

MC raised the glass to his lips and drank a small mouthful.

'It's drugs,' he said.

Drake swallowed more coffee and waited.

'They bring in drugs and that bastard Rosen was up to his neck in it. Don't know how they did it. Not yet anyway.'

MC stared at the glass.

'Stay out of it, MC. The drug squad should be involved.'

MC snorted, raised his head and blinked hard before pursing his lips. 'Prisons are full of drug dealers. And they think being sent down is an occupational hazard for them.'

'Don't go after this MC. It's not a battle you can ever win.'

'I shared a cell with a con who was doing a fifteen-year stretch. If they'd caught him the day after he was nicked they'd have found four times as much cocaine and heroin. He was just happy to do his time and then get out, dig up the drug money and retire to Spain.'

'Every time we bang one of them up, it's one less on the streets.'

MC started drumming two fingers on the table. 'They treat it like a business. Measure the risk and rewards, all that shit. Except they're dealing with people's lives.'

'How's Sylvie?'

MC stared at Drake, his eyes cold and hard.

'In a fucking bad way. And once I know who got her hooked, then they'd better pray really hard. Because when I've finished with them it'll be worse than dead.'

Drake leant over the table and lowered his voice.

'Stay out of trouble. You don't want to go down again.'

MC finished his drink and they left the café. Drake watched MC striding towards a black BMW and wondered how his cousin could afford it. He was always surprised how expensive it was to run his Alfa and Sian's BMW on their combined salaries. MC gave him a nod and a brief wave when he drove past. Drake couldn't decide if the meeting had been worthwhile or not. He couldn't rely on the information but he couldn't ignore it either.

Initially Dave Howick had been surprised at the financial arrangements between Rosen and his wife. There was a 'domestic account' into which they paid unequal amounts each month from their separate bank accounts and from which the mortgage and outgoings on their home were paid.

Howick had been able to get Rosen's internet password from the bank, after several difficult telephone calls, eventually having to threaten court proceedings, which seemed to frighten the supervisor sufficiently to win her cooperation. There were direct debits, insurance premiums (perhaps his wife had, after all, arranged a contract killing), standing orders for his membership of the flying club, of a local golf club and others to *Investor's Weekly* and a *Penny Share Tipping Guide*. Howick felt his concentration waning after two hours, so he stretched his legs and went to the kitchen to make tea. It was the sort of laborious work he'd hoped to put behind him with a promotion to sergeant, and it was difficult finding the motivation for the day-to-day work in CID.

Returning to his desk Howick resumed the task of trawling through the papers, gnawing on a chocolate bar between mouthfuls of tea. Alongside each of the bank statements were pay slips and P60s, all neatly filed in plastic pockets. Howick found annual payments to the Automobile Association and one-off payments to a company selling holiday villas. The Visa card payments included restaurants, pubs and petrol, nothing out of the ordinary. By mid-afternoon he came across a single debit entry for £10 to what looked like an Irish bank.

'I cannot give you that information without the account holder's consent.'

The response from the call centre was predictable, but Howick was ready with his reply. 'You already have the consent of the personal representatives of Mr Rosen to discuss everything with us. This is a murder inquiry,' he added severely.

Eventually the information was forthcoming. The transfer was to an account in the name of F. Rosen at the First Mutual Savings Corporation in Liffey Street, Dublin. Howick felt smug and self-satisfied that his hours of toil had produced something of interest. He now had to find out why Rosen had an account in Ireland, and why there was no other paper trail. After several futile telephone calls Howick found himself talking to Breda. She had a warm accent and he idly speculated whether the investigation would justify a trip to Ireland. Unless something remarkable turned up, it was only likely that the inspector would get the benefit of overseas travel. A couple of hours had gone by as Howick compiled a report for Drake when the telephone rang.

'It's some Irish bird for you,' announced the male receptionist.

'Is that Detective Constable Howick?' Breda almost sang down the phone.

'Yes, is that Breda?'

'We've had some trouble tracing this account. We don't have the address you gave us on any of our databases. Have you got a date of birth?'

Howick imagined Breda with dark hair to her shoulders, long legs and a fair, clean complexion. She promised to call him back after she'd verified the data and within an hour the telephone rang again.

'We found him,' she said simply. 'But the address you gave me was wrong. We have Mr Rosen living at an address in Rathmines. It's a suburb on the south side of

Dublin. I'll email the statement through in the next five minutes. If you need any more help, Detective Constable, please call.'

The last few words seemed to hang gently on his ears, caressing his hearing, enlivening the image he already had of Breda.

The email was straightforward enough, confirming the details of the initial deposit and the address Breda had given him on the telephone. He opened the attached statements and as he read them Howick's heart started to beat a little faster.

Drake stood in the kitchen at headquarters, looking at the coffee granules descending slowly in the cafetière. He'd recently changed the time he allowed for coffee to brew from two minutes to three and a half: apparently research he'd read in a Sunday supplement suggested this was the optimum time.

After pouring the dark liquid into his mug he returned to his office, adjusted the coaster to sit exactly square to the edge of the desk and plonked the coffee on top. He fiddled with the mouse until he scrolled down to the calendar. He'd been trying to ignore the memo that simply said 'TH'. A reminder from Price, before he'd left, about the counselling: it meant that he couldn't miss it – there was no justification for cancelling it.

Drake read through the membership list of the Anglesey Flying Club. He recognised the names of solicitors and estate agents, realising that addresses in the expensive parts of North Wales were only to be expected. There were a few *Jones* and *Williams,* but he guessed that for the average citizen of Anglesey the only flying they ever did was on their annual holiday. He cross-referenced the list of members to the syndicate supplied by Ellis-Pugh and stopped when he read the name of John Beltrami. He drank the final dregs of the tepid coffee and then sat back in his chair, wondering if there really was a connection to the Beltrami family.

From the Incident Room he heard the sound of Caren and Howick returning after lunch and soon Winder joined them. Drake grabbed the membership list and stepped into the Incident Room. Winder opened a chocolate bar before taking a large mouthful and sitting down. Howick had an expectant look on his face and Caren was staring at the cluttered board.

Drake had insisted on pinning to the board a cross-section drawing of the ferry, showing a complete layout of each deck. Alongside it was a list of all the crew members and another list of all the passengers. He had instructed that the lists had to be printed on sheets of A4 with a large font that made it possible to read the names without having to lean down and squint at them.

'I've made some progress.' Howick said.

'So have I, of sorts,' Drake said. 'John Beltrami is one of the owners of the plane that Rosen flew regularly.'

'The *Beltramis*?' Caren said.

Winder immediately began sorting through some papers on his desk. 'The family from Rhyl?'

Drake pinned the list of the members of the syndicate to the board. 'You said you'd made progress, Dave?'

'Got it,' Winder said too loudly.

Drake gave him an annoyed glance. 'What's wrong, Gareth?'

'I thought the name Beltrami rang a bell. I found this in Rosen's file,' he said, holding up a sheet of paper. 'It's a reference for Rosen when he applied for the job of chief engineer. Signed by John Beltrami.'

'So he must have known him very well,' Drake said.

'References can be meaningless.' Howick sounded a cynical note. 'And what's more important is that Rosen had a bank account in Ireland. It had over €150,000 deposited.'

'How much?' Drake said, incredulity in his voice as Howick pinned an A4 sheet of paper to the board alongside the photograph of Frank Rosen.

'€150,000,' he said, drawing his hand over the sheet with a flourish.

Winder, standing behind Drake, let out a brief whistle of surprise. Caren stared intently at the figures on the board, her face a mixture of surprise and interest.

'Frank Rosen had over €150,000 in the First Mutual Savings Corporation.' Howick stood back from the board.

'What's that in real money?' Winder asked.

'£129,538,' Howick announced.

'What are the details, Dave?'

'Frank Rosen had an address in Ireland that he used for opening the account. An initial ten pounds was sent electronically from Rosen's account. The rest of the deposits were made in cash.'

Winder joined Drake and the others in staring at the board. The money changed everything, always changed everything.

'Over what period of time were the cash deposits made?' Drake said.

'Last three years,' Howick replied.

'And the amounts?'

'They varied. The smallest could be €5000 and the largest €12,000.'

'Can we find out anything about the payments?'

'I've asked the bank to trace paying in slips and any other paperwork they've got. I suppose we need to make contact with the police in Dublin.'

'You'd better call the Garda. There'll be a contact name and number for a liaison department.'

'He was blackmailing somebody,' Caren said.

'One of his rich flying buddies,' Winder added, having sat down, his feet propped up on the edge of the desk.

Drake paced slowly back and forth before the board,

his mind focusing on various lines of enquiry, blanking out the prospect of the imminent counselling session. The possibility of cancelling crossed his mind – pressure of work, new important case – but he imagined how Superintendent Lance might react and, more importantly, what Sian would say.

'Maybe he won it on the horses.' Winder again, grinning.

Howick laughed, Caren snorted a dismissive comment and Drake ignored the banter, continuing to pace before the board.

'I want details of his flying companions up on this board. Straight away. You just don't have a shed load of money in a bank account without somebody knowing about it.'

'I wonder if Janet Rosen knew about this money?' Caren said.

Drake looked over at Howick and Winder. 'Both of you, find the syndicate members on this list.' He turned to Caren. 'Tomorrow we go and talk to John Beltrami.'

Chapter 10

Drake drummed the fingers of his right hand on the steering wheel to the beat of Bruce Springsteen's 'Thunder Road'. He'd noticed an odd smell as he got into the car that morning, hoping that Caren hadn't carried in something from the farm on her shoes. He reassured himself with the knowledge that he'd be cleaning the car the following morning.

Caren sat in the passenger seat, looking out over the sea towards the wind turbines, as they drove towards Rhyl. He took the junction off the A55 and soon found himself passing the box-like homes popular with the retirees from Manchester and Liverpool. Each seemed identical, patterned net curtains in the windows and small cars in the drive.

For a town with little more than a flat sandy beach, Rhyl had earned its nickname, BBC – beer, bingo and chips – by opening pubs and arcades filled with slot machines. Drake turned left, along the seafront, eventually finding a parking space outside an enormous amusement arcade.

'Did you notice the furniture shop we passed on the corner?' Drake said.

Caren shook her head.

'Belongs to the Beltrami family. And they've got a carpet shop.'

Caren bent forward, looking out of the window. 'This arcade must make them a lot of money.'

'The Economic Crime Unit has been after them for years. But they've never been able to bring a prosecution.'

The Beltrami family had hovered on the edge of criminality for many years, attracting the keen but discreet interest of the Wales Police Service. No investigation had ever developed into anything of substance; usually the version of events from complainants would change, memories would suddenly become unreliable.

'Let's go and see what John Beltrami has to say for himself.'

Drake and Caren walked through the arcade; it had a thick, warm atmosphere heated by hundreds of bulbs and various machines, and the occasional punter staring at the machines, willing the winning combinations to appear.

A girl with heavy black eyeshadow, which made her look like an extra from a zombie movie, sat behind a glass screen at the far end. Drake tapped on the glass and she gave him a lazy look.

'Mr Beltrami's expecting me,' Drake said.

She picked up the telephone and said no more than half a dozen words, before nodding towards a door behind her. Drake and Caren took the stairs to the first floor. A small woman carrying a folder full of papers stood at the top and led them down a corridor lined with box and lever-arch files, all neatly annotated. Drake could see why gathering evidence against Beltrami would be difficult, and why every successful criminal needed an accountant and probably the occasional dodgy solicitor as well.

She knocked on the door and, when she heard the shout from inside, stood to one side and pushed it open, allowing Drake and Caren to enter. The first thing Drake noticed were the two large indoor plants which had a healthy sheen, accentuated by the subdued lighting fitted to expensive-looking shades. Beltrami rose from behind a desk that would have suited the office of an important civil servant in a Welsh government department.

'Sorry to keep you waiting,' Beltrami said, sounding vaguely insincere. His voice had the rough, harsh edges of a Liverpool accent despite having lived in North Wales for years. Drake guessed he must have been mid-fifties; the expensive clothes made him look younger.

Drake reached out a hand. 'Detective Inspector Drake and Detective Sergeant Waits.'

'How can I help, Inspector?'

'I wanted to ask you about Frank Rosen.'

'Yes, yes. Terrible of course and how is his wife ...?' He stumbled to remember her name.

'Janet,' offered Drake.

'Yes, of course. How is she?'

'As well as can be expected. I believe you knew Frank Rosen quite well.'

'Only through the flying club. I've known him for four or five years. He's a good pilot and I'm a poor one. I've learnt a lot with him, as has my daughter who's flown with him more often than I have.'

On the wall Drake noticed framed photographs of a smiling John Beltrami in a dinner jacket with Richard Class, the first minister of the Welsh Government, another with UK politicians and several of Beltrami with various celebrities all beaming smiles to the camera. Drake thought about the job reference in the folder on his lap.

'Did you know he'd recently been promoted to chief engineer?'

'Ah ... I don't think ...'

'He never mentioned it to you?'

'He may have done. I can't honestly remember.'

Drake moved on, deciding he'd return to the reference later. 'Did you meet socially at any time?' Drake asked, thinking that there might have been a black-tie flying club dinner.

'Other than through the flying club no, I didn't.' Beltrami sounded vaguely surprised by the suggestion.

'Who were his friends in the flying club?' Drake continued.

'Well, I know he was friends with Tim Loosemore and I suppose Ellis-Pugh and the others in the syndicate. Have you asked Janet?'

Drake ignored the question. 'Did you know if he had any enemies? Anyone with a reason to kill him?'

'I suppose everybody has secrets. Something they

would prefer to keep that way. I've been in business a long time and people's motives and desires and jealousies continue to fascinate me, Inspector. But with Frank I really can't tell you anything. We all take risks, perhaps he took one too many.'

Drake hesitated; Caren squinted at Beltrami. She'd stopped making notes, clearly uncertain what he really meant.

'But you flew with him.' Caren made her first contribution. 'Did you talk about his personal life? Did he give the impression of having problems weighing on his mind?'

Beltrami gave Caren a sharp look. 'As I said, we only flew together.'

'Did you talk about his work?'

'No, I don't recall ever doing so.'

'And about his wife?' Caren continued, irritation in her voice.

'Again Sergeant, sorry. I knew who she was but he never talked about her in that way.'

'What way?'

Drake creased his forehead, uncertain where Caren was taking the conversation.

'The way you're suggesting. In detail, in conversation.'

'So what did you talk about? When you were together.'

Drake interrupted.

'It's important Mr Beltrami. There must have been times when you stopped overnight. You *socialised* then.'

'Yes, but I don't keep track of the conversations.'

Drake opened the folder on his lap and handed a sheet of paper to Beltrami. 'We found this job reference in the personnel file of Frank Rosen.'

For a moment, Beltrami looked uncertain. 'Of course. I was happy to provide Frank with a reference for the promotion.' Then he drew a hand over his Rolex, in an exaggerated gesture. 'Is there anything else Inspector? I am very busy.'

He rose to his feet and took a couple of steps towards the door. Caren gathered her papers and as Drake turned he noticed a framed photograph of Beltrami shaking hands with the Irish Taoiseach, and another with a couple of Oscar winners. A smaller picture that was hanging to one side had Beltrami with his arms over the shoulder of a young man and a woman who were standing either side of him.

'Family photograph?' Drake said.

'That was taken at the officers' mess in the RAF base near the flying club. Ellis-Pugh had organised a dinner when Jade qualified as an instructor. And that's my son, Jack.'

Drake noticed the photograph of Beltrami with Jenson Button and he bent forward, trying to identify the racetrack where the image had been taken.

'Are you interested in F1?' Drake said.

'Yes, I try and visit a couple of the races each year.'

'I've been to Silverstone a couple of times. And I went with a friend to Monaco a while back. But the demands of family make it difficult to find the time,' Drake replied, thinking to himself, *and the money*. 'Where was this taken?'

'Silverstone. We had a hospitality suite and some of the executives from the International Development Agency in Cardiff came along. We were able to get Jenson Button to attend – you know, press the flesh.'

Beltrami pulled open the door and made another of the smiles that Drake had seen in all the photographs. Downstairs the young girl in the glass box didn't look up as they passed, the room was still stifling and Drake was relieved when he saw that the Alfa was still in one piece and unscratched.

After returning to headquarters Drake spent the rest of the morning trying to fathom out what the codes could mean. There had to be logic to them. He wanted to think like Rosen. But not knowing him made it difficult to know how his mind worked. There had to be a reason for making the record. They were valuable enough to have been stored safely.

06	10	8
G	N	G
LK	WX	D
1589	3985	15146
0630	0524	0218
351	1652	2568

The numbers at the top could be the months of the year, or days, but which months did they relate to? So he scribbled NUMBER on a notebook and then below it LETTER. There were two sets of letters and for a moment he considered whether he should add another section for the letters that Rosen had put into the third cell of his spreadsheet. Then he decided to print out the spreadsheet and waited as the printer hummed into life. Seeing the details on paper was different somehow.

He laid the paper out on the desk and thought about the number combinations. It was like his sudoku but without the ground rules. There must be a pattern, though, and the meaning must be hiding behind the pattern. And, Drake was certain, these numbers had cost Rosen his life. Maybe Rosen had, after all, been blackmailing a member of the flying club. Drake could imagine that trips away for wealthy men could lead to indiscretions that they'd prefer to keep secret. But were they enough to kill for? And did Rosen have friends capable of murder?

He looked again at the paper on his desk, as his mind ran down the list of the flying club members that read like a who's who of North Wales. But they had to have some connection before they could make progress. The final sets of numbers troubled him. He experimented with putting the numbers together in the hope they might suggest a solution. He dismissed the notion that they could be telephone numbers. Then he thought they might be bank account numbers that Rosen had jumbled up for some reason, so Drake spent time building a spreadsheet from Rosen's statements before deciding that Winder or Howick could finish the task the following week.

He was doodling on the side of the paper when he recalled the comments from MC, that it was all about drugs. He quickly dismissed the possibility that Rosen was a drug dealer – he'd never keep records.

Rosen might have been lucky on the horses or successful with betting on football matches or had a winning streak in some poker syndicate. But there was still the question of the motive for Rosen's death and he dismissed idle conjecture as quickly as the drug dealer possibility. Next week would mean fresh minds and tomorrow was a Sunday, which he planned to spend with the family. He hoped he'd have a better insight after a day away from headquarters.

Then he noticed Caren, by his door, tapping on her watch.

Drake sat opposite Second Engineer Robert James in a small interview room. Suspects were taken into the custody suite at Area Control, but for now Drake kept an open mind on whether James would ever be formally interviewed. Caren carried three plastic mugs of coffee into the room. James picked up the cup she offered him, and blew on the mug before taking a sip.

James had thin, dark hair and small hooded eyes and was about Rosen's age.

'How did you get on with Frank Rosen?' Drake said.

'Okay, I suppose.'

'Frank Rosen and yourself both applied for the chief engineer's job?'

'Yes.'

'But Frank got the job.'

'He was lucky.'

'Were you annoyed?'

'At first I was. I'd been with the company a lot longer and on paper I was better qualified.'

'Were you angry?'

'For a while. I badly needed the promotion. I'd been doing all the right courses and I'd got the right certification and I always went out of my way to do things right. Even my last appraisal said that there was nothing wrong with my work.'

'Did you tackle Rosen?'

'What do you mean?'

'We have witnesses who refer to an incident where they heard an argument.'

'Yeh.' James looked down at the mug on the table.

'Tell us about what happened.'

'The promotion went to his head. He wouldn't sit with us in the mess. Had to sit with the captain. Sometimes he'd come into the mess, see nobody to sit with and then leave.'

'So what did you argue about?'

'He was cutting corners all the time. And he'd be late getting to the engine room. A couple of times I saw him on the car deck. Couldn't work out what he was doing there.

And he was knocking off one of the girls.'

Drake paused, deciding to pursue the work angle first. 'Did anyone complain about his work?'

James took another sip from his mug and grimaced. 'Of course not. If anything went wrong, the junior engineers got the blame.'

'And who was the girlfriend?'

'Mandy Beal. Once he got his claws into a woman he seemed to have a hold over them.'

'Where did you argue?'

'In his cabin. I told him straight that I thought he was swinging it, but it turned into a blazing row.'

'Did you threaten him?'

'No, of course not. He threatened me, told me he had friends who'd sort me out if I complained to management.'

'And did you?'

'You must be joking.'

'Where were you working between 5.00 – 7.00 a.m. on the morning Rosen was killed?'

'I was in my cabin at five, that's for certain. I'd had breakfast and I'd have been waiting to start the return trip to Holyhead.'

'What time did you go to the engine room?'

'I can't remember exactly. It would have been about an hour before we sailed. There are checks to run, records to update.'

'Did you see Frank Rosen?'

'Of course. He came into the engine room. Looked around as he always did. Nodded in that smug way that's so annoying. He took a telephone call and he left.'

'Who rang him?'

'How would I know?'

'Did you stay in the engine room?'

'Yes. The engine room crew will confirm that.'

Drake found his enthusiasm for the interview diminishing and he resolved that without further evidence there was nothing further he could achieve. He thanked James and finished the interview. Caren followed Drake out into the car park.

'I don't remember interviewing Mandy Beal on the ship,' Drake said.

Caren shook her head. 'Nor do I. Maybe she was ill.'

Drake stood by his car and turned to Caren. 'Find out where she lives.'

'Do you believe him?'

Drake opened the car and looked over at Caren. 'I wonder what he meant by *badly needing promotion*?'

Chapter 11

Sian had given Drake a hard stare when he announced that he'd have to excuse himself for an hour that Sunday morning and see Lance at his temporary home in Fort Belan near Caernarfon. The superintendent had made the invitation for coffee sound like an order and Drake had little alternative. There'd been some publicity and controversy when the owners of the old fort had succeeded in getting planning permission to convert the derelict old boat sheds by the dock into luxury properties.

He left Sian and his daughters at his parents' farm and drove down to Dinas Dinlle. As he approached the beach, childhood memories came flooding back of afternoons with his grandparents throwing pebbles into the sea and drinking milky coffee in the café. He pulled into the car park, left his car, and stepped up over the sea wall to look over Caernarfon Bay. To his right the long beach stretched for miles, beyond it was the mouth to the Menai Strait and in the distance, shimmering in the early morning sun, was Llanddwyn Island and the forest at Newborough. It wasn't the beach that made Dinas Dinlle magical but the mountainous backdrop behind him. The seafront didn't seem the same now as he remembered it. It was more dingy, more dismal; it didn't have the charm it had when he was a boy.

Back in his car he made his way past Caernarfon airport and along the track to the fort. He'd never been to the old place before, although his grandfather had complained about the aristocratic family that had once owned it often enough. They had been the freeholders of the family farm at one time and his grandfather had struggled to raise the money they'd demanded for its purchase.

He skirted around the main entrance to the fort and pulled up alongside a Mercedes parked next to a silver Porsche. He found the signs for the old dock. Lance stood by the door to one of the new properties, talking to a tall man with a pink sweater draped over his shoulders who walked down to the adjoining property when Drake approached.

'Good morning, Ian,' Lance said.

When Drake had learnt about Lance's secondment he'd expected a South Wales accent but he'd been surprised with the hint of a northern English tone to his voice. Drake stood by the dock and looked down at a handful of expensive motor launches. Down the Menai Strait he could see a yacht, its sails furled, making headway under power against the heavy tide.

'Amazing place,' Drake said.

'Let me show you around.'

Lance took Drake over towards a line of cannons pointing over the sea. 'The fort was built by Lord Newborough in 1775 to repel the Americans at the time of the war of independence.'

Drake knew something about the Newborough family. They had given their names to streets and public houses all over the county. Drake looked out over the bay and saw walkers on Llanddwyn beach.

'There are cottages in the main fort buildings. I used to come here with my grandfather every year.' Lance led Drake down a flight of slate steps and through an enormous wooden gate and into a courtyard. The sound of a radio played from an open window. 'He loved coming here. We'd go fishing and walking.'

Drake knew that his own grandfather could never have afforded a stay at the fort. He had a vague recollection of his grandfather going once to Blackpool for a week and hating it. Lance walked back towards the dock down a narrow passage framed by thick stone walls.

'Where were you brought up?' Drake asked.

'Warrington. But I went to university in Cardiff, met my wife and joined what was then the South Wales Police. Of course, all before the Welsh government and this devolution business.'

'Is your wife staying with you?'

Lance found the key to his property and unlocked the door. 'We're divorced, Ian.'

The superintendent motioned for Drake to sit down as he pulled a cafetière from a cupboard. Drake watched intensely as he made coffee. A tray was brought over to the table and immediately Lance plunged the filter. Drake almost said that there hadn't been enough time for the grains to brew – he'd been counting the seconds – but kept quiet.

'So they found the missing laptop?' Lance said, filling two mugs. He sat back and stared at Drake.

'It was hidden in a cupboard.'

Lance fingered the bone china coffee mug. 'I see.'

Drake had the uneasy sensation that Lance didn't want to talk about the laptop.

'Mike Foulds doesn't think there is anything of value. The hard drive was cleaned.' Drake picked up his cup.

'Let me know as soon as you have anything to report.'

'Of course,'

'How is Mrs Rosen? It must be difficult, losing her husband and having her house ransacked.'

'She's been staying with her brother.'

'Do you think they found whatever they were looking for?'

Drake wished he knew the answer. 'There's obviously a connection. But …'

Lance nodded. 'Of course. Too early to tell.'

Drake sipped on the coffee. Despite having not brewed long enough it had the strong, bitter taste of expensive beans.

'Inspector, now that Superintendent Price has left us, I thought it might be an opportunity to get clear how I want things done.' Lance set his hands down one on top of the other. 'I expect things to be done by the book. I want regular reports and all the paperwork needs to be up to date.'

Drake caught sight of his own name printed on the side of an orange file lying on the table, realising that Lance had been reading his personnel records. A brief flicker of annoyance ran through his mind and then a worry that Lance wanted to discuss the counselling.

'I know that there have been *issues* with certain inquiries you've undertaken.'

'Issues, sir?' Drake could feel his chest tightening.

'The use of informants in those burglary cases.'

Drake relaxed and hoped that Lance wouldn't notice him breathing out heavily.

'I don't expect anything like this to happen again.'

'Yes, sir.'

After they'd finished Drake walked back to his car feeling rather dazed. He had been accustomed to Price and now Lance was changing everything, reminding him of *issues* from previous cases and demanding results, and Drake worried what interference he could expect in the investigation. A helicopter flew above and in the estuary a procession of ducks floated away into the distance. He looked up and stood for a moment as the sun broke through the clouds and illuminated the summit of Snowdon.

Drake noticed his father's rheumy eyes and his pale complexion as soon as he entered the large kitchen where the family were waiting for him around the table. His father Tom was sitting at one end, and Drake, casting his gaze in that direction, realised that he must have lost weight again, judging by the sunken cheeks and loose skin around his neck.

Helen sat at her grandfather's side; she had blonde hair like her mother and a warm, round face that reminded Drake of his own mother when he caught her holding her head in a certain position. He watched his father and his daughter sitting together; Drake had been older when his own grandfather had died but the memory still lingered.

'Helen, will you help *Taid* with the potatoes?' Mair Drake said.

Drake watched as Helen reached over and heaped potatoes onto Tom's plate. The regular chemotherapy had been having an effect on his father and Drake hoped that the appointment with the consultant for the following week would mean good news.

Megan was a year and ten months younger than her sister and she'd insisted that morning on having a pony tail exactly the same as Helen's. Drake hoped there'd be many more family meals around this table but then dismissed the thought.

'What was Fort Belan like?' Tom said.

'Fascinating old place.'

'I walked up to the top of the beach and looked in from the outside when I was a boy. It was still owned by Lord Newborough then.'

'There's a small dock there.'

'They had a yacht there years ago. I remember my father telling me about the parties Lord Newborough had and how they'd entertain their guests sailing on the Menai Strait.'

The roast Sunday lunch was still a ritual that Mair Drake liked to follow. Drake saw sadness and worry in her eyes and occasionally she fussed too much. She ate little and then insisted on clearing the plates while Drake took his father though into the parlour to sit down.

Within a few minutes Tom Drake was fast asleep. Sian and the girls were busy helping Mair in the kitchen. The Sunday newspaper was full of the latest details about the renegotiations of the UK's treaty with the European Union. Once the cleaning had been finished they made to leave, Drake kissed his mother and reassured her that he would be with her and his father when they saw the consultant the following week.

Chapter 12

Drake sat in the waiting room darting glances at every visiting patient, hoping he wouldn't recognise anyone. It was lunchtime and Drake had spent the morning allocating tasks, worrying what would happen in his absence. Background checks were underway on James but he sensed that it was a dead end. He hoped that talking to Mandy Beal would be more constructive. He looked around and saw posters for a mental health advocacy service and an announcement about the NHS zero-tolerance policy on abuse and intimidation from patients. Drake glanced at his watch, knowing he was a few minutes early, but still his impatience was building.

'Mr Drake. You can go through now,' a voice said, above the chatter of the reception staff.

He walked down the corridor towards a room at the far end, passing a doorway piled high with brown boxes marked 'medical supplies'. Drake glanced through a door into a small kitchen and saw a pile of dirty mugs and plates littered with empty crisp packets. When he entered 'Meeting Room 2' Tony Halpin rose from one of the two chairs and greeted Drake. He wore a grey shirt underneath a thin sweater and a pair of well-worn chinos.

'Ian, it's good to see you again.' He stretched out his hand.

The two chairs in the middle of the room were identical – wide wooden arms and low, soft seats. Drake sank back into the chair and folded his arms and then unfolded them and placed them on the armrests and then on his knees.

'How has your week been?' Halpin asked.

'Busy,' Drake replied, deliberately avoiding the real question that Halpin was asking.

'Ian, did you find the first meeting helpful?' Halpin asked casually, flicking through his notes as he spoke.

The session had been at the end of the day, following a tricky interview that had only got worse when the prisoner had had an epileptic fit in the custody suite, cracking his head open on the door of his cell. The prospect of an independent review by another inspector, although standard procedure, had meant Drake had been on edge.

'Yes. Of course.' Drake tried to smile.

'Have you been keeping a notebook, as I suggested?'

'No. Ah … not yet.'

Halpin gave him a resigned look, as though Drake's reply was entirely expected.

'It will help.'

'By next time.'

Drake still had his hands on his knees, but they felt heavy and he suppressed the urge to move them onto the armrest. It occurred to him to cross his legs but he left them where they were, trying to second-guess what Halpin was thinking, how he might interpret the body language.

'Have you been more conscious of the rituals since we last talked about them?'

'Yes. I suppose so. It's been very busy at work.'

'I guess it must be busy all the time.'

'Always.'

Drake allowed himself a brief moment of relaxation.

'Good. Now we need to discuss some background. I mentioned trying to identify an event in your past.'

Drake nodded.

'Did you have a happy childhood?'

Drake looked at Halpin and hesitated. Nobody had ever asked him this before. It sounded so clinical, so remote and now he did move his hands, almost without thinking, and intertwined the fingers of both hands together. Drake spent half of their allotted time explaining about his schooling, adolescence and his extended family. Halpin made notes, occasionally smiled and nodded and then tilted his head, a quizzical look on his face.

'Tell me about your grandparents.'

'My grandfather died when I was twelve.'

Halpin slanted his head again and gave Drake a curious look. 'Were you close to him?'

'Yes. Looking back, I suppose I was. It's not something I thought about at the time.'

Halpin gave him an understanding nod of his head.

'He would show me how to mend fences and look after the sheep. He was the one who insisted that I be up all night to see a lamb being born in his shed. My mother didn't approve – she thought I was too young. He'd show me how the weather could affect the farm and he'd tell me how water could damage the field if the ditches weren't kept clear. He knew all those sorts of things about the land. They were important to him – to his way of life.'

Drake hesitated. Halpin waited.

'I suppose it's a way of life that we won't see any more. He was a kind man. I never heard him say a cross word, except if I didn't learn fast enough. He never liked that – always wanted me to pick things up quickly. He taught me the names of all the fields in the farm. And he could tell when there was rain in the wind. Didn't need a forecast. He could almost sense it.'

Drake slowed.

'He wasn't ill for very long. It was cancer. I remember everything as if it was yesterday. The coffin in the front parlour and all the old men gathered in the kitchen to express their condolences with my grandmother. She wore a black dress and my parents made tea and there were cakes and sandwiches.

'And they made me see him in the coffin. I remember being shocked. Wanting him to get up. I can never forget his face.'

Drake paused and silence filled the room. He looked down and realised that he was gripping his hands together so tightly his knuckles were white.

Drake sat by the window in a café near the surgery, his mind exhausted. He didn't want to talk to anyone. He couldn't remember what he'd ordered until a waitress arrived and put a coffee mug on the table. Then he stared out of the window, wanting to order his thoughts, knowing that he had to believe the session with Halpin had been constructive. But he wasn't feeling any better: he just felt bruised. Halpin had asked about the numbers, as he'd done in the first interview, which had only caused him to relive his last murder case whereby a four-digit number had dominated the whole investigation. Everywhere he turned there seemed to be numbers and now the death of Rosen had thrown up more numbers and he worried whether he really could carry on.

He didn't notice the weak coffee and he hardly registered his mobile when it first went off. 'Drake.' He had already recognised Caren's number.

'Where are you, sir?'

For a second he didn't know what to say. 'I'll be back in ten minutes.'

'Mandy Beal is dead.'

Immediately he stood up, some of the coffee spilled as his knee jolted the table, and he headed for the door.

Over an hour passed before Drake drove into the small estate of two-storey semi-detached houses and killed the sound of Springsteen's *Hungry Heart*. Caren pulled up behind him as he parked on the pavement. Drake paused, noticing the old cars parked in the drives and a large crack down the gable of the house opposite him. When he paid real attention to the houses he could see that they all needed painting, new windows and work on the gardens. He guessed they'd been built in the seventies, when the nuclear power station nearby had been built and money was easy to come by for new housing developments. A yellow police cordon tape flickered in the breeze and behind it the front door into Mandy's house was ajar.

Drake turned and watched Caren, remote in hand, locking her car before walking towards him.

'What are the details?'

'The body was found by one of her friends first thing this morning,' Caren said, lifting the tape for Drake.

He pushed open the front door and met Mike Foulds fidgeting with a box of equipment next to a door that was open a few millimetres, a strong rancid smell of stale urine coming from the toilet beyond.

'She's upstairs,' he said.

'Anybody else live here?' Drake said.

'Some girl. Hasn't been here for days. She's been staying with her boyfriend. Something about being home from the oil rigs for a week.'

Drake nodded.

'I'll take you upstairs,' Foulds said.

The stairs squeaked and Drake noticed a couple of loose spindles as they made their way upstairs. Chunks had been torn out of the woodchip wallpaper, and from the bathroom Drake heard the sound of movement and the clicking of a digital camera. Foulds stopped at the door and looked in.

'DI is here,' he said and the CSIs left the bathroom, carrying a tripod and a bag of equipment.

Drake took a couple of steps inside: at least it didn't stink. He looked down into the bath and saw the wrinkled body of Mandy Beal lying in the water; her head flopped to one side. Her stomach was flat and her legs slim. Submerged under the water and resting on her feet was an electric radio, its power cable draped over the side of the bath.

'We've disconnected the juice,' Foulds said. 'We wanted to wait for you to see her before we did anything else.'

Drake scanned the bathroom. A hurried count told him there were over twenty candles dotted at various locations. An enormous towel was resting on the seat of the toilet and on the tiles beneath it were two bottles of bath salts.

'There's an empty bottle of pills in the kitchen and the remains of a bottle of whisky,' Foulds said. 'And a suicide note.'

'Really?' Drake turned towards Foulds. 'So she drinks a skin full of whisky. Pops some pills and then has a bath and fries herself with the radio.'

'Looks that way.'

Drake took a final look around the bathroom. 'Where's the note?'

Foulds led them down the landing and into a bedroom: it was a dark colour, fashionable thirty years before but now faded with age. A double bed covered in a creased duvet dominated the room. Foulds stepped over to a cupboard pushed against the wall, covered with bottles and creams, and picked up a plastic evidence pouch. He handed it to Drake. 'We found it on the table by the bed.'

Caren stepped to Drake's side and peered down at the line of scrawled handwriting.

'*I can't go on without him,*' Caren said, reading from the page.

Drake pushed the paper towards Caren and turned to Foulds. 'And how long has she been dead?'

'Few hours maybe. Doctor was here before you. Certified death and left in five minutes flat.'

Drake and Caren left Foulds and walked back along the small landing to make their way downstairs. The lounge was dark and damp and two brown sofas had been pushed against the walls. A small table sat in the middle of the floor, the rings from hot mugs or damp glasses evident on the wooden surface. A family liaison officer sat with a young girl who was alternating between grabbing a handful of tissues from a multi-coloured box and blowing her nose and sobbing.

'Did you find the body?' Drake said without introduction.

'This is Debbie,' the liaison officer said.

Drake glanced quickly around the room. A small bookcase against a wall by a window held various DVDs and CDs, and on the shelves were some Catherine Cookson novels. The leaves of a pot plant were turning dark brown. Drake didn't notice any sign of heating in the room and guessed that there must be a radiator behind one of the sofas, which were disproportionately large for the size of the room.

'When did you arrive home?' Caren said, sitting by Debbie's side on the sofa after darting a glance at Drake.

'It was early.'

'What time?'

Debbie was perched on the side of the sofa, her legs tucked tightly against the edge of the leather. She had a pallid complexion, long blonde hair that stretched down over her shoulders, and a loud voice that put Drake on edge.

'Don't know,' Debbie said.

'Well, the call was received by Area Control at 7.30,' Drake said. 'So you must have been here by then.'

'Suppose.'

'How long was it after you arrived home before you discovered Mandy's body?'

She grabbed another tissue and sobbed some more. 'I needed to visit the toilet and ...'

Caren bent forward and pitched her head slightly towards Debbie. 'It's all right. You didn't realise she was home?'

'I thought she was working.'

Drake butted in. 'Did Mandy have a boyfriend?'

'Not a regular boyfriend. She'd had an affair with some creep on the boat and he'd dumped her. She used to tell me what he was like. He made her think she was the one. That she was really special and that there was no one else for him.'

'Do you know who it was?'

'Frank something. I never met him,' she crumpled a tissue and balled it tightly before dropping it onto the table.

'Do you know of any reason why Mandy would want to kill herself?'

Debbie swallowed hard and started crying again. 'I've never seen a dead body before.' Her voice broke.

Drake ran his hands along his trousers and then around his collar and pushed out his chin, trying to make himself feel comfortable. He wondered how quickly he would be able to get clean after this.

'It's important Debbie,' Drake said.

'I don't know ...'

Caren reached over and put a hand over Debbie's shoulder. 'I know it's difficult.'

'She was happy. She had her parents and her job and she was talking about buying a house. Last year, when she was with the *creep,* she said things about going away and what it would be like to live somewhere warm. I don't believe it. She would never kill herself.'

Drake knew from previous cases that suicide notes could be distressing and that often they assuaged guilt or explained why a person couldn't continue. Mandy's note had seemed straightforward enough. *I can't go on without him.* Drake wondered whether the *him* was the creep Debbie disliked so much.

'Did you read her suicide note?' Drake asked.

Debbie took in deep lungfuls of breath and grabbed the box of tissues, as though holding it was a comfort.

'I ... picked it up ...'

Caren inched closer to Debbie. 'I know how difficult it must be.'

Debbie nodded and darted glances at Caren and then

Drake.

Drake could hear the muffled conversations from the undertakers moving the body down the stairs and once he thought they were finished he said, 'I need you to go into Mandy's room again.'

'I can't ...'

Caren reassured her. 'Don't worry. I'll go with you.'

'I can't live here any more.' There was a pathetic, lost look in her eyes.

Drake stood up and waited for Debbie to compose herself and blow her nose one more time. The upstairs of the house was quieter now, but Debbie still looked frightened as Drake pushed open the door into the bedroom. She gave the bathroom a frightened look as she passed. Drake wasn't sure if taking Debbie into the bedroom was going to help and the odd glance given to him by Caren earlier had reinforced his suspicion that it might be a waste of time. But he was paid to be suspicious and maybe Mandy hadn't committed suicide and maybe the connection to Frank Rosen's death was too convenient.

'Is everything here?'

'Sorry?'

'Is there anything missing? Anything at all?'

'I don't know ...'

'Have a good look around.'

Debbie took a couple of steps around the room. 'It looks like Mandy's room. I don't ... I can't ...' She began to sob again and Caren gave Drake a sharp look, before taking Debbie by the arm and leading her out of the bedroom.

Drake stood by the bed and focused on everything in the room, the bedclothes, the bedside table, then the mirror on the cupboard and the row of bottles and cotton buds and mascara and eyeshadow. He'd never noticed whether Sian had this number of bottles and potions and he studied them again, wanting to believe that something was out of place, something misplaced. Without any real reason he began opening the drawers of the cabinet, hoping to find something to reinforce that feeling that Mandy's death had not been suicide, but all he found were neatly stored clothes. He stood, looking at the room from another angle, and realised how small it was with a double bed taking up most of the floor, its bedclothes neatly piled into one corner. Drake caught himself thinking about who would deal with Mandy's belongings, sort out her clothes – charity shop, maybe – and her finances. Who was going to mourn her passing? He stepped towards the window and looked down at the CSIs milling around the Scientific Support Vehicle while on a drive of the house opposite were two men, deep in conversation. Caren emerged with Debbie and walked with her to a car parked on the pavement nearby.

Drake didn't have the resources for the normal house-to-house inquiries. There was a suicide note after all, so the coroner's officer could do any work needed. He walked downstairs and out into the spring air. Debbie dragged heavily on a cigarette and outside her gaunt and pale complexion was even more striking. He turned to Caren. 'Let's go and see her parents.'

Drake rubbed his hands over his forehead then examined his palms as though he'd captured something. Then he tugged at his trousers before sitting down. He ran his fingers around his collar before straightening his tie.

Caren had noticed these particular habits earlier when they were sitting with Debbie, but now she was certain he'd repeated them. And it only reinforced what she already knew about Drake. It had taken her a while to really notice the rituals, the neat columns of Post-it notes on his desk, the little regular adjustments to the framed pictures of his daughters whenever he left or arrived in his office.

They sat in a small room warmed by a coal fire. Mr and Mrs Beal sat on a sofa, a combination of fear and uncertainty in their faces.

'I'm very sorry to have to break bad news, but Mandy has been found dead,' Drake said.

Caren thought that he could have got a little more emotion into his voice.

The colour drained from Mrs Beal's face and she started crying until the tears ran down her face and then she grasped her husband's hand, as he blinked away tears.

'What? I mean how did she …?' Mr Beal asked.

'She left a suicide note.'

Caren wanted to interrupt Drake and tell him to put more sympathy and feeling into his voice. They had lost a daughter, after all. She gave Drake a brief smile that was supposed to tell him she was going to say something; she doubted that he really noticed these things.

'Can I get you a glass of water or some tea?' Caren said.

Mr Beal gave Caren a stiff look and straightened his back, but his wife mumbled that water would be fine. In the kitchen, Caren filled a glass and returned to the sitting room where Mr Beal was adding coal to the fire. Caren sat down by his wife and handed her the glass.

'I know it must be a shock,' Caren said. 'We'll need to ask you some questions about Mandy, when it's more convenient.'

'When is there a convenient time to discuss death?' Mr Beal said, his eyes dark.

'Do you have any other children?' Caren said.

'She was my only daughter,' Mrs Beal replied.

They spent another fifteen minutes with Mr and Mrs Beal, Caren trying to interject as much sympathy into the conversation as she could. As they left the house and travelled back to headquarters Caren thought how utterly uncomprehending the pain would be to lose an only child.

Drake arrived home in time to read to Megan and Helen but his mind was awash with the conflicting emotions following the counselling with Tony Halpin and the images of Mandy Beal. He couldn't remember the last time he had read to his daughters at bedtime and Sian's comments, that one day he'd regret not spending time with them when they were young, had made him feel guilty. That evening he sat with Megan who'd reached for two books – one in Welsh and another, in English, about endangered animal species that she had bought at the trip to the mountain zoo at the weekend.

'Did you like those lemurs, Dad?' Helen said.

Drake flicked through the pages of the book, hoping to find a section that he could read quickly.

'They were cute,' Helen continued. 'I want to go and work in the zoo when I get older.'

'We'll see.' He'd found a page about various gorillas but decided against reading the text.

'That's what Mam said. She doesn't like animals.'

'That's not true.'

Helen pulled the book away from his hands and gave him the Welsh paperback. After removing the bookmark he started reading and soon found himself in the author's make-believe world. It amazed him how adults could write for children. At the end of a chapter he closed the book and kissed Helen on the forehead. It wouldn't be long before she wouldn't want him to read to her.

Megan, nearly two years younger than her sister, was already yawning when he sat on her bed. She passed him a Welsh book and she sat quietly as he read until he could sense that she was ready for sleep. He stood at the door and looked back at her as she settled under the duvet. He was pleased that the girls spoke Welsh to each other: it reminded him of his own childhood. Halpin had asked him about his family that morning and it had been painful talking about his grandfather. His rumination was broken when he heard Sian calling from the kitchen and he walked downstairs.

'How did it go with Tony?' Sian said as he entered the kitchen. She made her question sound detached, anonymous even. After the WPS had insisted that Drake have the counselling she had given him an I've-told-you-about-this-before look. She had even threatened that he might need medication if things didn't improve with his rituals.

She turned to finish plating a chicken stew.

'Fine.' He attempted brevity as he sat by the table.

She stepped over towards him. 'What do you mean? He is going to see you again?'

'Yes, of course.'

'Does he think he can help?'

Drake reached for the bottle of Sauvignon Blanc and poured two glasses. 'I suppose so.'

'Ian, it is important. I hardly ever see you. The children hardly see you. And you need to be in charge of your rituals or it'll destroy your life.' She put the food down, sat on the chair and pulled it up towards the table. 'And mine.'

Chapter 13

Drake drummed his fingers on the desk and then looked at his watch for the fourth time in as many minutes. Caren stood by his door, waiting for him to say something and he sensed her struggling to find the right words. The radiator behind Drake was hot despite the increasing temperatures outside.

The telephone rang and Drake snatched it from its cradle. 'DI Drake.'

'Thought you ought to know we've had some results from Rosen's clothes. There's evidence of drugs,' Foulds said.

'His work clothes?'

'No, his clothes at home. If it hadn't have been for the break-in we'd never have found them. We're sending them to the forensic labs for a detailed analysis.'

Drake replaced the handset after thanking Foulds. He stared at the telephone for a few seconds – MC had been right. Now he couldn't ignore what his cousin had told him. And it meant telling Lance and possibly even the drug squad. He looked at Caren. 'Mike has found drug residue on Rosen's clothes.'

'Really?'

'I saw a cousin of mine last week. He called me when we were eating at that place in Holyhead. He warned me that Rosen's death was drug related.'

'How would he know?'

'He's just been inside. And his girlfriend's an addict.'

'So how does this fit in with Rosen? Was he a supplier? Was he bringing drugs in through the port?'

'Or maybe on the plane.' Drake could see Howick in the Incident Room casting the occasional glance towards Drake's office. Winder was late and Drake was annoyed.

He'd often heard the young officer talk about the video games he played and from his frequent yawning and the deep bags under his eyes, it wasn't difficult to conclude that Winder spent half the night chasing goblins around some imaginary castle.

'How long before the ferry?' Caren said.

Drake glanced at his watch. 'I need to leave in an hour.'

Caren turned her back on him and returned to her desk.

A worry nagged at him, that perhaps he should be sending Howick or Winder to interview the bank manager in Dublin. But he had to be certain that the right questions were asked. He needed to be certain that everything was double-checked. He drew his tongue over his teeth, convincing himself they were dirty and that, because he would be away all day, he had to clean them again. He scrambled in the bottom drawer of his desk and found a toothbrush and toothpaste.

He got up and walked in silence to the bathroom. Pleased that it was empty, he cleaned his teeth vigorously and then stared into the mirror. He was almost able to see Sian staring back out him, with one of her looks. He threw the toothbrush in the bin and returned to the Incident Room. He stared at the board onto which a scale drawing of the decks on the ship had been pinned. He turned to Howick. 'Get another board set up. This looks a mess.'

Howick didn't have time to reply as Winder strode into the Incident Room, holding a hot pasty wrapped in a napkin and sat down, ignoring the dark glances of warning that Howick fired in his direction. A piece of the pastry fell onto the desk. Drake managed to contain his irritation long enough to clear his throat.

'Late night, Gareth?'

'Ah ...'

'I did say eight. You're late.'

Winder discarded the paper napkin into a bin and sat up straight. 'Sorry, sir. The alarm …'

'Shall we add Mandy Beal to the board?' Caren said.

Drake looked at his watch before turning to stare at the image of Rosen fastened into one corner of the board.

'I thought it was suicide,' Winder said, dabbing a corner of his mouth.

'Wasn't there a note?' Howick added.

'There was no sign of a forced entry or a struggle. And there was a suicide note so for the time being we keep an open mind. At least until we've had the results of the post mortem.'

'She might have been overtaken by grief,' Caren said.

Drake cast another glance at his watch. 'Caren. I need you to get background checks done on Robert James. All the usual financials. I want to know everything about him.' Drake turned first to Winder and then to Howick. 'How did you get on with the flying syndicate members?'

'We only saw Eddie Parry. Aylford's on holiday in his olive farm in Spain,' Winder said.

'And?'

'Parry was cut up about Rosen. Said he liked him. But he hadn't seen him much.'

Drake folded his arms and got some aggression into his voice. 'So what about Parry? Who is he? We are investigating a murder, Gareth.'

'He's a rich farmer. He's got a business letting out holiday homes and then he's got a restaurant and—'

'I get the picture,' Drake said. 'But do some background checks.'

'Yes, boss,' Winder sounded uninterested.

'And Aylford – what does he do when he's not picking olives?'

'Dentist. He's got three practices from Llandudno to Bangor. Lots of people working for him. Must be coining it.

Last time I visited the dentist it cost me fifty quid. And I was only in for ten minutes.'

'Dave,' Drake said. 'Make a note to contact Aylford when he's back and concentrate on the tapes from the CCTV on the ferry. Gareth, I want you focusing on Rosen's background. And Caren, talk to Mr and Mrs Beal again.'

Before leaving, he checked his desk and his office one more time. Then he got out his mobile and photographed his desk and the empty bin on the floor. That would be a reminder for later, a reassurance of how he had left the office. No uncertainty then playing on his mind, no niggling worry that things weren't tidy when he'd left.

He sat before starting the engine, considering his journey to Holyhead. He took out Springsteen's *Darkness on The Edge of Town* from his CD wallet, wiped the surface and slid it into the car stereo, ready to have his mind absorbed by something other than the case. He was about a third into playing the CD a second time as he parked outside the terminal. After checking through embarkation he sat in a first-floor lounge with a few other passengers, a couple of men in suits and a group of youngsters with enormous rucksacks and hiking clothes. He didn't have to wait long before an announcement called the passengers along a tunnel and then onto the fast ferry. He found a comfortable seat and fumbled for his mobile. No messages, but he looked at the photograph he'd taken earlier and, reassured, he closed the image.

He dipped into his briefcase and produced a book of sudoku puzzles before struggling to find a pencil. Behind him he heard the noise of the sea water powering through the turbines as the craft moved out of the harbour. It wasn't a ship – no conventional hull, but a vessel driven by a water jet engine that shortened the travelling time to Ireland by an hour.

He concentrated on the sudoku before eventually going in search of a coffee. He answered a couple of messages from Caren and then watched as the Kish lighthouse appeared in the distance before the outline of Dun Laoghaire harbour became clearer.

After half an hour, though it felt longer, Drake had shuffled through the terminal building, passing the watchful gaze of Irish customs and Special Branch, and finding himself standing in the main entrance hallway just as a man with long curly hair stepped towards him.

He stretched out his hand. 'Inspector Drake?'

'Yes.'

'Jesus. I'm sorry I'm late. The fucking traffic is diabolical. Detective Sergeant Malachy O'Sullivan. We haven't got much time, if you're to see everybody before the boat back tonight.'

Before Drake had a chance to say anything, O'Sullivan had turned on his heels and was marching out of the building, turning up the collar of his jacket against the chill wind whipping around the building.

'Car's over there,' O'Sullivan said, jerking his head towards a line of parked vehicles.

As he opened the door, Drake hesitated. The seat was filthy and the footwell covered in grime and dirt and pebbles.

O'Sullivan jumped in and fired the engine into life. Drake fought the desire to brush his hand over the car seat before sitting down and closing the door.

Drake noticed the heavy, clammy smell in the car and, casting a surreptitious glance, he noticed two empty McDonald's drink containers shoved into the glove compartments of the doors. Malachy O'Sullivan squinted through the windscreen as though he badly needed glasses.

'How far is the bank?' Drake said.

'No more than half an hour. In normal traffic. But today, Jesus.'

Drake glanced at his watch. 'Do you think we should call and tell him we might be late?'

O'Sullivan braked hard by a set of traffic lights. 'Did you see them fucking lights change?'

'Ah ...'

'The manager'll be okay. Yer man's only working in a bank after all.'

Drake counted another five sets of orange lights turning to red that O'Sullivan drove through before they reached the middle of Dublin and the car was squeezed into a small parking space. O'Sullivan had a looping stride that made him appear taller than he really was. Drake followed the Garda officer into the bank and then to the rear where he peered down through a small window and shouted a greeting that Drake couldn't understand.

Seconds later, the door was opened by a young clerk who had a wispy beard and a frightened look in his eyes.

'This way, please,' he said.

At the end of a corridor Drake heard the shouts of a man swearing down the telephone. O'Sullivan stopped by the door and the clerk raised a hand, pointing into the room. A portly man with a mass of jowls under his chin with some effort lifted his feet off a desk and waved his hand. O'Sullivan and Drake sat down as the man finished the call and replaced the handset.

'Detective O'Sullivan.' He stretched out his hand. 'And this is Inspector Drake from Wales.'

'Sam England.'

'We want to ask you about the account opened by Frank Rosen,' Drake said.

'Sure thing.' England ruffled the papers in front of him. 'It was an ordinary account. Because he was a non-Irish national he had to open the account with a bank transfer.'

'You told me there was an address,' O'Sullivan said.

'Of course.'

England fumbled through the papers, cursing under his breath as he searched for the information.

'The account was opened a couple of years ago,'

England said, the relief evident in his voice. 'Yer man gave an address in Rathmines.'

'I know, you gave me that information. We want to see everything. Stop messing and pass over them papers,' O'Sullivan said, leaning over and grabbing the file. He started going through each one, giving England the occasional defiant glance and then passing individual sheets over to Drake.

The file had various coloured forms with different numbers and codes.

'What's this one for?' Drake said, holding up a pink form.

'That's the DS12/6.'

'I can see that. What's it for? Haven't you got protocols for establishing people's identity?'

'Sure thing. We have to get three forms of ID, all the usual: utility bills, passport, etc.'

Drake took a moment to flick through the papers before asking, 'So what did Rosen produce for this account?'

'I'm not sure. Let me have a look.'

Drake passed over the folder and waited. England looked flustered as he went through the file. 'All I can find is the—'

'Tenancy agreement,' Drake said.

'That's right.'

'So the procedures weren't followed—'

'I wouldn't say that.'

'Well how would you say it?'

'It must have been busy when yer man came into the branch.'

'There are laws about money laundering, you know.'

The look of astonishment on England's face turned to fear. 'There must be something missing. I'll get the clerk who opened the account,' he said, dialling a number.

'Is Deidre Banks there?' England waited until eventually he let out a gasp before exclaiming, 'For fucks' sake. How long? … Jesus.'

'Let me guess,' O'Sullivan said. 'She's on lunch.'

'Australia. She moved there after the bank made lots of redundancies.'

Drake, realising they were making no progress, riffled through the papers again. 'Were all the deposits in cash?'

'Every one, so far as I can see,' England said after a cursory examination of the statements, his equilibrium returning.

'I thought there were limits on how much cash a person could deposit?'

'He was under the limit every time.'

There was a cheerful note to England's voice that Drake found annoying.

'How many deposits were there?'

England paused again. 'Jesus, I'd have to count them all. Must be a couple of dozen.'

'Didn't that pattern set alarm bells off?'

England managed an unconvincing shrug. 'It must have been busy. We're right in the middle of Dublin, Inspector. The place gets packed during the day. People in and out.'

O'Sullivan cut in. 'So you basically ignore the regulations.'

'It's not like that,' England protested.

After getting copies of everything in the file, Drake and O'Sullivan left. Standing on the main street, Drake heard the sound of trams clattering over points and, after the warmth of the office, the spring sunshine felt fresh on his cheeks.

'That was a waste of fucking time,' O'Sullivan said, striding back to his car. 'Let's hope yer man in Rathmines is more helpful. And what sort of fucking name is England anyways?'

Caren sat across from Peggy Beal, who was wearing a thick fleece she'd pulled up close to her chin, even though the house was warm.

'Is your husband in?'

Caren had decided that enquiring about his whereabouts was sensible, especially as they'd declined the offer of support from family liaison. And Caren knew that when families did that there'd be problems in the future.

'He had to go out,' Peggy said, without looking at Caren.

'I'd like to know about Mandy.'

Peggy Beal looked up, a distant look in her eyes. 'She was always very independent. We got on well. She would come over on her days off and we'd have something to eat and then sometimes we'd go out shopping.'

'Did she ever tell you about her boyfriends?'

Peggy found a handkerchief in her pocket and crumpled it in her fingers, taking her time to find the right words. 'I knew there was someone. She mentioned *someone special.*'

'Did you meet him?'

'No. And she never said much but I'd guessed he was married.' Peggy stared over Caren's shoulder through the window. 'As otherwise she would probably have told me more about him.'

'What did she say about him?'

'She never said much. That's what made it odd. I knew there was something wrong. But what could I do?' Peggy stared directly at Caren for a moment. 'It would have been nice to have had grandchildren,' she added.

Caren didn't know what to say, so decided to move the conversation on. 'Did Mandy ever give you any reason to think she had problems that would—'

'You mean was she mentally ill? That's what your

boss would have said. Rude man.'

Caren avoided her comments about Drake. 'Suicide is always difficult to discuss.'

Peggy nodded. 'There was nothing that made me think she might kill herself.'

There was finality to her tone that carried more conviction and certainty than the grief of a mother. Caren could see Peggy hurting as her mouth quivered and then tears filled her eyes. Caren decided on one final question.

'Do you think there could be anyone who might want to see Mandy dead?'

She hadn't noticed Philip Beal standing at the door of the lounge, and when he answered, it took Caren by surprise.

'Mandy had no enemies. She was just an ordinary working-class girl. She worked hard and liked to enjoy herself. What makes you think she might have been killed? Because if there's nothing, then don't suggest it. It's not bloody right.'

'I'm sorry Mr Beal. I didn't mean to cause offence. We haven't had the post mortem yet. Because your wife said there's never been anything to suggest Mandy might have killed herself then—'

'There was the suicide note after all.'

'Yes, of course.'

'Well, you people better stop making all sorts of accusations that aren't proper and get out of our lives.'

Caren noticed Peggy dabbing the handkerchief to her eyes, staring straight ahead. She promised to keep them informed and left. As she pulled the car out of the drive she saw Philip Beal standing, arms crossed, staring at her through the window.

The journey from the Beal household to Janet Rosen's house meant Caren had to use narrow back-roads, and she had to consult a map, a task that in normal circumstances she left to Alun. She drew up by a junction, uncertain whether she should take a left turn or continue straight ahead. She eyed the map, wondering whether, if she turned it upside down, it would make any difference. She powered the car ahead and eventually her decision was rewarded when she pulled up by a junction on a main road she recognised. For a moment she let the traffic pass until the road was clear. She thought about whether she would have any children. And how her parents might feel about having grandchildren. The alpaca farming hadn't been the success she and Alun had hoped and often she contemplated whether Alun was really cut out to be a farmer and a businessman. For now he seemed happy enough driving. At least it gave him a regular income without any hassle.

Twenty minutes later she pulled into Janet's drive; the slate waste of the drive looked damp and Caren noticed the newly soaked flower beds and a hosepipe lying nearby. Janet stood up from behind a low wall wearing an old blouse, its collar turned up under a thick fleece. She gave Caren a brief smile and Caren could see the curiosity in her eyes. She'd kept her telephone call deliberately short when she asked to see Janet.

'Coffee?' Janet said.

Caren nodded. They went inside and sat down by the stripped-pine kitchen table. Janet filled the electric kettle and flicked a switch.

'Did Frank ever talk about his trips to Ireland?'

'Not really. He was away for a couple of nights. If they flew to Scotland or France, then it might have been even longer.'

'Did he ever tell you where he was staying?'

'Might have mentioned the occasional hotel, but he kept in touch by emails or he'd call me on his mobile.'

'Nothing about his friends? Who they were?'

The kettle boiled and Janet reached for mugs and instant coffee. 'They usually paid for the hotel. That's what he told me.'

She skimmed a coaster towards Caren and placed a bowl of sugar onto the table with a spoon.

'Can you remember who was with him on these trips?'

Janet gave her a helpless look. 'As I said before, the men from the flying club. Beltrami, Ellis-Pugh, Loosemore and the others ...'

Caren realised the frustration in Janet's mind at how little she knew about her dead husband.

'What did they do in Ireland?'

Another feeble look. 'They'd go out for meals. Frank got excited once when he saw the guitarist from U2 in some nightclub. This isn't helping, is it?'

Caren sipped her coffee. It was stronger than she liked, but would have been too weak for Drake. 'Janet, I need to ask you about something.'

Janet cupped a mug of coffee and waited.

'Frank had over €150,000 in an Irish bank account.'

She put the mug down on the table with a thud. 'What?'

Caren made certain she was watching Janet's response; if she was acting, then Caren decided she was good at it.

'The account was opened a couple of years ago and the deposits were made in regular small sums.'

'I'm amazed. I had no idea. Where did he get the money?'

'That's where we were hoping you could help.'

O'Sullivan dragged heavily on a cigarette and blew the smoke out of the window. He'd parked fifty metres down from the address in Rathmines, behind an old BMW with a flat tyre. Drake looked over at the row of houses along Westfield Avenue: he could have been in any suburb of any major city. There were wheelie bins jammed into doorways, vertical blinds on windows and an anonymous feel. A young woman with heels that clicked on the pavement passed them without a second glance, despite the careful attention O'Sullivan paid to her legs.

The smoke drifted over towards Drake and tickled his nostrils.

The car was still untidy and he'd found himself sitting quite still, hoping that by doing so less of the dirt might permeate his clothing. O'Sullivan drew on the dying embers of the cigarette and threw the stub out onto the pavement.

'Let's go and see yer man,' he said.

The house was an old-fashioned property, spread over three storeys and Drake guessed that it had been turned into bedsits and flats long ago.

Drake heard the muffled sound of the doorbell ringing somewhere in the building. After a couple of minutes, the door opened.

'Are you Paul Maguire?' O'Sullivan asked.

The man nodded. 'Sergeant Malachy O'Sullivan and this is Inspector Drake from Wales.'

Maguire's haircut had left a dark shadow over his head where he'd recently shaved. His skin was a pallid grey and he stared at O'Sullivan with black, almost moribund, eyes.

He pushed the door open to let both men into the house.

'Come through into the kitchen,' Maguire said. 'I don't know how I can help.'

'I'm investigating the death of Frank Rosen, one of your former tenants,' Drake said.

Maguire sat by a table and Drake and O'Sullivan did the same. They weren't offered coffee and Drake could see O'Sullivan taking in the room.

'He rented a room from me.'

'How did he find the room?' Drake said

Maguire drew a hand over his mouth and then clutched both hands together, as if buying time. 'I don't remember, just now. Small ad probably.'

'When was it?'

'I checked my records after the Garda rang me. It was three years ago.'

'What did he say?'

'I can't remember.'

'It must have been odd. Someone from the UK renting a bedsit.'

'Why? I've two Poles and a Latvian in the house.'

'Did he tell you anything about himself?'

'Of course not.'

'Did you ask?'

'Why should I? I rent bedsits by the month. He paid three months in advance and I gave him the keys.'

'Did he ever have any mail?'

'Don't remember.'

Maguire sat back, folded his arms, and let out a long gasp as though his patience had run out. 'He paid the rent and I gave him the keys.

Drake kept his annoyance barely in check. 'Did you notice anyone staying with Frank?'

Before Maguire could reply O'Sullivan chipped in. 'Try and remember as much as you fucking can. Wouldn't want anyone to think you'd not been cooperating.'

'I keep odd hours. So I never saw him come and go.'

Drake again. 'How long did he rent the room for?'

'Six months, then he left.'

'Any explanation?'

'He just left.'

A radio started playing somewhere in the house. Maguire sat and stared at Drake. O'Sullivan pushed back his chair and stood up. 'Have you got a list of your tenants?'

Drake looked at Maguire as he fumbled through a folder and passed a neatly typed list over the table.

O'Sullivan and Drake followed Maguire back through the house, retracing their steps out onto the front doorstep. Drake zipped up his jacket and turned to Maguire. 'Where do you work?'

'In one of the nightclubs in town.'

'Have you got time for a pint before the boat, Ian?' O'Sullivan said, butting in across Drake. 'I've got a powerful thirst.'

Moelwyn Carol Hughes had never liked his Christian names. The first was the same as a range of mountains in the middle of Wales and the second was a girl's name. There were too many Welsh boys' names that were also girls' names in English for his liking. If he ever had children, they'd be Michael or Justin or Donna or Tracey, anything easily pronounceable in English.

Nobody called him Mr Hughes, except the screws in jail. He was MC to his family and Hammer for everyone else after an incident late one night in a pub when a drunken Scouser had taunted MC about his name. He'd called out all over the pub that MC's father must have been a paedo to give his son a girl's name, until there was an embarrassed silence and the man was dragged outside for his own safety. MC said nothing, but later took a hammer and smashed every window and dented every panel of the man's Mercedes.

Then repeated it twice more, each time the Scouser replaced the car.

Nobody saw anything and he soon moved back to Liverpool.

Now MC sat in a car, newly stolen from Birmingham, cleaned and then fixed up with fake plates. Once he'd finished MC would return the car and it would be cleaned again and another set of plates attached.

The street lights cast a sporadic glow over the cars

parked in the road. The occasional drunk meandered over the pavement. MC had a baseball bat under the passenger seat and his mobile in the cradle clipped to the dashboard. He drew back the cuff of his leather jacket and read the time.

Not long.

Chapter 14

Drake had little choice when he thought clearly. The drug squad had to be notified. And much as he didn't relish the prospect, he had to contact Inspector Glyn Newman. He picked up the telephone.

'Ian, keeping well?' Newman said.

The greeting sounded forced. Drake's frustration felt like a pin in his mind, trying to keep his thoughts in place. Maybe Glyn Newman knew already. Maybe his informers made him one step ahead of anyone else in Northern Division.

'I need to see you, Glyn.'

Ten minutes later Drake was sitting opposite Newman. The smell of stale tobacco hung in the air. Newman's herringbone jacket badly needed a visit to the dry cleaners. He undid his collar button, before pulling his tie down and then sat back, staring at Drake. For the first time Drake noticed that his eyes had a natural menace, a coldness polished to a keen edge. Nobody mentioned his successes because it was only his failures that came in for criticism by the judges, but somehow, each time, Detective Inspector Glyn Newman survived.

'I'm investigating the murder on the ferry in Holyhead.'

'I know.'

Drake hesitated; it was the sort of remark that suggested Newman knew a lot more.

'The chief engineer, Frank Rosen, was killed on the car deck. There are traces of cocaine on his work clothes and one of his jackets and his shoes.'

There was no flicker of interest from Newman, no raising of eyebrows or furrowed forehead: he sat and waited. Drake guessed that Newman took a particular interest in riling his colleagues, but he wasn't going allow him to feel that he was succeeding.

'How can I help?' Newman said eventually.

There was a knock on the door and another officer walked in. He wore an open necked shirt under a navy fleece and chewed gum vigorously.

'You know DS Wallace, don't you?' Newman said.

Jeff Wallace dragged a chair over to the desk and sat down. He gave Drake a lazy smirk. It had been two years since Drake had worked on a case with Wallace and the passage of time had only hardened Drake's resolve never to work with him again.

Drake looked over at Newman. 'I need to know if Frank Rosen has ever been of interest to the drug squad?'

'I haven't heard the name. What's the date of birth and address?'

Newman scribbled the details as Drake dictated the information.

'Anything going on in Holyhead that I should be aware of?' Drake said, casting a glance at Wallace.

'Nothing,' Wallace said.

'The town had a bad drug problem when I was there.'

'Like I said, nothing. Except the usual day-to-day, small-scale.'

Drake speculated where Wallace and Glyn Newman drew the distinction between low-level drug dealing and something more serious. Years of working in the drug squad had probably blurred the balance.

'Can you get your officers to ask around?'

'You know what it's like, Ian,' Wallace said. 'We put the occasional supplier inside but another takes his place and the men at the top who run things never get their hands dirty. The addict on the street just has to get his fix. What can we do?' Wallace had stopped chewing by now.

'I need to know whether there's a drug connection.'

Wallace pushed the gum onto his lips and then back

into his mouth. 'I'll ask around. But the statistics speak for themselves: sixty per cent of all crime, maybe more, is drug related and the rest is booze related. If we're lucky we might get one of the main suppliers making a mistake. And then – top-of-the-class drug squad.'

Wallace sat back. There was a cynical edge to the comments that Drake found unsettling.

Newman nodded slowly. 'Send me a copy of the forensic report. And a full list of people of interest and suspects. Have you got any?'

'I'll send you a summary of the forensic analysis. Just get back to me soon as you can.'

Drake stood up.

'Send me everything you have,' Newman said, leaning back in his chair. 'I can't work without complete information.'

Drake had no intention of providing the drug squad with details of his investigation. 'Thanks for your help, Glyn.'

Drake didn't bother with handshakes. He turned and left.

Alun's text reached Caren's mobile as she sat at her desk, with her second coffee of the morning. He was leaving Dover on his way to Dublin and planning to stop at home for a couple of hours on his way, if he was making good time. She smiled and thought about the prospect of seeing him again, sensing his kiss and the warmth of his skin next to hers. She replied, telling him she was in work all day.

She found her concentration lapsing as she punched the individual details of the crew members into the Police National Computer. After inputting twenty names, she had the first positive result as a 'possession of controlled substance conviction' flashed up against the name of one of the junior engineers. She straightened in her chair and stored the details.

Soon after him there was a spate of drink driving convictions that popped up – mostly twelve-month bans and fines of several hundred pounds. An able seaman had a conviction for assault as a juvenile and then several for common assault, all in Liverpool City Magistrates court.

She stopped when the results for the name of Darren Green appeared on the screen. She read down the long list of previous convictions, which included a caution for assault when he was sixteen, culminating in a six-month sentence for carrying an offensive weapon when he was twenty-one. But it was the conviction for supplying Class B drugs that drew her attention.

After Drake returned from his meeting with Inspector Newman he had buried his head in various papers in preparation for his briefing with the new superintendent, and Caren anticipated that he'd want to know everything about Green. Deciding that she needed more background and maybe intelligence, she called a liaison officer in Merseyside police, explaining that she needed the information as part of an important inquiry.

She replaced the handset and looked at the time, eager for the hours to slip past. An hour later her telephone rang.

'Sergeant Waits?' She didn't recognise the voice. 'DI Keith Charnwood, Merseyside police.'

Caren hadn't been expecting a detective inspector to call her back and it sharpened her attention as she listened.

'You've got an interest in Darren Green.'

'Yes, sir.'

'He's a bad fucker.'

'Sir?'

'You've got his precons I take it.'

'Yes.'

'Well, treat that as the icing on the cake. We didn't have half the evidence on Daz Green that we'd have liked.

He was implicated in a conspiracy to murder when a drug deal went tits-up. He was part of a gang that bundled a man into the back of a van that drove from London to Toxteth, telling him he was going to be skinned alive. The guy had to sit in his own shit and piss for five hours while they joked about killing him.'

Caren scribbled notes, blocking out the noise from Winder and Howick in the background.

'Then there was the armed robbery in the night club. Daz Green has a nasty habit of sticking shotguns into people's mouths.'

'Did you have enough to prosecute?'

'No, unfortunately. But he's implicated in at least three murders. And then there was the drug dealing we could never prove – he had the best brief in town. So what's he done?'

'A chief engineer on a ferry from Holyhead to Ireland has been killed. Daz Green is an able seaman on the ship.'

'And you're checking all the crew.'

'That's right, sir.'

'Be careful, sergeant. Daz kept some nasty company.'

Caren printed off an A4 sheet of paper with Daz Green typed in bold font along the top. Underneath his name she added MAJOR PRE CONS and pinned it to the board in the Incident Room, just under the photograph of Rosen. Drake would want him noted as a person of interest, but even so she kept ploughing her way through the other crew until she'd finished. The afternoon had passed more quickly than she'd anticipated. Her mobile buzzed into life and her mood lifted as she read the message from Alun, telling her he could stop for an hour. She'd changed the sheets of the bed that morning, had laid out clean towels in the bathroom. It would be another couple of hours before he'd arrive – just enough to call into the pharmacy on the way home.

Howick gazed at the numbers and letters, wanting to convince himself that he could make sense of everything. The disappointment at failing the sergeant's exams hadn't passed. Just being in work felt like a punishment and he'd struggled to find his motivation ever since. His wife had been making comments about his surly attitude and kept pestering him, asking if there was anything wrong.

He opened a spreadsheet and started inputting Rosen's bank account numbers and their various PIN numbers. It surprised him that Rosen had so many different accounts, and once he'd finished he scanned the numbers, looking for any pattern he might recognise. Then he tried the dead engineer's credit cards and investment bonds, looking for the numbers that might trigger a pattern. But the more figures he gathered onto the spreadsheet the more confused he became.

He tried a Google search for car journeys around North Wales: from Rosen's house to the port, then to Mandy Beal's house, and then out of desperation to the local supermarket and then the flying club. Another spreadsheet was opened with possible variations for journeys in miles and another in kilometres, but he couldn't see any pattern nor anything to suggest an explanation for the numbers and letters.

A strong coffee didn't help and neither did comments from Winder who was annoying him with his fidgeting. He'd always got on with Gareth, but it had always been on the basis that he assumed his own promotion was imminent. And now he was stuck as a constable at the same rank as Gareth, who seemed quite content with his role.

Another hour passed as he made a list of everyone who had contact with Rosen. Their first names, surnames and addresses – he even added telephone numbers and home addresses. Recalling something Drake had said, he made a list of initials and tried to cross-reference them with details about Rosen's life, but his mind wasn't thinking clearly.

Chapter 15

Drake couldn't help prioritising the numbers over the letters. He stared at the board and knew the team behind him were also staring at the notes and photographs, but he doubted whether they saw the numbers as he did.

'Who's reorganised the board?' he said.

He heard the scrape of a chair leg and then someone stand up. Howick was on his feet, as though summoned by a headmaster for punishment.

'Thought it would tidy things a bit,' he said.

The original order had been changed and that had unnerved Drake. 'Just ...' Drake realised that he was going to sound lame.

He noticed Caren fiddling with her mobile.

'Caren?'

She kept looking at it.

'Caren,' Drake continued. 'You said you had something about one of the crew.'

After another glance at the phone Caren stepped up to the board, tapping the note she'd printed up earlier.

'Darren Green. I spoke to a DI from Merseyside. They've got a mountain of intelligence but never enough to successfully prosecute him for everything he was involved in. He's quite the gangster.'

'Then we look at him in more detail.'

'What could be his motive?' Winder asked, still sitting by his desk.

'What are his precons?' Drake said to Caren.

'Violence and lots of it. Implicated in three murders and a drug-dealing skirmish that didn't get past a slick lawyer.'

'Drugs.' Drake spoke to the board rather than to his colleague.

Howick was still standing but by now he'd plunged

his hands into his pockets and he stumbled over his words. 'What did the drug squad have to say, sir?'

Drake thought of the dark stares that Newman had given him. He'd followed procedure and involved the right team but it wouldn't be reciprocated and he resolved that he'd have to talk to Lance, formally record the position, protect his back.

'They'll keep us informed of any links to known drug activity. DI Newman didn't recognise Rosen's name.'

'Maybe you should ask him about Green,' Winder said, having hiked his feet onto his desk. Caren was still staring at her mobile.

Drake nodded and mumbled a reply, already having decided that that was the last thing he would do. It occurred to him that he needed to find out where Rosen had flown to on his trips with the high-rollers of North Wales. There'd be records of course, flight plans, so he made a mental note to contact Ellis-Pugh for the information.

Caren's mobile beeped and she read the message. Then abruptly she grabbed her bag and coat.

'Sorry, sir. Got to leave early tonight.'

Drake nodded.

'Oh. On a promise?' Winder said, grinning and then nodding at Howick who smirked back.

Caren sneered at Winder and left.

Drake returned to his offices, slumping into the chair behind his desk, checked the Post-it notes and reached for the sudoku, knowing he had two incomplete squares. Then he read the time and realised that he was already late for the appointment with the consultant and his parents. He dragged on his coat from the stand by the door and hurried out.

The hospital seemed quiet, less busy than a normal week day and Drake hoped the consultant really wouldn't be as annoyed as his secretary implied he might be at having to work late into the evening. Drake recalled clearly the initial diagnosis of his father's bowel cancer, when the consultant had used terms that Drake had never heard of before like *colorectal surgeon* and *multi-disciplinary teams*. Since then there had been regular chemotherapy treatments every few weeks.

But Drake knew something was wrong. It was in the way his father walked, spoke and looked at his family. And now they were expecting the results of the blood test following the last chemotherapy session.

An elderly couple sat holding hands across from Drake and his parents. They gave Drake the faintest of smiles before the man patted his wife's hand. Drake couldn't work out which of them was the patient, until the woman gave her husband a brief frightened look once her name was called.

Tom Drake sat impassively between his wife and his son. Time dragged and Drake could feel a burning behind his eyes and suppressed a yawn. Patients arrived for the oncology clinic and Drake hoped he'd think clearly when the time came to speak with the specialist.

But he simply didn't want to think about his father's illness.

'Mr Drake.' The voice sounded soothing.

Tom Drake looked over towards a door in the far corner of the waiting area. A nurse smiled at him and the three of them got up and walked over.

The consultant had a dark-navy suit and a shirt with blue links in the shape of an open-top coupe. Drake caught the smell of sweet cologne in the air.

'Do sit down.' Alec Harrison waved to the chairs in front of his desk. Drake pulled one of the chairs to one side for his father.

'I've had a chance to look over the results of the CT scan from the follow-up appointment last week and we've had the results of the blood test. I'm afraid that it's not good news,' Harrison began.

Drake glanced over at his mother and thought he saw a tear in her eye. Having been married for over forty years, she would have already known.

'The blood tests indicate that you're anaemic which would account for your tiredness. But the scan indicates that the cancer has spread to the liver and lungs.'

Harrison ran through a protracted explanation of the results, giving more details of the results. Drake felt numb. He heard what Harrison said but didn't listen. It wasn't what they wanted to hear. Drake could see his mother playing with her fingers, as though she were trying to warm them, her eyes blinking at nothing. She turned, caught Drake's gaze and gave him a narrow smile, but it quickly faded.

'We can continue with the chemotherapy, but it won't be a cure. At best it will slow the disease from spreading.'

Tom Drake crossed his legs and put one hand on top of another on his left knee. 'How long have I got?'

Drake noticed Harrison swallowing. The consultant seemed relieved with Tom's question and his tone became bolder, less edgy.

'It will be palliative chemotherapy. And we can organise for you to have as much support at home as is possible. The Macmillan nursing service in this area is second to none.'

The words cut deep. He thought about his grandfather and his funeral and then all of the pain that the session with Halpin had resurrected. His father's voice had sounded calm and clear, as though he was asking about the weather. A tear dragged its way down his mother's cheek.

Once they'd finished and stepped out into the spring evening, he walked with his parents to their car. He kissed his mother and gave his father a hug. He watched them drive away and as he choked back the tears his mobile rang.

'Drake.'

'MC Hammer's been busy.'

Chapter 16

Caren woke that morning, having had the best night's sleep for months. Although the bed was empty by her side she could still smell Alun. She buried her head under the duvet and stretched her legs out into the warmth of the bed, remembering the roughness of his hands against her legs. A faint tang of diesel oil on his hair had clung to her hands after she'd pulled his face to hers and kissed him as though it had been the first time. He'd put on some weight in the four weeks since she'd seen him last and she'd prodded the developing paunch, joking that he'd have to exercise.

After a shower she stood in the kitchen making tea and toast, wondering what Alun was eating in the cabin of his truck that morning. The farmhouse felt empty without him. She finished clearing the dishes, stacking the dishwasher, as her mind gradually turned back to the deaths of Rosen and Mandy. She had been involved in suicide cases before, but there wasn't a pattern so it was never easy to judge what had driven a person to take their own life. She stopped for a moment and stared out of the window; it looked warm: wispy white clouds hung in the sky, like shredded cotton wool. A breeze moved the tops of the sycamores in the paddock; living in the farmhouse had made her appreciate the natural order of the seasons, and the rhythm that living in the country imposed.

She found the car keys lying under the cushions on the sofa and she smiled as she thought of the piles of clothes that had been strewn around the floor within minutes of Alun arriving home. Once she'd pulled the door closed behind her she walked to her car and then threaded her way down through the narrow lanes of Conwy Valley. She opened her window and felt a cooling breeze on her face and then the acrid smell of manure from a neighbouring field. The countryside shimmered a lush green as she made her way towards headquarters. It was a journey she never tired of and even headquarters, with its roof bustling with radio antennae and busy car park, had a fresh, clean look in the early spring sunshine. A few minutes later, she pulled a chair up to her desk and sat down. Winder looked up and she noticed the bags under his eyes, the pasty expression on his cheeks and the developing jowls. It would only be a matter of time before Drake or perhaps even the new superintendent would make some comment about Winder's obvious tiredness and poor timekeeping.

'Good morning,' Winder said.

'Lovely spring morning.'

'Good night last night?'

Caren noticed the hint of a smile on Winder's lips, but before she could think of a clever reply Howick lurched into the Incident Room holding two mugs of coffee. 'Do you want one?' he said.

'No, thanks.'

Howick wore a clean white shirt and, unlike Winder, had a tie folded into a wide knot that made his long neck look thinner than it actually was. Caren glanced over at Drake's room, his door firmly closed.

'Where's the boss?' she asked.

'He's gone to the hospital,' Winder said.

'I thought he went last night?'

Winder shook his head. 'Apparently the guy – called Tom Vigo – was unconscious. MC kicked the shit out of him, *allegedly*. Medics thought he'd be well enough to interview this morning.'

Caren nodded. Top of her to-do list that morning was finishing her work on the syndicate members, so she booted up her computer and typed the name 'Tim Loosemore' into a Google search. Within seconds she had a series of entries and she settled into the routine of scanning, recording and making notes that she could follow up later.

All the results on the first page related to

Loosemore's investment in Lyfon Pharmaceuticals. Caren noticed half a dozen newspaper articles covering the creation of three hundred jobs in an area near Cardiff described as 'disadvantaged' or 'depressed' or 'post-industrial' and each had an image of Loosemore smiling broadly, shaking hands with Richard Class, the economic development minister at the time. It had been the first pharmaceutical company ever to have a base in Wales and Caren read the promises from the politicians in Cardiff that 'Wales was a place to do business'. By the end of the second page of results the references to Tim Loosemore became more obscure, referring to his numerous directorships. Caren spent a couple of hours compiling a list of the companies of which he had been a director, doubting whether Drake had been sensible in prioritising this exercise.

A second mug of coffee was getting cold on her desk as she read about Loosemore's charitable work, and Caren speculated whether he had a study lined with photographs taken with presumably important and influential people. By the end of the fifth page Caren had resolved that she would do one more page and then have lunch; her stomach was turning over already. But she read her way down the sixth page, disappointed that there was nothing further to attract her attention. Feeling guilty that she had arrived late for work that morning, she decided to stay at her desk and typed 'Lyfon' into a Google search.

The entries on the first page related to the company's website, its eponymous Facebook page and various newspaper articles. On the second page, there were LinkedIn accounts, more Facebook pages and a link to images of an animation character. She was about to close the search when she noticed a BlogSpot reference to Lyfon Pharmaceuticals at the end of the third page and she clicked it open.

Caren lost track of time as she read through the various blog entries, going back a number of years – her interest piqued by the less-than-complimentary comments made by the author about Loosemore and his business activities. Winder and Howick returned from their lunch, dropping a sandwich onto her desk.

'They only had a cheese and pickle left.'

Caren mumbled thanks and pushed some coins across the desk towards Howick, without taking her eyes off the computer screen. She blanked out the joking and laughing from her colleagues, and she carried on reading until she decided to speak with the author. Another hour's searching finally gave her the name of the newspaper where Harvey Speed worked.

'He's not here right now.' The voice sounded tired, the accent flat and dull.

'Can I get hold of him? Does he have a mobile?'

'Like I said. He's not here.' Caren could hear the irritation developing in the woman's voice.

'Is there someone who supervises his work?'

'You mean an editor.'

Before Caren could reply the line went dead.

'Marcus Oldham's phone.' This time the voice sounded more cultured.

'I'm trying to get hold of Harvey Speed.'

'I don't think he's in right now ...'

'Will he be in later?'

'He's working on ... Who are you anyway?'

'Is Marcus Oldham his editor?'

'Look. Just call back in an hour.'

The time seemed to drag as Caren ate her way through the sandwich. After returning from the kitchen with coffee she resisted the temptation to eat the chocolate bar in the pocket of her coat, settling instead for an apple. She sent a text to Alun, surprising herself when she felt annoyed that he didn't reply immediately, forgetting that he was probably driving. Barely an hour had gone by when she could hardly contain her patience any longer.

'Just a moment.' The receptionist's voice sounded as though she had the cares of the world on her shoulders, but a couple of clicks later and Caren heard a man's voice.

'Harvey Speed.' Caren could make out the accent: it sounded like it came from the north-east of England, maybe Durham or perhaps Newcastle.

'I'm Detective Sergeant Caren Waits of the Wales Police Service – Northern Division. I was reading your blog recently about Lyfon Pharmaceuticals. I was …'

'How do I know that you're a police officer?'

'You can call headquarters. The number is …'

'I can find the number.'

'You've written some blog entries about Tim Loosemore …'

'What interest have you got in Loosemore?'

'I'm doing some background work …'

'Who's your superior officer?'

'Inspector Ian Drake. Why do you ask?'

'I'll call you back.'

Caren sat looking at the handset, wondering if she'd actually achieved anything. Maybe her interest in Tim Loosemore was another wild goose chase. She got up and stretched her legs, realising that huddling over the computer for most of the morning had made her feel stiff and uncomfortable.

Less than half an hour later her telephone rang.

'Detective Sergeant Waits.' Speed sounded almost friendly. 'Sorry that I had to sound so defensive. Dealing with people like Tim Loosemore means you have to be very careful.'

'What can you tell me about him?' Caren hoped she could conceal the interest that Speed's comments had sparked in her mind.

'When I started investigating Lyfon and Loosemore I began to get some very unpleasant attention from solicitors acting for the company and for Loosemore himself. Telling me I had to be very careful, threatening libel proceedings, substantial damages because they could prove that I was malicious and that I wanted to ruin his reputation.'

'When was this?'

'A couple of years ago. I've got everything documented. Anyway, why are you interested in Loosemore?'

'He's a person of interest.'

'In what sort of investigation?'

'I wouldn't be able to …'

'Financial irregularities, fraud, perhaps?'

Caren noted down the precise words used by Speed.

'Lyfon Pharmaceuticals was given favourable treatment and generous grants.'

'I thought that sort of thing was against the regulations. European directives.'

'You must be joking. There is one rule for most of us and another for people who are friends with Richard Class.'

'Why were you interested in Tim Loosemore's company?'

'I'm a financial journalist. A reliable source told me there was a story to be written. Once I began to do background checks and research, Loosemore and his cronies threatened to bring the world down on top of me.'

'Is there any material you could send me?'

'You need to talk to Detective Superintendent Adams in Cardiff. He might be more of a help.'

Drake called Ellis-Pugh but the answer machine had clicked on. The accent still sounded like a voice-over from a 1960s black-and-white documentary. Drake stumbled over the right thing to say until eventually he left a message, telling Ellis-Pugh he'd be calling at the flying club later that morning.

Then he telephoned the hospital in Bangor and after

some initial confusion about which ward Tom Vigo had been admitted into the receptionist put him through. A sharp voice answered: 'Intensive care.'

'Has Tom Vigo regained consciousness?'

'Not yet. Can you try again later?'

'How long?' Drake said.

'I can't tell you. It's impossible to say.'

Drake sat in the car outside the shop where he stopped every morning, the newspaper on the passenger seat open at the usual page. Frustrated at the possibility that his morning might be wasted, he decided to call at the flying club first. It was a clear, crisp morning, the temperatures were rising and the forecasters on the radio promised the first of several fine days. As he drove along the A55, he couldn't help but think about the session with Halpin and the fact that he hadn't made any notes. He'd even bought a small Moleskine notepad from a stationers but it was languishing unopened in his jacket pocket.

After forty minutes, he turned into the car park at the flying club and saw the old Ford parked alongside a sign that said 'Club Chairman' and from the plates he quickly calculated that the car must have been ten years old.

In the distance two RAF fire engines stood in the corner of the runaway and Drake saw activity in the modern control tower nearby. He drew up outside the old buildings and almost immediately the door opened and Ellis-Pugh strode out and then stopped, the surprise evident in his face.

'I didn't expect you so soon,' Ellis-Pugh said.

'I need some more details from you. It won't take long.'

'Of course.' Ellis-Pugh turned and led Drake into the building.

Drake heard the sound of a jet aircraft in the air.

'Training sessions,' Ellis-Pugh explained, looking at the sky.

Drake could smell the faint odour of furniture polish

in the small room which had 'Admin- Private' screwed to the door.

'How can I help?'

'I need the records of all the flights that Frank Rosen made in the last two years.'

'Of course.'

Ellis-Pugh started opening filing cabinets and reaching for folders tucked tidily into the suspension files. One wall was lined with photographs of what Drake guessed were club members smiling at the camera. He noticed a large group, all in black tie, glasses raised as a toast. John Beltrami was smiling broadly alongside his family. Two other men, both in their sixties, stood alongside Ellis-Pugh.

'Special event?' Drake said.

'That's Lewis Aylford and Ed Parry. Both are in the syndicate. The next photographs are of the wing walkers when they came to an air show we attended last year. Hairy stuff, I can tell you. Wouldn't catch me doing that.'

By the time Drake had looked at every photograph, Ellis-Pugh was sitting at his desk with various files in front of him. Drake guessed he'd need more time to assemble a complete list, so he sat down on a stiff metal chair to wait.

'Damned regulations. Health and Safety'll be the death of me,' he said, grinning at his own joke.

Ellis-Pugh pulled a sheaf of papers from a folder and handed them to Drake who was impressed by how quickly Ellis-Pugh had found the documents.

'It pays to be organised,' Ellis-Pugh said.

They shook hands and Drake left, feeling the chill of the spring morning on his face when he stood by the car. A training gnat was landing; its tyres screeched, watched by a fire engine and ground crew. In the distance Drake saw the mountains, perhaps even the remains of a snow flurry from the cold snap the week before.

A monitor standing alongside the bed beeped occasionally, its LED display flashing various numbers. A drip was attached to the arm of the man lying on the bed in front of Drake. A message asking him to call Glyn Newman urgently had been left unanswered. The night staff at the hospital had warned Drake that Tom Vigo might not recover enough to provide a reliable witness statement. A part of Drake knew that MC could have assaulted Vigo, but he wanted to dismiss the possibility until there was evidence. Real, hard, concrete evidence that the Crown Prosecution Service would sign off without hesitation.

A nurse entered the room and Drake took a step back as she moved towards the bed.

'You're wasting your time,' she said, her back to Drake. 'He's not going to be fit to interview for days.'

Drake drew a hand over his mouth, tightening his jaw. Drake knew that MC had a temper, but he'd never assaulted anybody. MC never had to: the prospect of crossing him was enough to stop most people.

'What does the doctor say?' Drake said, staring at the nurse.

She turned and gave him a defiant look, daring him to question her professional judgement.

'Same,' she said, through clenched teeth.

A sudden raft of sunshine poured through the window and Drake looked down at Vigo, thinking about the man's previous convictions, which stretched over two pages of a Police National Computer printout. Vigo was a person known to the police as a fixer, the sort of low-level toe-rag that would push the drugs around the pubs for suppliers who wanted to keep a clean profile.

'You'll need to leave soon,' the nurse said, hardening her eyes.

Reluctantly, Drake buttoned his jacket and left the ward, after extracting confirmation from the nurse that if Vigo regained consciousness she would contact him immediately. He'd put as much menace into his voice as he thought appropriate but it had little effect on her.

As he turned out of the corridor, he came face to face with Glyn Newman and Jeff Wallace.

'What are you doing here?' Newman said.

'I could ask the same about you,' Drake said. 'Both of you.'

'This is our case,' Wallace said, through a mouthful of gum.

'And why is the drugs squad involved with a simple assault?'

'This is my case.' Newman moved past Drake towards the ward. 'Don't interfere. And make no mistake, MC is going down for this.'

Outside Drake walked over to his car, a worry working its way into his head that MC was becoming a danger. If there was enough evidence to justify prosecution, questions might be asked about why he had been at the hospital. And why his recent contacts with MC had not been properly recorded. He tried MC's number again, but it rang out.

After cleaning his hands vigorously with an alcohol gel he kept in the glove compartment – he was never happy using the hand pumps on the wards – he drove away from the hospital and then on impulse turned towards Llanberis. Talking to MC's mother would give him the opportunity to find out what else was going on in MC's life. After turning left by the long boundary wall of the Vaynol estate, once the home of the slate owners that had employed thousands of men in the quarries of North Wales, he powered the Alfa Romeo up the hill. The mountains of Snowdonia appeared in front of him as he negotiated various roundabouts until he reached the turning for Llanberis. A thin veil of grey cloud hung over the summits, promising dampness, even rain, to those hardy enough to be walking on the hills.

He parked by the kerb in a small estate of

bungalows. He strode over the road and pressed the front doorbell. The chiming stopped after a few seconds and he heard a shout from the rear of the property. A couple of minutes passed before Gwen Hughes answered the door.

'Hello, Auntie Gwen.'

She looked older than Drake remembered. And thinner too. A brief moment passed before she recognised Drake.

'Ian, I didn't recognise you, *cariad*.'

She turned and led him through into a small back kitchen that smelt musty. Then he noticed the dog hair over all the chairs and an overweight Labrador sitting at the far corner, barely able to raise its head when it noticed a stranger in the house.

'How are you?' Drake said.

'My knees aren't so good.'

'Are you managing okay?'

She nodded weakly and sat down by the table. 'Do you want tea or something?'

Drake shook his head; the prospect of instant from a mug covered with dog hairs extinguished his need for coffee.

'I saw Moelwyn recently.'

A dark cloud passed over Gwen's eyes. 'How's your father?'

Drake hesitated. He could imagine the anguish she must have felt, the embarrassed glances in the shop and the awkward looks in the chapel on a Sunday morning.

'He's not very well.'

'I'd heard. And Mair?'

'Mam's coping,' Drake said. 'I need to see Moelwyn. I've tried his mobile and I need to contact him. I don't have his new address.'

Gwen gave him a vacant, almost surprised, look.

'You haven't heard then?'

'Sorry. What do you mean?'

'She's had a stroke.'

Drake could guess what had happened and he could guess how MC would react. 'Do you mean …?'

'Sylvie was very sick,' Gwen said, looking into the middle distance through the window. 'There was nothing of her. Thin as a … what has the world come to …?'

'What's Moelwyn's new address?'

She got up from the seat and heaved herself over towards a dresser by the wall. She fumbled through a couple of drawers until she found a battered address book and read out the details.

Drake stood up and made to leave.

'But he's probably at her house,' Gwen said, reading out a second address, before negotiating her way back to the chair by the table.

Drake left Gwen in the kitchen, thanking her for her help, promising to call again. Outside the spring morning had a cold tinge to the air. The mountains above the small town were grey and bleak in the morning sunshine. To his right, high up the mountain, he saw the outline of the gaping hole made by the Penrhyn quarry.

He suppressed a guilty feeling that he'd only called because he needed something. He wondered what Gwen was going to do for the rest of the day and then he remembered that he had to call his mother and find out how his father was.

But first he needed to find MC.

Chapter 17

'I'm early.'

Hannah gave Drake a weak smile. 'I'll tell him you've arrived.'

She reached for the telephone as Drake sat on one of the visitor chairs, the comfortable variety with padded armrests, and a significant improvement from the plastic chairs in the Incident Room. Hannah didn't seem too disappointed with the absence of Wyndham Price, despite the rumours about their close working relationship. Two well-thumbed editions of a popular walking magazine were lying on a table beside a publication from a major supermarket chain featuring their latest baking recipes.

After a couple of minutes – it felt longer – the telephone rang and Hannah swivelled in her chair. Drake noticed her slender legs and as he stepped towards the door into Lance's office he admired her neat and tidy desk. Had he been seeing Wyndham Price she might have smiled, but now she kept her comments brief.

'He'll see you now.' She darted her eyes towards the door before returning to stare at the computer screen on her desk.

Lance was sitting by the conference table in the middle of the room, a formality that Wyndham Price kept for important meetings.

'Please sit,' Lance said, nodding towards the chairs at the end of the table.

Drake did as he was told. Lance had a long, thin head and a pronounced chin, as though stretched by some invisible weights, but what Drake hadn't noticed on their first meeting was how dark the superintendent's eyebrows were, and that one was higher than the other. A pair of cufflinks with a Welsh dragon emblem made a tapping sound as Lance moved his hands across the table, turning over the pages of the report in front of him. Drake tried to guess the superintendent's age – it was difficult to tell: his hair was greying, crow's feet clustered around his eyes and there was a hint of flabbiness under his chin.

'You think there might be a drug connection?' Lance said.

'There's sufficient residue on Rosen's clothing to justify that assumption. And I've spoken— '

'Yes, I know. Inspector Newman kept me in the loop.'

'He told me that Rosen has no links whatsoever to any known drug supplier,' Drake said.

'I'm worried about the allocation of resources. If you take this investigation over budget the finance department won't be pleased.'

'I appreciate that, sir.' Drake could recall the memoranda that choked his inbox from the accountants when his last investigation went over budget. He wanted someone to tell the criminals to be considerate enough to allow the Wales Police Service to carry out its investigations on time and within budget. Drake had always been impressed how inventive the accountants could be in setting budgets when no one could tell how long a case might take. 'We're looking at all the passengers and crew. And then we'll look at Rosen's associates and friends.'

'I know. I know. I've seen the references to Beltrami. From the little I've read about him you need to be careful.'

A fragment of gossip from another DI over lunch the previous day had told Drake that Lance had spent two periods in the Professional Standards department in Newport – policing the policemen, although Drake knew that usually one posting to that department was enough to help any career.

'I had some intelligence that suggested there was a drug connection,' Drake said.

'Is that from your source MC Hughes?'

'That's correct, sir.'

Lance propped his chin on steepled hands before giving Drake a steely glare. 'I know that Superintendent Wyndham Price allowed you a certain *flexibility* in the way you dealt with informants. You won't find me so generous. If he's an intelligence source everything has to be recorded properly, no matter what. Otherwise it could be a disciplinary matter. Do I make myself clear?'

'Of course, sir.'

Lance pulled out a red folder and examined the sheets as though he were looking for a highlighted section. 'Was your trip to Dublin essential?'

Despite the innocent-sounding question Drake sensed that Lance had something more specific on his mind.

'In my judgement.' Drake summoned as much legal jargon as he could manage. 'It was important for me to establish the basic facts. Rosen had a substantial sum of money in a bank account. Scant attention was given to the money-laundering regulations.'

Lance looked up from the papers and raised an eyebrow.

'What did the Garda say to that?'

'Not a great deal.'

Lance pursed his lips, Drake could see his mind working; Price would have picked up the phone and complained like hell to an officer of a similar rank in the Garda. But he could see that Lance was going to ponder, consider the angles, weigh up the options.

'They were cash deposits. Which suggests a connection to drugs,' Drake said.

A silence hung around the table. 'Everything being equal, Inspector, I still think a junior officer could have visited Ireland.'

Drake wasn't certain what to say. Lance started clicking the top of a chrome biro, and the sound filled the void over the desk.

'From now on I shall assume the role of SIO. You'll be my deputy.'

Drake could feel his shirt contracting round his neck. Lance stared at him. Drake wanted to blink as he thought how to react. It was his case. *Had* been his case.

'And any contacts with other departments all come through my office,' Lance continued.

Drake sensed grime on his fingers and he desperately wanted to wipe away the grease he was sure lay along his hairline. Lance had returned to shuffling his papers.

'Mandy Beal,' Lance said eventually.

Drake didn't reply, uncertain whether he needed to say anything, relieved when Lance continued.

'We haven't had a post mortem report?'

'No, sir.'

'I'll chase the pathologist.' Lance scribbled on a yellow pad. 'Is there any question that it wasn't suicide?'

'No forced entry, no sign of a struggle. And nothing missing, so far as we can tell.'

'What's your gut feeling?'

'Sir?'

'You know, your immediate gut reaction. You must get them.' Lance peered towards Drake.

'Of course. It's …'

'Too much of a coincidence.'

'I suppose …'

'And it looks too neat.'

'The evidence we've gathered so far all suggests that Mandy wasn't the suicide type.'

'And what sort is that?'

Drake knew there was no simple answer; there wasn't a standard description and typical characteristics of a person likely to commit suicide.

'She didn't have any problems. Didn't complain to

anybody. She broke up with Rosen, was upset but she got on with life.'

Lance tidied the papers which Drake took as a signal that the meeting was over.

'Any contact you think is necessary with the drug squad comes through me. And before you leave, fix a time with Hannah for the next review.'

Drake noticed Lance reaching for another set of files as he pulled the door closed behind him. Hannah gave him an enquiring look as Drake stood by her desk.

'He wants me to diarise another meeting,' Drake said.

Hannah nodded. 'He's very meticulous,' she said in a whisper, clicking open the calendar on the computer. 'He's asked for so many different files, going back years. It's very odd without Wyndham … I mean Superintendent Price. I've sent you an email with the date.'

Drake left the senior management suite and threaded his way back to the Incident Room, his thoughts all tugging towards the fact that Lance knew all about his rituals.

As Drake returned to the Incident Room he called MC. Drake debated leaving a message when the messaging service clicked on but in the end killed the call. He'd sat for an hour outside MC's house earlier that morning, until eventually he'd decided to call at Sylvie's. It had taken him longer to find the small terraced house than he'd expected and after hammering on the door he'd peered into the front window and then, walking through a warren of back lanes, he'd pushed open the wooden back gate only to find that he couldn't see anything through any of the rear windows either. And the neighbours either side had no idea who lived in the property.

In the Incident Room he stared at the board, hoping for inspiration. Rosen's photograph pinned in the middle of the board made him look older. The names of the co-owners of the plane had been scribbled to one side, and lists of the crew and passengers printed in a medium-sized font dominated one-half of the board. It gave Drake an odd sense of comfort to know that he knew where to find the killer. All he had to do was find the evidence linking Rosen to one of the names on the board. It should be easy; all it required was patient police work.

His concentration was broken as Caren pushed open the door, followed by Winder and Howick joking loudly. Their conversations died as Drake looked over, and Caren went to stand by his side.

'All we have to do is find the connection,' Drake said. 'Somebody on one of these lists killed Rosen. So we know who it is.'

'Bit like one of those Agatha Christie films, you know, *Death on the Nile*,' Winder said beaming.

'And a ferry from Holyhead to Ireland is exactly like a boat travelling down the Nile, is it?' Howick said, sitting down.

'And I've got a list from Ellis-Pugh of the flights that Rosen made in the last couple of years.' Drake said. 'I need sense made of these. There might be something that matches up to the codes. An address or city or destination.'

'There are protocols about flying to Ireland,' Howick said. 'Special Branch have to be notified. They need to be sent the passenger list for every journey.'

Drake remembered about the CCTV coverage and looked over at Howick. 'Have you finished going through the CCTV yet?'

Howick adjusted his position on the chair. 'Not quite finished.'

Drake gave him a dark look. 'I need them done and finished by tomorrow. Even if that means you're here all night.'

Howick gave Drake a brief, sullen look.

Irritation built in Drake's mind. Why had Lance taken over the role of SIO? Was it something Lance had read about him? A realisation hit him that there must be something in his personnel file that was influencing Lance.

'I've also spoken to a journalist who's investigated Tim Loosemore,' Caren said. 'He got really spooked when I made contact. Wouldn't speak to me until he'd rung reception to check I was really a police officer.

Drake stood silently looking at the board. Caren gave a quick glance around at the others.

'Sir. Tim Loosemore.'

'What?' Drake said.

Caren cleared her throat and repeated herself.

'Did you contact Superintendent Adams?' Drake said once she'd finished.

Howick and Winder were standing by their desks listening intently to every word.

'Yes, sir. He confirmed there was an investigation, but wouldn't give me the details. It had to come from you.'

Drake nodded; another call to be put on his to-do list, another Post-it note to be added. He looked again at the list of passengers and crew. He turned to look at Winder. 'Gareth, let's get the names of all the passengers into groups.'

'Any suggestion, boss?'

'Foreign nationals, lorry drivers, families, businessmen. And Dave ...' He looked down at the list of crew members before looking at the young officer. 'I want you to do the same with the crew members. The killer is there so let's narrow it down. Tick the boxes. Complete the paper trail.'

Drake strode over to his office, avoiding the glances exchanged around the room at his final comments.

The routine was always the same: move the telephone a few millimetres, adjust the photographs of his daughters, draw a finger over the frames to check for dust before his mind could allow him to settle. Files of papers had been placed in neat piles and the Post-it notes were still in their proper place. He found the number Caren had given him for Superintendent Adams but the soothing professional tones of the officer's answer machine contrasted sharply with the brusque message Drake left on MC's mobile. Deciding to call again later, he left no message and turned his attention to his emails. Every circular email was meticulously read and scrutinised for its relevance and then, when he was assured it could be safely removed, he pressed the delete key. A second call to Superintendent Adams was unsuccessful and Drake circled the officer's name on a Post-it note with a green highlighter.

It was after ten when the Macmillan nurse brought the conversation to a close. Drake felt an odd mixture of emotions, pleased that she had left but daunted by what he might say to his father. An uncomfortable few seconds passed before his mother stood up.

'I'll make tea,' she announced and left the room.

'She's finding it hard,' Tom said.

'I know.' Drake felt a lump forming in his throat.

'It comes to us all.'

Drake felt like telling his father that clichés were no comfort.

'You'll look after your mother once …'

'Dad. Don't say that.'

'I know, but …' Tom blinked rapidly but he failed to hold back the tears. 'It's just so unfair.'

When Mair Drake returned with a tray of tea mugs Tom had brushed away the tears. She turned to Drake. 'And how are Megan and Helen?'

Drake reached for the tea. 'They're fine.'

'And Sian?'

Drake took a mouthful of hot tea, wondering how his

mother could be normal after a discussion with a Macmillan nurse about end-of-life care.

'She's busy.'

Tom was nursing his mug as Mair finalised the arrangements for Drake and his family to visit on Sunday. 'Your father can't travel now,' she said as though he wasn't in the room.

Soon enough Mair ushered Tom to bed and Drake left. It was a clear cloudless night and as he turned at the top of the lane down towards Caernarfon he noticed the shimmering lights from the farms and cottages. There were people preparing for bed, boiling kettles, eating biscuits, watching the evening news, kissing loved ones – doing the ordinary things of life. The things that his father wouldn't be doing very much longer.

He passed through Caernarfon, the various supermarkets with their lights blazing, the occasional pedestrian walking home, another eating chips. Once he was clear of the town, he accelerated towards the A55. He slowed and then pulled the car into the main carriageway behind a truck with Polish plates. When the road was clear, a couple of minutes later, he signalled and overtook the lorry. By the time he was nearing Llanfairfechan his mind was full of reminiscences, memories of childhood, sadness even at the happy times he'd had.

On impulse he signalled left off the dual carriageway, followed the road into Llanfairfechan, and then down towards the beachfront. He parked and wrapped himself up against the evening chill. Behind him the lights of the houses stretched up the hillside, a train thundered through the station and in the distance he saw Llandudno illuminating the night sky. He walked along the concrete path thinking about his father, remembering the childhood trips to the seaside. The sound of the tide lapping against the rocks on the shore mixed with the occasional car horn. He stepped away from the concrete path and onto the rocky shoreline. He leant down to pick up a couple of large rocks and turned them through his fingers before discarding them and walking on. A heavy shadow drew itself over his mind as he contemplated how he'd react if he had months or weeks or maybe just days to live.

He had read about people facing death with equanimity but he supposed it was something no one could ever prepare for. The Macmillan nurse had wanted to sound helpful, constructive, and he could remember that she made regular eye contact, was warm and approachable. She'd used soothing language about palliative care and doing everything to support the family that made it sound so remote. But it was like reaching out for something elusive, chasing clouds, yet his father's illness was real enough.

Out across the bay he caught the faintest outline of Puffin Island and then along the coast the flickering lights of Beaumaris and the villages on Anglesey. He shivered in the cool evening air, stepped down towards the shoreline and found half a dozen thin flat stones that he skimmed along the surface. His father had shown him how to do that as a boy. And now, walking back to his car, he wondered what his father was thinking about at that very moment.

Chapter 18

Noticing Drake's freshly ironed shirts and carefully folded ties made Howick realise the inadequacies of his own wardrobe. The night before he'd bought two new shirts – one white, the other a light blue – and sombre ties with subdued stripes.

That morning he'd half expected some sarcastic comment from Winder and had been pleased when his colleague had barely given him a second glance. The bags under Winder's eyes were beginning to carry a nasty black tinge and even before he sat down, he'd complained of being tired. Caren hadn't commented either but then she always looked as though she'd been pulled through a hedge so Howick assumed that she wouldn't notice.

Six hours of CCTV coverage from four different cameras had meant three full days stuck in front of the computer screen. Howick had managed two four-hour sessions in the previous couple of days but he had now decided that a complete day had to be dedicated. A spasm of worry had crossed his mind that his decision to view the images from quite so far back in time may have meant delays, but he had wanted to be thorough and now he had to make progress. Carefully pinned to the Incident Board were the lists of various groups he had created from the crew rota. He had taken a certain pride in being as methodical and as thorough as he thought Drake expected.

A plan of the ship pinned to the board had highlighted the location of each CCTV camera in yellow. Another list summarised their locations and the areas they covered. Howick had spent a couple of hours at the beginning of the inquiry identifying which camera promised the best images. A camera located at the bow of the vessel recording the activity on the car deck had been quickly relegated to the bottom of his list. Another had been screwed high up above the middle section of the car deck, unable to film the immediate area surrounding the position where Rosen's body had been found.

The stern and the area adjacent to the office were covered by two cameras. Howick clicked the images into life from the first and watched as the occasional crewmember passed by, their chests swollen by high-visibility jackets. He glanced at the time on the screen and knew that the ferry would have been alongside at its berth in Dublin. He stretched his arms out over his head as the minutes ticked by but the screen remained blank. After an hour, he could feel an ache in the small of his back and he got up, found his way to the kitchen and made a coffee – just an instant, not the sort of real coffee that Drake fussed over. He turned a couple of teaspoons of sugar into the brown liquid and took a heavy slurp.

Winder didn't look up as Howick returned. He rubbed the palms of his hands over his eyes before a couple of clicks brought the screen to life. Another glance at the clock told him that the vessel would soon begin embarkation. He resisted the temptation to fast-forward the images and a sense of relief descended as he noticed activity commencing. Men darted around the trucks, silently and slowly moving down into the car deck. Some of the faces he recognised, despite the poor quality of the images. He ticked off the names of the crew members that should have been on the car deck. Then it struck Howick that all the crew had their backs to the camera once they were working.

Turning to the final images, Howick decided to start viewing the images from the point at which activity had commenced on the earlier tape. He'd had enough of looking at an inactive screen. Returning to the earlier tape he found the time and, reverting to the final coverage, scrolled to the right time and started playing. He took a mouthful of cold coffee, Winder was still staring at his computer screen although Howick had noticed him stifling a yawn earlier.

The Incident Room felt unnaturally quiet. Ten minutes after he'd started the clock an image appeared on the screen of a man standing talking to someone out of sight of the camera. The man raised his arms, turned and then walked towards the main section of the car deck. Howick froze the image, trying to force his mind to remember the man's face. He reached for a notepad and scribbled down the time, somehow believing it had relevance. It was half an hour before the boat was due to sail. Just about the time when Rosen had reached the engine room.

Another few moments passed and then Howick saw a shoulder of a man in a one-piece work suit – no high-visibility jacket – moving through one corner of the image. Immediately he pulled up his chair and focused on the screen. He clicked back carefully until the screen showed the image again and he let the coverage run on. Whoever it was had been careful, no face turned to the camera, the body shielded from the CCTV camera. He stopped the coverage for a moment, ran his tongue over his drying lips, wondering if he had just seen Rosen's killer.

He clicked again and when the man's head turned the light caught on what looked like a piece of jewellery in his right ear. Howick's pulse raced for a moment. He lowered his head again, staring at the screen.

Gotcha.

After an hour of trawling through the photographs of crew members, ignoring Winder's invitation for lunch, Howick sat back and weighed up what Drake would say. He would have to check one more thing, so he picked up the telephone.

It took four telephone calls to find the hospital that had admitted Sylvie. The nurse in the high dependency unit refused to give Drake any information and, despite considering the possibility of demanding to speak to a consultant, he rang off.

The need to speak to MC was imperative and, guessing that he might be at Sylvie's bedside, Drake drove to the hospital. After parking he followed the directions for the HDU and, pushing open the doors, strode over to the nurses' station.

'I want to see Sylvie Whatmore,' he said, holding out his warrant card.

She raised a hand and pointed down the corridor. 'Number four, at the end.'

Drake found Sylvie in one corner of a small ward; a drip fed a clear liquid into her body and a dull hum emanated from the equipment alongside the bed. A woman with a short haircut and long earrings was sitting in one of the visitor chairs. He looked around, hoping that MC might suddenly appear. Sylvie was thin and drawn, her cheeks hollowed and her eyes were closed. It was difficult to tell if she was breathing.

'And who are you?' The woman did not get up.

'Detective Inspector Drake. I know MC.'

'I was ... am her drug support worker. Sam Croft.'

Drake pulled up a chair. 'How is she?'

'Not good.'

'Has MC been around?'

'Not today.'

'What's the prognosis?'

Croft gave a long sigh. 'Like it is with a lot of drug addicts. You hope that things will get better, but they never do.'

'Have you been working with her a long time?'

She shrugged. 'It seems a long time. But once MC was inside she was as vulnerable as hell and the pushers got hold of her. She'd go out with friends, borrow money and then she started small-scale until she got hooked on heroin. She was really a nice girl, but by the end of MC's term in jail she'd hit rock bottom. And the pushers and dealers were taking advantage of her ...'

She let the last few words hang in the air. Drake understood what she meant and a sense of unease built when he pondered if MC knew as well.

'She had to sell everything. Clothes, even the nice expensive stuff that MC had given her and all her furniture. Everything – gone, and in the end she was using a sleeping bag on the floor. I did everything I could to help her. I even stayed with her overnight once. But it was no good and useless – as soon as I'd left the pushers were back. Do you have any idea the evil that drugs can cause?'

Sylvie moved in her bed and let out a sigh. Drake looked over at her and saw her shoulder blades protruding from under her nightgown. 'Do you know where I can contact MC?'

Croft gave him a puzzled look, as though the question was unexpected.

'No. No, I don't.'

Drake got up. 'I really need to speak to him. If you see him get him to call me.'

Croft stared at him. He looked over at the bed. Sylvie's eyelids flickered briefly.

On the journey back to headquarters, Drake found his mind wondering why Mandy's death was dominating his thoughts. Various unanswered questions ran through his mind. But there wasn't enough to suggest anything other than suicide. Soon he couldn't justify any further resources investigating her death – he would have to turn the case over to the coroner. Sitting at his desk Drake watched the coffee grounds descending in the cafetière. He looked over at the photograph of Sian and the girls, realising that he should add a photograph of his parents as well. He tried to think where he could find a photograph of his mother and father with his wife and the girls. Sian could find one, he was sure, and he made a mental note to ask her later.

Lance had emailed him several times during the morning and Drake spent more time reading the emails than he would have done on Price's. Ahead of him was the task of telling the team that Lance was now the SIO, creating yet another knot of tension to deal with. There was no reasonable explanation for his demotion, and he tried to calculate what Lance might have read about him in his personnel file.

An email from Malachy O'Sullivan reminded him to send a photograph of Mandy Beal, so he spent time trawling through the folders until he attached it to a reply. He was suddenly impatient with everything about the investigation. And there was an odd smell in his room, of that he was certain. Unless he could determine its source it would distract him for the rest of the day. Moving the bin and rearranging the chairs had little effect and even adjusting the latch on the window didn't help.

He was standing in the middle of the floor, staring at his desk, when Howick knocked on the door.

'Something you should see, sir.'

Drake frowned as he turned to look at the young officer. His pulse increased a notch at the thought of having to speak to the team.

'I've been looking at the CCTV coverage from the boat.'

'It's a ship,' Drake said, repeating Captain Seymour's admonishment.

Howick blinked a couple of times, obviously uncertain how to reply. 'It's on the computer,' he said eventually.

Drake walked over to the board. 'I think you should know ...' He could feel a lump developing in his throat. 'Superintendent Lance has assumed the role of SIO for the duration of the inquiry.'

Winder glanced at Caren. She puckered her cheeks and then frowned slightly. Howick stuck his hands into his pockets, but said nothing.

'Is there any reason?' Caren said.

Drake had been thinking exactly the same himself. A heavy atmosphere hung in the room. Winder bowed his head slightly and looked at Howick. Another spasm of doubt ran through Drake's mind that maybe his team knew something about this turn of events. They might have heard some gossip.

'We get on with the investigation,' Drake said, stepping towards Howick, who sat down and started clicking through various CCTV clips. Winder walked over and stood next to Drake.

Drake said nothing as he concentrated on Howick's screen. Caren put her tea down on the desk and fumbled noisily with the wrapping of an Eccles cake. Drake gave her a sharp glare.

'Dave's got something important,' he said, raising his voice.

Without turning his head, Howick started a detailed explanation of the CCTV coverage. After five minutes Drake cut across him. 'What exactly did you want to show us?'

'It's the cameras near the stern door.' Howick sounded flustered.

More images of men in high-visibility jackets filled the screen. Howick explained that the ship was loading, ready to leave the port. Drake turned to look at Caren, the half-eaten pastry in her hand, the rest floating around in her open mouth.

'Look at this, sir,' Howick said, freezing the image of a man, stationary below the camera, his hands outstretched, a defensive posture to his body language. 'I think this is Rhodri Owens, the ship's deck officer. Something doesn't look right.'

'Have we got any statements?' Drake said.

'I've gone through the statements from the other officers on the deck, but nobody mentions Rhodri Owens.'

'But all we asked them about was Rosen.'

'There may be an innocent enough explanation to all this,' Caren added, leaning on the back of the chair alongside Drake.

'What else have you got?' Drake gestured towards the screen.

Howick clicked again until the image of the earring appeared. 'That's Darren Green.'

'And who is he?' Winder again.

'Able seaman,' Howick replied.

'How do you know it's Green?' Caren asked, moving closer to the screen.

'He wears an earring. I checked with his photograph.'

Caren balled the remains of the cellophane wrapper and discarded it in the bin by her feet. 'And if the intelligence from Merseyside police is reliable, he should be our number one suspect.'

'So what are you thinking?' Winder asked. 'What time was this?'

'It was half an hour before the ship was due to leave.'

'Just when Rosen went missing,' Drake said. 'I think we need to talk to Green.'

'I've spoken with the ferry company already. He's coming off shift at six in the morning,' Howick said.

Drake turned to Caren. 'Better get an early night.'

Chapter 19

Drake pulled back the sleeve of his Barbour jacket and read the time. He knew from a Google search that sunrise was at 6:16 a.m. and, looking eastwards, he saw the first faint shards of light. At least it wasn't raining as it had been the last time he'd stood on the quayside. He thrust gloved hands into both pockets, but there was no escaping the bitter wind blowing through the harbour. Caren, standing by his side, alternated between blowing onto the surface of a coffee and then sipping loudly. Even at this early hour, he was irritated by her eating habits. She had given him one of her usual odd glances when he'd declined the offer of coffee.

The noise from the approaching ferry increased and he took a couple of steps towards the ramp. The sound of seawater that was churned by the bow thrusters smothered the broken speech from voices on radios used by the shore staff. Lights flashed and sirens wailed as the stern doors of the vessel slowly heaved open. Behind Drake engines of tractor units roared into life. Another five minutes passed until the ship had been secured and the ramp lowered towards the car deck. Drake saw familiar faces as he walked down into the body of the vessel.

'Captain Seymour's expecting you,' one of the deck officers said to him, leaning towards Drake's left ear to make himself heard. 'Go up to deck A.'

Drake and Caren heard the heavy pneumatic door closing behind them as they climbed the stairs through the vessel. He unzipped his jacket, removed the gloves and after five flights, taken too quickly, he stood on deck A, his heart pounding. The door opened and Captain Seymour strode towards them.

'How can I help, Inspector?'

'We need to interview Darren Green,' Drake said, regaining his composure.

'The AB?'

Drake nodded.

'He's not on board.'

'We were told he was working.'

'He went off watch early. I think he's got the flu. So he left twelve hours ago.'

'Why the hell didn't anyone tell us?'

Seymour looked surprised. 'I was told to expect you. But not that you wanted to speak to Green.'

'Didn't he tell you ...' Drake didn't finish. 'Thanks Captain,' he said, before turning back towards the stairs.

The car deck was a throng of activity. Drake hurried towards the ramp, but had to wait as a lorry with Lithuanian plates slowly hauled its way onto the quayside. He cursed silently his decision not to give Captain Seymour advance warning. Walking up from the car deck Drake could make out the silhouettes of the harbour buildings from the sunshine breaking over the horizon.

The Alfa was still parked by the small office building, now alive with activity. He unlocked the car before joining the stream of lorries threading their way back to the main entrance.

'Find the address,' Drake said to Caren, as they turned towards the middle of the town.

After a few minutes Drake pulled the car onto the pavement near Green's house, a two-storey end of terrace.

'There'll be a back lane,' Drake said, knowing that every terrace in the town seemed to have access from the rear. 'You go to the front.'

At the opposite end of the terrace of five houses, Drake found the narrow tarmac-covered lane. He broke into a brief jog until he reached a junction and saw another lane running behind the properties. A tall black bin was lying on its side, spewing out its contents and there was a strong smell of dog urine. He reached the end of the lane and peered towards Green's house. But there was no sign of life, no lights or movement.

He tried the latch on the gate but it wouldn't budge. He pushed it, hard. Nothing. He thought he heard the sound of the doorbell and guessed Caren was trying to raise Green. He stepped back, concluding that the wall was well over two metres. Retracing his steps, he kicked away some rubbish from the bin before upending it and dragging it towards the entrance to Green's backyard. He scrambled to the top of the bin, hoping it would hold his weight. The plastic sagged a little but, ignoring the angst that his Barbour would be ruined and that his brogues would probably be badly scratched, he climbed over the wall and fell heavily into a flowerbed full of nettles. He felt his hands burning and cursed.

He reached for the mobile in his pocket and dialled Caren's number. 'I'm in the backyard.'

'No sign of him. I've tried the bell and hammered on the door. Curtains drawn on the front window.'

Drake had reached the back door by the time Caren had finished.

'The back door is open. I'm going in.' He killed the call and put the mobile back into his pocket before pushing open the door and stepping into a small room with a washing machine and tumble dryer. To his right there was a narrow door that he gently prodded with his foot. There was a foul smell from the toilet behind it, so he pulled the door closed.

Moving to his left he stepped into a kitchen and shouted Green's name, only for a moment wondering about whether he'd entered lawfully, and whether he'd have the lawyers on his back. But something wasn't right. He flicked on a light switch and a shadeless bulb illuminated the kitchen; a pile of empty lager tins lay on the kitchen table alongside a takeaway pizza box.

There was a musty smell to the hallway, as though nobody had cleaned for months. He called out Green's name again before nudging open the first door he came to. It was empty apart from an old table, no chairs and no covering on the small window.

The second door was to the room at the front of the house.

Drake looked at the light switch, smudges of grease over its surface. Forcing himself, he flicked the switch, filling the room with a pale haze. He only took one step before seeing Daz Green sitting in a chair, blood covering his chest, a bullet wound centred in his forehead.

Chapter 20

A yellow tape marking the outer perimeter of the crime scene was already in place when Drake and Caren arrived back after a hurried breakfast in the local police station. One of the young uniformed officers they'd left at the house in their absence was standing alongside the Scientific Support Vehicle talking to an elderly man; a small overweight dog sat on the pavement by his feet. Drake could see the back of a white-suited CSI standing in the doorway.

Winder and Howick arrived and as Drake gave them instructions his mobile rang. Recognising the number he took two steps away from the other officers, hoping he could talk privately.

'I know who did it.' MC's voice was clear.

'What do you mean?'

'Don't you want to know who killed Green?'

'Of course, but—'

'We can talk now.'

Drake turned and looked down the street. MC was fifty metres away, standing on the pavement, mobile pressed to his ear, legs astride. A couple of elderly women jostled past him.

'And I want to talk to you about Tom Vigo. I'll get my sergeant.'

'No way.'

Drake clenched his jaw, anger building with his cousin. Family loyalty was one thing, but he couldn't take the risk of talking to MC alone. Drake's attention was drawn to Foulds emerging from the house and when Drake looked back towards the main road MC had gone. Drake killed the call and cursed. He stood for a moment, conflicted. Caren strode towards him. 'Problem, boss?'

'Nothing. Let's go inside.'

But he couldn't rid himself of the thought that MC

might know something important, something that might help. Foulds was waiting for him by the front door.

'Good Morning, Ian.'

'Mike.' Drake was still thinking about MC. Perhaps he ought to talk to Lance; he worried about the consequences of *not* getting MC to talk to him and then worried about the consequences *of* talking to MC. They stepped into the front room, which was still curtained.

'Lots of blood and signs of a struggle,' Foulds said.

But Drake wasn't listening. He stared at Green sitting in the chair, blood scarring his face. It was too hot in the room; he glanced over at the curtains, wondering if the neighbours had heard anything and then he considered whether the house-to-house would turn up anything of value.

'Is the pathologist on his way?' Caren asked Foulds.

Drake turned as he heard her voice and focused again on the task in hand.

'Should be here in an hour,' Foulds said.

'We're going to look around,' Drake said, making for the door.

He walked through into the kitchen, snapping on a pair of latex gloves. He'd paid no attention to the empty pizza boxes and discarded cans of lager strewn over the kitchen table when he'd first entered the house that morning but the smell hadn't changed. He ran a finger over various pieces of crockery on the drainer before moving to one side half-empty boxes of cereal discarded on the worktop – there had to be something rotting somewhere, but he couldn't find the source.

'What's that smell?' Caren said as she started to open wall cupboards.

Drake didn't say anything. Even the window looking out over the garden was dirty. He itched to wash from head to toe but was unable to even turn on the tap to wash his hands – there were black rings of mildew around its base, and old water pooled next to the sink. Stepping out into the rear garden he smelt the feline urine that hung in the air. A radio played in the distance and he could hear the muffled conversations from the rear yards of nearby houses. Opening the gate, he stepped into the lane behind the house and wandered down to the junction with the tarmac path that lead behind the main street. He stood, looking at the rear of the houses, noticing the occasional loft conversion and dilapidated gutter. Green's killer could have gone left or turned right and disappeared up the side streets and rear alleyways. No CCTV camera for miles. Retracing his steps back to the house, he found Caren finishing in the kitchen.

'Disgusting,' she said simply.

'Let's go through.' Drake nodded at the doorway.

They worked through each room in the house. It looked as though Green hadn't entered the living room at the rear for months, maybe longer. Dust had settled in thick waves over every surface, plastic bags were piled into a corner and the theme of disorganised chaos continued in the bedrooms upstairs. Two large speakers had pride of place either side of a large television screen, strategically placed so that Green could watch television propped up in bed. Drake didn't want to think about what was causing the smell in the bathroom. After half an hour Drake and Caren stood on the front doorstep, the sound of crime scene investigators busy inside the house drifting outside. Drake heard a noise behind him and saw Foulds emerge.

'Bloody hot in there.'

'Anything?' Caren asked.

'Nothing yet. It will take us all day.'

By the junction with the main road, Drake saw Winder and Howick comparing notes. Arms were raised, fingers were pointed and they set off in different directions.

'Let me know soon as you're finished,' Drake said to Foulds. 'And we will need to retrieve his personal details as soon as we can. He was single, but he must have had a family somewhere.'

Foulds nodded before taking a deep lungful of clean air and stepping back into the house.

'The ferry company should have details about his next of kin,' Drake said.

It was a short walk to the port office and as they approached the railway bridge a train slowly pulled out of the station. The ferry company had a building overlooking the port, squeezed between two platforms of the railway station. After buzzing an intercom Drake introduced himself and the door clicked open. A small woman with fierce black hair stood in a doorway of the first-floor landing.

'Anne Hegarty,' she said, offering Drake her hand, its nails painted pillar-box red.

'I want to speak to the port manager.'

'Is it about that man Daz Green?'

Drake hesitated, knowing he shouldn't have been surprised that the news had spread so quickly. It was a small town, everyone knew each other's business and Green would have acquired more friends in death than he probably had alive. Rumours would become half-truths, confirmed in the pubs from reliable sources and by the evening there'd be a dozen versions of the events circulating.

'Did you know him?'

'Not personally,' she said. 'But one of the girls that works in the office used to be part of the on-board catering staff.'

Hegarty led them into a small office with a round table and waved a hand towards plastic chairs as an invitation for them to sit down. Drake stood and leant his hands on the back of a chair.

'We'll want the personnel file.'

'Of course.' Hegarty's gaze floated over the chairs.

Once she'd left Drake stepped towards the window and looked down at the port below. The sun's rays glistened on the engine oil floating on the surface of the harbour.

'Have you worked in Holyhead, sir?' Caren said.

'Custody Sergeant, hated every minute.'

In the distance Drake could see a narrow bloom of smoke rising from the funnel of the ferries berthed at the far end of the harbour. Drake heard voices in the room behind him and turned just as Mortlake entered, followed by sheepish-looking Hegarty.

'Inspector Drake,' Mortlake said, sitting on one of the chairs and tossing the buff-coloured folder he was carrying onto the table. 'I hope this doesn't mean you're going to stop our ferries running.'

'What do you know about Daz Green?'

'Not a lot.'

'Is that his personnel file?'

'Anne will make photocopies for you. The original stays right here.'

Hegarty left, taking the file with her and Drake stared at Mortlake, wanting to believe there was something likeable about him, but the accent was too crass and Drake was convinced the man wanted to goad him.

'We'll wait,' Drake said, pulling out the chairs and nodding to Caren for her to do likewise. 'How long had he been working for you?'

'A few years. He was an able seaman, what more can I tell you?'

'Any good at his job?'

'You don't need a degree or any qualifications to be an able seaman. Do you think he killed Frank Rosen?'

'Is there a connection between both men?'

Mortlake sat back, rubbed his fingers over his mouth and gave Drake a tired look. 'Next you'll be telling me there's a connection to Mandy Beal's suicide.'

Drake was spared having to reply as Hegarty returned with Green's file and a pile of photocopies.

'If we can be of any more assistance,' Mortlake said, pushing the copies towards Drake and standing up at the same time.

'Thanks.' Drake scooped up the papers.

Taxis were beginning to arrive outside the main port building and Drake guessed a train was due to arrive.

'I'm starving,' Caren said as they walked up to the bridge. '*Paned*, boss?'

That word suddenly made him think of Sian, that Welsh word for an invitation to join someone for a cup of tea or a coffee, and one of the first Welsh words his wife had learnt. Using it had a universal usage even if you didn't understand Welsh. Caren had already started towards the café in the old chapel and Drake followed, noticing the look of anticipation on his colleague's face as they walked into the café where the staff welcomed them as regulars.

Drake found a newspaper with an untouched sudoku and settled into solving the puzzle, feeling his mind resting as he began filling the squares. Even the instant coffee tasted acceptable and he blanked out the noise from Caren eating a sandwich by his side while simultaneously flicking through Green's personnel file. He didn't notice when she'd stopped eating and concentrated on a single document.

'You won't believe this, sir.'

Drake's irritation had developed to exasperation when one of the squares proved troubling.

'Sorry?' Drake said, his mind still on the sudoku.

'You need to read this.'

'What?'

'Reference for Darren Green.'

Drake picked up the document she pushed over the table.

'Signature at the bottom, sir.'

Drake suddenly forgot all about the troublesome puzzle as he read the name and the familiar signature above it.

Chapter 21

Caren suppressed a yawn as she marched over to the window and unfastened the catch, allowing cool air to brush her face. It worked for a moment to make her feel less tired and she wondered where Alun was. The absence of a text during the day had unsettled her, so she found her mobile and started composing a message as Winder and Howick marched in, each holding a steaming mug. Winder carried a bag of pastries and Howick threw a couple of chocolate bars onto his desk.

'Do you want a coffee?' Winder said to Caren.

She nodded. 'The usual.'

Winder trooped off to the kitchen, passing Drake in the doorway.

'Coffee, boss?'

'No thanks.'

Drake put the file he was carrying on a nearby desk and began rummaging through the papers. Caren watched as he fumbled to insert a photograph into a plastic stationery pocket before pinning it under Green's name on the board. Drake's suit jacket was a rich navy and Caren guessed it was expensive: his clothes were always neat – no creases or folds and Caren often puzzled how he managed it. On their journey to headquarters Drake had spent time finalising a sudoku puzzle, ignoring her attempts to discuss the case. She had tried small talk, but her reference to a popular crime drama on the television produced a blank expression so she had given up and they drove on in silence.

Winder returned, dumping a mug advertising a local firm of solicitors onto her table. Drake turned away from the board.

'How did you get on with the house-to-house inquiries?' Drake alternated his gaze between Howick and Winder.

'We'll have to go back again, boss,' Howick said. 'I spoke to one guy who was convinced he'd seen the killers driving away as he left for work. He works in one of those chicken factories in the middle of the island. He starts his shift at five in the morning, preparing and gutting chickens all day. The company gives him four seconds to skin and prepare a chicken fillet.'

Winder stopped eating a Danish pastry and looked up. 'Four seconds? That must be bloody monotonous.'

'He'd been out of work for four months since they closed another abattoir on the island.'

Caren recalled the article in the local paper and the press reports when three hundred jobs had been lost. Local councillors and union leaders had repeated the usual warnings about the effect of unemployment on the local population. Everyone seemed to be waiting for the nuclear power station to be approved, creating jobs and giving the economy of the island and North Wales a boost.

'Did he have a description of the drivers of the car?' Drake said, a weary tone to his voice.

Although he didn't show it, Caren guessed he was as tired as she felt.

'I'm on the case,' Howick said.

Drake nodded. 'Anything else?'

Winder licked the tips of his fingers after finishing the last of the pastry. 'I spoke to the occupants of the houses opposite Green's place. There was a fussy woman with teenage children and a husband who didn't say anything. She'd seen a lot of people coming and going from the house. But I wasn't convinced she was telling me the truth.'

'Why?' Drake said.

'You know how it is, boss. Somebody wants to be helpful but they embellish everything.'

'Check with the other houses next door.'

'Sure thing. Then I got talking to this old man. He had a small dog who could hardly move, just sat in the middle of the floor, panting.'

Drake folded his arms and cleared his throat. 'I don't want to hear about the dog.'

'No, sir.' Winder moved in his chair. 'He kept talking in code. Asking me if I knew where places were in Holyhead and whether I remembered certain people.'

Caren made her first contribution, sharing Drake's impatience. 'Get on with it, Gareth. He was probably a bit lonely.'

'Anyway, he told me that the woman who cleans for him might be able to help. She goes in three times a week, helps with his cleaning. And the cooking sometimes.'

Drake was rubbing his temples as though he were trying to relieve a headache. 'I can't believe that nobody saw or heard anything.'

Howick threw the crumpled wrapping paper from the second chocolate bar into the bin by his feet. 'The man next door wasn't at home. He'd left early and when the uniformed officer in the back lane spoke to him, he told her he'd had an urgent call from a relative. So I'll go back and see him tomorrow.'

'This is the middle of Holyhead,' Drake said, ignoring Howick's last comments, an edge of despair to his voice. 'If the pathologist was right and he'd been dead for over ten hours when we found him, then he could have been shot as people watched television last night. So the killer parks nearby, walks down the street, knocks on the door and kills Green in his front room.'

Winder and Howick exchanged glances that suggested they didn't know how to respond. Caren stood up and walked over to the board, drawing a link between Green and Rosen.

Caren stepped back from the board. 'We know they worked on the same ship.'

'On the same watch,' Howick reminded them.

'And if Green killed Rosen, what was the motive?'

Drake said.

'So what's the connection between Green and Rosen?' Howick asked.

Drake flicked through his file of papers, a pleased look crossing his face as he removed a single sheet. 'This is a copy of the work reference given to Green when he started in the ferry company. I quote "Darren Green is a reliable and conscientious individual who I have known for some time" and it goes on in that vein. Signed by J. Beltrami".'

Winder let out a low whistle; Howick stood up, folded his arms and gave the board a serious look.

Drake continued. 'So Caren and I are going to pay Mr Beltrami another visit.'

Drake had paid scant attention to the gossip about Superintendent Lance. *Cold fish, arrogant, distant* had been some of the comments he'd heard, but at least working with Lance meant that he knew nothing about Drake or about his routines. He had already been waiting ten minutes when he glanced at his watch for the third time, knowing that he would be much later getting home then he'd promised Sian when he'd spoken to her earlier. Her monosyllabic replies only reinforced his irritation, that this meeting was unnecessary.

Lance stared at him through humourless eyes as Drake brought him up to date. Drake thought he detected a glimmer of recognition – perhaps the faintest move of an eyebrow – when the name Beltrami was mentioned. Price would have said something, reacted, suggested a strategy but Lance kept his fingers tightly laced together, nodding occasionally.

After a few long minutes Drake ran out of information to share with the superintendent. They shook hands, Lance reminding him to provide regular updates and Drake left. The Incident Room was quiet; Drake heard the sound of a vacuum approaching in the hallway. After adjusting the Post-it notes on his desk, he tidied all his files then scanned the room one final time before leaving.

Drake allowed his senses to enjoy the smell of the recently cleaned leather seats and the thrill of driving the sports car too quickly on the short drive home. He pulled the Alfa into the drive alongside Sian's BMW. His eyes were burning and his shoulders ached. Once inside the house he could hear the television from the sitting room. Sian emerged from the kitchen, a troubled expression on her face.

'Where have you been?' she almost whispered.

'What's wrong?'

'Your cousin's here. I did text you.'

A knot of anger formed in his chest. 'Do you mean—'

'You know. Auntie Gwen's son. The one your father likes, for some reason.'

'Where is he?'

Sian nodded towards the sitting room door. He pushed it open. MC sat in one of the armchairs, Megan and Helen on the sofa opposite. Both girls looked up at their father, gave him a brief smile and then returned their attention to the television programme.

'Nice to see you, Ian,' MC said. 'I've been reading to Megan and Helen.'

'Apparently Moelwyn has something important for you,' Sian said.

Drake could feel the pulse hammering in the side of his neck. He wanted to pick up Moelwyn by the scruff of the neck and throw him out of the house.

'Let's go to my study,' Drake said through clenched teeth.

MC stood up. The jeans were a designer variety, fashionably faded, his black brogues spotless. MC picked up the same leather jacket he'd worn when they'd met for breakfast.

Sian stood frowning in the hall, her offer to make coffee or tea or something stronger dismissed by Drake. He slammed the door of the study closed.

'Don't ever come here again,' Drake said. 'You know I can't talk to you.'

'Rosen nursemaids the drugs on the ship. I don't know how he does it but I'll find out.'

'Did you assault Vigo?'

'He's a slimeball.'

For a second Drake thought he'd heard a confession. He even started rehearsing the usual warning for suspects once they'd been arrested – *you don't have to say anything, but if you do ...* But it wasn't enough for an arrest.

'This is insane. I'm going to call Newman.'

'This is family, Ian. Sylvie is lying in the hospital because she's an addict. And I know the fucking smackhead that got her hooked. And do you want to do anything about it? Or do I have to sort it out myself?'

'How many times do I have to tell you? There are procedures I have to follow. If you tell me anything it's not intelligence I can use.'

Drake realised that even if he did try and arrest MC, his cousin would march out of the house. He didn't have any handcuffs, and he didn't want the children to see a skirmish.

'You'll find a way.'

'Don't be an idiot. You have to leave.'

MC threaded his arms into his jacket and stepped towards the door. 'I was there last night.'

'What do you mean?'

'Near Daz Green's house.'

'Where were you?'

'At a mate's.'

'Why?'

'Doesn't matter.'

Drake drew a hand over his mouth. 'Did you see who went into Green's house … Or was he on the streets just walking around with a gun …'

'Don't be a knobhead, Ian.'

'So what did you see?'

'Question is, what are you going to do about it? Nothing of course. Nothing you can do because of those *regulations* and *protocols.*'

'If you want anything done, then you need to tell me.'

MC reached for the door. 'I saw him last night.'

'Who, for Christ's sake?'

'I kept a good distance. I lost sight of him for a while, but then I heard him talking in the backyard. He's got a really squeaky voice.'

'In Daz Green's place?'

MC nodded.

Drake stared at his cousin. 'You'll need to tell me who it was.'

Chapter 22

Drake sat at his desk that Monday morning wishing he'd slept more over the weekend.

On the Sunday morning he'd woken up dreaming of MC and Lance, his mind heavy with the possible repercussions of having seen his cousin at home. The day hadn't improved as Sian fell into a sullen mood, making clear her disapproval of MC's visit until eventually she took the children to visit her mother without including Drake in the arrangements. Instead he wasted an afternoon watching an old film on television and then a rugby match, followed by the local news that featured a piece on the fundraising efforts of the Ellis-Pugh family to pay for treatment for their daughter's rare illness. Sian had arrived home as Drake pressed a second film into the DVD player. Her mood hadn't improved and they barely spoke for the rest of the evening.

He'd arrived early and spent the first hour interrogating the computer system for intelligence reports on the man MC had named.

Martin Valencia.

There was a certain mysterious quality to his name. European. Exotic even. But the intelligence reports were straightforward enough. A major player on the drug scene, clever enough to keep himself clean.

But this time it was different of course. MC couldn't be relied on as a witness and Drake knew the CPS would dismiss his evidence.

He was frustrated that he wasn't seeing what was really happening. There had to be a motive to the deaths. Drake knew that they still had to establish whether Green had actually killed Rosen and if he had, what was the motive? And what did the codes and numbers and letters really mean? He stared at the single sheet of paper on his desk, on which he'd written the word MOTIVE in capital letters. He agonised at the possibility that they might never establish who killed Rosen. MC's threats and the possibility that his cousin was out for revenge also filled his thoughts.

His concentration was broken, his mind set on edge, as the telephone rang.

'Inspector Drake?'

He struggled to recognise the voice.

'Sam Croft. We met at the hospital when you saw Sylvie Whatmore.'

'Yes, of course.'

'She's dead.'

Immediately, Drake thought of MC talking about revenge two nights earlier. There was no doubt that MC would now be past the 'talking' stage.

'Does MC know?'

'Yes. I spoke to him yesterday. And there was another policeman asking about him too.'

'Inspector Glyn Newman?'

'No. I don't think—'

'Jeff Wallace?'

'Yes. There's going to be a post mortem this morning. God knows why – there's nothing left of her.'

All Drake could think of was trying to contact MC.

'I've got to find MC. Do you know where he is?'

'You're the police. Surely you can find him.' Sam Croft didn't wait for a response and the line went dead.

He sat holding the handset for a few seconds before replacing it on the cradle. It occurred to him that he should call Auntie Gwen again and ask if she'd seen MC. Perhaps he should contact Newman or Wallace but investigating MC wasn't his case.

The telephone rang again and he snatched the handset and snarled an introduction. It was Hannah's voice. 'Superintendent Lance wants to see you.'

'I've got a meeting scheduled at midday.'

'Now. He wants to see you now.'

Drake replaced the handset after telling her he'd be there as soon as he could. He pondered whether to wear a jacket but decided against it and then walked through headquarters, taking the lift to the top floor.

'Good morning,' Hannah said once he'd arrived at her desk. 'You all right?'

'What do you mean?' Drake sounded nonplussed.

'You sounded ... well, doesn't matter. He's got company.' Hannah nodded at the door to Lance's office, Drake could hear the muffled sound of conversation.

Drake knew that he had to tell Lance about MC as soon as he could and that this meeting was the ideal opportunity to do so. He pushed open the door and saw the face of Andy Thorsen looking over at him. Drake realised that the lawyer's presence was probably the reason for the rearranged meeting. The crown prosecutor was one of those lawyers who Drake could never make out and he often thought that being cross-examined by Thorsen would be a non-event.

'Good morning, sir.'

'Ian, you know Andy of course,' Lance said.

Thorsen nodded an acknowledgment, which Drake returned with a brief smile.

'Andy needs to leave for a court hearing in Mold, hence the need to reschedule. First, can you bring me up to date with the Green murder?'

'We are almost certain that Green killed Rosen. We've been able to piece together his movements from the CCTV camera footage and it looks like he was on the car deck at the time that Rosen was there. CSIs are at Green's house at the moment.'

'And the motive?' It was the first thing Thorsen had said.

'That's what we're working on at the moment.'

'Could it be related to the codes you found on Rosen's data stick?' Lance asked.

'We simply don't know. And I don't want to stop the inquiry into Rosen's death until we can be absolutely satisfied that Green killed him.'

'Any connection between Rosen and Green?' Lance again.

'None that we know of, but it's what we're working on now. Caren has gone to see his next of kin in Liverpool today. There has to be a link of some sort.'

'You've been to see John Beltrami?' Thorsen said.

Drake took it as a question. 'He was one of the owners of the plane that Rosen flew regularly.' Drake waited until Thorsen could reply, sensing there was more coming.

'I was prosecuting in the crown court last week. You know, that mortgage fraud case, involving that surveyor and the mortgage broker who defrauded building societies of over ten million?'

Drake nodded, recalling how he'd overheard a DI in the economic crime department boasting about the successful outcome.

'Well,' Thorsen continued, 'I was approached by the defending barrister with the solicitor for one of the defendants – Jade Beltrami, no less – and they began to ask if I had anything to do with the investigation and if I'd reviewed the case and the evidence. Because, and they made this very clear, if we treated John Beltrami again with the same sort of aggression and discourtesy as was shown by the *investigating officer*, there'd be a complaint faster than you could say Jack Frost.'

Silence hung in the room.

Drake hesitated, replaying what he'd said to Beltrami. He had been courteous and normal and he struggled to think on what grounds Beltrami could complain. 'I can't imagine what he means. Rosen was his friend, for Christ's sake.'

'They've asked me to formally respond.'

'Hence me asking Andy to look over the case,'

Lance said.

'We need to speak to Beltrami again,' Drake said slowly. He noticed Thorsen's face. Nothing, no reaction. 'He gave Green a reference when he applied for a job with the ferry company.'

Lance moved a biro through his fingers. 'Don't do anything until Andy's had chance to look at the papers.'

Drake cleared his throat. 'And there may be an eyewitness to Green's killing.'

Howick resolved that once this case was over he would get back to his studies and retry the sergeant's exams. He was becoming cynical. Plus, listening to the woman sitting opposite him droning on about her dog, its feeding habits and how her husband hated the animal made him realise he really didn't want to do house-to-house for the rest of his career. The room was excessively tidy and the coffee table in the middle of the floor had streaks from recently applied polish. The only consolation was that Jean Fox wore a skirt short enough to accentuate her thin, attractive legs.

'He's a strange one,' she said, crossing her legs but barely moving the dog sitting on her lap.

'What do you mean?'

'Nobody goes in and out of the place. The lights can be on in the middle of the night.'

'How do you know?'

'Freddy was ill a couple of months ago,' she said, stroking the dog's head. 'I was up with him all night, poor thing. I'm sure he was constipated. I took him for a walk a couple of times. Just up and down the street of course; it was the middle of the night after all. But it's a nice, safe street here. Or it was. Anyway, the lights in the upstairs bedroom were on. And, another thing, he always keeps the curtains closed.'

'On the night Darren Green was killed did you notice anything?'

Jean Fox looked away from Howick towards the street beyond the window, as though she were hoping for inspiration. Howick realised that he had to move on, to the next house, wondering whether Winder was having greater success.

'If you do remember anything, please contact me,' Howick said, standing up and handing her a card.

The dog gave out a snapping sound as Jean Fox closed the door behind Howick. He glanced down the street, quiet now after the chaotic scenes the day before. The Scientific Support Vehicle was still parked on the pavement outside Green's house and Howick caught a glimpse of the forensic team inside the bedroom on the first floor. He glanced at the notes from the morning briefing and calculated that it would probably be late afternoon by the time he visited the Beal family. Drake had insisted he visit them and ask if they had something with a sample of Mandy's handwriting to be compared with the writing on the suicide note. Howick had decided it was probably a waste of time – everything was electronic these days: he couldn't even remember when he'd last written anything. In the meantime, he had more of Green's neighbours to interview.

The elderly couple next door to Jean Fox were expecting him and Howick gradually felt his boredom hit new levels as he listened to their incessant small talk. After ten minutes he'd found out that Mr and Mrs Williams had gone to bed at nine-thirty on the evening of Green's death, and hadn't heard anything, as both were hard of hearing. It occurred to him that he was to them a social service, listening to their complaints, keeping them company, admiring the photographs of their grandchildren who lived in Australia.

Once he'd finished he consulted the list of residents and, realising he still had to see Green's next door neighbour, strode over the road and knocked loudly on the front door. Howick guessed Hywel Liscomb was single as soon as he opened the door. His hair was cut neatly. He wore a dull grey sweater and dark grey trousers that had never been fashionable. A pair of oversized spectacles were perched on the bridge of his nose. His cheeks had a pale complexion, made worse by a chubby face and double chin. He gave Howick an inquisitive stare.

'Detective Constable Howick.' He flashed his warrant card.

Liscomb gave it a cursory glance before pushing the door open and directing Howick to sit in the parlour. The room was clean but full of old furniture and a screen covering the fireplace.

'I need to ask you some questions about your neighbour.'

'Of course,' Liscomb said, as though being interviewed in a murder investigation was an everyday occurrence.

'How well did you know him?'

'Not at all really.'

'Can you tell me anything about him?'

'He was a Scouser,' Liscomb said, adding as an explanation, 'From Liverpool. And he worked on the ferries. There are lots of them, Scousers, I mean, working in Holyhead. I used to work in the ferry office.'

'Did you ever speak to him?'

'Occasionally, if we arrived at the house the same time. Or sometimes in the summer in the back lane.'

'Did he have a lot of friends?'

'I don't know that I can answer that. There was certainly a lot of people who came and went from his house, especially through the back lane. My bedroom's in the back – always has been. My parents slept in the front bedroom.'

'Are your parents …?'

'Both dead.'

'How often would people come to the house?'

Liscomb tightened the narrow navy tie up to the frayed collars of an old white shirt, which complemented his grey V-neck sweater. 'I always go to bed after the ten o'clock news. Then I read. Usually a Welsh novel but sometimes I'll read some Agatha Christie. Since I've been retired I don't need to get up so early.'

Howick squinted at Liscomb, wondering how much practice it took to be this old-fashioned.

'Did you ever see these visitors?'

'No, of course not. The rear gate to his backyard makes a noise and I sleep very lightly and they'd be talking.'

'And did you hear anything on the night Green was killed?'

Liscomb seemed to relax at the prospect of telling Howick about the evening of the murder. 'I was in the parlour, watching television. I was watching *Pawb a'i Farn*. Do you know the programme? How good is your Welsh?'

'I understand a little ...'

'Well, it's the Welsh equivalent of *Question Time*.' Liscomb sounded pleased to be informing Howick. 'It started at about nine twenty-five. I especially wanted to watch it that night because there were local councillors in the audience. I worked with a lot of them.'

'So did you hear anything?' Howick raised his voice slightly.

'Oh, yes. There was an argument and then shouting. After that it sounded like furniture was being moved and then somebody banging like a hammer, a couple of times. So I put the sound up on the television.'

Howick forced himself to concentrate – at least they had a time.

'This could be very important. That could have been the sound of gunfire. Did you see anyone leaving the house?'

Liscomb chewed his bottom lip, hesitating; his skin had got greyer very quickly.

177

'Darren Green was shot twice. Did you hear anything after the "hammer-like sounds"?'

Liscomb shook his head.

'And after you went to bed, did you hear anything?'

'Not a thing.'

Howick walked through the house to the front door and paused on the threshold before thanking Liscomb, who'd also stepped outside with him.

'Have you found his girlfriend?' Liscomb said.

Howick turned and stared at him.

Drake spent the rest of the morning failing to block out the look in Lance's eyes when he'd heard about MC. Pretending that he could un-cousin him wouldn't work and Lance's demands that he cut all contact wasn't going to work. MC was family after all. There'd been nothing he could have done to stop his cousin calling uninvited and taking the flak made Drake feel sore.

He redoubled his concentration on the paperwork on his desk, occasionally pausing, annoyed that the investigation was on hold until Thorsen had reviewed the papers. There might be an innocent explanation for the employment references, but nothing could be left unresolved.

He drew a mind map and down one side of the same A4 sheet of paper he'd written the codes from Rosen's computer, but the more he stared at them the more jumbled they became. Each letter seemed to stand apart and then the numbers appeared to be floating around the page. Abruptly he stood up and stepped towards the window. There had to be a logical explanation for the codes. He noticed a couple meandering on their bicycles around the perimeter of the parkland and he spotted an old man with a large dog pulling at a leash. The weather seemed cool but he had no idea what the forecast had been. He hadn't watched television for days and although two weeks had passed since Rosen's murder he didn't feel he was making progress.

Returning to his desk and finding his mobile, he hoped Caren was having more success but her messaging service clicked on. He turned his attention to whether Green had stolen Rosen's laptop. It must have been a risk. Someone might have seen him. He would have been out of place in the crew quarters when he should have been on the card deck.

He found the list of crew and began scanning through the names and their working titles. Ignoring the night crew who were sleeping, he tried to find some thread that might link them to the theft. After a couple of hours, he was no further forward. The crew quarters weren't covered by any CCTV and it had been too easy to assume that Green had stolen the laptop. And maybe he had, but then there could also be someone else involved. To an extent Drake was relieved because he could ignore the passengers, but then he still worried that it might not have been Green after all.

He ate a sandwich at his desk at lunchtime and drank from a bottle of fizzy water. An apple stood by the photographs of the girls, by the telephone. He was about to turn his attention to the codes again, thinking he'd personally work through Rosen's bank accounts and then go through all his papers, when the telephone rang.

'Ian, how're doing?' He recognised the voice of Malachy O'Sullivan.

'I'm good.'

'You sent us over that photograph.'

'Of course.'

'We spoke to Maguire. Never seen her before.'

'Anything from the other tenants in the house?'

'One of our lads is doing some checks but we're real busy.'

'Thanks.'

Drake clicked off and sat thinking about the flat in Dublin and why Rosen had needed to rent the bedsit. He was still deep in thought when the telephone rang again.

'Ian.' He recognised Mike Foulds's voice. 'You need to get over here now.'

Chapter 23

The Scientific Support Vehicle dominated the pavement outside Green's house. Drake found a parking spot on the opposite side of the street. He ran over towards the front door while pointing the remote back towards the Alfa and, after carding the unfamiliar CSI, he stepped over the threshold. He took the stairs to the first floor two at a time and discovered Foulds standing in the main bedroom. What furniture Green had was stacked to one corner, the rolled-up carpets propped against them.

Alongside a section of exposed floorboards was a pile of carefully stacked packages: Drake could guess their content.

'Heroin,' Foulds said.

'How many?'

'We found at least twenty so far.'

'That makes Green one hell of a supplier.'

'We've done the rear bedroom.' He nodded towards the door. 'But we've still got the attic room.

'Anything else?'

Drake heard the floorboards creaking behind him and glanced over, expecting to see a white-suited CSI but instead he saw Detective Sergeant Jeff Wallace.

'What are you doing here?' Drake said.

Wallace made a narrow, mean smile, obviously pleased with the annoyance in Drake's voice. Wallace had small, dark eyes that seemed to stare unblinkingly. He was short for a policeman, no more than five foot six. His skin looked thin, his hair a sharp grey and trimmed close to his skull.

'This could be of interest to us.'

'This is a crime scene. I want to know what your interest in this is?' Wallace's very presence put Drake on edge.

'Drugs.' Wallace nodded at the packets on the floor. 'I liaise with Special Branch in the port.'

Drake clenched his jaw. He felt like picking Wallace up and pushing him downstairs. 'And why do Special Branch have an interest in this?'

'Looks like Green was bringing drugs in through the port.'

Drake said nothing, calculating exactly how he could get rid of Jeff Wallace, who continued. 'If there's anything to suggest he was bringing drugs into the port then we need to know. Inspector Newman would want a full report.'

Drake's irritation increased to the point where he was in danger of saying something he'd regret.

'You'd better leave, now,' Drake said. 'I'll make certain I send a report *direct* to your inspector.'

Wallace stood for a few seconds before nodding slowly. He turned his back and strode towards the stairs. Drake heard him slam the front door behind him.

'What was that all about?' Foulds asked.

'What did he say when he came in?'

'Told me he'd had a call, asking him to attend.'

'He had no right … Anyway, what did you tell him?'

'Get off my back, Ian. The guy's a Special Branch officer. If there's a problem, you sort it out.'

'I want all these packages secured overnight. I'll get uniformed officers to accompany you back to headquarters.'

Foulds gave Drake a puzzled look. 'We have done this before, Ian.'

'And I'll get two of my officers to stay here all night.'

'But we probably won't be finished until—'

'Doesn't matter,' Drake said, reaching for his mobile.

On his way downstairs Drake passed two CSI's filling plastic cups from flasks, a tired look in their eyes.

They nodded. He stood on the front door threshold and called Lance's office where Hannah put him through immediately.

'I need to see you this afternoon,' Drake said, almost stumbling over the right way to explain Wallace's presence. After telling Lance about the heroin he paused. 'When I arrived, Sergeant Wallace was at the crime scene.'

'Who?'

'Jeff Wallace. He's with the drug squad, but he liaises with Special Branch.'

Drake detected a sharp intake of breath down the telephone.

After finishing his call Drake rang operational support, demanding that they arrange for two officers to attend at the scene. Half an hour passed before two young junior officers arrived.

'I don't want *anyone* contaminating the scene,' Drake said, watching the nervous expressions on their faces. 'Anybody asks for access, I need to be called.'

The traffic had been quiet and, when he thought it was safe, he'd broken the speed limit frequently on the drive back to headquarters. Despite attempts to order his thoughts, Drake could feel his mind a jumble. The discovery of a large quantity of a Class A drugs changed things. But the apprehension that it meant the involvement of Newman and Wallace in the investigation was something he didn't want to contemplate. If Green had killed Rosen it meant someone had a motive. And the codes, the letters and the numbers were driving him mad. He had printed out duplicates of Rosen's numbers, just in case, and everywhere he turned, they were there – in the glove box, on his desk, on his computer screen, next to the bed at home.

He spotted Lance's BMW in one of the spaces reserved for the senior officers. He had no idea what car

Glyn Newman drove; it was probably a Mondeo or a Vauxhall. When he reached the senior management suite Hannah gave him a tentative smile.

'I've got a meeting with the superintendent.' Drake stood by her desk.

Hannah nodded towards the door.

The pile of folders and files on the table by Lance's side had doubled in size since Drake's last meeting with him. He was certainly keeping himself busy, and Drake wondered whether Wyndham Price was matching his replacement's diligence in the West Midlands. As Drake sat down he noticed how thickset Newman had become, his face and jaw puffy; spiders of burst blood vessels ran over his cheeks. He wore the same battered herringbone jacket.

Lance made eye contact with Drake first and then Newman. 'This was a significant discovery. Why wasn't Green on your radar?'

Newman didn't flinch. 'He's obviously been very careful.'

'Careful?' Lance repeated, as though he were weighing up every nuance that the word implied.

'This amount of Class A heroin makes him a major dealer. It must've come in through the port.'

Drake detected the slightest unease in Newman's eyes.

'And who is Sergeant Wallace?' Lance said.

'He acts as a liaison between Special Branch and the drug squad.'

Lance replaced the top of the expensive-looking fountain pen, placing it carefully on the table, before folding his arms. 'And why was he at the crime scene?'

'Because there was a connection to the port. There's been so much terrorist activity through the port in the past, anything that might be related gets the attention of Special Branch. And with his background in the drug squad then it's only right he should take an interest.'

'It should have been cleared with myself as the SIO first. I want procedures followed to the letter.' Lance spoke directly to Newman.

Drake nodded, appreciating the superintendent's rigour. Procedures had to be followed, protocols enforced, especially if he wasn't the SIO. The possibility of telling Lance about the unenviable reputation of Newman and the drug squad played on his mind. But that was a job for the Professional Standards unit in Newport, with officers who could smell the fear in a corrupt police officer from an adjacent room.

Newman had managed a smirk, which Drake hoped Lance would have noticed.

'Of course.' Newman sounded offhand.

Lance moved in his chair, unfolding his arms, bringing the meeting to an end. 'I will liaise with drug squad. All the briefings from Ian's team will be directed through this office.'

'Yes, sir,' Drake said.

'I want regular formal reviews. Hannah will email you with dates and times. That's all.' Both inspectors pushed their chairs away from the table and left.

Caren got up as soon as Drake walked into the Incident Room.

'When did you get back?' Drake asked.

'I tried to call you when I was driving back from Liverpool. There's something you need to know,' Caren said. Drake waved her into his office.

Caren sat, hair dishevelled, clothes crumpled even more than usual. Drake realised that she must have been tired after hours of travelling.

'I spoke to Daz Green's mother. She's had no contact with him for years. Then I spoke with his sister. She didn't react at all when I told her about her brother's death. What she did tell me was that one of Green's associates was a Terry Beltrami.'

Drake stopped fiddling with the column of Post-it notes and stared at her. 'What?'

'Tex Beltrami is John's brother. I did a search on him—'

'And, nothing turned up.'

'That's right. But then I spoke to DI Charnwood in Merseyside police and he's one of their top-ten targets. The DI that nails him can retire early.'

Drake fingered a red Post-it note. 'Let's talk to Gareth and Dave.'

They walked out into the Incident Room.

'Things have changed,' Drake announced. 'The CSIs called me earlier, after they discovered a pile of drugs in Green's house. It makes him a major player.'

Howick was the first to respond. 'Do the drug squad know anything about him?'

'No, nothing.'

Howick gave a puzzled look. Caren raised her eyebrows. Drake could guess what they were thinking, but none of them had ever referred to the reputation that clung to the drug squad like a bad smell.

'And we know that one of Green's earliest associates was Terry Beltrami. So we concentrate on establishing the motive for killing Rosen. Maybe even Green was instructed to kill Rosen.' Drake turned to look at the board behind him, his mind starting to compute the possibilities.

'But why kill Green?' Caren said.

Drake hesitated. 'I know. Last night MC was waiting for me when I got home. He told me that he'd seen a Martin Valencia in Green's house the night he was murdered.'

For a few seconds nobody in the team said anything. Winder was the only one who moved in his chair; it squeaked as one of the casters rolled along the floor.

'We can't rely on the evidence of MC Hughes, can we boss?' Howick said.

'Why don't we just go and arrest this Martin Valencia?' Winder asked, standing up.

'Because MC won't give a statement and if he did the CPS wouldn't sanction a prosecution. Can you imagine MC being cross-examined? I've already spoken to Superintendent Lance who had Andy Thorsen with him. It's simply not going to run. And with the drugs found in Green's place, the investigation is changing completely. If there's a drugs angle, the superintendent wants everything investigated before we make arrests. So we look at every single person of interest again: we go through everything a second time. It's an ever-increasing web,' Drake said, turning a paperclip he'd found in his pocket through his fingers.

'And I spoke to Green's next door neighbour today: he says Green had a girlfriend.'

'Could be someone off the ferry,' Caren offered.

'Check it out tomorrow, Dave. Show him the crew photographs.'

Howick nodded energetically.

Drake's mind darted from Rosen to Mandy Beal and then to Martin Valencia, hoping that he could find the connection. The thread that pulled everything together. He looked at his watch and, realising the time, abandoned the prospect of calling at his home before travelling to visit his parents. But the prospect of seeing his sister filled him with dread.

He was back at his desk when his telephone rang and he heard Newman's voice. Even the sound of his nasal accent put Drake on edge.

'I meant to tell you earlier, Ian,' Newman said slowly. 'Tom Vigo regained consciousness yesterday.'

Newman paused. Drake said nothing.

'We took a statement of complaint that implicates MC Hughes. We've issued an arrest warrant, of course. Any idea where he might be?'

'None and if I had—'

'Of course. Happy days, eh? MC Hughes behind bars again very soon.'

The line went dead and Drake grasped the handset tightly. He stared at it, hoping that the anger at Newman would dissipate and then wondering where MC had got to. As soon as he replaced the telephone, it rang again and Drake snatched it, ready for Newman. But he heard Lance's voice and the tension throbbing in his chest fell a couple of notches.

'Andy Thorsen approves a second interview with Beltrami.'

'Thank you, sir.'

For the first time that afternoon Drake felt pleased; he'd already been rehearsing how to tell Lance about Terence Beltrami. For now that could wait.

Chapter 24

A grey drizzle fell like a dirty net curtain as Drake drove to his parents' farm. On his journey he skirted round the medieval castle in Caernarfon, accelerating past the narrow-gauge railway station and finding himself following a route he'd travelled hundreds, maybe thousands, of times before.

The mountains of Snowdonia caught the last of the sun as it set over Isle of Anglesey, before he threaded his way through villages of slate-roofed houses, low stone walls and narrow cottages. They could look sad and dreary, but in a few weeks' time it would all look so different in the summer sunshine.

In the distance he could see the flat landscape of the Anglesey spreading into the horizon and the expansive beach and forest at Llanddwyn. He slowed as he drove down the track, but immediately felt uneasy when he saw an unfamiliar car, a year-old Audi, silver-blue with expensive alloy wheels, parked by the rear door. Realising that his sister had made good time from Cardiff he pulled up a little distance away from her vehicle.

His mother was standing by the open back door.

'How is he?' Drake asked.

'Come in,' she said.

'Has the nurse been today?'

'In an hour or so.'

'I take it Susan has arrived.'

Mair Drake nodded. 'She's in the parlour with your father.'

There was a sense of inactivity in the kitchen that Drake found oddly unsettling. He had been accustomed to the bustle of a busy household, but his mother seemed distracted. There were two fruit loaves still in cellophane wrapping sitting on the kitchen table.

Susan sat next to Tom Drake and their conversation

fizzled out when Drake walked in. They embraced without enthusiasm and exchanged pleasantries. Her journey had been long, the traffic busy and there'd been sections of the drive with no mobile signal that had annoyed her intensely, necessitating, she explained in exaggerated terms, that she had to make urgent calls when she arrived.

Drake guessed that his mother would have been responsible for the temperature in the room being a couple of degrees too hot. He loosened his tie and sat down.

'I was telling Dad that we have to get as much help in the house as we can,' Susan said.

His sister's attitude compounded Drake's feeling of suffocation in the small, hot room.

'Mam can't do everything,' she continued, as though Tom Drake wasn't in the room.

Drake glanced over at his father who said nothing, a blank, expressionless look in his eye, his gaze fixed on a point on the carpet by Susan's feet. He listened with growing impatience to his sister who detailed how things should change and what had to be done. Eventually, Drake interrupted. 'How long are you staying?'

'A couple of nights. George can't possibly cope on his own. As it is I had to make a freezer full of food for him and the children.'

'And when are you going to be up next?'

Susan tried a world-weary look, as though she was solving everyone's problems single-handedly. 'I'll let you know,' she said, managing to sound dismissive.

Drake heard conversation in the kitchen, recognising the voice of the Macmillan nurse. Tom Drake's eyes looked like they were only able to focus on the past – and as though they wanted nothing to do with the future.

Joe Birch enjoyed the sensation of fingering the calfskin wallet. There was something reassuring in its natural warmth. He flicked through the contents, wondering if two hundred pounds would be enough. Cash was king, he'd heard some business guru say on the television. In Joe's business that was all he had. Mounds of it. But he kept himself discreet. His girlfriend had shares in a Chinese takeaway restaurant and each week cash would find its way through the till and into the bank accounts. She took a wage from the business, of course, and did some work on the books but it wasn't demanding and she could please herself.

And on her days off she'd look after the terraced houses he'd bought and put into fictitious names. They had tenants that she needed to keep an eye on. Rent paid in cash of course. No cheques or BACS payments and definitely nobody on benefits. Since the new money-laundering regulations he'd decided to *diversify* his business interests: more small businesses with tills where people handled money. He'd even thought about a pub. He fancied himself as a publican.

Joe had three small cannabis operations. He'd learnt from his mates, who'd become too ambitious, that large scale meant more people and activity, which in turn meant the attention of the Wales Police Service. And he liked to think of them as *operations* – it sounded businesslike and professional. He had cover stories for all premises where lofts had been converted into hot houses, but even so he moved them around and he was always looking for new locations. Every week he handled over two thousand pounds in cash from satisfying the demand for cannabis in North Wales. And then he had the regular income from heroin addicts and the cocaine users.

Most weeks he'd help Martin Valencia with some discreet managing of his *stock*. Another bit of jargon he'd heard was 'working more cleverly' and he thought it described perfectly how he and Valencia did things.

Joe usually went drinking with his mates on a Friday and Saturday night, but it was a special birthday so a crowd were going to Llandudno to tour the pubs and the nightclubs. He stared at the clothes hanging in the wardrobe before choosing the dusty-pink Lacoste polo shirt. Then he found a pair of Lacoste chinos, recently dry-cleaned and pressed. In fact, nearly all of his clothes were Lacoste and the cash that had accumulated over the past month meant that he and his girlfriend could really do with another shopping trip. Maybe stay overnight in Manchester – take in a movie and eat in a swanky restaurant. His mother-in-law could babysit.

He pushed open the door of Chelsea's bedroom but she was already asleep. He stepped over to her bed and knelt down to kiss her. Her skin felt warm and he smiled as she moved her lips slightly. Kieron, a year younger than his sister, had fallen asleep with his head on his favourite teddy bear. Joe moved it to one side and stood looking at his son. It had surprised him how much he enjoyed being a parent.

He heard the sound of a horn outside and padded downstairs. He kissed his girlfriend, curled up in front of the enormous flatscreen television with a bottle of chilled Prosecco and a large box of chocolates.

The minicab was a small van, already nearly full, and he squeezed into a seat by the door.

After half an hour, they reached Llandudno and headed for the first of the pubs where Joe fished out a wad of notes and ordered the first round. He never worried about buying too many rounds of drinks. He had enough cash to enjoy himself and provide a decent life for Marie and the kids. One of his friends had shown him photographs of his recent holiday in Florida and Joe had decided they'd have a decent family holiday next summer– the kids would enjoy a big pool.

It was gone eleven by the time they staggered towards the nightclub at the far end of the town. Joe should have gone into the toilet before leaving the restaurant where he'd eaten a thick steak so he excused himself from his friends, waving them on and telling them he'd catch them up.

He walked up an alley by the side of a guest house and unzipped his fly. A cloud of steam rose as he pissed onto the wall, being careful not to hit his three-hundred-pound loafers. He heard something behind him, but he was almost finished so he made a half-hearted glance over his shoulder. The last thing he heard was the gentle swish of a baseball bat.

Chapter 25

By the end of his four-hour journey Drake had convinced himself the trip was going to be a waste of time and that he was chasings shadows.

More smoke and mirrors.

Nothing seemed to fit. It was like building a sandcastle too close to the approaching tide. A wave would always come eat away at the edge.

Initially he thought he'd been given the wrong address as the sat-nav took him into an industrial estate. Then he noticed the car breakers and the flooring warehouse mentioned in the email with the directions. Behind a factory unit that made home-made yogurt, he turned into the car park of an anonymous building. After squeezing the Alfa into an available space he walked over to a door with an intercom. A large sheet metal panel hung on hinges next to the door and then Drake noticed the bars on the windows and the CCTV camera high up near the gutter.

Once he'd spoken into the intercom, the door buzzed open and a young woman escorted him through the building. There was sense of unnatural calm about the place, as though it were the paperless law firm where everything was done by emails. No telephone calls and chaotic meetings: just officers ploughing through paperwork in front of large computer screens. The woman knocked on a door and after a shout she pushed it open and Drake stepped in.

Bryan Adams was a tall man with broad shoulders and he pushed a large hand towards Drake.

'Inspector Drake. Good morning. How was your drive?'

'Slow, sir.'

'I know, but isn't the scenery wonderful? Not many people realise that driving through Wales is one of the best kept secrets.'

Drake approved of the order in Adams's office. He had folders with neatly typed labels on the spines and books in cabinets all at the exact same distance from the edge of the shelf.

Adams sat down. There was a directness in his eyes that drilled into Drake.

'How do you think Loosemore might be connected to your inquiry?'

'He's part owner of an aircraft that the murder victim flew. We're doing background checks and his name came up. I know this could be a waste of your time.'

'Initially our contact came through the Serious Organised Crime Agency, on a referral from the FBI no less. They had some intelligence about Loosemore being connected with the Mafia and their drug operation. SOCA didn't want to get involved, so they passed it down to us. We set up this special unit to deal with large cases, mostly economic crime. We've got specially trained officers from all over Wales and accountants on secondment from SOCA. It became impossible to unravel all the strands of his financial empire. We had nothing to go on and I was getting pressure from the force accountants about my budget. It got to the point that we were going to close the investigation when we had a complaint, initially from local councillors, about a property transaction involving Lyfon Pharmaceuticals.'

'That's Loosemore's business.'

'Of course. And everyone thinks it's a great success story for South Wales.'

Adams began weaving a pencil in and out of his fingers. 'And then we had referrals from the auditor general about the conduct of certain officials relating to the property transaction behind the establishment of his business.'

Adams spent an hour taking Drake through every stage of the investigation. A development grant and Welsh government loan had facilitated the establishment of a research facility for Lyfon Pharmaceuticals on an industrial park that had been empty for several years. The company had moved from its base near London, promising to create jobs, boost investment and raise the profile of South Wales, creating the right atmosphere for other inward investment.

Adams took a break from his monologue, picked up the telephone and ordered coffee, asking Drake at the same time if he wanted to order sandwiches for lunch, and explaining about the catering company that supplied the unit. A few minutes passed until a junior officer returned with mugs of coffee.

'The industrial park that was sold to Lyfon Pharmaceuticals was given a "realistic" price tag,' Adams continued. 'Within a year Lyfon lodged a detailed planning application to convert most of it into residential property, a public house and a nursing home.'

'And the planning application was successful?'

'Of course. And it made the company millions.'

'How did Lyfon buy the land so cheaply?'

Adams sat back in his chair and rubbed his forehead just above the top of his nose in a circular motion.

'It was pushed through. Protocols were broken, shortcuts taken. Somebody wanted the deal to go through at all costs.'

'He must have had friends in high places,' Drake said, thinking about the photographs adorning Beltrami's offices.

Adams hesitated, his eyes developing a hard, steely look. 'The whole deal was pushed through by Richard Class when he was the economic development minister.'

'Are you suggesting …?'

Adams nodded his head.

'But it gets worse. The land was transferred into a property company partly owned by Lyfon Pharmaceuticals. It was one of those joint ventures, intended to maximise returns for all the participants.'

'And the other companies involved?'

The same junior officer returned with plates of sandwiches, a chocolate bar each and an apple recently cleaned judging by the water glistening on the skin. Adams gestured his hand towards the plate, inviting Drake to help himself.

'This is where it gets interesting. We found three companies directly involved. All of them owned by offshore companies or trusts. And all based in Dublin. Have you got an Irish connection in your case?'

Through a mouthful of chicken salad sandwich Drake mumbled. 'I don't believe it.' Drake swallowed. 'We've got money deposited in an Irish bank account owned by the dead engineer, which his widow knows nothing about.'

'The police in Dublin had a link to a trust set up in Prince Edward Island.'

'Where?'

'It's one of the Atlantic provinces of Canada.'

Drake nodded.

'But the Garda couldn't prove anything. They had a suspicion that it was all linked to organised crime from the United States.'

'Have you got any names of individuals in Dublin or Irish companies? Can you give me a contact with the Garda?'

'I've organised a room for you to read some of the files. And a word of warning. Richard Class is a very powerful politician. He's been able to survive all sorts of embarrassment, including being warned about kerb-crawling years ago.'

Drake raised his eyebrows, picked up the rest of his lunch and followed Adams to a small room with a desk, a reading lamp and boxes of files.

'It shouldn't take you more than a couple of hours to read the relevant sections.'

Drake slumped into the chair by the desk, realising that there was little chance of him returning to Northern Division headquarters as quickly as he'd hoped.

Chapter 26

Winder stifled a yawn and lowered his head, pretending to concentrate on the papers piled on his desk. Like every addict, he promised himself that he could change; he didn't really need to be playing computer games until the small hours – he could stop, of course he could. The night before, a takeaway pizza had arrived by seven – extra ham and fiery peppers and by ten p.m. he had drunk half a litre of a soft drink, demolished most of the pizza and then gone in search of ice cream from the freezer. Another two hours passed before he gave his watch a cursory glance, promising himself he would finish in half an hour.

It was never that easy. The tranquillity of the early hours, and the ability to escape imprisoned his mind. A friend from school had become a computer games designer, spending hours shooting aliens, jumping off imaginary buildings and driving cars too quickly. Winder often thought it was the ideal career choice. He'd glanced at the clock on the screen and given a double-take in surprise when he saw it was two in the morning; his mind was still fizzing with activity. He'd tried to sleep but his make-believe world intruded.

Winder wanted to avoid any possibility that Howick or Caren might realise how tired he felt. Luckily, Inspector Drake was in South Wales, Caren was in Merseyside for the second time recently and Howick was engrossed in the tasks Drake had assigned the day before.

Howick's telephone rang, and hearing the one-sided conversation jerked Winder from his lethargy. He didn't want to think about how much sleep he had actually managed. Looking at the papers on his desk, he tried to concentrate. He heard a voice in the background but ignored it.

'Gareth.' This time the voice was louder.

Winder looked over his shoulder at Howick.

'What's wrong with you?' Howick said. 'Are you half asleep?'

Winder mumbled an incoherent reply.

'Do you want a coffee or something?'

'Yes, yes of course,' Winder said, pleased that it was nothing more important.

Once Howick had left for the kitchen Winder stood up, put his hands to the small of his back and stretched, then rubbed both hands over his eyes, hoping the tiredness would disappear before yawning violently.

Winder was sitting again, biro in hand, when Howick returned.

'You look like shit.'

Winder's heart sank. He reached for the mug and took a large mouthful, gathering his thoughts and thinking how best to reply.

'Not feeling too good.' Winder added a brief frown to his expression of feigned illness.

Howick gave his friend a who-are-you-kidding look and sat down.

Winder returned to building a picture of Darren Green from the papers on his desk. There was another boxful on the floor.

The policy of the CSIs to dust everything at a crime scene meant every possible piece of paper had a sticky sensation. Winder had never had a case where fingerprints had been recovered by this scattergun approach and the papers of Darren Green were no exception.

Winder found council tax bills going back several years, all with letters complaining about outstanding payments. It was a similar pattern for the utility bills. And the bills seemed high, especially as Green lived on his own but then Winder recalled the enormous television screen and the PlayStation on the bedroom cabinet. A brief twinge of jealousy crossed Winder's mind, as he thought of the possibilities of playing games on an enormous screen.

He spent the rest of the morning sorting the paperwork into various piles, before storing them in the lever-arch files. So much for the paperless office – someone should have told Green to join the twenty-first century.

He fished out of the box by his feet catalogues from clothing companies, special offers from all the local takeaway Chinese and Indian restaurants and a folder two inches thick with details of the claim Green had made for his payment protection plan. Winder read through the various exchanges of correspondence about the loans Green had taken to buy his car and then the surround-sound system and television. After some negotiation, the claim had been paid in full and Winder hoped that his own claim for the loan he'd taken to reschedule his credit card would be paid as quickly.

It struck Winder as completely unnecessary to keep bank records for more than a few months and, working through each page of Green's financial activities over five years, his concentration waned. Petrol was bought at the local supermarket, regular payments to the local pizza takeaway, often more than once a week, together with standing orders to internet music providers and a mobile phone company.

By the time Winder reached the credit card statements it was almost lunchtime and he still had hours of work. Howick had left for Holyhead after lunch and Winder had hoped that he could finish early and get home to bed. It was like peering into someone's grave, prying into their personal life, with no one to complain. When Winder first noticed the payment in euros to the Blue Parrot he thought it was another chat line or maybe even an escort agency. Various telephone calls to the credit card company, each in turn requiring him to prove who he was and why he needed the information, led eventually to someone promising to call him back. By the middle of the afternoon, when he'd finished the call that gave him the information he needed, he felt pleased.

He decided to recheck things again and started with the bank statements.

It had been a day when Drake had initially doubted why he was travelling to the other end of the country to talk to an officer in a department that dealt with chasing money from one international bank account to another. But he'd settled easily into reading the papers and found his mind focusing on the link to Ireland and the drug suppliers that operated in the city. There were reports about organised crime taking control of the drug scene and references to the terrorist groups having fuelled their activities from selling drugs.

By the time Drake had read the name of a Fergal Connors a dozen times he knew he'd have to visit Dublin again. A call to the department of the Garda in Dublin, which had been dealing with the case, had proved futile – nobody was available so he'd call back tomorrow. He made notes, photocopies and found himself getting familiar with the jargon of the forensic accountants from SOCA. Beltrami's name appeared as a footnote to all the activity as a shareholder in a freight company with Connors.

It was late in the afternoon when he'd satisfied himself that there was nothing else he could achieve. He sent a text to the team and called Sian, telling her he'd be late. He thanked Adams and left, dreading the four-hour journey home. As it turned out, the traffic was light and he made good time, but his hands were sweaty and damp on the wheel. His fingers were grubby from photocopy ink, his shirt was crumpled on his back and his face felt dirty too. He yearned to get back to the order that awaited him in his office.

He should have gone straight home and then to bed, but he pulled into the car park at Northern Division headquarters instead. The building was quiet and calm. There were muffled shouts from cleaners somewhere in the building and lights burnt in the senior management suite. In his room he found a pleasing smell of polish; the bin was empty but the desk needed tidying.

He'd only managed to tidy the papers on the cabinet in his room before he heard a noise in the Incident Room and a face appeared at the door.

'For Christ's sake, Ian. What are you doing here?' Lance said.

Chapter 27

Drake stood by the board in the Incident Room and tugged at the double cuffs of his shirt. It was light cream, the links dark crimson and the tie was a solid navy variety fashionable with politicians. Caren wasn't certain if she'd seen the dark grey suit before. When she'd started working with Drake it always surprised her how many shirts he had and how many suits there must be hanging in his wardrobe. Caren had seen Drake fussing over his clothes and, in an odd way, it had made her less interested in looking tidy.

Caren walked past him, exchanging pleasantries, before dropping her handbag by the chair of her desk and mumbling an acknowledgment to Winder. She'd tried calling Drake last night, after returning from Liverpool, barely able to contain her excitement but his mobile had rung out.

'Any luck with Super Adams?' Caren asked.

'I spent hours going through paperwork about the international money laundering ring that the FBI thinks Loosemore is involved with.

'FBI?' Winder said. 'Bloody hell.'

'Loosemore is involved with some serious American gangsters. They think they bankrolled his company. He struck a fantastic deal to buy some land from the Welsh government. And then he got planning permission and made millions.'

Behind him the door opened and Howick walked in, collar open, tie loosened.

'Sorry I'm late, boss,' he said, flashing Winder a glance and raising his eyebrows to Caren. 'Have I missed anything?'

Drake ignored him.

'Loosemore was a big fish and maybe he still wants to be a player. So Gareth, I want you to chase down the contact in the Garda and get as much information as you can about him. And include Beltrami in that too.'

'I found another link to Ireland,' Winder said, striding over to the board and pinning up an A4 sheet with 'Blue Parrot' printed on it.

'And what's the Blue Parrot?' Drake stared at the paper.

'A nightclub in Dublin where Green used his credit card.'

Another link to Dublin.

'Eight times, over an eighteen-month period,' Winder added.

'Gareth, you'd better add the Blue Parrot to your list.'

Caren's chair made a squeaking sound as she moved. 'Quite the party animal.'

'How did you get on yesterday?' Drake said, turning to face her.

'I didn't finish until quite late,' Caren said, enjoying the build-up to her revelation. 'Green had put down that his next of kin was his mother and his father. His real father – a Mr Beal.'

'Bloody hell,' Winder said. 'Not?'

Caren nodded. Drake had a pained look in his eyes, as though he were trying to work out all the connections. Howick leant back onto his desk before clearing his throat. 'I spoke to Liscomb yesterday, sir.'

'Who?'

'Lives next door to Green.'

Drake nodded, signalling for him to continue.

'I showed him the photographs of the crew members and, bingo, he recognised a face.'

'And?' Drake said, watching Howick getting up from behind his desk and stepping towards the board.

'Liscomb may be a bit of an old woman, but he recognised Mandy Beal,' he said, pointing at her photograph.

'Tick. VG,' Drake said.

Caren was accustomed to Drake's shorthand of *very good* but she wasn't certain if the praise he intended was deserved. All they had was more loose ends.

'More work then.' Drake kept looking at the board as though a message would appear, telling them how to proceed. 'Dave, anything on the handwriting?' he said, still looking at the board.

'Graphologist coming in later.'

'Graph what?' Winder said.

Drake ignored him. 'And Gareth, you make progress with the Irish link. And remember to ask about the Blue Parrot.'

'Janet Rosen mentioned something about a nightclub that Frank visited,' Caren said.

'We can see her again and get all the details,' Drake said. 'First let's go and see an Italian Scouser.'

Drake pulled the car to a halt alongside a group of youths in hoodies and jeans hanging midway down their thighs, turned off the engine and waited without saying a word. He looked around the street, into the rear-view mirror and then leant over and glanced at the youngsters again. It was the sort of situation that Caren found difficult to read. She felt like asking if everything was all right but thought better of it, as she had when he'd greeted her with an odd look as she had got into the Alfa that morning. It was a pained expression, as though he was uncomfortable with her presence in the car. When she sat in the passenger seat the smell from the cleaned leather and polished plastic tickled her nostrils: the car always looked, and smelt, as if it had just been delivered from a showroom.

The seafront of Rhyl stretched in front of them. In another couple of months the streets and amusement arcades would be full of holidaymakers hoping for a big win on the slot machines, eating fish and chips and drinking industrial quantities of lager. In the winter months the tourists stayed away, but the poverty and depravation remained. Rhyl, like the other resorts along the North Wales coast, needed police officers with a certain attitude and Caren had, so far, avoided a posting to the town.

She looked over at the penny shops and the arcades and contemplated how much of the drugs that Green had brought through Holyhead had found their way to Rhyl. The town featured more prominently than anywhere else in the reports and intelligence updates circulated through the emails of the officers of Northern Division. She looked over at the offices of John Beltrami on the opposite side of the street, recalling their first visit and wondering whether Drake had been wise not to warn of their visit. Nobody had ever been able to prove anything against Beltrami, but no one believed that he'd built his empire from the honest businesses he purported to operate. Knowing that someone laundered money through myriad cash businesses and campsites, fuelled by the visitors from Manchester and Liverpool, and proving where all the cash came from were two very different things.

'I did some research on Beltrami. He makes a lot of political donations.' Caren broke the silence.

'Really. Buying friends?'

'Maybe he wants to change the world.'

Drake turned and gave her a hard look. 'No one changes the world in Rhyl.'

'Even so, I think we need to be careful if he's got political clout.'

'We'll ask the questions and we'll see what he says.' Drake's tone telling Caren she shouldn't argue.

They left the car and he squeezed the remote. A gentle clunking sound locked the car before Drake took a final look around. Caren had noticed that his fastidiousness about the car extended to regular checks of it, including where he'd parked. She had an eight-year-old estate car that Alun occasionally used for the farm, which was handy for taking the dogs for walks in the woods. She dismissed the notion of Drake having dogs: keeping the car clean would be impossible.

This time, there was a tall man, no more than eighteen, standing in the booth in the arcade, a dragon tattoo stretching down one arm. She noticed fine dark roots to the band of flame-coloured hair on the centre of his head when he lowered his face to look at Drake's warrant card.

'Wait here,' he said, the accent thick from the streets of Anfield.

Behind her she could hear the springs from fruit-machine arms being released, bells and chimes from successful attempts and she thought of Alun who always tried his luck on the machine at the local rugby club.

'You know your way,' the youth said eventually.

Caren followed Drake up the stairs to the first floor. The same diminutive woman who met them the first time stood at the top and gave them a blank stare. She led them a second time to Beltrami's office.

Beltrami reached a hand over the desk. The cloth of his pinstripe looked heavy, the stripe a delicate off-white. The prospect of watching Drake being riled by another witness had exercised her mind as they drove to Rhyl and she'd decided to intervene if she thought she had to.

'We're here to discuss the deaths of Frank Rosen and Darren Green,' Drake began.

No response. Then Beltrami blinked. 'I've told you about Frank. We have discussed him already.'

'Tell us again.'

A flash of irritation passed over Beltrami's eyes. He narrowed his lips and repeated practically word for word what he'd said before. Caren checked the notes she'd made from their first meeting, thinking that the answer was either the truth or incredibly well rehearsed.

'Did you know Darren Green?' Drake asked, as though he was of secondary interest.

'Who?'

'Darren Green. Originally from Liverpool. Your neck of the woods, Mr Beltrami.' Drake had opened the folder on his lap and didn't notice the annoyance in Beltrami's eyes. Caren guessed that Beltrami wanted to leave behind his association with Liverpool, all as part of his campaign for respectability and success in Wales.

'Who the hell is he?'

Caren detected the vaguest hint of the harsh Scouse accent.

'He was killed in his home. Gunshot wounds to the head.'

'Look, Inspector, I'm a busy man and—'

'Green worked on the same ferry as Rosen.'

Beltrami was tapping his fingers on the desk. 'And how would I know him?'

Caren strained to figure out Beltrami. She decided to prompt Drake about the letter so she found a copy and passed it to him. The faintest shadow of uncertainty crossed Beltrami's eyes, nothing more.

'This letter was in the human resources file of the ferry company.' Drake handed the letter over the desk.

Caren noticed Beltrami's frown, which quickly turned to surprise and then recognition.

'This is a letter—' he began.

'It's from your company. In fact it's more than that. It's from you personally, as a reference for Darren Green when he applied for a job.'

Caren winced to herself as she thought the initiative had been lost.

'We give lots of references. I have a lot of employees and it's not always—'

'But it's a coincidence, don't you agree? You socialised with Frank Rosen and provided him with a job reference. Darren Green also works for the ferry company. And there's another job reference from you.'

Beltrami turned a hand in the air, buying time. Caren watched Drake squeezing the folder of papers on his lap.

'You have to understand, Inspector, that we have a lot of employees. A lot of people—'

'Did you know Darren Green?'

'I can certainly find out—'

'Did you know Green personally or not? Simple question.'

Caren watched the face of Beltrami, straining to see what he was thinking, how he would react, what excuse he would make.

'I'll need to check our records—'

'Don't avoid answering my questions. There could be serious consequences.'

Caren saw Beltrami's jaw tighten.

'I'll get someone to check the HR records and get back to you.' Beltrami was on his feet.

'Are you refusing to answer the question?'

Caren felt like saying, *for Christ's sake, sir, let it go.* But she could tell Drake wanted answers.

'Of course not, Inspector. You have to realise that these things need to be checked.'

Beltrami had refound his confidence. Mixing with politicians had at least given him some bullshitting skills, Caren could tell. Beltrami moved around the desk, straightening his back, smoothing his tie, wanting them out of his office.

'I'll have someone onto this immediately,' he said, walking with them to the end of the corridor.

Caren felt a mixture of relief and annoyance at an opportunity wasted, as they walked back to the car. Drake examined every panel, checked for dents and scrapes and, only when satisfied, opened the car.

At reception in headquarters one of the civilians working on the desk stopped Drake.

'There's three people in the main conference room wanting to see you.'

'Who are they?'

'One is a Jade Bel-something-or-other.' The woman handed over a glossy business card. 'And there are two men with her. They say it's urgent.'

Drake turned to Caren. 'You go and see Janet Rosen. I'll deal with our unannounced visitors.'

Caren turned on her heels and headed out for the car park. Drake sprinted up to the Incident Room only to find Detective Inspector Newman standing by the board, hands on hips, his jaw tight.

'Your fucking cousin has really done it this time,' Newman began. 'Kicking the shit out of Tom Vigo was bad enough. But this time we've got so many eyewitnesses that not even MC Hammer can weasel his way out of a life sentence.'

'What are you talking about?'

'Joe Birch. That's who. We've been after him for years. But he was really good. Very slick and we never had enough evidence on him. Didn't you watch the news this morning?'

Drake frantically tried to think.

'Body found battered in Llandudno,' Newman continued.

Drake didn't like where this was going.

'Birch was killed with a baseball bat on his way to a nightclub in town. But there are eyewitnesses that saw MC walking out of the alley. It's in the middle of Llandudno for Christ's sake.'

'Have you found him?' Drake said.

'Only a matter of time. And if he contacts you, then tell him I need a chat.'

Chapter 28

Drake slumped into the chair by his desk and thought about his family. A sense of impending disaster crept into his mind. And he also felt helpless, knowing that there was nothing he could do and that MC had to be arrested. How would Auntie Gwen cope with her son locked up for life? Would she ever visit him? But he doubted that she had even visited MC when he had been in prison. His father liked MC and Drake had never really known why. He'd have to tell Sian of course, and make certain she called operational support if MC ever went near the house.

Then he remembered the visitors in the conference room and it jolted him out of his lethargy. He grabbed a notepad from the desk, straightened his tie and headed for the lift.

When he opened the door a tall man with a shaved head, wearing an immaculate navy suit, turned to look at him. He had a perfectly trimmed goatee beard and when he held out a hand to Drake the cuffs of his shirt exposed a glistening Rolex.

'Jocelyn Peters,' he said, with an accent honed by an expensive private education. 'I'm counsel for Mr Eddie Parry.' He briefly turned his head to the man sitting by the table. 'And you know Jade Beltrami of course.'

Drake didn't, but he looked over at Jade sitting next to Parry. He recognised her face from the photograph in her father's office which had flattered her, as the camera often did. Drake couldn't fathom out why on earth a barrister had turned up at headquarters with Eddie Parry.

Peters continued. 'Mr Parry is one of the joint owners of the light aircraft that Frank Rosen flew. You've been enquiring about my client. And he wants to make a full statement.'

'But we need to schedule this in properly.'

'I need to do it now.' Parry had an unusually deep

bass voice. Beads of sweat had formed on his forehead, even though the temperature was cool.

'There have been so many rumours flying around North Wales. Mr Parry wants to be able to say quite clearly that he isn't involved. And that you have eliminated him from your inquiries.' Peters spoke as though there were no room for argument.

'You know that won't be possible,' Drake replied.

'Look, Inspector. We want to make a statement.'

Drake glanced over at Jade who had the barest hint of a smirk on her lips. Annoyance was making his pulse increase. Abruptly he stood up. 'I'll get my papers: stay here.'

He stalked back to his office, hoping that he could keep his anger at bay. *Think clearly.* He gathered all the files he needed, convincing himself that he would be calm enough to undertake a meaningful interview.

Drake returned to the conference room and sat down. He noticed Parry almost crushing a plastic cup with a thick-fingered hand. Peters was holding a plastic water bottle and gave Drake a brief smile without opening his mouth.

'Mr Parry wants to make a statement,' Peters began.

'We'll come to that in a minute,' Drake said, looking over at Parry. He had a stylish suit, too smart for an ordinary farmer.

'What sort of farming do you do, Mr Parry?' Drake said.

'Cattle mostly.'

'My grandfather was a farmer. Only a smallholding, not enough these days to make a decent living.'

Peters interrupted. 'Mr Parry wants to make a statement.'

'All in good time.' Drake shuffled his papers. 'How many acres do you farm?'

'Two thousand.'

Now Drake knew how Parry could afford a share in

a plane. Drake sensed Peters getting impatient. When Drake looked over at Jade she gave him an untroubled look.

'What are prices like at the moment?' Drake continued.

'I sell directly to one of the main supermarkets,' Parry said, as though every farmer did that.

Peters put his water bottle down by the papers on the table. 'We'd like to get this finished as soon as we can.'

'Of course.' Drake gave Peters a brief acknowledgment before turning back to Parry. 'Do you know Frank Rosen?'

'Of course. He was a good pilot.'

'Did you fly with him a lot?'

'Hardly ever. My wife didn't want to me to buy my share in the plane. I only did it because Lewis Aylford thought I needed to socialise more. "Get out," he said. "Have more fun".'

'Who flew with you on these trips?'

'John Beltrami. Rosen, of course, and Lewis.'

'Did you ever go to Ireland?'

'Inspector, I really must protest. Mr Parry came here to make a statement and you're interviewing him.'

'Mr Parry has nothing to hide. So he won't mind answering some general background that might help with the inquiry. Unless, that is, he doesn't want to cooperate.'

'Really. This is no way to treat us. We shall have to consider how to respond. It may well be that the Assistant Chief Constable needs to hear about your approach.'

Drake smiled at Peters, happy that he'd riled him. He turned back to Parry. 'So did you ever go to Ireland?'

'Yes, once or twice.'

'Did Tim Loosemore go with you?'

'Yes.'

'How often?'

'I can't remember.'

'Come on, Mr Parry. You don't fly very often and

yet you can't remember how many times Tim Loosemore was a fellow passenger.'

'Inspector, what exactly are you trying to establish? What are the lines of enquiry in this investigation?' Peters said.

Drake felt like telling the barrister that he would conduct the investigation in any way that he wanted, but the prospect of another meeting with Lance and Thorsen made him take a reluctant step back.

'Did Rosen ever talk about his life?'

'Not that I can recall.'

'He never mentioned money?'

Parry shrugged.

'I'll take that as a no.'

'You can take it any way you please, Inspector. This is not an interview under caution and Mr Parry wants to read this statement.' Peters pushed a sheet of paper over the desk.

Drake gave it a cursory glance. 'What did you do when you were in Ireland?'

'Nothing much.'

Drake gripped a biro tightly – he hated being lied to and Parry wasn't telling the truth.

'Did you visit nightclubs, pubs?'

Jade began making notes on a pad and Peters tapped the plastic bottle on the table.

'No. I'm teetotal, Inspector.'

Drake could imagine that the highlight of Parry's social life was an enormous rump steak with a plateful of chips at his local restaurant, washed down with tap water. Parry sat back and picked up the statement. Peters nodded for him to read. For the first time Drake noticed the strong Anglesey accent and the slow, measured tones Parry used. There was a lilt to his voice that Drake could remember his grandfather using whenever he spoke English. By the end of the discussion Drake had heard that Parry's interest in flying had quickly waned once he realised that he'd have to spend large amounts of money to keep the plane operational and then there were hotel costs, fuel bills and insurance.

When Peters brought the meeting to a close Drake saw a hint of uncertainty in the barrister's eyes. He watched them leave headquarters and he headed back to his office unable to decide if challenging Parry had really achieved anything.

It was a clear spring afternoon, the hedgerows starting to blossom; tractors were at work in fields and the lanes of Anglesey were free of holiday traffic.

At a junction Caren indicated and turned into the road that led to Janet Rosen's cottage; her heart sank when she saw a tractor in front of her pulling a flat trailer. She changed down the gears and decelerated. She found a radio station playing country music and accepted that the last few miles would be taken at a crawl.

Rounding a corner just before Janet's home the tractor in front accelerated and Caren slowed in anticipation of turning into the slate-covered drive. But she saw a large Jaguar parked by Janet's car and a man who looked familiar standing by the driver's side. Her mind raced until she recognised Tim Loosemore from the Incident Room photographs that hung alongside Ellis-Pugh and the other members of the flying club. Caren's pulse quickened and immediately she made the decision to drive on, hoping Loosemore wouldn't notice her. She tilted her head away, peering in the opposite direction. As soon as she could, Caren pulled up in the entrance to a field and adjusted the rear-view mirror. The reflection caught the entrance to the driveway although the front of the Jaguar was hidden from view. She didn't have long to wait until the car pulled out, Janet sitting in the passenger seat. Pleased that the car wouldn't be passing her she quickly turned her own vehicle around and followed them.

Approaching a T-junction by an old chapel Caren worried that she'd lost them, until she saw the rear of his car caught behind an oil tanker to her left.

She fell back and Loosemore reached the A55 and then accelerated hard eastward. Caren did likewise, but kept three cars between her and the Jaguar. She rather enjoyed the chase; it reminded her of the American crime dramas her mother loved so much. Eventually she followed Loosemore towards his home overlooking the Menai Strait. The electronic gates closed behind them and she drove on before parking and reaching for her mobile.

Chapter 29

Lance had left Drake with an odd feeling that there was too much going on in the background. The investigation was slowly sliding out of his control. They'd made no progress, the paperwork was mounting up and soon enough another senior officer would be called in to do a review. Lance would know the procedures and Drake was certain that if the deadline came without progress Lance would instigate a review without hesitation.

The next session with Halpin was imminent and Drake had been shuffling the notebook around the various drawers of his desk, only occasionally thinking that he should record something.

And having Lance discover him at headquarters late the night before hadn't helped.

He fingered the pages of the notebook, reading the words that he had dutifully scribbled. *Order* and *clean* and *coffee* repeated themselves too often and he worried what the counsellor would make of it. The sound of a conversation interrupted his thoughts and he heard Caren's voice louder than usual, and, intrigued, he marched through into the Incident Room.

'I've just followed Loosemore in his Jaguar from Janet Rosen's cottage.'

'And let me guess,' Winder said. 'Janet was with him.'

Caren nodded.

The door burst open and Howick almost fell into the room.

'Dr Collins is here, sir.'

For a moment Drake didn't connect.

'The graphologist I mentioned,' Howick said, just as a middle-aged man followed him through the door.

Winder opened a bag of pastries that filled the air

with a warm, sweet smell. Howick made the necessary introductions and Dr Collins stepped towards the board.

'I must say Inspector, that you were very lucky to have a sample of Mandy Beal's handwriting.'

Howick's smile broadened.

Drake recognised the holiday postcards Mandy had sent her parents and that Collins was pinning to the board.

'The paucity of the text I had to consider must be a restricting and eventually limiting factor in the gravity of my conclusions,' Collins said.

Howick's smile waned. Winder had a pained expression on his face as he chewed on a doughnut. Caren stood watching Collins intently. He stood back and admired the cards before turning to Drake.

'Weighing up all the evidence and, as thin as it is, I've concluded that the author of the suicide note and the postcards cannot be the same person.'

'So someone else wrote the suicide note?' Drake said.

Howick nodded slowly.

'Or someone else wrote the postcards,' Collins said.

It was the sort of comment that only an academic would make.

'How can you be certain?'

'Nothing is certain, Inspector, only taxes and death. But it's simple – one is written by a left-handed individual and the other by a right-handed person.'

'Thank you Dr Collins,' Drake said.

Howick escorted Collins to reception and once he'd left Winder blew out a lungful of air. '*Someone else wrote the postcards,*' he said, mimicking Collins's thin voice. 'As if. Guy's a Muppet.'

Drake stepped to the board. 'So she was killed. Another murder suspect. We'll need to tell the family.'

'Caren, you go and see Mr and Mrs Beal again.'

'What, this afternoon?'

'You can ask him about Green,' Drake said, turning to Winder who had a thin band of sugar covering his upper lip. 'Anything on the Irish connection?'

'The department in the Garda have got nothing on Loosemore. But the Blue Parrot hit the jackpot. Owned by a Fergal Connors and the Garda have a whole team onto him. And he's friends with Beltrami no less.'

Caren parked the car and sat watching a man helping his elderly wife as she struggled into their car. She wondered how many of the other bungalows on the small estate were occupied by retired couples, hoping for a contented retirement away from the bustle of the cities of England. Once she'd locked the car her thoughts turned to Alun and whether their final years would be spent in a home with a neat front garden, driving a small, neat car and worrying about what the neighbours thought. She liked her farmhouse perched on the side of the Conwy Valley and she found it difficult to imagine moving from there. But with Alun away so often, she had begun to feel lonely and was contemplating the possibility of selling up.

She walked down the paved drive decorated with the occasional terracotta pot. She reached a hand to the doorbell.

How easy would it be to tell Mrs Beal that her daughter had been murdered?

'Must be important if you're working so late,' Philip Beal said, standing in the doorway.

'Good afternoon,' Caren said.

'She's sleeping,' Beal said, lowering his voice.

'I'd like to talk to you.'

Beal frowned, but drew the door open after a delay and then pointed Caren towards the conservatory. A section of horizontal blinds fluttered noisily beneath an open section of the roof, cooling the temperature. Caren narrowed her eyes against the sunshine and sat down opposite Beal.

'We've had a report from an expert about the suicide note Mandy left.'

Philip Beal let out a brief grunt. 'What sort of expert is that?'

Caren ignored him. 'I'm afraid I have some difficult news. We don't believe that Mandy killed herself.'

Philip Beal sat impassively, his eyes hard.

'We were able to compare the handwriting from the postcard you gave one of my colleagues against the handwriting on the suicide note and the expert is convinced they were written by different people.'

'Are you sure?' Beal asked.

Caren nodded slowly and adjusted her position on the chair so that she sat on the edge.

'We're treating the inquiry as a murder investigation.'

Beal nodded again, but kept eye contact with a look that sent a shiver down Caren's back. As though there was no emotion in the man.

'I need to ask you about Darren Green.'

Beal didn't flinch and it surprised Caren.

'He worked on the same ferry as Mandy. You've read about his murder I take it? It was in all the newspapers.'

Beal curled the fingers of both hands together.

'I've read the Merseyside police file: you're named as his next of kin. He was your son.'

The statement inviting confirmation hung in the air. Caren waited and saw Beal blinking and then swallow, as though he was preparing to say something. Then he nodded briefly.

'From my first marriage. I didn't know him. It wasn't like we were close.' The Liverpool accent seemed to get harsher as he recalled unhappier times.

'How did Mandy find out?'

'She found some old papers. And then she was like a dog with a bone. Wanted to know all about it and where and when.' Beal bowed his head slightly. 'Eventually she traced him to the family in Liverpool. I was amazed when she told me he ... Darren ... was working on the ferries.'

Beal ran out of energy and Caren could only guess at the pain of losing two children within days of each other, even if one was a person you'd never known. Never had anything to do with. Never had any part of their life.

'She was full of it. Wanted us to meet him.'

'Did that ever happen?'

'No. She ... Peggy ... wouldn't contemplate it.'

'What did Mandy tell you about him?'

'She liked him. He told her about his past and she saw him quite often. What's going on?'

It was the first time Caren had seen vulnerability in Beal's face, a tremor in his voice which made this the hardest part of her job.

'We don't know, but Mandy didn't kill herself.'

'I never thought she did.'

Caren hoped that he had more to say, but he stood up abruptly.

'I'll show you out.'

'Will you tell ... ?'

Beal nodded as he opened the door. Outside she felt the cool evening air on her face as she walked up the drive to her car.

Drake ignored the first and last single letters on the codes, deciding that it was utterly impossible to try and guess what they could mean. He had already spent hours trying to work out if they related to place names and if so, where. There had to be logic to this, like solving a crossword, a Rubik's cube and he'd recently downloaded the Rebus game onto his tablet computer, but that was about finding the right words. Now what he had were letters and numbers.

He started with the initials of everybody that may

have had contact with Rosen.

JB – John Beltrami
LA – Lewis Aylford
RJ – Robert James
EP – Eddie Parry

Then he finalised a list with the initials of other crew members. First the captain Jonathan Seymour – JM, then the engineers and some of the deck officers. Drake decided against including the cabin staff, but added MB for Mandy Beal.

It must have been an event. In the past or perhaps in the future, but why did Rosen record the activity? There must have been a significance. He turned to the dates, thinking that he of all people ought to be able to make more sense out of the numbers. He scribbled on the pad 4520 and then, interchanging the last two set of digits, came up with 2045. And 3018 became 1830. Then the numbers looked like times and he double-checked the sailing times for the ferries. But then there were two other ferries travelling from Holyhead and he spent an hour building a spreadsheet with the departure times of each. At the end of this task he was no clearer and in fact thought that he was more confused.

Then he spent another hour writing all the names backwards, so 4520 became 0254. But still the significance of any combination of these numbers eluded him. He leant back in his chair, considering the possibility that there was some computer expert somewhere who might have a piece of software into which they could punch the data and wait for a reply.

He read through the background notes to Rosen's career, hoping there might be some clue. Maybe the numbers were his regular combination for the national lottery or a combination to a safe they hadn't found. The numbers didn't relate to the PIN numbers of Rosen's various cards. They'd already eliminated that as a possibility.

The exercise needed clearer thinking so he walked

through to the kitchen and flicked the switch on the electric kettle. He reached for the coffee grounds, measured accurately, allowed the timer on his mobile phone to ping after a minute and then poured the hot – not boiling – water over the coffee. He fiddled again with the timer on his mobile and waited, thinking about the numbers, resolving that they had to be dates and times. He was still staring at the coffee pot when the mobile sprang to life with the sound of an old car engine that he'd chosen as the tone.

Returning to his office, he stood for a moment looking out over the parkland surrounding headquarters. Patrol cars were leaving, a Scientific Support Vehicle pulled into the long drive down to the main building, and along the pavement by the main road two joggers ran past. The coffee tasted sweet and bitter: he'd just changed the variety of grounds, experimenting from an online supplier.

It occurred to him to reread some of the reports and he found his mind wandering to the post mortem of Rosen and Green and thinking that he hadn't spoken to the pathologist about the death of Mandy Beal. Some joined-up thinking was needed, he concluded, realising the possibility that all three reports needed to be read with the same critical eye.

He picked up the telephone and dialled the number of Lee Kings. He'd never particularly liked Kings, who could be over-familiar with the occasional clumsy innuendo about Sian that only resulted in Drake wishing there were more pathologists in North Wales.

'How are you keeping, Ian?' Kings said.

'I needed to talk to you about Rosen and Green.'

'What about them?'

'We're working on the basis that they are somehow linked. I know it's not the same MO. But there's a strong possibility Green killed Rosen. And if somebody wanted Rosen dead, they may then have disposed of Green.'

'Everything is in the report. I don't think I can add

any more.'

'And we are treating the death of Mandy Beal as murder now.'

'The stewardess on the ferry? Attractive girl.'

It was the sort of comment that annoyed Drake. He stood, peered out of the window and saw a BMW the same colour as MC's passing in the main road.

'Anything to link those three deaths together?'

'No nothing, nothing. Is this helpful, Ian?'

Drake knew that thinking about MC prompted his next question. 'Did you do the post mortem on Sylvie Whatmore?'

'Yes, why do you ask?'

'Her boyfriend is a relative.'

'Small world.'

'You know how it is.'

'She died of a stroke. But she'd been developing pneumonia and she'd had such a dependency on heroin her body gave up. The manual evac didn't help.'

'Manual evac?'

'She had a miscarriage in her twentieth week. At the time doctors thought she was lucky to have carried the child so long. They operated under general anaesthetic to remove all the products of conception. The procedure's called a manual evacuation.'

Drake grasped the telephone a little tighter. He was certain that MC knew nothing about the pregnancy.

'Does MC Hughes know about this?'

Drake heard the sound of Kings flicking through some paperwork. 'I spoke to him at the start of the week.'

'How did he take it?'

Kings didn't need to reply: Drake already knew the answer. He had to find MC. Quickly.

Drake knew he couldn't ignore the possibility that once MC

had learnt about Sylvie's pregnancy he had reacted badly. And the likelihood that Newman had been right about MC killing Birch became more of a probability. Newman had sent Drake Vigo's statement – for the sake of completeness the email had said – naming MC as his attacker and making clear how MC enjoyed using a baseball bat. Protocols meant that he should notify Newman, and it crossed his mind to send an email but then he recalled the hard, determined look on Lance's face, making it clear that any contact had to go through him.

He left his office and took the lift to the senior management suite. Hannah gave him a surprised look when he asked to see Lance.

'He's very busy.'

'It's important.'

She picked up the telephone and spoke tentatively, explaining Drake's presence. She motioned to the door to his room.

'I've just spoken to the pathologist. Apparently he told MC Hughes about his girlfriend's pregnancy. I'm sure MC didn't know she'd become pregnant when he was inside.'

Lance sat back into his chair. 'And that gives him the inclination for murder?'

Drake nodded. 'I was going to call Glyn Newman but—'

'I'll do it.'

Drake turned to leave.

'Ian. About the other evening. How are you coping? I know that double murder case hit you hard. And Wyndham gave me some background but I need to know you're dealing with things.'

'I'm fine, thank you, sir.'

Drake didn't say anything to Hannah as he left and he headed straight for the car park.

It was a short drive home, his suit jacket folded

carefully on the rear seat, the newspaper on the seat by his side. He pushed a Springsteen *Greatest Hits* CD into the player and flicked idly through the songs, playing no more than a minute or two of each. By the time he drove into the estate where he lived he was already on the tenth song. He noticed an Audi parked on the pavement outside his home and immediately thought that MC had visited again. After last time he didn't think his cousin would have dared to return. But he needed to speak to him. His mind was rehearsing what he would say to MC as he pushed open the door, the realisation striking him that if it was MC he'd have to arrest him on suspicion of murder.

Voices from the kitchen were unfamiliar. Certainly not MC's accent. For a moment he relaxed, pleased that it wasn't his cousin and that he would avoid the inevitable confrontation.

He only took a couple of steps into the kitchen before stopping and staring in disbelief.

Detective Inspector Glyn Newman sat at the table, Jeff Wallace by his side. Newman managed a sneer while Wallace narrowed his eyes. Neither man moved and Drake saw the notepads in front of them on the table. Sian looked up at Drake, uncertainty clear in her eyes.

'I understand that Moelwyn Carol Hughes was here last week,' Newman said. 'As you know Ian, he's the only suspect we have for the murder of Birch.

Drake stood for a moment, suppressing the urge to shout at Newman.

'I did try to call you earlier to arrange this discussion with Sian,' Newman continued. 'But you weren't available. Busy, I suppose.'

Drake balled a fist with both hands.

'We haven't been able to find MC Hughes yet. He seems to have *disappeared.* His whereabouts are critically important.' Newman narrowed his eyes, obviously implying that Drake and Sian knew something valuable.

Drake wanted to lunge over the table, pick up Newman by his dirty jacket and throw him outside. Instead he settled for taking a step towards Sian, then leaning on the table.

'You can fuck off right now. Leave my house and don't ever pull a stunt like this again.'

Chapter 30

'Why were they here?' Sian said, drawing her fingers around a glass of water.

Drake's mind felt paralysed. Sian was being dragged into the investigation and he was powerless to prevent her involvement. It was lucky that Megan and Helen were at a party.

'Newman thinks that MC killed Joe Birch.'

'And did he?' Sian brushed away the last of her tears.

'There's evidence—'

'He wanted to know all about the time MC was here.'

'What did he ask you?'

'He wanted to know if I knew where Moelwyn was and whether I could contact him.'

Drake breathed out heavily.

'And he wanted to know what you'd talked to Moelwyn about.'

'What!'

'And why did they want to talk to me? Was I *helping with inquiries?*'

Drake wanted to scream at Newman. He'd call Lance immediately, tell the superintendent what had happened and demand that Newman keep away from his family.

'Am I going to be arrested because of your awful cousin? I wish I'd ...'

Drake briefly pondered what she meant.

'He said he tried to call you. Why didn't you answer?'

'It was a lie. He didn't call me. He was just saying that.'

'Why would he do that? I can never get hold of you.

Most women can reach their husbands on the telephone. They answer their mobiles.'

Drake knew that he'd explained a dozen times before that it could be difficult reaching him on the telephone and that ... Well, he wasn't certain he could explain. He couldn't compare himself to an accountant or an estate agent who kept neat hours and never had to go out and look at dead bodies for a living or comfort grieving families.

Sian ignored him for the rest of the evening. She worked on some papers for the practice, called her mother and put the girls to bed. Drake killed time around the house, finding aimless chores, until he sat in the study, holding the notebook in his hand and hoping he would feel inspired to write something.

Overnight Sian's mood had not improved. She barely looked at him over breakfast and ignored him as he tried small talk, so he left the house and headed for headquarters with a gloomy mood enveloping his mind.

He took the usual route into Colwyn Bay and as he stopped by a traffic light his mobile rang. He peered down at the screen and a flicker of anger registered as he read MC's number.

'Where the hell are you?' he said, answering the call.

The lights turned to green, so he pulled away.

'Behind you.'

Drake darted a glance into the rear-view mirror and saw a black BMW behind him. He could make out the hands-free cable hanging from MC's ear. Drake slowed the car and started indicating.

'Just keep on driving,' MC said.

Drake glanced around again, hoping there weren't any patrol cars that might stop him for using a mobile while driving.

'Did you kill Birch?' Drake said.

'Have you arrested Valencia yet?'

Drake slowed instinctively as he approached another

set of traffic lights showing red. But they changed to green and he had to drive on.

'If you've got any intelligence we'll need to go through all the correct procedures.'

'Fuck that. You know it doesn't work like that. Not for the likes of Valencia. I've been doing some digging around. Vigo and Valencia are only part of the operation. You should know that and I'm sure your friends in the drug squad know that too.'

'I spoke to Dr Kings yesterday.'

No reply. Drake glanced again into his rear-view mirror. MC had dropped back. His voice was softer now when he did reply. 'Those bastards killed her. And there's nothing you can do about it. The likes of Valencia and Birch get away with murder.'

'Stop this now. You know I'll have to speak to Newman about this call.'

Drake saw a refuse lorry pulling out into the main road so he slowed.

'Just don't tell him then. Birch is out of the way now and—'

They were almost at headquarters. Drake hoped a patrol car would turn out and follow them.

'Turn right,' MC said.

Drake cursed and indicated, hoping that his cousin would want to talk to him face to face. Then he could overpower him and make an arrest. They were approaching the seafront, the best place to stop and park.

'Just keep going,' MC said as Drake slowed. 'Have you made the link to John Beltrami, the wonderful upstanding citizen of North Wales? He's in the middle of it somehow and it's only a matter of time before I work it out. And if he was involved then I owe it to Sylvie.'

'Are you mad?' Owe her what? To spend the rest of your life in prison – and what about your mother?'

Drake swerved to miss a couple of cyclists in front

of him, just as his attention was drawn to two joggers running past the car. He glanced in the mirror again, but MC was gone. He slammed on the brakes. He made a three-point turn in the middle of the road, gesticulating wildly to the oncoming traffic to stop. He fired the car up the only road that MC could have taken but it was clogged with the early morning traffic of mothers on the school run.

He opened the window and then slammed his palm against the steering wheel.

Hannah gave him a less-than-enthusiastic smile when he arrived unannounced at Lance's office.

'I don't think he'll see you,' she said.

Lance appeared at the door of his office and raised an eyebrow when he saw Drake. 'Do we have a meeting?'

'It's urgent, sir.'

Lance turned to Hannah. 'Hold my calls.'

Drake pondered what he could have done differently. Could he have stopped and forced MC to park? But he'd have simply driven away. Drake stood up and followed Lance back into his office. The room was cool but there was the faint smell of vaguely sweet cologne.

'What so urgent?'

'I thought you should know that as I was driving into work this morning I was followed by MC Hughes.'

Lance stood by his desk and leant his hands on a pile of papers. 'I see.'

'He made allegations that John Beltrami was involved with Valencia.'

'Did you stop him?'

'He was driving.'

Lance raised an eyebrow.

'We spoke by telephone.'

'Whilst you were driving? Did you ask about the Birch inquiry?'

'Of course. I told him to surrender himself immediately.'

Lance sat down. Drake waited for Lance to point at the chair in front of the desk. Drake noticed a muscle twitching at the back of Lance's jaw. 'Is there anything to suggest that Beltrami is involved with drugs?'

'There's intelligence about his business interests over the years, but nothing that we could develop into concrete evidence that would stand up in court.'

'Anything in *this* inquiry, Ian.'

'No, sir.'

'Then we need to find and arrest MC Hughes on suspicion of murder. I'll call Newman. And remember, everything comes through my office.'

Drake stared at Halpin's red trousers. Then he noticed the striped socks and the brown brogues: the left shoe had a heavy scuffmark of a clumsy walker down one side. It was late in the afternoon and when he'd entered the room Drake had noticed the faintest tacky smell. He'd resisted the temptation to run a hand over the seat of the chair before sitting down.

'Have you been able to keep notes as we discussed last time?' Halpin tilted his head slightly, giving Drake an inquisitive glance.

Drake reached into his jacket pocket and pulled out the Moleskine notebook. 'It's not that easy. I don't seem to get the time.'

Halpin was nodding his head very slightly, offering a smile of encouragement.

'Tell me about the rituals since I saw you last.'

Drake turned the notebook in his fingers. 'I was in the office late, the night before last. I hadn't been there all day.'

'Where had you been?'

'In South Wales, with work. I got back and I knew I just had to check my office. Make certain that the papers were tidy. That everything was organised. That there wasn't just chaos all over my desk.'

'And was there?'

Drake looked over at Halpin, who waited for an answer.

'It made me feel in control. As though I was in charge again, having been away all day.'

'And did you find this helpful?'

'Yes. But the superintendent was working late. I was sorting papers on the floor when he …'

'What did he say?'

Drake looked over at Halpin and shrugged. 'He ... he told me to go home.'

'What do you do when you feel the rituals wanting to dominate your mind?'

Drake hesitated but after ten minutes he'd explained to Halpin how the intrusive thoughts could control his mind and that it was never easy to manage his rituals. Halpin made the occasional note, nodded and smiled. He flicked through the papers on his lap.

'How is your father?'

'He's not well. I found myself on the beach in Llanfairfechan after visiting him.'

'Does he like to go there?'

Drake was surprised by the question but then appreciated that Halpin knew him better than he'd realised.

'Yes, he does. We used to go there as children.'

'So did visiting the beach help?'

'In a way.'

'Visiting places that have links to your past with memories good or bad will be one way for you to handle the stress.'

Drake nodded.

'Do you have someone you can confide in?'

'Not really ...'

'I know you were let down by someone in the force, of course.'

Drake drew his tongue over his lips. The memory was still raw.

'And it's never easy to discuss these things with a wife. I suggest that one way to manage the stress is to have a 'safe place'. It needn't be a *place* of course. It could be a change to your routine. You could simply take a file in your hands and walk round headquarters for a few minutes.' Halpin looked over at Drake; another kindly look crossed his face. 'Nobody would think it odd. And it would give you time away from your office.'

Drake folded his arms, pulled them tight into his chest and contemplated what Lance or Newman might say if they found him walking around headquarters with a file under his arm. Slowly, the possibility that the coping mechanisms, as Halpin called them, might work.

Chapter 31

Drake woke with a start and for a moment could not remember which day it was. It was a Sunday of course and he had promised Sian and the girls that after visiting his parents he'd spend the rest of the day with them. He stared at the clock, realising it was still early. Sian was sleeping by his side.

He reached out from under the duvet and turned off the alarm before the clock buzzed into life. He padded downstairs and flicked a switch on the kettle, before picking up the news section from the previous day's newspaper. A headline about the ongoing arguments about the rebate from the European Union dominated the front page. The kettle switched itself off just as Sian appeared in the kitchen.

'Breakfast?' Drake asked.

Sian stood at one end of the worktop a little way from Drake, her arms folded. 'What's happening to us?'

'I'm sorry?'

'Why did Newman want to question me?' Sian stepped over to the table and sat down.

'He was—'

'Ian. I just don't know what's going on. It's all too much.' She put her head in her hands.

Drake should have known from Sian's taciturn mood since Friday evening that Newman's visit was still preying on her mind. There was a worn-out look in her eyes.

'Only I don't want them to call again. This is my home. Our home and …'

'It won't happen again.'

'Is there something you're not telling me? Can't tell me, I suppose.' She drew her hand in the air, a gesture of helplessness. Exasperation. 'Have you done something …?'

'No, of course not.'

'Then why did they call? Do they think I'm involved

in some way?' She looked up at Drake.

'Glyn Newman was making it awkward for me. He's a difficult individual—'

'I thought you were supposed to work together?'

'He's probably heard that Lance is the SIO and he was throwing his weight around.'

'He was an odious little man.' Sian stopped and played with the nails of her right hand. Drake poured water from the kettle over the coffee grounds in the tall cafetière and brought it over to the table with two mugs. 'And another thing. I don't want to see Moelwyn Carol here again.'

Drake nodded. Sian looked at him again.

'I didn't expect things to be like this …'

Drake felt the inside of his mouth drying. He didn't know what to say.

'Are you going to be able to switch off today?' Sian said, sitting by the table. 'One morning this week Helen actually asked whether you'd slept here the night before. Both girls had gone to bed before you got home and you left before they woke. It's not much of a life is it?'

'Look, I told you. Sylvie had had a miscarriage.'

'It can happen, Ian.'

'I know, but it must have happened while MC was in jail.'

'You mean the conception.'

Sian sounded remote, detached, even though they were talking about his cousin.

'And MC didn't know about it until a couple of days ago.'

'Yes, yes, I know. You went through all of this last night. Do we have to rehearse it all again?'

On the worktop behind them there was a pinging sound as two pieces of perfectly browned toast emerged from the Dualit machine. Drake found a low-fat margarine spread and a pot of marmalade in the depths of the American-style fridge freezer.

'If he's bearing a grudge against anyone because of what happened to Sylvie, then he's mixing with some dangerous people.'

Sian folded her arms, pursed her lips. 'You need to get a grip, Ian. Get a perspective. All these obsessions are getting the better of you. I just hope that Halpin can help.'

They ate the toast and finished the coffee in silence.

'What time do we have to leave?' Sian said, without much enthusiasm.

Drake looked at the clock on the wall. It was still early.

'A couple of hours, I guess.'

Sian left Drake clearing the dishes and he heard her moving around upstairs and then the sound of running water from the shower. He couldn't remember the last time they'd showered together, but the memory was still vivid, of taking a soapy sponge over her breasts before squeezing her nipples gently. But she'd complained he was too rough, so he'd started washing her thighs, moving her legs gently apart as they'd kissed and he'd gasped as she gripped his erection. The memory quickly faded as he heard the sound of young footsteps descending the stairs. He adjusted his dressing gown, making certain the girls wouldn't notice how aroused he'd become.

He'd finished loading the dishwasher when the telephone rang.

Drake recognised the voice of Mike Foulds. 'We've found MC's car.'

Sian had given him a stare worthy of the Spanish Inquisition when he'd left the house and no amount of apology had improved her mood. Helen and Megan had looked confused and his mother had sounded disappointed on the telephone, when he'd explained that he wouldn't be calling when Sian and the girls visited later.

It took Drake an hour to reach the disused quarry above Bethesda. Two marked police cars blocked the entrance and as Drake walked over he heard the sound of a car behind him and stopped when he saw Caren. She pulled the car behind Drake's Alfa, but unlike Drake she didn't bother to lock hers.

They walked towards the quarry, past the police vehicles, into a narrow entrance that led onto a wide, flat plateau of land surrounded by steep cliffs and a tall screed of different-sized rocks and pebbles. Wisps of smoke still escaped from the remains of the BMW. Drake recognised the number plate and the apprehension gathered in his chest. A uniformed sergeant stood at a safe distance from the smouldering remains.

'Good morning, sir. Sergeant Wilkinson,' he said.

'Who found the car?'

'A couple of guys out hiking. The car was ablaze. They guessed something was wrong.'

'Have they been interviewed?'

'Not yet.'

'Why not?'

'We haven't got round to it.'

'Send me a copy of the statements as soon as.'

Wilkinson nodded. 'The CSIs should be here any minute.'

Drake and Caren walked around the car, getting as near as they could. Behind them they heard the sound of tyres on the loose shale and then more footsteps until two CSIs joined the uniformed officers.

Drake stared at the car: he didn't know what to conclude. It didn't make sense for MC to abandon it. He reached for his mobile and dialled MC's number. It rang out again, as it had done several times the day before. Drake felt he was on the edge of the dark world MC had got himself into. He turned his back to the car. 'Let's go.'

He kept to the speed limit as he drove through the

main street of Bethesda, passing the occasional shopper visiting the convenience stores and children riding their bikes along the pavements. Soon enough he reached the outskirts of Bangor and waited for Caren to park behind him before leaving the car and walking over to MC's house. He thumped on the front door but there was no reply.

'I'll go round the back,' Drake said, before jogging down the street.

The property was in a row of recently built terraces all with neatly paved front gardens, no more than a couple of metres square, all with weeds pushing through the paviours. At the end of the terrace Drake found a narrow alley leading behind the houses. The back gate into MC's yard opened easily enough. Drake noticed a small padlocked shed. The back door and windows were all a fading white uPVC. His mouth dried out as he peered into the empty rear rooms.

He reached for the handle of the door and pressed it slowly. It gave way under his pressure and he breathed out. He had grounds for entering the property, reasonable grounds to suspect that something had happened to MC. His calls had been unanswered, the car found burnt out and MC's girlfriend had recently died. There was more than enough to justify a lawful entry.

Stepping over the threshold, he noticed immediately the cool temperature. The house had two ground-floor rooms, both small and box-like. The rear was empty but the front had a sofa, a couple of chairs and a large television.

Back in the hallway he recognised Caren through the glass in the front door. But there was no way of opening it and, looking around, he couldn't see a spare key so he shouted for her to use the rear. A coat stand by the front door had two fleeces alongside a waterproof jacket, but he couldn't spot the leather jacket MC loved. He heard his colleague's footfall inside the house.

'Anything?' she asked.

'Nothing downstairs.'

Drake reached for the bottom balustrade and took the stairs to the first floor. The sound of each creaking step seemed to reverberate through the small stairwell. At the top Drake hesitated. To his left was a bathroom that he guessed was over the kitchen and alongside it a small box room filled with old furniture and suitcases. In front of him were doors to two bedrooms. He reached out a foot and gently pushed open the door of the bedroom at the rear. He took a step inside and saw a single bed pushed into a corner; alongside it was a cabinet with a small light still blazing.

Caren stood by the closed door to the front bedroom, an uncertain look in her eyes. Drake nodded. She covered the handle with a handkerchief she'd found in a pocket. There was the barest sound of creaking hinges as she pushed the door open. She let out a long breath as her shoes echoed noisily over the bare floorboards of the empty room.

Chapter 32

The start of a new week should have meant clear thinking. A Monday morning always meant a busy surgery for Sian and she had barely spoken more than a few words as she raced around the kitchen organising breakfast, before checking that Helen and Megan had everything they needed for school.

Drake left home that morning, knowing that the weekend had done nothing but complicate the investigation. Foreboding gnawed and scratched at his mind every time he thought about MC. There was always a motive for murder and in this case he struggled to find clarity for the deaths of Rosen, Mandy Beal and Green. If Green had killed Rosen then why had Green been killed and who killed Mandy Beal and why? He cursed MC who must have the answer. Finding his cousin and gathering a witness statement had to be a priority.

On his way to headquarters frustration built until he drove straight past the turning and travelled down into Colwyn Bay before realising where he was. He stopped and retraced his journey before parking next to Winder's black Ford, knowing that the young officer always made an effort to be in promptly during the beginning of the week and that by Thursday or Friday he'd be late once again. A few minutes later Drake walked through the doors of the Incident Room.

Winder was talking to Caren.

'What's the latest about Janet?' Drake said.

Caren replied. 'She wasn't at the cottage over the weekend. The uniformed lads from the local station made regular trips to check.'

'And Loosemore?'

'Behind the locked gates in his mansion.'

'All weekend?'

Caren nodded and then stepped towards the board,

tapping the picture of Frank Rosen with the top of her biro. 'I wonder if there was anything going on whilst Frank Rosen was alive?'

Howick was the first to respond. 'Maybe Loosemore wanted Frank Rosen out of the way. Talks to his friend Beltrami, tells him he *has a problem* and Beltrami puts him in touch with his favourite gangster Darren Green, who dutifully obliges by killing the husband.'

'Don't be daft,' Winder said. 'How'd you explain Green's death?'

'Somebody else,' Howick replied.

Drake cleared his throat, aware that this sort of conversation could go around in circles. 'We've missed something,' he said, stepping towards the board. 'Let's go back and look at Rosen's death again.'

Drake turned to Howick. 'You go through the CCTV images this time, and Gareth ...' He looked over at Winder. 'You go through the statements. Caren, check all the passengers.'

The coloured Post-it notes were in the same long columns on his desk as he'd left them, but he was convinced that the cleaners had been shuffling the furniture around, lifting files and folders. Sitting by the desk he reached over to the telephone, which he moved a few millimetres before adjusting the photographs of his daughters and switching on the desk lamp. He booted up the computer and watched the flickering images of the set-up routine. He wondered whether Frank Rosen watched catch-up television and classic movies. Then Drake found himself thinking about the laptop.

Abruptly he got up and strode out in to the Incident Room.

'How did Green steal Rosen's laptop?'

Winder glanced over at Howick, who frowned. Caren stopped chewing on a piece of gum and sat back in her chair.

They had missed something. He looked at the drawings of the ship and the various decks. If Green had killed Rosen then he must have got access to the engineer's cabin when he wasn't there, either before or after Rosen had left for the engine room. He stared at the plan, oblivious of the stares behind him. What if it wasn't Green? So he stared at the list of the crew.

He turned and saw the three pairs of eyes peering at him.

'What time was Rosen last seen?'

Caren was the first to contribute. 'In the engine room, about half an hour before the ship left Dublin.'

'Yes, of course, of course.' Drake wrote something furiously on the board. 'How long would it take him to walk down to the engine room?'

'Ten minutes max,' Howick replied.

Drake sensed the developing concentration in the room, minds beginning to focus.

'So whoever trashed Rosen's cabin would have known when he had to leave.'

Winder piped up. 'That could have been anybody on the crew.'

Drake spun round. 'No. That can't be the case. It's not likely that the catering staff would know the movement of the engineers. And they'd be taking a risk going into the officers' quarters, even though they've got access to everywhere on the ship with those key cards.'

Howick interrupted him. 'All part of the security regime. I've got all those details from the office staff—'

'I know Dave, but then there's the CCTV. We've got hours of CCTV footage of everywhere in the ship.'

'You don't mean?' Caren asked.

Drake turned again to the board, knowing where to look but realising it would take hours of work. He tilted his head forward, nearer the board. 'Let's isolate the officers' quarters. I want a list of all the officers separately and then identify where they were half an hour before Rosen went down to the engine room. I want to know how many of them were in their cabins and how many were on the car deck or on the bridge and or in the engine room.'

'But it could take—'Caren protested.

'No choice.' Drake pointed at the layout of the ship. 'There are cameras covering the entrances to the officers' quarters. We'll need to get all those records sent over now.'

He turned around, pleased with himself for the clear thinking despite the gloominess he'd experienced earlier. Winder had a resigned look while Howick frowned slightly, puzzlement in his eyes, and Caren was searching for something in her notebook. Drake had made progress and he hoped that by the end of the day his quest for the thief responsible for taking the laptop wasn't another waste of time.

'Then we need to go through all the interviews and statements from the crew. Everyone, but start with the deck officers and the engine room staff. I want a list of the crew who have cabins in the decks below the engineers.'

He left the Incident Room, ignoring the exasperated glances. There seemed to be more order on his desk now that he'd returned. He turned to the messages swamping his inbox and began scrolling through them. There were a dozen emails, maybe more, from the Police Federation and he read one asking for his support against the latest cutbacks to policing numbers. Even the ritual of making good coffee gave him no pleasure and he returned to the desk thinking about MC. So he called his cousin's mobile, but it rang out.

The earlier clarity soon disappeared when Drake returned to his desk after visiting the bathroom to clean his hands from the grime of the Incident Room board and the dust on the computer keyboard. He needed to double-check everything, but there wasn't the time. And his plans to travel to Dublin the following morning only meant another day away from his office.

He went back to the beginning – it was a good place to start and he cursed himself for not having focused on Rosen and Janet sooner. He spent the rest of the morning trying to think clearly, but the more he contemplated the threads of the case the more they turned into a thick mesh. When the telephone rang he stared at it, his mind still entrapped. He answered it after the third ring.

'Drake.'

His mother sounded tired. 'Ian, will you be able to call tonight?'

'Of course.' Immediately his heart felt heavy and the guilty feeling, that he had been unable to see his father the day before, returned.

'How's Dad?'

'He's still in bed. You know, it's not easy. He gets very tired.'

'I'll see you tonight.'

'Good afternoon, Inspector.'

Even Drake could sense the impatience in Sergeant Wilkinson's voice.

'Is there anything back from forensics yet?'

'Nothing. And frankly I think it's unlikely. If MC Hughes torched the car himself to destroy evidence, then he's probably done a pretty good job, I'd say.'

'What do you mean?'

'Exactly that, sir.' The sergeant's tone changing to defiance.

'Have you spoken to MC's friends?'

'Of course, first thing we did.'

'And what about his time in prison?'

'Look, sir, I've got a team of officers involved.'

Drake couldn't stop himself from interfering and knew that the sergeant could complain.

'Has there been any contact with Sylvie Whatmore's family?'

'Oh yes. They don't want *anything* to do with MC or his family.'

After extracting a begrudging agreement from the sergeant to keep him informed, Drake finished the call. Every instinct wanted him to work on his cousin's disappearance. The last conversation he'd had with MC had riled him more than he realised. He should have arrested MC when he had the chance, regardless of the evidence. He found himself chewing heavily on his thumb nail when the telephone rang.

'That solicitor is here again. But with someone else this time.' The receptionist's voice sounded uninterested.

'Who?' Drake looked at a small bead of blood on his thumb.

'Jade Beltrami.'

'Okay, and who else?' Drake stuck his thumb into his mouth.

'A Mr Aylford. Beltrami said you'd definitely see him.'

Drake mumbled an instruction for them to wait in the conference room.

Satisfied that his thumb wasn't going to bleed all over the paperwork, he found a writing pad before telling a surprised-looking Caren they had an unexpected interview. The unplanned visit began to irritate Drake as soon as they walked into the conference room.

'Good morning.' Jade Beltrami smiled. 'This is Lewis Aylford. He wants to make a statement.'

'Come on Jade,' Drake said. 'You know this isn't routine.'

'Mr Aylford is aware that Frank Rosen was a regular pilot for his syndicate and that you have him as a person of interest—'

'I'm not telling you who is of interest in my

247

investigation.' Drake sensed he sounded annoyed.

'Inspector. This is a murder inquiry and I'm sure you'd want to eliminate Mr Aylford from the inquiry.'

'I'll be the judge of that.'

Drake noticed Caren opening her notepad. Drake stared at Aylford, knowing that he and Parry must have agreed between themselves to attend voluntarily. It riled him to think that someone else wanted to interfere.

'We've got a statement,' Jade said.

'Of course, you have,' Drake said. 'Let's get some preliminaries done with first. You're one of the owners of the plane that Rosen flew.'

'That's right.' Aylford had a mellow Irish twang to his voice, and Drake wondered if he had a connection to Dublin.

'What part of Ireland are you from?' Drake said.

Aylford looked nonplussed. 'Galway.'

Jade broke in. 'We've come to make a voluntary statement.'

'About the Rosen killing.' Drake stared at Aylford, various permutations crossing his mind.

'Yes, of course.'

'And how long have you lived in the UK, Lewis?'

Jade rustled the papers on the table. 'Mr Aylford wants to assist with your enquiries.'

'I'm sure,' Drake said. 'Do you go back to Ireland very often?'

Aylford wore a black pinstripe, the sort a successful barrister might choose. The stripe was dark red, his shirt had a faint pink tinge and the tie had been knotted perfectly. The edginess Drake had felt earlier was returning and Aylford wasn't helping. He stared at him, waiting for a reply.

'I haven't been—'

Jade cut across him. 'We've got a prepared statement.'

'I'm sure Lewis wants to cooperate. That's why he's

here,' Drake continued, oblivious to the open-mouthed astonishment Caren was trying to hide. 'How long have you lived in North Wales?'

'It's been twenty years.'

'You're a dentist?' Drake continued to stare at Aylford.

'I have a practice in Llandudno.'

'And Colwyn Bay and Bangor, I understand.'

Aylford nodded.

Jade moved more of her papers and gave Caren a sharp look. 'What is this about, Inspector?'

'Lewis is cooperating fully with us so that we can eliminate him from our inquiries. Do have any family in Dublin?'

'Ah ...'

'Easy question. Yes or no?'

'Well, my sister lives outside.'

'And is she married? Children? Where does she work?' Drake said, trying to work out if there might be a connection to Fergal Connors.

'She's a nun.'

Drake played with a biro. 'Any other family then, cousins, etc.?'

'Ah ...'

'Did you fly to Ireland very often with Rosen?'

'Yes.'

'Who would be with you?'

'It could vary. John Beltrami, Tim Loosemore and sometimes Eddie Parry.'

'And what did you talk about?'

Aylford shrugged. 'It's impossible to talk on a small plane.'

'You know what I mean. There was plenty of time either side of the flight. Come on, you must have talked about something. Football, rugby, the weather.'

'I don't remember.'

'Did Rosen talk about money?'

Another shrug. Drake could feel his pulse increasing.

'I don't think so.'

'You don't think so?' Drake raised his voice.

'Where did you stay with Rosen?'

'Different hotels—'

Drake's annoyance was building. 'And did you ever go the Blue Parrot nightclub?'

'I don't—'

'So if I requisition your credit card statements and bank accounts there'll be no reference to that night club?'

For the first time Aylford looked worried. 'Well. I don't remember names like that but we did visit various restaurants and clubs. So I could well have gone there.'

'Ian. We are going to read this statement.' Jade raised her voice, before shuffling a single piece of paper over the table to Aylford.

Drake squinted occasionally, knotted his brow and doodled with the biro while Aylford read the statement which was more or less identical to the one he'd heard Parry read. Drake glanced over at Caren and noticed her irritation too. By the end Aylford had confirmed his various trips to Ireland with Beltrami and Loosemore and Rosen. Drake noticed the time on his watch, judging that he'd wasted almost an hour. Once Aylford finished Drake placed the biro on the table and leant forward.

'Just one more question.'

Jade smiled. 'Of course.'

'Did you kill Frank Rosen?'

Chapter 33

Drake listened to the safety announcement and smiled to himself as he recalled the look of utter disbelief on Aylford's face, as though he'd been told he only had hours to live. Children were chattering behind him and he'd placed the morning's newspaper on the seat by his side, ready to start on the sudoku. The announcer continued in smooth calming tones, explaining the emergency evacuation procedures. Children came running past him towards the front of the vessel – the same enormous catamaran he'd used on his last trip to Ireland – parents oblivious to the suggestions in the video that youngsters shouldn't run around unaccompanied.

Drake finished the sudoku quickly, soon regretting his decision not to slip a book of puzzles into his bag, and once he'd read the news section he went in search of a coffee. The girl behind the counter smiled, took his order, then flicked some switches until a plastic mug filled with an Americano. It had a plastic taste that hung around in his mouth. The journey passed quickly and once the vessel had docked he filed through to the terminal entrance.

'How was your trip?' Malachy O'Sullivan said, shaking Drake's hand.

'Good.'

Drake followed O'Sullivan out to the car.

'I've got some good news. We found one of the tenants from Rosen's Dublin house. It was dead fucking lucky – seeing as he had no idea where any of them had gone. Anyhow, one of the lads was doing some background checks and an address pops up.'

Drake opened the car door: the smell was the same as the last time. O'Sullivan fired the engine into life and drove off. 'Colm Harrison remembers a woman visiting a couple of times. He worked from his flat, finishing a novel or some such bullshit – sounds like an excuse for idleness to me. He clocked them straight-off as a philandering husband – younger woman, etc. etc. He had all that jargon about people screwing people they shouldn't.'

They reached a set of lights and the car braked hard. O'Sullivan took a left and then another sharp corner before pulling the car abruptly to a halt. They got out and Drake followed O'Sullivan up a short path to a door at the rear of one of the terraces. The Irishman banged his fist a couple of times before the door opened.

'Colm. This is DI Drake from Wales. He wants to talk to you.'

Inside Drake saw cluttered work surfaces and an untidy kitchen as Harrison led them through into a room with a desk under a window and a single bed pushed against a wall. Drake showed the image of Mandy Beal to Harrison, who nodded.

'That's her all right. I saw her with the guy from the other photo.' He nodded again when Drake showed him the image of Rosen.

Harrison happily described his working day in the ground-floor bedsit in the house owned by Maguire. He'd be at the computer first thing and write all day. Drink too much coffee, eat too many biscuits, and surf the internet when he was distracted.

'I've got a good memory for faces. Occupational hazard of being a writer.'

'Have you had anything published yet?' Drake asked.

'Still not finished. I even included a description of her in the book.'

Once Drake had finished jotting down the details he made to leave.

'There was another woman too,' Harrison said. 'She wore a uniform and carried a green shoulder bag.'

'Really.' Drake's mind was racing, thinking how he'd get photographs of the crew. 'I'll need to speak to you again today.'

'OK. I'm only going as far as the computer,' Harrison said, nodding towards the screen on his desk.

Outside the temperatures were warming. Drake and O'Sullivan strode back to the car.

'I need to call my team and get them to email you photographs of all the female crew members,' Drake said.

'You can do that from the office.'

Eventually, O'Sullivan turned the car into a narrow residential road and then through a wooden drive to an old house set back in its own grounds. O'Sullivan parked and looked through the windscreen.

'And this is the An Garda Síochána unit that deals with all the high-end white-collar crime that no bugger understands. I'll see you to the door. I'll pick you up later.'

O'Sullivan tapped a code into the red painted door and ushered Drake inside. The building had the same tranquil intensity he'd felt in the unit headed by Super Adams, with its flickering monitors and air-conditioned luxury. The first floor was open plan with large boards and wide tables. Daylight filtered into the room through barred windows and Drake guessed there were cameras he couldn't see, recording everything.

O'Sullivan pointed to the far end of the room. 'That's Super Mallin. He's expecting you.'

When Superintendent Mallin got up from behind the desk Drake was surprised how small he was. His hair was cut short and the shirt sleeves, a single-cuff variety with long button-down collars, hung down past his wrists. He stood wide-stanced like a scrum-half in a rugby game, ready to catch the ball.

'I'll see you later.' O'Sullivan nodded to Drake.

Mallin pointed to a chair and Drake sat down.

'You want to know about Tim Loosemore and John Beltrami?'

'They're suspects,' Drake said immediately,

regretting that he had made the case sound clear-cut.

Mallin sat down and looked over at Drake. 'We've got investigations ongoing with the WPS and the FBI into various companies involving Beltrami and one of our home-grown crooks – Fergal Connors. Beltrami owns a business with Collins, and Loosemore's name crops up occasionally. So much of what goes on is shrouded in offshore trusts and front companies that the best we can do is hope they make the occasional mistake. I've got everything ready for you.'

The door to the room had 4/A/C written on it in large letters and inside two large box files had been dumped on the desk. Mallin explained where Drake could make coffee and find the toilets.

'Any questions, please ask me.'

Howick returned from a brisk walk, knowing that he had to concentrate. His career depended on it.

After the first couple of hours of staring at a flickering computer screen, his concentration was lapsing. The last thirty minutes had passed in a complete haze. He was sure Winder didn't feel this kind of urgency: Howick reckoned his colleague would be quite happy to finish his thirty years as a constable. But Howick wanted the promotion more than anything.

Returning to the Incident Room with two mugs of coffee, double strength just in case the dose of fresh air needed assistance, he put one down on Winder's desk.

'Good walk?' Winder yawned and stretched.

'I needed the fresh air,' Howick said. 'Any progress?'

Winder leant back and, folding his fingers together, and put his hands behind his head. 'Hours of the bloody stuff. Never realised a ferry had so many cameras.'

They'd widened the time frame suggested by Drake by ten minutes, but it had added over an hour to their work.

By the end, Howick had drunk a second cup of powerful coffee and they had the beginning of a spider chart of who was where on the car deck and the approximate times. Cross-referencing whether any of the crew had left the car deck meant watching the coverage from other cameras nowhere near where Rosen's body had been found.

A call from Drake asking Howick to email the images of the female crew members to Ireland had been a welcome distraction.

'I watched that film *Murder on the Orient Express* on Saturday,' Howick said.

'What?'

'You know, the Agatha Christie story, involving murders on the Orient Express train. Poirot knows the killer must be on the train. All he needs is the evidence.'

'But we know Green killed Rosen.'

'Can't be certain.'

'Come on. We've seen the earring – had to be him.'

'And we know the identity of the person who took Rosen's computer. Snag is that it could be one of twenty crew members.'

'Isn't Poirot French?'

'Belgian,' Howick corrected Winder.

'I thought Belgians were really French?'

'There's Walloons who speak French and Flemings who speak Flemish. And Brussels – that's bilingual.'

'Bit like Wales then.'

'Lots of controversy over language. Same the world over.' Howick returned his attention to the screen in front of him.

A spreadsheet entry was created for each deck officer and his movements tracked until they had a list of officers they knew were on the car deck in the half-hour before Rosen's death.

The exercise to track the catering staff took much longer as they moved around the vessel, darting from one area to another. Watching the crew swiping their entry cards was one thing, but not knowing where they might exit the secure area was quite another. And when Howick tried to follow one of the crew, he found himself having clicked from one camera footage to another for twenty minutes without knowing where the crew member had gone.

'I've found this girl leaving one of the entrances to the crew quarters about an hour before the ship leaves,' Howick said.

'So about half an hour before Rosen was killed.'

Howick scanned the photographs. 'Vicky Church. Works in one of the cafeterias. She's part of the permanent staff on the ferry.'

'Think we should talk to her?'

'No harm I suppose. Ask her what she was doing there?'

Another couple of hours passed until they had two more names. Howick and Winder stood by the board, staring at the crew list, before pinning the small passport-sized photographs of the engineer Robert James and the deck officer Rhodri Owens underneath Rosen and Green.

Howick tapped James's image with his biro. 'Robert James goes into the crew quarters when he should have been down in the engine room. One of the deck officers said something about Owens being late.'

'He's on that coverage from the car deck,' Winder said, turning back to his computer screen and searching until he found the relevant section. 'Hey bloody presto. Look at him,' Winder said. 'Holding out his arms. He's late. Been somewhere he shouldn't have been.'

'Tick.VG,' Howick said, mimicking Drake, and making the Nike-brand sign.

Sergeant Jeff Wallace stood under the shelter and regretted the day the politicians banned smoking inside buildings. It was cold and damp and having a smoke wasn't a pleasure any more, not that he was considering stopping – just that he had loved the old days when smoking was a necessary qualification for being in CID.

Political correctness gone mad, he had said at the time to anyone wanting to listen. He shivered and then fastened two buttons of his jacket against the chill of the afternoon – the shelter was on the north of the building, well away from any sunshine.

He didn't know Frank Rosen, but he'd guessed who was behind his death. It had taken Wallace a long time to get where he was and there was so much at stake that he didn't want to contemplate the possibility of things going wrong. He had another ten years till retirement and his pension and the lump sum that would swell the nest egg he was accumulating. He fancied a place in the sun, somewhere where you could still smoke inside.

Drake was out on a limb. Everyone knew that he was only the Deputy SIO on the case. If he carried on like this he'd soon be in Traffic. That would suit Wallace just fine.

Chapter 34

Normally, by late in the afternoon in his office Drake's eyes would have felt gritty, his hands greasy, forcing him to visit the bathroom and clean, but he found the coolness of the air conditioning calming. By six o'clock Drake had read everything on the closely typed single sheet of A4 prepared by Mallin, cross-referencing to the files from the various boxes. Drake knew that Rosen must have learnt or heard or just guessed something that had given him enough bargaining power with Loosemore or John Beltrami or now even Fergal Connors. There could always be a simple explanation; Frank Rosen could have got lucky on the horses at Leopardstown racecourse.

Fergal Connors had perfect teeth that glistened when he smiled and, from the photograph on the cover of a glossy magazine, he looked healthy, his arm wrapped carefully around a pouting super-thin woman with skin like leather. Drake skimmed the magazine article on Connors, noting that his portrayal as a property developer and entrepreneur was more complimentary than the Garda description he'd read earlier. Connors had property all over Dublin and in the boom years had been able to extend his empire to London – a mews house in Chelsea – and various hotels and apartment blocks in Spain and Portugal. The latest venture to capture public attention was a film company that promised to bring in Hollywood blockbusters, creating hundreds of jobs. And there was a building company, a couple of golf courses and the freight business

'Impressive, don't you think?' Mallin said, leaning against the door, arms folded.

Drake turned to look at Mallin. 'He seems to be everywhere. This freight company is just small beer for him.' Drake patted the file on the table.

'For a man who came from Athlone fifteen years ago

with nothing he's built one hell of an empire.'

'Where is Athlone?'

'Middle of nowhere.' Mallin stepped towards Drake. 'But it was the year he spent in the States that made the difference.'

Drake flicked through the papers, knowing that he'd seen a timeline for Connors.

'We have no idea what he did or really where he went. But what we do know is that when he came back Fergal Connors had enough money to make himself a fortune, marry a trophy wife, etc. etc. Did you read about his Easter holiday?'

Drake shook his head.

'Fergal Connors hires a one-hundred-foot yacht in the Caribbean, complete with crew, including a captain and a five-star chef. Just a touch under one hundred thousand euros a week. But instead of flying economy class or taking a charter like the rest of us, he hires a private jet.'

'Nice.'

'It's all drugs. That's where all the money comes from. Every little smack head, every lawyer or journalist sniffing their cocaine and every homeless heroin addict from here to Belfast and Cork is contributing to Fergal Connors's lifestyle.'

'How near are you to building a case?'

Mallin grunted. 'Who knows? Sometimes it feels like we'll never get him.'

Drake's mobile beeped. Mallin picked up one of the sheets from Drake's file, printed with Rosen's codes. A knot of worry crossed Drake's mind when he read the message – *ferry cancelled collect you in twenty.*

'They're the printed records we found on Rosen's data stick,' Drake said, looking at the mobile and wondering whether he should reply. 'We can't make any sense of them.'

'Looks easy enough to me.'

Drake's initial excitement when Mallin declared he could decipher the code waned when he realised that it was only part of the problem. But Drake's exasperation was tested further when O'Sullivan arrived and announced. 'That is *so* fucking obvious.'

Interspersed with the single letters and numbers were sets of Irish registration numbers, and Mallin sat by the desk assembling a full list. O'Sullivan clutched the sheet of paper, giving it a studious stare.

'The first number, 04, is the year of registration – 2004 and the letters afterwards are for the county of registration. C is for Cork, D for Dublin and LH for Louth. Do you get the picture?'

'How many counties are there?'

'Twenty-nine, but some won't have many vehicles registered.' Mallin carried on scribbling.

'And the numbers?'

O'Sullivan piped up. 'They're sequential numbers. Shame about your ferry. You'll either have to stay overnight or take the ferry in the middle of the night – quarter past two. Jesus, that's no fucking time to be travelling.'

Drake couldn't afford to lose another day. 'I think I'll go back on the ferry tonight.'

'Let's find out something about these plates,' Mallin said, turning to the computer screen.

He tapped the numbers and letters into his keyboard, stopping occasionally and hitting the print key. Drake heard the muffled sound of a printer in another room. Once he'd finished Mallin got up and trundled out to the adjacent office, returning with a handful of papers. Drake could barely contain his excitement that this was some sort of progress. Mallin slumped into his chair and started flicking through the sheets, blowing out a lungful of breath as he finished.

'Interesting.'

'Are they cars or lorries or what?' Drake said.

'Most of them are lorries owned by a haulage company in County Cork. This could be very useful.'

'Why?'

'The company is another small part of the Connors empire.'

Mallin set the papers down on the table. 'You've got your connection to organised crime, Ian. All you have to do is work out why he kept this list.'

Drake didn't have time to reply before O'Sullivan piped up. 'And I think it's about time we visited another part of the Connors empire.'

Drake rang Caren first but her messaging service clicked on; he called Howick but the number was engaged, before he finally succeeded in speaking to Winder.

'We need to get a full list of all the vehicles that have passed through the port in the last twelve months. Find someone in the ferry company who can get you the data.'

'Do you realise the time, boss?'

'I don't care what time it is. Contact that runt Mortlake and if he fails to cooperate, then tell him I will personally arrest him for obstruction. I'll be back in the morning. And Gareth, nobody except our team gets to hear of this.'

Drake heard the silence on the other end of the telephone. Being unable to explain to his team that he'd had specific orders not to involve any other department was going to raise eyebrows, maybe even already had.

O'Sullivan stood by the front door waiting for Drake and Mallin.

'Are you coming, sir?'

'You must be joking. Connors would recognise me,

and the Garda Commissioner would think I'd gone mad.'

Drake was developing an uneasy feeling that visiting the Blue Parrot might not be such a good idea. But O'Sullivan had insisted and he had hours to kill before the ferry.

'We need to see Harrison,' Drake said, as they stood outside by O'Sullivan's car.

'Jesus, almost forgot.'

O'Sullivan drove the car too quickly around the streets of Dublin until they found themselves outside Harrison's home.

The door opened as O'Sullivan raised a fist.

'Heard the car,' Harrison said.

The remains of a chocolate bar and an empty packet of crisps were the only evidence of activity in the flat since their earlier visit. Drake sat down uninvited and passed over the photographs from his papers. O'Sullivan walked over to the desk.

'So what are you writing? Is it like that Stieg Lawson guy from Norway?'

'He was *Larsson*,' Harrison said, without looking up. 'And he was from Sweden.'

O'Sullivan didn't reply.

'Do you recognise any of these?' Drake said after a couple of minutes.

Harrison stopped at one photograph and tilted his head slightly. 'She's the one.' He pointed at the page.

Drake had dialled Winder's number before they reached the car.

'Vicky Church,' Drake said.

'How did you know?'

'You're not making sense, Gareth.'

'She's on the CCTV leaving the officers' quarters.'

'And I've spoken to an eyewitness who saw her staying in Rosen's flat. Find out if she's working on the ferry from Dublin tonight. If not, find her. Quick.'

'Sounds like she could be in trouble,' O'Sullivan said, leaning over the car door.

Drake nodded.

After a journey of half an hour, they reached the suburbs and O'Sullivan drew the car to the kerb by a fish and chip shop.

'My expense account wouldn't buy a salad leaf at the Blue Parrot,' O'Sullivan said. 'So we're eating in my favourite restaurant.' He nodded towards the queue on the pavement.

Drake waited in the car, hoping Winder would reply and cursing the weak signal. O'Sullivan returned with the containers of food. Drake picked at the salty, fatty food without much enthusiasm.

'Now I've got one powerful thirst,' O'Sullivan said, wiping the back of his hand over his lips once he'd finished.

O'Sullivan turned the car into the long driveway that curved its way towards the front entrance of the Blue Parrot. He parked next to a dark-blue Mercedes. They paid their entrance fee to a tall girl with long earrings and a hangdog appearance and walked past bouncers with enormous chests and cables hanging from their ears.

'Eastern Europeans,' O'Sullivan said under his breath.

The main room was a large oblong shape with a sunken area to the right that had an array of gaming tables. Thin women with high heels and perfectly manicured faces hung off men in dark suits.

'Jesus, place is full of hookers tonight.'

At the far end, behind a narrow screen, were tables policed by an officious-looking man in a dinner jacket.

'There's yer man.' O'Sullivan nodded to the far end of the restaurant.

Drake searched the diners for the face of Fergal Connors. He was smiling at a group of young women on the table with him. O'Sullivan reached the bar and caught the attention of the barman. After ordering his own drink, O'Sullivan turned to Drake.

'What's your poison?'

'Guinness.'

'Very sensible.' O'Sullivan turned to the barman and mouthed the word 'two'.

The drinks arrived and they stepped away from the bar. Drake took a mouthful of the black liquid, enjoying the warm, mellow flavour in his mouth. A man approaching them from the gambling area seemed familiar and Drake recognised Paul Maguire, despite the dinner jacket.

'Hello, Mr Maguire,' Drake said.

Maguire stood rigid for moment, began blinking nervously, and then looked around as though he was searching for someone.

'Gentlemen. Have a pleasant evening.'

'What was that all about?' O'Sullivan said.

'Did you know that Maguire worked for Connors?' Drake's pulse beat in his neck.

Before O'Sullivan could reply, Drake saw another face he recognised. He put the Guinness down on the nearest table. 'We're leaving. Now.'

O'Sullivan opened his mouth to protest but Drake was already walking towards the door.

Chapter 35

By one a.m. Drake felt an ache in the small of his back, his mouth was dry and he could feel a headache developing all over his temples. And, after the nightclub, he needed to clean. He was convinced that the hand wipes he'd used had left a sticky residue over his hands. He'd finished the sudoku from *The Irish Times*, which he'd scanned unsuccessfully for photographs of Fergal Connors. The puzzle had been described as difficult, but Drake finished it in half an hour and wondered what the paper's fiendish version would be like.

He hated the feeling of not being in control. And the codes and numbers were still dominating everything and the fact that the battery on his mobile had run out earlier had put his nerves on edge.

The call from Winder, before his mobile died, confirming that Church wasn't on the ship and that in fact it was a completely different ferry, only made his edginess worse. The terminal lounge had uncomfortable, narrow, upright chairs. He thought about lying down to sleep, but worried he might sleep on and miss the ferry. He walked around. He stared blankly at the television high up on the wall playing the same music videos over and over. He watched the faces of the other passengers. Two students with backpacks and hiking poles were holding hands while watching a tablet computer. A handful of other passengers sat around the lounge, trying not to look bored, and others lay on the chairs or on the floor, arms tucked under the heads.

After boarding, Drake hurried to the information desk on one of the upper decks, deciding that there might be cabins and that two hours' sleep had to help. A woman behind the counter yawned at him and then nodded, telling him the cost, debiting his card and passing over a small key before pointing to a door across the hallway.

He couldn't remember falling asleep, but a sharp knock on the door and a shout woke him just before arriving at Holyhead. At first he couldn't focus his eyes, and his mouth was still parched. He disembarked in a blur and found the Alfa where he'd parked it the night before. Fretting that he couldn't stay awake long enough to drive home, he opened the window and suffered the cold air streaming over his face.

He pulled into his drive just before seven and as he entered the house, he heard the alarm by the side of his bed.

'Martin Valencia.'

Drake looked at the faces in the Incident Room. Caren's eyes were piercing and Winder stood, his feet wide apart. Howick had his arms firmly threaded together. There was an edge of expectation that Drake hoped signalled that progress was being made.

'Valencia is a known supplier. The WPS have been after him for years. Flashy bastard has a Range Rover and he wears white suits. But in the past every case against him has collapsed. He was sitting bold as brass in the Blue Parrot last night with Fergal Connors.'

'Did he spot you?' Caren said.

'Don't think so. I want to know everything about Valencia. And this goes no further than our team. Understood?'

Drake looked at each of them in turn, knowing that soon he'd owe them an explanation. Once he had one from Lance. Drake turned to the board and tapped a sheet printed with one of the codes. 'I had to go to Ireland to make sense of these.'

He leant over and circled a section with a yellow marker. 'The number is for the year. So 05 is 2005, etc. and then the letter or letters refers to the Irish county. So WW is Wexford and KK is Kilkenny.'

'And I thought that was something to do with the Ku Klux Klan,' Winder said.

'You watch too many DVDs.' Howick sounded serious.

'The Garda were able to build a list of the vehicles and they all belong to a haulage company that's owned by Fergal Connors. The police in Dublin have a complete unit looking into him. But what's interesting for us is his link to Beltrami. The freight company they own carries freight regularly through Holyhead.'

Drake turned to Winder. 'Gareth, did you get hold of Mortlake?'

'He was really pissed off. Doesn't like you, boss.'

Drake allowed himself a brief moment of satisfaction as he thought about interrupting Mortlake's domestic routine.

'The lists you're after only arrived about an hour ago. Dave and I are working on them at the moment.'

'What about the rest of the codes?' Caren asked.

'Once we work that out, we'll …' Drake took a glimpse at the board, wondering whether the Garda had any chance of prosecuting Connors. 'Tell me about the CCTV footage, Dave.'

'The only two deck officers we could see that might be of interest are Robert James and Rhodri Owens. But it could take hours to build a complete picture of the movements of all the crew. There are so many cameras over the ship and all the crew had key cards to get access to everywhere. We need more bodies to do the job properly.'

Drake couldn't tell how Lance would react to a request for more resources, but he could easily imagine the pained look Superintendent Price would have given him, before letting off steam about the bean counters in finance. So Drake ignored Howick and stared at the board, hoping for more inspiration, and the prospect of a meeting with Lance later that morning preying on his mind.

'Did you find Vicky Church?'

'Wasn't at home last night.'

Caren said out loud to no one in particular. 'I'll talk to her family.'

Drake hesitated. 'We need to find MC and I want all the statements and house-to-house inquiries around Green's property looked at again.'

The earlier anticipation of progress had mellowed into a realisation of the scale of the work they needed to get through.

'Are we any further forward, sir?' Caren said, a frown on her face.

'We need additional resources to work on establishing where all the crew were at the time of Rosen's death.'

Lance stared at Drake without interrupting, but now Drake noticed his raised eyebrows. He persevered until he'd explained how many cameras there were on the ship. Drake even managed to dredge from his memory comments made by Mortlake and Captain Seymour about the different levels of security they worked to when the ship sailed.

'Interview Owens and James initially. Then we'll review.'

'The Garda have a lot of background on Fergal Connors and his involvement in organised crime. There's a connection to Beltrami and there's a real possibility that they're moving drugs through the port.'

Lance was nodding now.

'And shouldn't we be bringing in the drug squad and Special Branch for this, sir. This is developing into a major organised-crime investigation.'

It had troubled Drake before that Lance wanted to keep this operation under his direct control. There were protocols about team working and shared objectives that Lance was ignoring and Drake hoped that none of this was going to impact on his own career. He tried to decipher the look in Lance's eyes, to interpret what was going on, but, as always, he struggled.

'I will liaise with Special Branch in Cardiff. But murder is always top priority.' Lance was staring at Drake now, his jaw clenched. 'I don't want you making contact with any other department. And that includes drug squad.'

Drake thought about requesting confirmation in writing, but knew that within an hour Lance would have sent him a formal memo.

'But there are—'

'And that goes for your team as well. Make certain they all understand it. We're talking about three murders here.'

Drake thought about the practicalities. 'I know, sir, but—'

'It's a direct order, Inspector.'

Chapter 36

Drake hoped he could quell his frustration with Lance. He slammed closed the door to his room, ignoring the puzzled looks on the faces of his team.

A light drizzle fell on the window. It would only be a matter of time before the lack of sleep would affect him. Something was very wrong, but trying to rationalise the thoughts that were competing against his rituals only made him more anxious. He had to make some progress and he had to get the team to make progress.

He marched out to the Incident Room and over towards Winder.

'Gareth, have you finished cross-referencing the ship's manifests against the registration plates of the lorries?'

'Should be finished later.'

'Come on. Get on with it. We've got three murders to solve.'

'I spoke to some of Mandy's friends,' Caren said. Drake gave her one of his troubled expressions. 'They said she'd been talking about moving to somewhere warm.'

'What does that mean?' Drake said.

'Bournemouth, probably,' Howick chipped in.

Caren ignore the comments. 'One of them said that Mandy had an old laptop. But there was no sign of it in the house.'

Drake nodded.

Winder had more to say. 'We've been digging into Rhodri James.'

Drake raised his eyebrows, hoping that whatever Winder looked so pleased about wasn't another dead end.

'Until ten months ago Rhodri Owens owed a shed load on his credit cards.'

'How much?'

'Twenty grand.'

'And?' Drake realised Winder had more to say.

'All of it has been paid off in varying amounts. And now he's only got a couple of thousand left. Apparently his marriage fell apart a few years ago. He took it badly, especially when his wife took the children to live in Florida. Every chance he gets he goes to see them. But it's expensive.'

'We'll have to interview him.' Drake looked at the smiling faces of Howick and Winder. 'Get on to it right away.'

He turned and left without looking at the face of either officer. In his office he sat down and clenched his hands together. His eyes burnt. His shoulders were heavy. The need to follow his usual rituals tugged at his mind until he thought about Halpin and he reached for the notebook in the top left-hand drawer and opened a new sheet – always a clean page for every new entry. He wrote *sudoku* and *desk-tidying* before scribbling *how do I stop myself?*

Slowly he unclenched his fingers.

He cleared his desk and found the codes from Rosen's computer. He opened an Excel spreadsheet and copied the data into three columns before printing the single sheet, which he placed in the middle of his desk. He placed the fingers of each hand against his forehead, as though, by applying pressure, his concentration would increase. He stared at the numbers and letters.

06	10	8
G	N	G
LK	WX	D

1589	3985	15146
0630	0524	0218
351	1652	2568

He deleted the data that related to the Irish vehicles and stared at the bare details with the empty cells.

G	N	G
1589	3985	15146
0630	0524	0218

He ignored the letters. The numbers would be easier. He began constructing a spreadsheet of possible alternative scenarios. And, realising that he'd wasted an hour before recognising that the letters and numbers had to be taken together, he headed for the kitchen, knowing that he would be comforted by the repetition of his usual routine.

Rejuvenated by the bittersweet taste of the coffee from Columbian beans coating his mouth, he opened another spreadsheet and entered the entire alphabet down one side, guessing that Rosen may have converted letters into numbers. He chose the letters that corresponded to the number and filled out the spreadsheet, including the possible variations for the five-digit entry.

1589	3985	15146
AEHI	CIHE	AEADF
		OANF - 15,1,4,6
		AENF - 1,5,14,6

0630	0524	0218
FC?	EBD - 5,2,4	BR - 2,18
	EX - 5,24	BAH - 2,1,8

He looked blankly at the result of this exercise, thinking that there was something familiar about the second line with the four letters. But the final number had three permutations and none seemed to help him. The line of letters under the second row of numbers filled him with even less enthusiasm than the first set of four letters. He remembered a training session with a management consultant who'd referred to the preponderance of TLAs in every walk of life. It took a while for Drake to realise he was referring to Three Letter Abbreviations.

0630	0524	0218
3006	2405	1802

He ran a brief experiment
> FC? Football Club?
> EBD English Bottling Department
> BR British Rail
> BAH British Aerospace Hospital

There could be endless possibilities and the prospect that they'd never find an explanation filled him with dread.

It occurred to him to divide the last set of numbers into pairs and reverse them – he even considered the possibility of matching pairs from different columns. As he read the second line of digits an excitement grew at the possibility that dates were emerging. And, if he was right, then what had motivated Rosen to keep this record?

'Gareth,' he shouted.

Moments later Winder appeared at the door.

'I need that list of all the dates of the flights from RAF Mona.'

'Yes, boss.'

Drake could hear the rustling of papers and the twanging of lever-arch files. Then Winder stood at the other side of the desk and slipped over the sheets he'd asked for. He could feel the anticipation that something *had* to add up from all the hard work.

His pulse quickened as he read that Rosen had flown on the thirtieth of June and on the eighteenth of February, but disappointment that no flight had been recorded on the twenty-fourth of May. Drake searched for the names of the plane's passengers but then realised that he had been given a list of the flights only.

'Gareth,' he shouted. 'I need the details of the passengers on this list.'

Winder stood at Drake's door. 'We've never had that, boss.'

Drake stared at Winder, realising that there was a piece of the jigsaw missing. He wondered why the names of the passengers hadn't been provided. He picked up the telephone and dialled a man who could help.

Miranda Church was a perfect size ten, Caren concluded. And the well-pressed denims complemented her long, slim legs. It had taken all of Caren's motivation to unwrap herself from the warmth of Alun's body that morning and the next opportunity for a morning away from the investigation seemed a forlorn hope.

Miranda glided around the kitchen making coffee, then offering lunch, which Caren refused.

'I am so desperately worried.' Miranda flicked her blonde hair. 'Vicky has never done anything like this before.'

'When did you see her last?' Caren said, sipping coffee from a bone china mug.

'It was before she went to work on her last shift. But we speak every day.

'Does she have a boyfriend?'

'There was somebody on the ship, but it was never serious. I never wanted her to work *there*.' Miranda made it sound like a leper colony.

'Have you spoken to her friends? Maybe she's gone away from a few days. Is she due a holiday?'

'Look, I know this may sound old-fashioned but I know my daughter, sergeant,' Miranda said, managing to inject Caren's rank with maximum condescension. 'Her mobile phone is dead, and the landline wasn't answered all of last night.'

'Do you have a key to her house?'

'Of course,' Miranda said, shocked by the implication that she might not.

'And.'

'She's not there, of course.'

'Perhaps we should take a look.'

Caren followed Miranda out to a gleaming silver sports car. They turned west along the narrow lanes behind the town of Beaumaris, Caren in the passenger seat, who was gradually deciding that being Miranda's daughter would have driven any sane person to escape. Caren had heard the details about the annual sailing club ball, Vicky's favourite restaurant, how she had always been such a success at school and that now she was waiting to hear about a job opportunity in the Caribbean. The car slowed and Miranda pulled into a narrow driveway.

'It's just down this path.' Miranda pointed towards a narrow gate.

At the bottom of a narrow path of cream-and-custard-coloured slabs Caren saw the front of the two-storey farmhouse. It was sort of image Caren saw in glossy magazines at the hairdressers. Miranda pushed the key into the front door and Caren followed her inside. As she closed the door behind her, there was a sound of moving furniture from the first floor.

'Vicky, darling. Oh my God, are you there?' Miranda shouted out.

Silence.

They heard the sound of a window squeaking open and Caren took the stairs two at a time. The first bedroom was empty but she pushed open the door of the rear bedroom and saw Robert James struggling with the sash.

Chapter 37

Drake sat opposite Rhodri Owens in the small interview room at the police station in Holyhead. He had a long, thin neck and a large Adam's apple, which moved almost hypnotically every time he spoke. It had annoyed Drake more than he cared to admit that he'd missed the possibility that Green wasn't responsible for stealing Rosen's laptop.

Owens was wearing a green T-shirt under a half-zipped sweater and, judging from the frequency with which he scratched his ear, then his jaw and finally his nose, Drake knew that he was nervous. Drake took more time than he needed to prepare, fiddling with the cellophane wrappers of the cassettes for the tape-recorded interview, searching through the file of papers and then glancing at his watch. It gave him a brief moment of pleasure when he noticed Owens's gaze flashing around the room as he chewed on the forefinger of his right hand.

'Interview at Holyhead police station. My name is Detective Inspector Ian Drake. For the purposes of the tape, can you state your full name?' Drake looked over and saw a frightened, wide-eyed look on the man's face, as he yanked away a piece of nail with his teeth.

'Rhodri Owens.'

'We want to establish the movements of everybody working on the ship on the morning Rosen was killed.' Drake leant back in his chair and hesitated. 'Can you explain what exactly your duties are?'

Owens swallowed hard and gave Drake a rather pleading look.

'I am one of the officers responsible for making sure that the ferry is loaded correctly. We check that the cars and lorries get to the right place.'

Owens spent ten minutes explaining his job. Occasionally Drake had to cajole him for more details, until

Drake had learnt about the health and safety regulations, the need to get the vessel loaded quickly and the pressures from the port manager to get the ship sailing on time.

'But on that sailing you were a man short, weren't you?' Drake said, without taking his eyes off Owens.

'Ah. I … don't remember.'

'Well, that's what the first mate says.'

'Must be right then. We get so busy.' Owens was blinking again.

'When would you normally be on the car deck?'

'It depends.'

'Roughly.'

'Thirty minutes before sailing.'

'And before that where would you be?'

'It can vary. Eating or sleeping or in my cabin …'

Vagueness – always a good sign of guilt, thought Drake. 'And your cabin is G23?'

'That's right.'

Drake opened a layout of the ship on the table. He took the yellow highlighter, marking cabin G23.

'Where were you on the day Rosen was killed?'

The Adam's apple moved up and down again.

'I was in my cabin.'

'And do you remember when you got onto the car deck?'

'About the usual time.'

'That's not true, is it Rhodri?'

Drake noticed a shadow crossing Owens's face.

'You were late, weren't you?'

Owens gave a brief shrug.

'For the purposes of the tape, can you give a proper reply?'

'I … can't remember.'

'Let's have a look at this CCTV coverage to see if it will jog your memory.'

Drake opened the laptop and as it booted up he

noticed that the colour seemed to have drained from Owens's face. Drake navigated to the relevant file and waited until the images filled the screen.

'Can you see the timer?'

'Yes.'

'What time does it say?'

'Seven fifty-five.'

'And the ship sails at eight twenty.'

Owens nodded.

'For the purposes of the tape Rhodri Owens nodded his head in confirmation. I'll now run on the CCTV coverage.'

After four minutes – it felt like longer – Drake stopped the coverage, the image of Owens filling the screen.

'That's you isn't it, Rhodri?'

'Yes.'

'So the time is seven fifty-nine, which is twenty-one minutes before the ship sails. Let's have a look at the next minute of the tape.'

Drake clicked the machine into action. The screen filled with the images of Owens opening his hands, tilting his head, as if offering an explanation.

'You were late, weren't you, Rhodri?'

'I suppose.' Owens picked at his upper lip.

'So you lied when you told me you were on the car deck at the usual time,' Drake said, all traces of wanting Owens's cooperation having disappeared.

'It's not easy to remember.'

'What were you doing before you arrived on the car deck?' Drake watched Owens leaning on the desk, his shoulders hunched forward. 'You were lying when you told me you were in your cabin. You lied to me about when you arrived on the car deck and you're lying to me now.'

'It's not what you think.'

'I think you know all about Rosen's death. Do you know that the sentence for murder is life imprisonment?'

'I didn't kill Frank … It was …'

'Who was it, Rhodri?'

Owens's head slumped into his hands.

'You went into Frank's cabin, didn't you?'

Owens didn't lift his head. Didn't say anything.

Drake continued. 'You were the one that ransacked his cabin. You stole the laptop. The evidence is piling up against you being involved in Frank Rosen's death.'

'I never killed him. Never.'

'Don't lie to me again.'

Owens lifted his head; Drake could see tears forming in the corner of his eyes. Owens took a long, deep breath.

'It was a data stick. All they wanted was the fucking data stick.'

'They?'

'And the laptop. I had to check the laptop for them. It was something about Frank and what files he kept. I had to take out the hard drive and destroy it. That was all. There was no data stick. I didn't know …'

'I need you to tell me why and who else is involved.'

By the end of the interview, Drake had recorded all the sordid background of Owens's financial problems, which eventually, through a recommendation from Darren Green, led him to borrowing money from Martin Valencia. What he hadn't realised was that it was never that simple. Soon enough Valencia had wanted favours, a certain lorry parked well away from the main activity of the car deck and the occasional word to Special Branch officers, encouraging their enquiries away from various vehicles.

'Are you going to charge me with murder?' Owens asked, his voice breaking.

Drake left him in the small, hot windowless room.

The custody sergeant didn't need much persuasion to agree

that Owens be denied bail and charged with theft. Drake knew that he only had limited time available until he could either find evidence to link Owens to the murder or face a bail application that even a half-competent solicitor would win.

Drake left Holyhead and headed east on the A55. Springsteen was on going down to the river, but before he got very far Drake switched the music off. It was one of the songs that made him feel morose and he started thinking about Halpin and the implication of his comments about Drake's failure to make notes. He worried what sort of report Halpin would write, and whether Lance might read it. Maybe Lance would be transferred back to Southern Division before the sessions ended.

He turned left off the dual carriageway, but before finding his way to RAF Mona for his meeting with Ellis-Pugh he parked up and rang the Incident Room.

'We've finished that work on the ship's manifests,' Winder said.

'Anything?'

'All the lorries in Rosen's lists travel over on the ferries, regularly.'

'And what do we know about them?'

'The cargo manifests vary. Electrical goods, toys, kitchen equipment, and so on.'

'Any reports about MC?'

'Nothing boss.'

Drake could sense his chest tightening again.

'Meet me at MC's place in half an hour.'

'Of course.' Winder sounded puzzled.

Drake pulled into the entrance of RAF Mona and parked alongside an old Ford Fiesta. Rays of red sunshine were beginning to scour the evening sky and Drake calculated that sunset was probably in less than an hour. Ellis-Pugh emerged from the building holding an envelope in his hand.

'Sorry I'm late,' Drake said. 'Thank you for waiting.'

'Perfectly all right.' Ellis-Pugh handed Drake the envelope.

Drake extracted the sheets and scrutinised the various entries.

'You'll have to excuse me: we've got a Cessna arriving from the Isle of Man.'

'Of course,' Drake said, as Ellis-Pugh walked back into the building.

In the distance, Drake heard the sound of a small light aircraft approaching. He looked up and saw an aircraft slowly descending, its wings pitching slightly in the evening turbulence. Sunshine reflected from the canopy of the aircraft as it made its final descent towards the runway. The pilot dipped the plane, the wheels squealed as the brakes were applied and the engine raced.

Drake stared at the plane. A pilot and passenger were the only occupants. For some reason Drake walked down past the main building towards the runway. He watched the plane taxi, the engine now at a slower speed. He walked nearer again, knowing that he should be in his car, driving to MC's house. The plane turned so that the main fuselage was in his direct line of sight. And then he saw the plane's registration details and ran back to his car.

Chapter 38

'Do you realise the time, sir?'

'I don't bloody care. There is bound to be somebody, somewhere that can help. The civil aviation board or bureau or some public body that keeps a record of these things. Just get it done Dave. Drag somebody back to their office if you have to.'

Drake didn't remember the journey to MC's house. He couldn't put to rest the frustration that it had taken him so long to discover that the codes could be Rosen's record of the aircraft he'd flown. He parked, with two wheels on the pavement, outside MC's house and waited for Winder.

He of all people should have seen meaning behind the numbers, should have been able to work out what was going on. But why did Rosen make this record? And MC was the only eyewitness they had to Green's murder. More than anything, he had to find his cousin.

Drake noticed headlights as a car pulled up behind his vehicle. Winder joined Drake standing on the pavement.

'Any luck with Owens, sir?'

'He coughed to the theft of Rosen's laptop. And Valencia was looking for a data stick as well.'

A single, yellow sodium light cast a pallid glow over the backyards and lanes behind MC's house. Drake stood for a moment in the rear yard, disappointed that the darkness and the uncurtained windows meant the house was still empty. He tried the handle. It was still unlocked and they stepped inside. He hoped for any sign that suggested MC had been back, a mug with the remains of coffee or tea or a discarded takeaway, but once he'd looked around the kitchen he knew nobody had been there since his last visit.

'Gareth, you go upstairs. Check through all the cupboards and drawers. There must be something.'

'What are we looking for, boss?'

'If I knew, I'd tell you.'

Downstairs, in the room at the front, Drake sat on the sofa pushed against the wall. Across from him was a shelving unit, with slots for storage baskets and boxes. He got up and opened the first container, but it was empty. The second had a collection of DVDs which he absently moved to one side. The third was full of papers. Drake sat down and began flicking through the collection of bank and credit card statements, a P45 from the prison service, the insurance policy for MC's BMW and letters he'd received in prison from Sylvie.

Drake noticed that as the weeks passed Sylvie's handwriting deteriorated to a narrow scrawl and the length of her letters shortened from two or three pages to a couple of paragraphs. It struck Drake how helpless MC must have felt, reading the letters, knowing what was happening to his girlfriend.

At the bottom of the box there were invoices for a service to the BMW, printouts from a well-known sofa chain with prices for new furniture, and an invoice from an online electronics company. It was the description of the items sold – surveillance equipment – that caught Drake's eye. He stood up, kicking the box, which spilled its contents onto the floor, and shouted.

'Gareth, get down here. Now.'

He heard Winder's footsteps on the staircase.

'MC bought surveillance equipment.'

'What do you mean?'

'For Christ's sake, Gareth why would he need that sort of kit?'

Drake thrust the invoice towards Winder. 'Look at the details. *Recorder* and *cameras.*'

Drake started to look around the room. 'He must have some cameras hidden somewhere.'

'Did he have anywhere else? Garage or his girlfriend's place?'

'How would I know?'

'He must have the recorder somewhere.'

Drake marched out into the hallway, opening the small cupboard under the staircase. 'Any sign of anything upstairs?'

'No, nothing.'

'Have you opened every single cupboard?'

'Yes, boss.'

'Then go and do them all again.'

Drake heard Winder crashing around in the bedrooms upstairs as he stepped into the kitchen. He should start on the cupboards, but instead he stood for a moment, staring out of the window. In the dim light, he saw the brief outline of the shed roof.

He yanked open the back door and strode down the small path. Gripping the padlock in his hand, he hoped he could rip it away from the shed door without disturbing all the neighbours. He looked around the backyard for a piece of metal or something sharp that he could use as a lever, eventually continuing the search in the kitchen. From the back of a drawer he found an old kitchen knife, which he took outside, and, slotting it behind the clasp, began to pull and lever until he heard the sound of wood splitting. He gave the door a sharp kick, and the clasp and padlock fell limply to one side.

He pulled the door open and made out the outline of an old bicycle and a couple of patio chairs. As his eyes grew accustomed to the darkness he saw a grey sheet covering a box in the far end.

He reached down, removed the sheet and saw a small green light.

Drake stood immediately behind Flanagan who was sitting in front of the computer monitor, his jaw clenched. Caren came through the door into the Incident Room, her hair dishevelled and a harassed look on her face.

Drake turned towards her. 'So, what happened with Robert James?'

'Miranda Church had a fit, that's what happened. She went apeshit. Once she saw him in Vicky's room she launched herself at him. Fists flying and kicking. I've only just finished in the hospital and I haven't started an interview. She gave him a black eye and a broken nose and a cracked rib.'

Winder laughed out loud.

'Will he be okay to interview tomorrow?' Drake said.

'He's insisting on using a family solicitor from Liverpool who can't get here until mid-morning.'

'Maybe James will want to make a complaint of assault,' Winder said, a half-smile on his lips.

Caren gave him a weary look and turned to look at the screen in front of Flanagan, who cleared his throat.

'It won't be long,' Flanagan said. 'He must have rigged up the camera to the recorder in the shed. That took some planning.'

Drake squinted at the flickering monitor.

'Did you see any cameras?' Flanagan asked.

'Where would they be?' Winder squinted at the screen.

'They'd be very small.'

'Which means they could be easily hidden?'

Flanagan nodded. The image of a room with furniture filled the screen.

'That's MC's house. I'm sure of it,' Winder said.

A moment later MC walked into the room, directly into the line of the camera. He turned and looked towards the door. A figure walked in and Drake saw the smiling face of Valencia. Both men sat down, MC taking a chair with his back to the camera which must have been concealed high up on the wall. Valencia spoke first.

'I hear you've been busy.'

'Not as busy as your fucking toe rags.'

'You mean Birch, of course.'

'And Vigo. They supplied Sylvie when she was alive. It was those two arseholes that sold those drugs. And now she's dead.'

'But she was very grateful when she was alive. Very grateful. You get my meaning?'

Drake could feel his pulse pounding in his neck, more loudly with every second that passed.

'You won't get away with this. Why did you kill Green?'

'He'd become a problem. Just as you've become a problem.'

The tension turned up a couple of notches.

'I hate a grass.'

'Jesus Christ,' Drake said.

Valencia reached into his pocket and drew out a small pistol, which he pointed at MC.

'On your feet,' Valencia said.

MC stood up.

Valencia waved the gun towards the door. *'You're coming with me.'*

They watched as Valencia followed MC out of the room.

For a few seconds nobody said anything. Drake rubbed a hand over his mouth. 'We need to talk to Valencia,' he said slowly.

Drake returned to his office but his desk was chaotic – people had dumped papers all over it – and he couldn't think straight unless he could order it. Abruptly he stopped and thought about Halpin and his advice. He seized a folder of papers without checking its contents, hard enough in itself, and then he marched through the Incident Room towards the main corridors of headquarters. None of his team paid him any attention and then he found himself uncertain as to what he should be doing. So he walked briskly, determined not to make eye contact with anyone who passed him. The tension abated and, checking his watch, realised that he had managed to walk for ten minutes around headquarters, up and down three flights of stairs, without anyone noticing him.

Returning to his office, he focused on what he had to say to Lance. Drake had replied to Sian's text earlier, telling her not to expect him home until much later. He could never work out from her brief messages whether she was annoyed or just busy. He left his mobile on his desk and walked up to the senior management suite.

Once he'd finished explaining to Lance about the recording, he paused, anticipating that Lance would respond.

'I think we should arrest Valencia on suspicion of murder,' Drake said, tired of waiting.

'Don't be ridiculous.'

Momentarily Drake was nonplussed. 'But we know that Green and Mandy Beal have the same father. She'd been talking to her friends about tracing her family—'

'How the hell is that going to help us?' Lance said.

Drake gathered his thoughts, hoping he could capture the clarity he needed. 'Whoever killed Rosen was looking for something on the laptop. A piece of data. But what they don't know is that we have that data. We just couldn't work out what it could possibly be, not until the last couple of days.'

'What. The trucks and planes?'

'Yes. And one of Mandy's friends said her old laptop was missing.' Drake hesitated. 'Valencia thought Mandy, as Rosen's ex, may have had the information he needed, but she didn't. So he killed her. Green finds out and there's an argument in Green's house. Valencia sees the opportunity to tidy everything up and *bang*. He kills Green and hopes everything is done.'

Drake ran out of momentum and silence hung in the room for a few seconds.

'MC is the only eyewitness we've got,' Drake continued. 'But we can't trace him. Clearly we've got evidence to suggest that he may have been abducted, even killed by Valencia.'

'I warned you about MC. If we take this to the Crown Prosecution Service they'd think we were mad,' Lance said. 'MC'll turn up. Men like that always do.'

Drake opened his mouth to reply, but knowing that if he said something, he'd regret it. So he kept quiet, clenching his jaw in annoyance, feeling, oddly, that MC deserved to be taken seriously. At least they had a confession of some sort to the murder of Green.

'Keep focused on the codes and the connection to Loosemore and John Beltrami.' Lance leant forward, staring at Drake. 'Just imagine what evidence you'd use in any interview with Valencia.'

Drake drew a hand over his mouth, reluctant to acknowledge that the superintendent was right.

'What's the motive, Ian? There always has to be a motive.'

Drake sat in the car for a few seconds after parking on his drive. There had been normal days during the investigation, but they seemed a long time ago. His thoughts were a jumble, and he knew that he couldn't tell Sian about MC. A real sense of foreboding filled his mind as he recalled the image of Valencia pointing the gun at MC.

Sian was lying across a sofa, flicking through some papers. A pile of folders from the surgery lay strewn over the reclaimed-oak coffee table. Her blonde hair brushed the tall collar of her bold-striped cotton blouse.

'Busy day?'

Drake should have picked up the signals from the insincerity in Sian's voice, but he slumped on the sofa and then rubbed his palms over his eyes, realising how tired he felt.

'Helen and Megan asked about you earlier.' Sian made him sound like a distant uncle.

'Things are a bit hectic.'

'Tom rang as well.'

'How is he?' Drake felt a spasm of guilt that he hadn't spoken to his father for several days. He glanced at the clock on the mantelpiece, realising it was far too late to call

'He's not very well. He's feeling very tired, wretched.'

'I'll call in the morning.'

'He asked about MC, called him Moelwyn of course. He said that Auntie Gwen had called him – she was worried.'

All Drake could think about was the sight of Martin Valencia drawing a gun. The image kept repeating itself like an old-fashioned black-and-white film, replaying the same frame over and over.

'We don't know where he is,' Drake said, getting up, wanting to avoid further conversation. He returned from the kitchen, half an inch of whisky swilling around the bottom of a glass.

'How have you been coping?'

Drake was accustomed to her tone that mixed concern with medical objectivity.

'Okay.'

'I think you should make more of an effort to see the girls. They're not going to be young forever. And taking a couple of hours to see them in the evening isn't going to ruin your investigation, surely. And it might do you good.'

Drake waited for her to say *work-life balance* but she grabbed the papers on her lap and then tidied all the files on the table.

'I'm going to bed.'

Drake knew he had to sleep, but first he needed to eat and, spying the newspaper on the table, buried under Sian's files, realised that he had no choice but to complete a sudoku puzzle.

Chapter 39

At a little after eight that morning Drake stood before the Incident Room board with Lance's demand for them to establish a motive buzzing through his mind. Despite seven hours' sleep he still felt weary. He had replayed the scenario that Rosen had been killed by Green and Green had been killed by Valencia, so often that he hadn't thought about why. He had woken that morning knowing grudgingly that Lance was right.

'We don't know why?' Drake said, ignoring the puzzled look on the faces in front of him.

Howick was the first to contribute. 'You were right about the aircraft registration details, sir.'

Caren's interest was piqued and she looked over at Howick. 'What are the details?'

'There were twenty lists of codes. Like the one on the board. I've stripped away the codes relating to the vehicles from Ireland. Gareth has done work on matching the lorries to various manifests and journeys.'

Winder nodded seriously.

'All aircraft in the UK have a registration made up of an initial letter G, which we've got on fourteen of the twenty codes, followed by four letters. Perhaps it's no surprise that two of the twelve aircraft are registered to either John Beltrami or Tim Loosemore.'

'And what about the others?' Drake said.

'The prefix with an EI refers to planes registered in Ireland. The N prefix refers to the two aircraft initially registered in the US and the other two are from France.'

There was a nodding of heads once the interpretation was apparent.

'I'm waiting for confirmation about the ownership details.'

Drake knew it was progress, but wasn't certain exactly where it was taking them. 'Your turn, Gareth,' he said, still staring at the board.

Winder stood up and stepped around his desk, holding various sheets of paper in his hand.

'All the trucks that we identified from the codes in Rosen's computer have travelled across in the last twelve months on a regular basis. They all carry freight for various companies, but it's the haulage company that owns the vehicles which is of interest. It's owned jointly by Beltrami and Connors.'

'So it's giving us a link between Beltrami and Connors. It still doesn't explain the motives behind the deaths.' Drake said.

'Rosen must have been blackmailing Beltrami and Connors and Loosemore, and the whole fucking lot of them,' Winder added, sounding exasperated.

'You don't blackmail somebody like Beltrami or Connors, unless you've got insurance,' Drake said. 'And we've got these lists of letters and numbers.'

Winder raised a hand, waving the papers in the air. 'But we've got the evidence to demonstrate a connection. This is his insurance: he was keeping a record of all the lorries that came through the port with drugs or illegal immigrants or ...'

Drake began pacing in front of the board. Winder had run out of steam because there was nothing to link the codes to specific offences. Without the evidence, there was nothing they could achieve.

'If we are right that Rosen was killed by Green, then why was Green killed?'

'He knew too much,' Caren said.

Drake was the first to break the brief moment of silence that followed. 'That would certainly match Valencia's personality. But there's the connection to Mandy Beal. What if Valencia killed her and Green found out and ...'

'Maybe *she* knew too much?' Winder said.

Drake was pulling the tip of his nose, trying to work out what exactly would have been the motive for killing Mandy Beal. 'They were looking for something. Rhodri Owens was told to look for the laptop and a data stick. They must have thought she had it.'

'Who's 'they', sir?' Caren asked.

Drake rolled his eyes just as the telephone rang in his office. He hurried over and snatched up the receiver. The desk was tidy and the floor and bin reassuringly clean.

He recognised the gruff voice of Malachy O'Sullivan. 'Have you seen your emails yet?'

'No. Give me a minute …' Drake reached for the switch on the computer.

'We found the body of Paul Maguire face down in the Liffey yesterday.'

'Christ Almighty. How?'

The screensaver appeared on the monitor and Drake clicked through to his inbox.

'Shot in the head. And knee-capped for good measure.'

'What? Like the IRA did years ago?'

'That's right. Jesus, Ian, have you had that email?'

Drake clicked on O'Sullivan's message and saw the attachment.

'There's no message – just an attachment …'

'Open it. Maguire's sister flew in last night. Wanted an armed escort from the airport.'

'What for?'

The image was finally opening.

'She's got enough evidence to put Fergal Connors away for a thousand years. And she's got material you'll want to see.'

Drake heard O'Sullivan but didn't reply. He just stared at the screen.

Caren had secretly been pleased to have Drake out of the way with the door to his office firmly closed and instructions that he not be disturbed. It meant she could interview Robert James in her own time without the inspector's inevitable rudeness, but in the end she'd returned to headquarters frustrated that she'd wasted valuable time. Caren had guessed that Vicky had acquired the skills of manipulating inexperienced men from her mother. James had been saddled with a mountain of debt from regular holidays, refurbishing and redecorating Vicky's house, as well as buying her a new car. He had believed her protestations of undying love and when she had unceremoniously dumped him in favour of Frank Rosen, he had become incapable of clear thought.

The telephone rang just as Caren returned from a ten-minute lunch, where she'd bolted down a cheese sandwich that sat heavily in her stomach.

'There's someone in reception about that girl, Mandy Beal.'

Caren finished the glass of water on her desk, hoping it might help to settle her indigestion, before finding a notepad and a biro.

The receptionist pointed to a man sitting with a camera bag by his feet. Immediately he stood up and stretched out a hand.

'George Abbott,' he said, giving Caren a brief smile.

Abbott had the remains of acne under a wispy beard that was intended to make him look older but that succeeded only in accentuating his youthfulness. Caren guessed eighteen, maybe twenty at the most.

'I've been away on holiday in Malta with my parents. We live a couple of doors down from Mandy Beal. We heard that she'd been killed when we got back yesterday. Terrible, really terrible. She was so nice. Only, I know this might be nothing, but I saw her a couple of times with this guy.'

Caren led Abbott into an adjacent interview room.

He put the camera equipment bag onto the table. He was wearing a short-sleeved grey shirt under a blue gilet of heavily quilted material, its collar lined with leather.

'I saw him leave the house with her one morning.'

'Can you give me a description?'

'I saw him again with her a couple of days later.'

'Where was that?'

'In that fancy supermarket in Menai Bridge.'

'What, inside?'

'No, I was outside in the car park.'

'In your car?'

'Yes. I was working.'

'Working?'

'I'm training to be paparazzi.'

Caren knew that by now Drake would have been drumming his fingers on the desk, wanting to tell this time-waster to leave.

'What do you mean?'

'I'm doing a photographic course. And I want to go and take photographs of celebrities and important people. Really great pictures can earn a lot of money in the glossy magazines.'

Caren hoped that Abbott hadn't heard the gurgling sound from her stomach, so she decided it was time to stop humouring him and bring the interview to an end.

'Who were you hoping to photograph?'

'I know one of the staff there and they told me they were expecting a royal visitor.'

Caren nodded.

'And did you see Mandy?'

'Yes.'

'I'll get one of the detective constables to come and take a statement from you.'

Caren stood up.

'But don't you want to see the photographs?' Abbott said reaching for his case.

Drake had downloaded the large file onto his computer and began reading through the papers that Maguire had taken a long time to collect. There were statements and memoranda that should have been destroyed years before and Drake realised that this had been his attempt at a posthumous revenge. People like Connors didn't respond to threats and Drake doubted whether Maguire had even tried to blackmail his boss, an act which would probably have meant something worse than death.

Emails with references to Richard Class had been highlighted in yellow and, from what Drake could recollect, they tied into the dates of the activity involved with Lyfon Pharmaceuticals. Superintendent Adams would salivate at the prospect of threading all these emails into his papers. Perhaps there would be a realistic prospect of the CPS authorising a prosecution. There were dates of regular 'shipments' through Holyhead. Drake tried focusing on the evidence. He had three murders to solve. Three deaths that needed evidence to satisfy the prosecutors. Valencia was the killer of course, but without MC he just couldn't prove anything. Everything else was guesswork. There had to be a motive.

Drake tilted his head to one side as he began looking through the various photographs of Richard Class. In the first, a tall, thin girl with small breasts and erect nipples sat naked over Richard Class's buttocks. Drake could see the hairs on his chest and the outline of a paunch taking shape. His hands were on the girl's thighs. In the final couple of photographs, Drake could only guess that Class was still enjoying himself, as he couldn't see the politician's face, which was buried between the legs of a shorter Chinese girl.

By the end of the morning Drake had read enough and called Mallin.

'How did she get all this material?' Drake asked.

'Maguire sent her copies of everything he could get his hands on. He worked for Connors for five years in the club. Nobody noticed him. He was the sort of semi-invisible person the likes of Connors take for granted.'

'Where were the photographs taken?' Drake said.

'We can't tell. But we think it was at a nightclub years ago. The girls are all part of a Chinese prostitute ring that was active in the city years ago. They targeted Americans mostly, here on business or on golfing holidays.'

'So what's happening now?'

'Garda Commissioner's happy. And the DPP. Both so fucking happy.'

'What changed?' Drake said. It had been on his mind all morning as he'd read the papers.

'What do you mean?' There was uncertainty in Mallin's voice.

'What changed that made Connors have to kill Maguire?'

'Who knows? Who cares? He's going down for years.'

Drake still had a nagging sense that there was something he'd missed.

Chapter 40

Caren barged into Drake's room, Winder and Howick following in her slipstream.

Drake looked up from his desk: there was tiredness in his eyes that Caren hadn't seen before.

'We've got an eyewitness,' she said. 'I've got photographs.'

She held up the camera's memory card.

'What do you mean?'

'I've just interviewed a geek who takes photographs. He wants to be paparazzi *when he qualifies*. I'll show you.' She turned on her heels and pushed past Winder and Howick, before almost knocking over an office chair. She pressed the memory stick into her computer and clicked until the first image appeared on the screen.

Drake stood behind her, Winder and Howick to one side. Pictures of expensive cars and high-value SUVs filled the screen.

'Where were these taken?' Drake said.

'At that pricey supermarket in Menai Bridge on Anglesey. He was waiting to take photographs of the royals. Apparently he's friends with one of the staff who tips him off when they're likely to arrive. The manager always knows in advance, because the Royal Protection officers contact him. And they clear a parking space right next to the door.'

Caren scrolled through the images.

'Jesus, how many pictures does this guy need?' Winder said.

'All he needs is one picture and he could make a shed load of money,' Howick added.

Caren clicked through the images, still thinking about the enthusiasm on Abbott's face. 'That's what he said.'

After a couple of minutes she stopped. A Range Rover pulled into a parking slot and the still photographs ran into each other.

'He thought it was *them* because of the Range Rover.'

'None of the Royal Protection Squad around though,' Howick said.

Caren nodded. The excitement building in her voice. 'Take a look at these.'

Martin Valencia emerged from the driver's side of the Range Rover. From the passenger side Mandy Beal appeared, looked around and then pushed the door closed. She tossed her hair to one side and then threaded her arm under Valencia's.

'When were these taken?' Drake said.

'Two days before she was killed. Abbott went on holiday then for a couple of weeks. And when he got back he heard about Mandy's death. And he'd seen Valencia leaving Mandy's house one morning.'

Drake stepped over to the board and tapped the image of Valencia. 'So now we have evidence to link him to the Beal murder. And if only we could find MC.' He banged the board with his fist.

'Do we arrest Valencia?' Winder asked.

'We've missed something that ties everything together. Why kill Mandy Beal?' Drake peered at the board.

'Valencia was looking for her laptop. Maybe he thought that Rosen had given her something like a file or picture, maybe, or even a video,' Caren said, wanting to make her contribution. 'Maybe there was something incriminating that he wanted to dispose of.'

'I agree,' Drake said. 'Let's go through everything again. We've missed something.'

'And Valencia?' Winder said, a tone of developing disappointment in his voice.

'I'll talk to Superintendent Lance later,' Drake said, turning to face the team. 'We've got all the papers to go through again.'

Winder was convinced they should be arresting Valencia.

They had the evidence linking him to Mandy Beal, as well as the connection to MC and Green. It would only be a matter of time until forensics would dig something up. He glanced over at Howick and watched as his colleague stood up and tried doing some exercises to his back. Winder turned his attention back to the flickering images on the screen, convinced that there was nothing to be gained by revisiting the CCTV coverage. By midday his stomach grumbled and he turned to Howick.

'Lunch?' Winder said.

Howick glanced over at Drake's office, but the door was firmly shut. 'Ten minutes.'

The canteen was quiet and they took their trays to a table at the far end.

'Anything?' Winder said.

Howick chewed on a sandwich. 'Nothing. We've gone over all of this before.'

'I know. There's something not right. We should be arresting Valencia now and banging him up. The CPS are bloody spineless.'

Howick nodded slowly. Winder continued. 'If we don't lock him up now then he'll ...' He ran out of something useful to say and started on a cheese sandwich.

After fifteen minutes Howick drew back his shirt sleeve and checked the time.

'We're entitled to a lunch break,' Winder said.

Howick gave him a weak smile.

Drake spent the first half an hour preparing his desk. He placed the papers he wanted to read in a pile on the bookcase and then sat back, admiring the rows of neatly stacked Post-it notes. After carefully reading them, he divided them into piles, tearing up those in one pile and discarding them in the bin. Then he created a clear space in his desk and then started reading.

If he was wrong and there was nothing new, then he faced the task of persuading Lance that they had to arrest Valencia. But he could hear the reservations and the comments about the motive. But with a man like Valencia maybe there was no motive and perhaps he simply enjoyed killing. But he reckoned that explaining that to Thorsen, even if he could persuade Lance, was going to be impossible.

He decided to start with Rosen's bank statements and he found himself approving of the order and system he had used to file and record his financial affairs. Then he reached for the credit card statements, hoping that Rosen would have used the same cross-referenced order.

A couple of hours passed as he ran his fingers through the various pages. He read the entries for the cost of repairs to Rosen's car and the crate of wine brought from an online wine seller. Then a single entry for a payment to a company struck him as out of place, so he flicked through each month and, satisfied that it was a one-off, took another half an hour to establish if Winder or Howick had identified the recipient. When he couldn't find any reference to RacingStar, Drake sat back, hoping he hadn't wasted more time. But the name niggled and on impulse he googled it.

The first entry took him to a company offering cheap websites. He stared at the screen before surfing through the pages, wondering why Rosen had paid an internet company. The receptionist put him through to the Technical Support department and Drake listened to some soothing orchestra music as he waited.

'I'll need to check out that I can give you this information,' the man said, once Drake had explained his enquiry.

'I'll wait.'

After a couple of minutes the music stopped and he heard another voice, older this time. 'I'm Malcolm Coles, the senior technical manager. How do we know that you are who you say you are?'

'What's your email?'

Once Drake emailed Coles with Rosen's death certificate and a standard notification from the WPS, he knew he'd have to wait for the information. He reached over for the next file and started reading. It was the ferry company's HR file and the juvenile gratification at the memory of annoying Mortlake was broken when the telephone rang.

'Frank Rosen bought a domain name from us last year,' Coles said.

'What do you mean?'

'He bought a domain name. And paid in advance for two years' hosting.'

'What are the details?'

'I've emailed you.'

The line went dead and Drake hoped that this was something that justified the time he'd spent on the task that afternoon. His inbox pinged and he clicked it open. He read the simple three-line email and shouted for Caren.

'Why would Rosen need a website?'

Caren stepped into his room.

'What's the website address?' Winder said, through the open door.

'www.bwthyn1234.co.uk,' Drake said, forwarding Winder the email.

Drake left his room, ushering Caren out until they stood by Winder's desk. After a couple of minutes he raised his head. 'Site is behind a password.'

'There's a password on the email.'

Drake folded his arms and stared over at the board. 'What could Rosen possibly need with a website?' Drake felt excitement building in his chest.

A couple of clicks later the screen filled with various boxes and columns with messages about updates and the latest version of plug-ins for the website.

'Easy,' Winder said. 'Now let's see what you've got.'

He clicked on various tabs on the left-hand column and moved to a section called 'media gallery'. A row of entries showed up on the screen.

'Bloody hell,' Winder said.

'Well, what is it?' Drake asked.

'This could be what you're looking for.'

'Just fucking well tell us.'

Drake's swearing had the effect of stunning everyone into a momentary silence.

'There must be twenty voice files here. These are tape recordings of something. I'll click on the first.'

Drake stared at the screen; a voice soon broke the silence.

'Turn up the heating Frank.'

'Okay, okay.'

Sound of coughing and spluttering.

'Fuck's sake, Frank.'

Then the sound of a door opening.

'I don't know how this works ...'

Sound of metal squeaking.

'When's the stuff arriving?'

'You leave all that to us.'

The final voice slurred badly.

Drake didn't recognise all the voices on the tape but wanted to believe that he'd heard the voices of Loosemore and John Beltrami exchanging banter about the previous night in the Blue Parrot. He pulled his arms tight into his body and thought about whether this was going to give them the motive they needed.

'How long does this last?'

Winder squinted at the screen. 'This is twenty minutes and the rest are about the same – some longer.'

'I want them divided into five. That's four each and then we listen to them and make notes. I want to know if you can identify voices, names and dates. Anything really.'

Back in his office Drake sat heavily in his chair while he waited for Winder to distribute the various voice files around the team.

By the end of the afternoon the recordings were swimming around Drake's mind and he needed a break. He'd missed lunch but knew that to concentrate that afternoon, he'd have to eat something. So he left for the cafeteria and found a curling tuna sandwich and a cake called a millionaire shortbread, which got him thinking about Beltrami and Loosemore. And that millionaires were just like everyone else, greedy and jealous and risk takers. He justified to himself the ten minutes he spent on the sudoku as being necessary for his mind to get him back into the right routine.

Once they'd all finished, Drake stood facing the team. He tugged at the double cuffs on his shirt and then ran a finger around his waist band. He nodded at Howick who spent ten minutes summarising the recordings he'd listened to. Rosen seemed to be forcing whoever was listening into a discussion about the delivery of cocaine or heroin. On a couple of occasions there'd been talk about the delivery from 'our friends across the pond' and then flights had to be delayed and there was controversy and some arguments. Rosen was the only one that sounded sober. Winder had the same pattern to the conversations he'd listened to. It was always the same: Rosen getting his listener to confirm things that he must have known. Drake kept nodding his head as Caren confirmed much the same as Winder and Howick.

'Rosen wanted out,' Caren said.

'That's obvious,' Drake said. 'The recordings I

listened to are the same, except for one thing. There's something happening on the twenty-seventh.'

'It's the perfect motive,' Drake said.

Lance tapped a biro on the papers on his desk.

'We're transcribing the recordings as we speak but it's clear that Rosen wanted to stop flying for these guys. Obviously he wanted to get out and enjoy his money.'

'And Valencia didn't want any of it.'

'Started going on about respect and loyalty and family.'

'Jesus, these guys watch too many of the *Godfather* films.' Lance steepled his hands and hesitated.

'And Saturday's the twenty-seventh,' Drake said. 'Connors and Beltrami have three trailers booked on the early morning ferry. We've got enough to charge Valencia and Beltrami with conspiracy to murder. We should arrest them now.'

Lance put up a hand to stop Drake.

'Set up an operation to follow them off the boat. You've got thirty-six hours.'

'But,' Drake could see the certainty of an arrest disappearing. 'We might be losing the only opportunity.'

'It's an order, Inspector.'

Chapter 41

Caren looked at the ferry as it approached the berth, bow first. Gantries were dotted all over the hard standing, bathing the loading area with a harsh white light. A truck from Poland pulled up behind a lorry from Hungary, parked under one of the metal towers. The driver climbed out, stretched his back, waved his hands slowly in the air, relieving tired muscles, and then walked slowly towards the drivers' lounge tucked into the concourse. Caren's unmarked car was an old Ford that O'Sullivan told her was the best the Garda could arrange at short notice. She got out, felt the stiffness in the small of her back; an ache drilled deep into her right shoulder too.

She cursed Drake. Drake had narrowed his eyes when she'd suggested that having an officer on board with the suspect cargo might not be needed. He'd given her a look of exasperation that could be so annoying. On the crossing to Dublin she'd tried sleeping, but the sound of the engine and the creaking of the thin cabin walls had kept her awake. Caren had been met by O'Sullivan when she'd arrived the previous evening and after a briefing from Mallin she'd tried and failed to sleep on the narrow camp bed O'Sullivan had organised. He'd woken her before five and they'd travelled together to Dublin Port.

She stared into the gloom, hoping to recognise the plates of the three trucks. Once the ferry was near the berth she watched as the tugs raced over the tarmac towards the ramp and men in high-visibility jackets milled around. More lorries arrived and her concentration sharpened as she watched the trucks jerking to a halt. With an hour until departure she started to feel apprehensive that perhaps something had gone wrong and that the lorries wouldn't arrive and that the whole exercise would be a complete waste of time. She looked at her watch: another pang of worry. Then a lorry passed her, she recognised the plates and her pulse quickened. The mobile vibrated in her pocket, the message from O'Sullivan reading – *first one*. Another ten minutes passed until the second lorry arrived, followed quickly by the third. She left the car and wandered around the tarmac, hoping to catch sight of the drivers, so she weaved in between the various lorries until she almost bumped into one of the drivers as he lit a cigarette. He gave her a hard look and after mumbling an apology she pretended to be passing the time, stretching her legs. But she'd fixed the man's face in her mind. He had three days' stubble, thick, dark hair to his shoulders and eyes too close together – driver one.

In the adjacent lane, driver two was still in his cab, his head thumping to the music from the earphones. All she could see was the reflection of the cabin light off his bald head so she walked on, fearing that someone might think she was acting oddly. Luck was on her side with driver three. He was checking around the vehicle for loose brake connections. He wore a pair of baggy jeans and a thick fleece that Caren could see, even in the half-light, was streaked with dirt.

She carried on down the various lanes of lorries. Behind one she heard the sound of a driver urinating; cigarette smoke drifted in the night air. Eventually she returned to her car and watched as lorries, some hauling trailers, streamed off the ferry, followed by a mini bus and then cars. A tall man wearing a hard hat began directing traffic and soon she was driving down into the ferry, passing the gesticulating arms of the deck officer.

She found the bar near the lounge that was reserved for long-distance drivers and settled to read a paper. Driver three arrived first and sat in the lounge sipping a coffee and soon enough drivers two and one arrived. It was difficult to tell if they knew each other from where Caren sat. They sat separately, watching the television in the corner. Caren tapped out a message on her mobile and waited. She thought about eating when the smell of fried bacon drifted through from the cafeteria. When her mobile beeped she read the message and left for customer services.

Seymour was waiting for her when she arrived and he took her through into an office behind the bridge. A man with a brown T-shirt with 'New York' printed on the front sat before a computer screen.

'I was only told about *you* five minutes ago,' Seymour said edgily.

'I need access to the CCTV footage.'

'This is Mark Halton,' Seymour said. 'He's part of the night crew.'

Seymour said to Halton, 'Mark, I need you to help DS Waits.'

Caren turned to Seymour. 'And we need the car deck monitored.'

'The deck officer will cover the lower deck and the bosun is on the top deck.'

'We need two of your crew on the lower car deck for the entire sailing.'

'I can't do that. We simply don't have the manpower.'

'Wake someone from the day crew.'

Seymour glared at her. 'This could cause me big problems. I've got regulations to keep.'

'And we've got a murderer to catch.'

Caren sat down, rather pleased that it had been easy to get her own way. Whatever Drake had said to him must have worked. She started explaining in clear terms to Halton what exactly she needed.

Drake slept badly and when he woke his pulse began to hammer, so he got up without disturbing Sian. He'd woken twice – or maybe three times – in the middle of the night, noticed the time before cursing his mind for forcing him to wakefulness.

He sat at the kitchen table, a mug full of instant coffee in front of him, and his mobile by its side. Once Caren had texted he made various calls before showering. Sian was awake when he finished. He reached for a dark-navy suit and a cream shirt. He hesitated, not really knowing where he might be at the end of the day or whether he should wear a suit or not but indecision was replaced by a determination that Beltrami and Loosemore and Valencia had to be caught. He chose a heavily striped tie to match the shirt.

Breakfast passed in blur with Drake thinking all the time that he had to get to headquarters, even though he knew he'd have to wait. In the car he glanced at the clock on the dashboard: Caren would be on the ferry, waiting for it to depart. He drove to headquarters, barely concentrating on the traffic.

Lance was standing by the board in the Incident Room, which immediately put Drake on edge.

'Have you heard from Caren?' Lance asked.

'Everything went as planned.'

'No one else knows?'

Drake nodded, wondering whether he'd ever discover what Lance was doing.

They turned and blankly stared at the crowded board. Drake looked at his watch again, but only ten minutes had elapsed since he'd last read the time.

'How long will it take you to get to Holyhead?' Lance said.

'A little over an hour, depends on the traffic ...' Drake glanced towards his office. There was a sudoku in the drawer of his desk, which would be bound to calm him down, but with Lance there he couldn't get to it. His eyes fell on the notes arranged on his desk: after today was over he would sweep them all into the bin and start a fresh notebook for Halpin. He might even tell Halpin that he was okay and coping and that the rituals weren't suffocating him any longer. But he fretted about what Halpin would include in his report and then how the WPS and Superintendent Wyndham Price might react.

Lance looked at his watch. 'So you've got a couple of hours?'

Drake had already decided to leave as soon as Howick and Winder had arrived.

'Important case this, Ian,' Lance said. 'Keep me informed,' he added, as he made for the door.

'Of course, sir,' Drake said.

Howick bowled into the Incident Room just before Winder, who was clutching a coffee mug in one hand and a sausage roll in the other.

'Good morning, boss,' Howick said.

'Dave,' Drake said, before nodding to Winder. 'Let's go,' Drake said, before either man could sit down.

'But ... we've still got ...' Howick said.

Winder put the coffee onto the table and threw the paper bag with the remains of his breakfast into the bin.

Drake tried playing a U2 CD, but not even Bono's voice could make it a beautiful day so he settled for silence instead and thought about his father. As a child he'd been to Ireland for a holiday. He could remember his father fussing over filling the boot of the car with luggage and how his mother's impatience would be tested.

The journey to Holyhead passed quickly; occasionally he caught a glimpse of Winder's car in his rear-view mirror, and eventually he pulled up outside the same café where he'd received the first text from his cousin. They had an hour to kill and today, even bacon and eggs seemed appealing. Winder and Howick tried making small talk, but Drake had no interest in the prospects for Manchester United winning the FA Cup. He sent a text to Sian, but she didn't reply so he stepped outside for privacy and called his father.

'How are you?'

'All right,' his father managed. 'The bottom field needs to be fenced again this year and the ditch could be drained at the same time.'

Drake wanted to say that he'd come and help one weekend, but he didn't know what to say, so he mumbled something about being in Holyhead on business and that he'd call later.

Back in the cafeteria a waitress arrived with the coffee and the food he'd ordered.

'Is it time, boss?' Howick said.

Drake looked at his watch. As Lance had told them not to call at the town's police station, nor at the Special Branch office in the terminal, Drake decided that sitting in the café was preferable to sitting in their cars. 'Another half an hour.'

The time dragged until eventually they made their way down to the port. Passes were waiting for them at the security gate and Drake drove through the terminal entrance and over the link bridge. They drew up by an old building, near the admiralty arch built to commemorate a royal visit in 1821. Behind them they heard the muffled announcements from the public address system of the fast ferry as it lumbered its way out of the harbour on a delayed departure.

Forty minutes to go.

Chapter 42

Seagulls were pulling rubbish from an open bin near Drake's car. The air brakes of a lorry hissed as it stopped a few metres away. The salty bacon dried his lips and he regretted not having any water. He undid his top shirt button and adjusted his position in the seat.

Thirty minutes to go.

Drake watched Howick manoeuvring his car over the concourse before pulling up by the side of a minibus. Drake sat and waited. The ferry steamed into view and slowly began a broad sweep as she entered the berth, stern first.

Fifteen minutes.

Cramp sent a jolt of pain up his leg and he wanted to get out and walk around, but he thought better of it. Activity built on the concourse as the ferry approached until eventually Drake saw the stern doors open. He tried to bite back any trace of anxiety when he dialled Lance.

'Ship's arrived.'

'Loosemore and Beltrami haven't moved. And there's no sign of Valencia.'

Drake had been surprised when Lance had told him that three teams of plainclothes officers from Southern Division had been outside the men's homes since the early hours. It only confirmed to Drake that Lance wasn't to be trusted.

The first lorries headed off the ship and over the concourse towards the terminal exit. It crossed Drake's mind that there'd be a problem if the trucks were stopped at customs. But Lance had probably managed that as well, he concluded.

Another half a dozen trucks emerged from the ferry. Drake strained his eyes to see if he could spot Caren. Her silence was disconcerting. He checked again the registration plates of the trucks they needed to follow. Then he saw the first and he could hear his pulse beating in his head, pounding until the blood seemed to boil. A text from Caren startled him – *second on way* – and then he noticed the Dublin plates crossing the concourse, followed by a silver BMW.

The third truck followed very soon, Caren immediately behind it.

He followed them through the port, praying that the port police wouldn't stop them. Howick pulled in behind him. He let out a long lungful of breath when the vehicles passed through the check points undisturbed.

After negotiating the bridge and the roundabout on the outskirts of Holyhead the trucks fell into a line, keeping a safe distance apart.

Drake picked up the mobile on the cradle in the dashboard and dialled Caren.

'No problems, sir. Nobody went into the car deck or near the trucks while we were sailing. Two of the drivers ate an enormous meal of steak and chips and another played poker for two hours.'

The trucks kept a steady sixty miles an hour as they drove over the island towards the mainland. Occasionally trucks overtook them and Drake and Howick varied places and then fell back and turned off, only to circle and rejoin the A55. As they approached the Menai Strait the pace slowed and the traffic backed up, until it thinned out to cross the bridge in single file. Drake tapped his fingers on the wheel as he crawled along, sending texts to Caren and Howick in the queue. Lance called him again when the trucks were through the tunnels at Penmaenmawr and nearing Llandudno. Drake felt apprehension tugging at his mind. They powered on past Abergele and then inland away from the coast. Twenty minutes passed and they were approaching the border, and Lance would soon have to start making calls to counterparts in England.

Drake was at the front of the queue when the first of

the trucks indicated left off the dual carriageway. He followed, hoping that the indicating wasn't a mistake. He pulled into the off slip ahead of the truck, which appeared to be staying on the A55 until the last minute. Then, it turned in and slowed dramatically. Drake accelerated towards the roundabout at the top and on impulse turned left into the industrial park, a decision rewarded seconds later when he saw the first lorry following him.

He sped on until he found himself driving past one industrial unit after another. All around him were white vans and trucks pulling trailers so he slowed his speed just as the first truck indicated right for a junction. His mobile beeped and Drake read the text – *With them, boss.'* Drake pulled up before turning around and retracing his steps. He drove down the section of the industrial estate, watching Caren's car in the distance.

He hadn't realised how large the estate was until the wagons had negotiated four different junctions and then slowed by a collection of storage units. The trucks came to a halt and Drake jerked his car to a standstill a safe distance away. He could see Caren and Winder's cars parked on the pavement down past the entrance to the units where the lorries were manoeuvring slowly. In the rear-view mirror he spotted the van from the dog section slowing.

Drake dialled Lance. 'They've all stopped at a unit in the Deeside Industrial Park.'

'What's your location?'

Drake scanned for a notice board. 'Zone T12.'

'We'll check it out.'

Then Caren called him. 'What's happening, boss?'

Drake glanced over at the trucks. The first had completed a reversing manoeuvre to the concrete platform and the open doors of the industrial unit.

'We wait,' he said.

He called Lance. 'Anything on the location, sir?'

'Nothing yet. But Loosemore and Beltrami are on

the move.

'Drake felt a trickle of sweat beading under his armpit and he hoped the feeling of anxiety that was turning to real fear wouldn't last.

The second lorry had almost finished parking.

Fifteen minutes passed. He clicked on the radio, turned the sound down until it was barely audible and then switched it off. He opened the window, allowing fresh air into the car. He was convinced his breath must stink, so he rummaged through the glove compartment, hoping to find some chewing gum but only discovered a couple of dried-up wine gums.

Then another fifteen minutes had ticked by.

His mobile broke the silence.

'We've lost them,' Lance said. 'There was a car crash on the A55 and they managed to slip ahead of the cars following them.'

'Bloody hell. Any sign of them from the CCTV?'

'We're working on it.'

Twenty minutes later Drake knew something wasn't right. They should have arrived. The third truck had finished and its driver was now swinging the rear doors open.

He dialled Lance again, who picked up after the first ring. 'There's no sign of Loosemore or Beltrami, Ian. And the units are part of a storage and warehousing business. We haven't been able to find anything about the owners.'

'We can't wait any longer.'

Drake started the engine.

'I agree,' Lance said

Drake wound down the window and waved to the others as he powered towards the entrance. The trucks had been parked alongside each other, their tailgates open and the backs reversed towards the loading platform. He skidded to a halt and watched as Winder and Howick pulled up alongside him, both officers racing to the main entrance and leaving their car doors open. Caren drove past them beyond

Winder's Mondeo and the car jolted as she parked. The dog handlers' white van pulled up behind her. Another few seconds passed and a BMW squealed to a halt near them. Immediately Drake was on guard but, then, driver and passenger emerged wearing the standard WPS-issue holstered small arms around their waist and warrant cards held high. They shouted. 'Inspector Drake. WPS special operations unit, Cardiff.'

They ran to the main building and followed the SOU officers who kicked open the unlocked doors. They found Winder and Howick handcuffing three drivers and two other youths; officers with dogs panting at their leashes rummaged through the first lorry. A small forklift was still running and Drake reached over and turned off the engine. He walked over to an office nearby and pushed open the door. There was a desk and some filing cabinets and three wooden chairs. Within a few minutes the dog handlers returned.

'Nothing, sir,' one of the officers said. 'But that doesn't mean it's conclusive.'

It wasn't the answer Drake wanted to hear. The SOU officers returned with Winder and Howick.

'The trucks are full of toys and garden equipment. A full search will take hours,' Winder said.

Drake took a couple of steps towards a window and looked into the main part of the warehouse, unease crawling through his mind.

'What do we do next, boss?' Caren said.

Drake kicked a table leg.

Chapter 43

Drake drank heavily from a plastic water bottle.

'Where have Loosemore and Beltrami gone?' Caren said, standing by his side.

'There's no sign of them.' Drake wiped his lips with the back of his hand.

'But Rosen was so clear about the date.'

Drake looked over at the officers working through the pallets of children's toys and plastic tents and garden implements. With every minute that past, desperation deepened: what if the search wasn't successful and the failure of the entire operation was down to him? He thought about Valencia's voice on the recording. Maybe he knew that Rosen was recording their conversations. And perhaps the whole fiasco in the industrial estate had been one enormous tip off designed to divert their attention.

He threw the bottle into a bin by his feet and marched out to his car, talking to Caren who followed behind him. 'Let's go back to headquarters.'

'What about the drivers?'

'Seize their mobiles and arrest them on suspicion of trafficking. Get them into the custody suite where they speak to no one.'

Caren started to protest. 'But—'

'I don't want them talking to anyone until we've worked out what's going on here.'

Caren nodded and signalled to Howick and Winder.

Drake started the car and it skidded away too quickly. A dark, sullen mood enveloped him. There had to be an explanation and he had to find it. He was certain that Valencia was involved and that he was behind the killings. But without evidence there was nothing he could do and a sense of helplessness started to throttle his mind, stopping him from thinking in straight lines. He accelerated hard down the A55 westwards towards headquarters. He ignored the speedometer, but instinct told him to slow the car as he reached the turn-off for Colwyn Bay.

After parking he marched up to the Incident Room. There was a dull pain at the corners of his temple so he darted into the kitchen and drank a glass of water. The Incident Room was empty. Tranquil. He stood by the board, staring at it, forcing his mind to think.

It was the twenty-seventh.

The month after Rosen had made the tapes so it *had* to be the right date.

Valencia was bringing in a large consignment through the port in the wagons owned by Connors. Then he stopped and thought about the possibility that they'd followed the wrong lorries or that they'd got the wrong freight company. But Howick had checked out all the freight companies for all the sailings on the twenty-seventh.

He had to check. Howick had been sloppy recently. Sitting at his desk, he riffled through the papers until he found the details. But it took him back to what he knew. The only consignment for the twenty-seventh had been the trucks they'd followed that morning. He blanked out the telephone ringing in the Incident Room. He had to think. He shut out the noise from the rest of the building. *Maybe they were flying the drugs in, but without Rosen they had no pilot.*

He stood up, paced around, and then walked back out into the Incident Room.

The images of Rosen and Mandy and Green peered down at him. MC's photograph was pinned to the bottom corner. He had a narrow smile and intense eyes. The image of Valencia drawing a pistol in MC's house sent a shiver through Drake.

Maybe there was another ferry route that Connors and Valencia were using and they'd – *he'd* – wrongly assumed it was through Holyhead. Back in his office he googled the details of all the ferry operators from Ireland to the UK. A hectic few minutes of clicking took him to the website of a ferry company with a sailing from Dublin to Liverpool that arrived that evening. He checked his watch and realised they had over two hours until the ship docked. His mouth was dry and his chest was rigid with tension. The possibility of an informer struck him and he stopped and stared at the Post-it notes, his mind urging him to tidy and reorganise. Then he remembered how Lance had insisted he take over being the SIO and that everything went through his office. Drake decided that he was insane to think of Lance being involved and that there had to be another explanation.

He found the contact telephone number for the port manager in Liverpool. He stood up when the voice asked him to wait for the third time.

'Sorry, what was it you wanted again?'

'What's your name?' He raised his voice.

'Meg.'

'Well, Meg. This is an urgent police matter. Get me the port manager now or I'll arrest you for obstruction.' Drake dearly wanted to shout.

The line was quiet before Drake heard another frightened voice.

'How can I help?' The man sounded young and he had a broad Scouse accent.

'I need you to email me the inventory for the ferry that left Dublin this morning. And I want it done now. Is that understood?'

'And how do I know—'

'Don't give me any of that bullshit. Just call Northern Division headquarters and ask for me.' Drake dictated the number and slumped back in his chair.

He heard a noise in the Incident Room and saw Caren's face at his door.

'Everything taken care of?' Drake said without enthusiasm.

She stepped into the room and sat down. 'They were complaining like hell.'

Drake shrugged. 'There's a ferry from Dublin en route to Liverpool. We might have got it wrong about them using Holyhead.'

'But the connection to the crew …'

'I know. But …'

'They could be flying the drugs in. They could have another pilot lined up.'

Drake stared at her, realising that he had to check. He reached for the telephone and punched in the number of the flying club but the call rang out. As he waited Drake's mind ticked over the options. The drugs had to be coming in somewhere. Then, as he replaced the receiver, he thought of Caren's last comment.

Pilot.

It kept repeating over and over until he knew the answer. And then the image of Jade Beltrami smiling at him in the conference room came vividly to mind and he slammed his hand on the desk.

'That bloody bitch.'

Caren frowned and, startled by his behaviour, she moved in her chair.

He scoured the papers for a telephone number, growling at Caren's offer of assistance. Then he grabbed the handset again and punched in the numbers. The call was over quickly and he made a second. He almost threw the handset down and then turned to look at Caren.

'We had two visits from Jade Beltrami with her *clients* about the investigation and she was with that barrister. Guy with the expensive suit,' Drake said, his thoughts unordered. 'And she asked Thorsen to review the case. Damn.'

Caren looked bewildered.

'And each time she learnt more about the case,' Drake said.

'Do you mean?'

'Those two calls. She's a qualified flying instructor.

And she's got a plane registered in her own name. Damn it, she was right under our noses.' He slammed the other hand onto the desk.

'And do you remember talking to Beltrami about the second reference – the one for Daz Green?' Caren said.

Drake was standing now, hand on hips.

'I was convinced he didn't recognise it at first. Then he must have realised it was Jade's handwriting,' Caren added.

'You're right, you're right.'

'So where are they landing?'

'They must be flying into RAF Mona,' Drake said, reaching for his car keys.

'Too risky. You know what Special Branch in the port at Holyhead are like about the paperwork.'

They exchanged a look of shared suspicion.

'Do you think someone at SB is involved?' Caren said.

'It would make sense of all this secrecy with Lance.'

Drake reached for the car keys and strode for the door. 'You follow me once you've checked out the inventories from the ferry to Liverpool.'

He was out of the door before Caren had a chance to reply.

Drake blasted the car horn and screamed obscenities at a bus that pulled out in front of him just as he left headquarters. Ten minutes later he was driving on the outside lane of the dual carriageway, flashing his headlights at the cars ahead of him, nudging the Alfa to a hundred miles an hour. He guessed it would take him another forty minutes to reach RAF Mona. He dismissed the idea of calling ahead; he'd had enough of things not going to plan. He hoped the patrol car in the opposite lane would ignore him and even if they didn't, by the time they'd have turned round he'd be onto the island.

Approaching the bridge the traffic slowed to single file but soon he accelerated again. The car shook as he raced down the long, straight section of road for the turning he needed. At the junction he had to slow the car but the adrenaline was still hammering from the pace of his driving. *Another five minutes* he said to himself. It would be dark in a couple of hours so time was against him. There'd been an urgency in Valencia's voice on the tapes, a sense of purpose. Nearing the airfield he looked up into the sky, hoping that he might spot a plane about to land. But maybe they'd already landed and left and an unshakable doubt gripped him, that they'd done everything wrong so far.

He parked by the entrance alongside a couple of cars that he didn't recognise and the anxiety returned. He ran to the building, but it was empty, and then he emerged on the other side and saw a car in the distance in the hangar. He sprinted over the grass and tarmac, his lungs burning in his chest. He reached the hangar door and almost fell, gasping for breath. A van covered in the livery of an electrical contractor was parked near the door and two men looked up at Drake from beneath the engine cover of a light aircraft.

He bent double, his hands on his knees, before running back to the control building. This time the stitch in the right side of his body throbbed but he carried on before pushing open the door and running up the stairs. Halfway up he had to stop and draw breath. At the top he pushed open the door and found a young man sitting on a small chair, his feet up on a desk, reading a car magazine.

'Are you in charge?' Drake managed between gasps for breath.

The man hauled his feet off the table and squinted at Drake's warrant card.

'Are you expecting a flight from Dublin?'

'Nothing. I'm packing up once this training flight is finished.'

'So what happens if a plane was flying at this time of the day?'

The man peered out of the window of the control tower. 'But it's going to be dark soon.'

'What happens then?'

'They'd have to divert to RAF Valley.'

'What, the RAF base?'

'Yes. We haven't got lights on this runway at night.'

Drake peered out, hoping he could see something.

'Or they go to Caernarfon,' the man said.

Chapter 44

Drake stood by the bottom of the control tower, pondering. He thought he heard the sound of a light aircraft approaching and he lifted his head and watched as the small plane dipped towards the runway, the wheels hitting the ground with a squeal.

He fished out his mobile from his jacket pocket.

'Caren. Anything on the ferry?' he said.

'Just finished, nothing.'

'Nothing here either. They might be flying into RAF Valley.' He walked back to his car. 'It could be the perfect cover.'

'They land at night. Small bags never examined,' Caren said.

'Hell of a risk.'

'There'll be military police on duty.'

'Call the military police and warn them. I'm going over to Caernarfon airport. Meet me there. And find out where that operational support unit could be. Get them over there.'

Overhead he thought he heard the sound of an engine. He jerked his head skywards, hoping he'd see a plane approaching, but the visibility was poor and he could see nothing and having almost swerved into a refuse lorry, he decided to concentrate on the road.

Lance made single-word replies when Drake told him what he was doing. It only confirmed for Drake that he preferred, and missed, Wyndham Price. A long queue was waiting for him at the bridge and he cursed the early evening traffic. There was time enough for him to be thinking about the case and to ruminate at every wrong turn they'd taken. He thought about Jade Beltrami and then he slammed his hands against the steering wheel when the realisation struck him about Maguire. He had mentioned the name of the Blue Parrot to Jade at the first interview, or was it the second?

She'd drawn him into telling her where the investigation was going. And for a split second he thought that Maguire was dead because of him..

He was stationary in the queue. A horn sounded somewhere.

But, Drake realised, it had been Winder who'd discovered the link to the Blue Parrot. Valencia must have seen Drake in the club talking to Maguire. Killing him was probably just tidying up another loose end.

Another horn sounded. *Why don't you fucking shut up?*

He wanted to picture Maguire's face but somehow the image wouldn't focus. Connors must have had him killed because he could. Or was it because Valencia knew from Jade that they'd made the connection to Connors?

There were shouts now. Loud.

He looked out and saw the road ahead clear. More horns blasted and he fumbled to get the car into gear.

Dusk was falling when he approached Caernarfon. He glimpsed over towards Anglesey, convincing himself that the bright dot he'd seen in the sky was a plane heading for the airfield.

He pulled to a stop in a layby by the junction down to the airport. He called Caren.

'I should be there in ten minutes,' she said.

'And the SOU officers?'

'They'd already left for Cardiff. But I managed to get them to turn around and they should be with us in about an hour.'

'An hour!' Drake said. He peered out of the windscreen, certain now that he could see the flickering lights of an approaching aircraft. His hands were sweaty on the wheel but he couldn't decide if there was anything else he could do. If there was any other explanation. And more than anything he wanted to arrest Valencia for murder.

It was twenty minutes before Caren pulled up behind

him. She opened the car door and sat down and he pointed into the distance. 'There's a plane approaching now. Can you see it?' He pointed out over Caernarfon Bay.

Caren leant forward and squinted. 'How long have we got?'

'Call the SOU car.'

Caren found her mobile while Drake stared out into the greying sky. She spoke in short, incomplete sentences and then turned to Drake. 'At least another half an hour.'

Drake said nothing at first. He could just make out the light aircraft making its final approach to the airfield. He thought about Valencia and Jade Beltrami and the pleasure it would give him to arrest them. He pondered who else might be at the airport waiting. It had to be DS Wallace, of course. He had access to the Special Branch records, making it easy to disguise Valencia's trips to Dublin.

'We'll have to go in,' he said.' I'm not waiting half an hour.'

'But—'

Drake had already started the engine.

He headed down the narrow lanes around Dinas Dinlle that led to the airfield. He lost sight of the plane, guessing it had already landed. Along the seafront the road was straight; the houses and bungalows protected by a high sea wall seemed grey and lonely in the gathering gloom. A light flickered on in a bungalow down a lane lined with weeds. After a couple of sharp bends he reached the gate to the car park and braked hard. He jumped out and saw the fence surrounding the airfield. He thought he heard shouts and voices, but couldn't make them out. He ran between the old control tower and the main airport building towards the perimeter fence, hoping there'd be a gate. Caren stood beside him as he put his hands up against the tall fence, threading his fingers through the mesh. Caren's mobile rang and she fumbled to take the call. She turned to Drake.

'The SOU won't be long.'

He heard the sound of a car engine starting and he turned and ran back towards the Alfa, Caren following behind him. As he ran to the opposite end of the building he tried opening a metal door but it was locked and he cursed. At the far end another long fence stretched out along the perimeter.

He turned and hoped he could spot an entrance onto the airfield. The Museum building behind him was closed and an old jet aircraft stood towards one end of the car park. He had to get into the airfield. There was only one exit from the airport and no one had passed them so there was every possibility that the plane's passengers were still there. He raced over to his car, yelling at Caren to join him. He fired the engine, drove the car towards the fence before braking hard and parking alongside it. After getting out he clambered up onto the roof and then climbed onto the top of the fence and over and down onto the grass. He heard the cloth of his jacket tear and a shout from Caren, as she fell onto the ground beside him. He didn't want to think about the possibility that he'd lose them, so he ran.

By the time he reached the hangar door his chest was heaving, his pulse beating wildly. Caren was by his side taking deep breaths.

The lights were blazing, the door of the plane open and a BMW and Audi were parked in one corner. A radio was playing a pop song too loudly. He hesitated for a moment and then saw the office at the back of the hangar. He ran over and kicked at the door, hard, and it smashed open. He almost fell into the small room. Two men in white overalls playing cards by a table looked up at him.

Chapter 45

Drake held his hands onto his knees and breathed deeply, unable for a few seconds to say anything. Caren stood gasping by his side.

'Where have they gone?' Drake asked between deep breaths.

One of the technicians stood up. 'Who are you after?'

'The plane that just landed.'

'We didn't see them. They drove towards the old fort in a Range Rover.'

'What!' Drake said, straightening up. He ran out of the hangar and stared into the distance towards the sea and Fort Belan. It was dark and all he could see was the dim outline of the sand dunes as they stretched for miles into the bay.

Caren was by his side now. 'Should we tell the super?'

'We don't tell the super anything,' he said, turning back into the hangar and shouting as loudly as he could for someone to open the gate in the perimeter fence.

The same technician came running out and soon Drake was accelerating down the road towards Fort Belan.

'He could be up to his neck in all of this. He was living in that new development in the fort. I saw him there during his first week.'

Drake grasped the steering wheel and pressed the accelerator hard as the bits of the jigsaw all fell into place. He'd been removed as the SIO, Lance had wanted everything to be channelled through his office and any contact with Special Branch had to be his responsibility.

'Damn it. Why the hell didn't I see it before?' Drake said. 'He must be involved. The lying bastard.'

Caren gave him a troubled look. The car hurtled

towards the fort before speeding over the small causeway, the seawater lapping at the tyres. Drake drew the car to a halt behind the Range Rover just in front of the old wooden drawbridge. The pair ran over it and then through into the courtyard. There was a light in the first of the cottages on the left but otherwise the buildings were in darkness. He gripped the old door handle on the first cottage and stepped into a small hallway. A narrow staircase led up to a landing, light seeped around the door frame to his right, and there was a faint noise from a television somewhere in the building. Caren pushed open the door slightly but then stepped back, shaking her head. Drake motioned to the door in front of them. It led into a corridor that stretched the whole length of the building, joining all the old cottages together.

The television seemed to be blaring more loudly now. They walked down the passage. A door to Drake's right was locked when he tried opening it. They reached a small hallway and in a room to their left Drake saw an old toilet with a wooden seat. A faint electric light was on in the room and he pushed open the door further. He noticed a window with old glass, its surface rippled, and an old wash basin on a stand trimmed with mahogany.

Drawn against the far wall, hanging from the ceiling, were curtains that could be pulled around the huge Victorian bath which stood in the middle of the floor. Drake stepped over towards it and when he looked inside he caught his breath. Bile gathered in his throat and for a moment he stood, unable to think.

Caren moved towards him and peered down. 'Jesus.'

MC Hughes lay in the bath, almost unrecognisable, his face a mass of bruises and his shirt soaked a deep red. Drake leant down and touched MC's arm – it was cold and lifeless. Then he barged past Caren and out into the courtyard just as the two officers from the SOU ran over the drawbridge. He stood still, drawing deep breaths. In the distance they heard the sound of an engine.

'Let's get down to the dock.' Drake started to run down the same passage that Lance had used when he'd seen him. He considered what he might say to the superintendent, face to face. He balled a fist in anticipation of what he might do. They reached the dock but there was no sign of a boat. All the properties were darkened except for a small square of light from a narrow window in one of the old buildings in the far corner.

Caren followed Drake over the quayside towards the building, with the SOU officers trailing behind, their pistols drawn. As they drew closer they heard the sound of conversations and then laughter. Drake tightened his fist until his fingers hurt. He thought of MC and then he barged through the door.

Valencia turned sharply and gave a narrow smile, but Jade Beltrami couldn't hide the surprise in her eyes and the fear behind them. Behind them Inspector Glyn Newman sat at the desk. He got up and made for a gun on the edge of the table top. Before his fingers curled around the butt the SOU officers stepped into the room, pistols drawn.

Drake sat down at the narrow table and ran a finger along the tacky surface. His eyes were burning and he couldn't remember when he'd last eaten. He glanced over at Caren standing by the counter and ordering food from a pimply youngster. Winder came into the restaurant, Howick following close behind him. They said something to Caren that Drake couldn't hear and came over to his table.

'Great result, boss,' Winder said, slipping into the bench opposite Drake. 'And all three of them together.'

Howick came over with a tray holding four plastic drinks containers.

'I didn't think Newman was involved for one minute.' Howick slid a drink each towards Winder and Drake.

'It was only because of him that Valencia could operate on such a scale.' Drake examined his cup.

'And Special Branch in the port weren't involved at all,' Winder said.

Drake fumbled with the straw before piercing the top of the container. The cold fizzy drink felt refreshing. Caren arrived with various boxes full of burgers; Winder and Howick were the first to reach into the tray, lifting out their choices. Caren had eaten her way through half of her burger before Drake had touched his. She pushed over a small paper bag.

'Onion rings?'

He shook his head.

He finished his meal and for once hadn't noticed whether Caren ate with her mouth open. Perhaps she'd stopped that habit. Tiredness would hit him later, but for now he listened to her telling Winder and Howick what exactly had happened at Caernarfon airport. They each made exaggerated gestures of surprise when she recounted that Newman had mysteriously fallen and lost two teeth, sustained a couple of chipped ribs and acquired a black eye.

'That's what happens when you don't cooperate with an officer trying to restrain you,' Winder said.

'Wait until he gets inside,' Howick added.

Winder finished the last of his burger and licked the salt from his fingers. Howick was taking his food at a gentler pace and finished as Drake crumpled his tissue, discarding it in the food packaging. He straightened his posture, knowing that he felt better for having eaten, despite the fatty, greasy residue that coated his mouth and tongue. Tomorrow, it would be back to healthy eating.

'Job well done all of you,' he said, looking at each of them turn. Caren gave him a warm smile of acknowledgment, Winder blinked energetically, surprise evident in his eyes, and Howick gave him a serious-looking nod.

'Let's go,' Drake said.

Chapter 46

The following morning Drake couldn't remember whether he had dreamt the night before. It was a Saturday and Sian was sleeping by his side, the gentle rhythm of her breathing breaking the silence of the spring morning. He turned over and saw the time: seven-twenty, surprised that he'd woken so early. He still felt tired. His back ached and there was an aftertaste of burger in his mouth.

He slipped out of bed; he had to coordinate the interviews with Valencia, Jade Beltrami and Newman. It was going to be another long day.

In the kitchen he turned on the kettle and stood listening to its gurgling sound. Upstairs the floorboards groaned and he heard Sian's footsteps on the stairs.

'Are you going in this morning?' she said, wrapping her arms around herself. 'Only I hoped you'd be able to come with me to this charity lunch and auction.'

'I've got interviews with Valencia and Jade Beltrami.'

'Can't you spare an hour even?'

'It's going to be difficult.'

She sat by the table and let out a lungful of air. 'It's taking you over, isn't it?'

He poured water, just off the boil, over coffee grounds.

'I never see you. And when you are here it's as though you're not with us at all.'

He stepped over towards her, slid two mugs onto the table and then returned with the coffee pot. 'It's been difficult, I know. But with the arrests last night things should be wrapped up now.'

'We'll see.' Sian poured coffee and avoided his eye.

Drake drove to headquarters, wanting to believe that the

malaise in his mind was just post-arrest blues, that once he had the interviews finished, charges laid, and court dates fixed he'd feel better. Caren had arrived already and he parked next to her estate car. He walked over to headquarters and through the main building to the Incident Room.

Caren was sitting by her desk and Drake sat by Winder's, knowing that the junior officer wouldn't be prompt on a Saturday.

He looked over at the board.

'Custody sergeant told me that Jade Beltrami's gone to pieces. Kept sobbing and whimpering,' Caren said.

'Have they had solicitors making contact yet?'

'Don Hart was on the telephone first thing.'

Drake nodded at the name he recognised. 'Who does he represent?'

'Valencia.'

'Figures,' Drake said. 'I bet they'll feed Jade to the wolves. You know how it is.'

'Must have been *inconvenient* when Rosen wanted out.'

Drake nodded.

Caren continued. 'They had to find another flyer quickly.'

'It wouldn't surprise me if she wasn't involved right from the start – don't forget those references she forged for Rosen and Green.'

'But Valencia took a hell of a risk flying over to Ireland. If his name was on the passenger list, then Special Branch would have picked it up right away.'

Drake sat upright as soon as she mentioned Valencia. 'I didn't see his name on any of the lists.'

'Are you sure?'

Drake got to his feet. Reaching into a filing cabinet he pulled out a binder with the carefully filed sheets from the flying club. He checked them all, realising that Valencia's name was nowhere.

'He could have gone on the ferry,' Caren said as he reached the last page.

Drake nodded. 'Only one way to find out.' He strode over to his office and called O'Sullivan.

'Ian. How're doing? Connors is having the fucking time of his life in Mountjoy jail.' O'Sullivan started laughing.

'I need a favour,' Drake said.

Drake returned to headquarters after wasting three hours interviewing Newman. He blanked all of Drake's questions without even opening his mouth. Not even a 'no comment'. He refused all offers of water or tea or coffee. He just sat and said nothing, occasionally exchanging glances with his solicitor.

Drake knew there'd be more interviews and that by the beginning of the week Newman would be remanded in custody. To a prison cell. Segregated from ordinary prisoners for his own safety, sharing a cell with an equally vulnerable criminal. Maybe a paedophile or a wife beater.

Ordinarily Drake's patience would have run thin with a prisoner failing to cooperate, making a no-comment interview, but he took oblique pleasure in realising the sort of treatment Newman would receive in custody.

He bought a sandwich from the canteen and in the kitchen started the meticulous process of making coffee. Even while measuring the grounds, and counting the minutes, he convinced himself that Sian's criticisms were unfair. He took the cafetière back to his room and sat down. The columns of Post-it notes had been repositioned to one side, and an apple placed nearby. He checked his mobile, then his email, to confirm that there was nothing from O'Sullivan. Instead of feeling pleased that they had three suspects already in custody he could only concentrate on the notion that there was a missing piece of the jigsaw.

He'd managed a couple of mouthfuls of coffee by the time the telephone rang.

'You were right Ian,' O'Sullivan said.

Drake put the unfinished sandwich down on the plate, and waited.

'Special Branch never check the arrivals at the airport. The forms are emailed through from Special Branch in Holyhead and after that; fuck knows what happens to them.'

'And?'

'Yes. I'm coming to that.'

Drake glared at the phone, as though it itself was getting in the way of his progress.

'The man from the airport can identify Valencia as a passenger on a couple of the flights. He remembered the fancy cream suits.'

'Send me everything you have,' Drake said, before slamming the phone down. His pulse had increased: he knew what they needed to do. He shouted over at Caren and she appeared at the door of his office. 'You were right about the passenger lists. Valencia wasn't on them but he was on the flights.'

'What! How did that happen?'

'The lists sent to Special Branch were doctored. The information was wrong. Damn. I should have seen that. And it was Meirion Ellis-Pugh who sent all the forms in. So he must've been involved.'

'Do you know his address?'

Drake looked at his watch. 'Better than that. I know where he is.'

He snatched his car keys and then, unfolding his jacket from the wooden hanger, left the office, his sandwich unfinished.

'Do a search,' Drake ordered Caren, as he accelerated out of the car park.

Caren looked blank.

'On the phone. For Ellis-Pugh. He was on the BBC recently about his daughter.'

Caren tapped the instructions into her phone.

'Nothing so far.'

'Bloody hell, it must be there. Has to be. Try the news channel.'

'That's what I am trying.'

'Try it again.'

He left the outskirts of Colwyn Bay, as the soothing tones of Ellis-Pugh's voice came back to his mind.

'Got it.'

'Well what does it say?'

'It's a long piece and there's some video footage too. I ... *Sophie Ellis-Pugh diagnosed with high risk neuroblastoma ... Last week the family reached their £250,000 fundraising target to pay for the immunotherapy treatment ... specialist treatment in the US begins on Monday ...*' Caren read aloud about the operation Sophie needed. 'That was a month ago. There's a picture of her here. She looks very ill.'

Drake guessed that money from the pocket of Valencia had discreetly been fed into the fundraising campaign. And he only briefly thought about the practicalities of tracing money to the bank account of a hospital in the United States that treated terminally ill children. It wasn't going to be his problem.

Drake parked outside the front door of the hotel and marched through the main entrance with Caren, before noticing a sign for the charity function that pointed to the ballroom at the rear.

He pushed open the door and strode into the high-ceilinged room. He caught sight of some television celebrities, a couple of local assembly members and various businessmen. Drake scanned the room. He saw the puzzled look on Sian's face as he and Caren walked towards her.

'What's wrong?' she said.

'Is Meirion Ellis-Pugh here?'

'He left about an hour ago.'

'Did he say where he was going?'

'He was going to catch his flight I think.'

'Which airport?'

'Manchester. What the hell is wrong?'

Drake turned and rushed for the door, knocking over chairs as he left.

'I think we should call the airport police,' Caren said.

Drake was driving hard in the outside lane, flashing the headlights and blasting the horn at dawdling drivers. Caren was right, but his thoughts kept returning to the image of Jade Beltrami's face in the meetings with Aylford and Parry. It was the last one where he had mentioned the Blue Parrot and he could see the smirk and the contempt in her face. He may as well have killed Maguire himself. She'd made certain he was annoyed and once she learnt that they knew the Blue Parrot was involved they had Maguire killed.

'The airport police, sir,' Caren repeated, loudly.

It broke his concentration.

'Of course. Call them.'

Caren reached for her mobile. Drake sped on until eventually he was on the motorway, with only half an hour to the airport. He prayed for clear traffic and listened to Caren by his side dictating the details of what they knew. *Meirion Ellis-Pugh*. She gave a description. Age, 54. Destination, US, but she didn't know where.

'Connecting flights?' Caren said. 'We don't know. Just get an alert out to all the departure desks for them to notify you if he tries to leave.'

To their left as they sped along a long, straight section of motorway was a chemical plant, white smoke drifting out of tall chimneys. Drake saw the signs for the junction in the distance, no more than a mile away, to Liverpool John Lennon airport.

'What if he isn't going to Manchester at all?' Drake said.

'He can't suspect anything?'

He slowed the car and pulled into the inside lane.

'He's very careful. There's probably nothing to link the fund for his daughter to Valencia. Small enough donations to pass unnoticed and then a friendly bank manager who's supportive and sympathetic and isn't surprised when large amounts of cash come into the account.'

'But why take the risk?'

'Desperation. His daughter needs specialised treatment and the only place is the US. All he has to do is complete the forms for Special Branch inaccurately.'

'He knows that if Valencia's name is on them the SB would be bound to pick it up.'

'So he tells Sian and anyone else that wants to listen that he's going from Manchester. Just in case.'

Drake flicked the indicator switch. 'If he's in Manchester the police there can deal with him. Call Liverpool airport.'

Five minutes later he was crossing Runcorn Bridge and following the narrow road towards the outskirts of Liverpool. He battled as he drove with a clawing frustration, as he stopped at numerous traffic lights until eventually they saw the lights of John Lennon Airport. He accelerated towards the main entrance and braked hard. After slamming the doors closed they left the car and ran inside, dodging suitcases and trolleys.

The departure desks stretched out ahead of them in the main hall. Drake ran over the concourse, his heart hammering in his chest. People with luggage were in his way, shuffling in zigzag lines towards the desks.

Caren followed him towards the first of the departure desks – a flight for Alicante was scheduled for departure in an hour. Drake stood for moment, breathing heavily. Producing his warrant card he pushed his way past the protests of the security staff and walked down along the departure desks, peering at the faces of the waiting passengers.

Next were various flights to Poland. Nothing. The queue for the flight to the south of France was smaller and he heard French accents.

He hadn't reached halfway down the departure hall when he thought the saw Ellis-Pugh. The man was the same height, same bald patch, but when he turned he wore thick spectacles and a thick bushy beard.

Drake marched on.

A feeling that it had been a complete waste of time clouded his thoughts. He turned to Caren. 'Anything from the police in Manchester?'

She shook her head.

They passed a handful of passengers for a flight to an airport in one of the Baltic countries. At the far end a larger crowd was forming and Drake saw the departure details for two flights to Ireland. *Easy for connection to the US.*

He slowed, trying to concentrate and focus on spotting Ellis-Pugh. Over the public address system a woman's voice announced the boarding for a flight to Frankfurt. They could very easily have missed Ellis-Pugh already.

Then, in the middle of the crowd, he saw him.

Drake stopped, his breathing returning to normal.

Ellis-Pugh was pretending to read a magazine, but sneaking a glance from under a baseball hat on his head, a small holdall by his feet.

He raised his head slowly and looked at Drake. His lips twitched and he nodded briefly.

Chapter 47

Drake looked at his watch for the third time in five minutes; Caren was late and he was annoyed. And his annoyance hadn't been helped by the conversation he'd had with Sian the previous evening. She'd explained in a clear, logical way that the time was right for her to work full time in the practice and that it was the right time for them as a family. She made comments about his work-life balance and that he needed to prioritise more time for the family. How exactly he was going to achieve that with her working full time wasn't clear. This time, it was his home life that was crowding into his office one and it was stopping him from thinking clearly.

Caren appeared at his door, breathless. 'Sorry I'm late.'

He mumbled a reply, got up, and picked up his car keys. 'We need to leave.' Caren seemed more cheerful than usual and he even noticed that she looked tidier than normal.

Drake buzzed down the window a couple of inches and let the spring air rush over his face as he drove down to the A55. He turned westwards. The traffic was light.

'Did I tell you that Alun has got a job with a local company?'

Drake realised that this news must account for her high spirits.

'When does he start?'

'Straight away. More or less. He's got one trip to Poland and then he'll be back.'

'Does he enjoy all this driving?'

'He doesn't like being away.'

They reached the turning for Mold in good time and headed down the hill towards the crown court.

'Dave has booked a couple of weeks off to study for his exams,' Drake said.

'I know. He told me.'

'Do you think he'll pass?'

'His wife'll divorce him if he fails.'

'Seriously?'

'Dave thinks so.'

Drake pulled into the car park. A camera crew was standing by the main entrance. They watched as a prison van reversed towards the prisoners' entrance. Inside the main building it was cool and they passed witnesses and lawyers waiting for cases. Drake tugged open the door of the court room and they sat down. Andy Thorsen nodded a greeting at Drake. A pulse of anticipation ran through the court when the judge entered.

Drake looked over at Valencia, searching for any emotion in his eyes as the court clerk read out the three counts of murder: first Rosen, then Green and finally MC Hughes, but Valencia stared straight ahead. Forensics had proved that the gun Drake had taken from Valencia had killed MC, which meant he was going down for a long time even if they might have difficulty proving Valencia had conspired to kill Rosen and Green.

Drake watched the prosecution barrister lean back against the wooden bench. Occasionally he consulted his papers, as he addressed the judge in clear, persuasive terms as to why Ellis-Pugh should be denied bail. That, with the ongoing nature of the inquiry into the drug-smuggling operation, the interests of justice would not be served if Ellis-Pugh was released. The judge frowned when he suggested Ellis-Pugh might abscond.

Two prison officers stood at either end of the dock; Jade Beltrami sat next to Ellis-Pugh and stared at the floor. Valencia was wearing a dark suit and a carefully knotted tie. When he'd emerged into the dock from the cells below he'd given Drake a dark, intense glare.

The barristers for the three defendants stood up in turn, each adjusting their gowns and wigs before starting. Drake could tell by the way the judge narrowed his eyes at each that they'd have been better off saying nothing.

Drake looked over at John Beltrami sitting at the opposite end of the court building, arms folded, listening to every word. Valencia sat in the dock staring at the judge and then the image of Valencia pointing the gun at MC crowded into Drake's mind. Drake's mind drifted back to MC's funeral the day before, to the small cemetery in Llanberis under the trees and the spring breeze blowing in the faces of the mourners.

Drake had knelt down and scooped up a handful of fine clay. He'd straightened and opened his palm. He'd watched as some of the fine grains had fallen through his fingers. They had felt dry and chalky against his skin. With a single jerk of his hand he'd thrown the dirt into the grave and it had clattered over MC's coffin. A young girl had supported Auntie Gwen who had stood, tears filling her eyes, by the side of the minister conducting the funeral.

He felt someone prodding him, turned, and noticed Caren on her feet with the rest of the courtroom. The judge rose and left, and the prison officers bundled the three defendants down towards the cells.

'I don't suppose we'll ever be able to trace the money,' Caren said, as they left the building.

Drake nodded. The weather felt warm after the coolness of the courtroom.

'And Jade Beltrami wants to do a deal,' he said.

'Doesn't surprise me. The interviews were pathetic. Each blaming the other. But she's a sad character. In awe of her father and then seduced by Valencia. Now she's going to spend the next fifteen years in prison.'

Hannah was busy typing when Drake walked into the senior management suite. She gave him a brief nod.

'He's got someone with him.' She made her voice

sound mysterious.

After five minutes the door to Lance's room opened and a tall man in an expensive suit emerged. He had spotless shoes and he strode out of the room as though he was on a parade ground. His hair was neatly trimmed and the thin navy tie had been knotted severely. He gave Drake a brief glance. Drake noticed his clear blue eyes.

'Thank you, Hannah,' the man said, the accent straight from an officer's mess. He smiled briefly at her and left.

The telephone on her desk rang and she looked over at Drake, nodding towards Lance's door.

A tray with cups and saucers and an empty cafetière had been pushed to one side of the conference table. Lance looked up at Drake and motioned for him to sit down.

'All remanded safely into custody?' Lance said.

'They dealt with Newman by video link. I don't think they could guarantee his safety.'

Lance cleared his throat. 'Look, Ian. I know you might feel aggrieved about the way we ran the operation but Professional Standards gave us no choice. We had to flush out Newman. When Rosen's death happened it was an opportunity too good to miss.'

Drake's annoyance had passed and the knowledge that Newman was facing prison was reward enough.

'I've been discussing the evidence with the CPS.'

Drake braced himself for some crazy decision.

'There's nothing we can use against Loosemore,' Lance said. 'Certainly not in the murder investigation and I spoke to Superintendent Adams last night and his preliminary assessment is the same for their fraud inquiry.'

'I see.'

'The connections don't give us enough to build a case.'

'Of course, sir.' Drake knew Lance was right. 'But after I've interviewed Jade Beltrami and Martin Valencia I'll need to speak to John Beltrami.'

Lance cleared his throat. 'The CPS don't think it'll run.'

'What!'

'It's circumstantial and you know how difficult it is to rely on the evidence from a co-accused.'

'But the aircraft and the dates and ...'

Lance opened a notebook on the table, checking something. 'The ACC has spoken to a Mr Peters. He's a barrister representing Aylford and Parry who want to offer their complete help and assistance in any way they can. I take it we have nothing on either man?'

Drake shook his head slowly.

Lance flicked through his notepad again. 'And the interview with Janet Rosen merely confirmed that she'd started a relationship with Loosemore after her husband's death.'

Again, despite his nagging doubts, Drake knew that Lance was right.

'The Garda tell me that Connors's trial is going to be one of the most high-profile events ever in the criminal courts in Ireland.'

Drake nodded.

'The world will be a much better place with him locked up,' Lance continued. 'We've broken up an enormous drug-smuggling operation. Think of the lives that might have been ruined by Valencia and Jade Beltrami if they'd continued.'

Drake thought about Sylvie lying on a hospital bed, her breathing shallow, her will to live slowly vanishing. There would be other Sylvies, maybe even other MCs, but for the time being Connors and Valencia were off the streets. Drake had realised at MC's funeral that blaming himself wouldn't bring his cousin back, wouldn't solve anything.

'I still need to interview Class, of course,' Drake said.

Lance shifted his position and looked over at him.

'It's not going to happen.'

'What? We need to know if he knew anything.'

'What's the evidence?'

'The photographs. The emails.'

'The photographs prove nothing. I've had a clear directive that it's not going to happen. The security service have been involved.'

Drake remembered the man with the glistening shoes in Lance's office.

'Apparently there's going to be an announcement about his retirement. Family reasons – all the usual bullshit.'

'But they can't interfere in an investigation. It's a police matter.'

Lance said nothing.

Drake stopped on the way to his parents' home and looked out over Caernarfon Bay. The water looked calm and a yacht heeled over as it made passage south. He opened the window. There was stillness in the air, and he watched the outline of the wind generator at Caernarfon airfield turning slowly. Holyhead Mountain was a distant bump on the horizon. The ferries would still be ploughing back and forth and passengers would be travelling, unaware of the events that had recently unfolded.

As he approached the house he saw the Macmillan nurse on the threshold with his mother. Behind him he heard a car approaching and he recognised the local GP. A heavy mood filled his heart. He parked the car under the kitchen window, as he had done a thousand times. But this time things were different.

Made in the USA
Monee, IL
19 February 2022

91497151R10193